PURE OF HEART

Book one of the Faoladh Series

by

Danielle Parker

Copyright © 2015 Danielle Parker

All rights reserved.

ISBN: **1516916530**
ISBN-13: **978-1516916535**

DEDICATION

For Austin

CONTENTS

Prologue	I
CHAPTER ONE	9
CHAPTER TWO	23
CHAPTER THREE	35
CHAPTER FOUR	43
CHAPTER FIVE	51
CHAPTER SIX	63
CHAPTER SEVEN	75
CHAPTER EIGHT	85
CHAPTER NINE	95
CHAPTER TEN	103
CHAPTER ELEVEN	111
CHAPTER TWELVE	123
CHAPTER THIRTEEN	135
CHAPTER FOURTEEN	145
CHAPTER FIFTEEN	155
CHAPTER SIXTEEN	165
CHAPTER SEVENTEEN	177
CHAPTER EIGHTEEN	187
CHAPTER NINETEEN	197

CHAPTER TWENTY	205
CHAPTER TWENTY-ONE	213
CHAPTER TWENTY-TWO	221
CHAPTER TWENTY-THREE	229
CHAPTER TWENTY-FOUR	239
CHAPTER TWENTY-FIVE	249
CHAPTER TWENTY-SIX	257
CHAPTER TWENTY-SEVEN	267
CHAPTER TWENTY-EIGHT	275
CHAPTER TWENTY-NINE	283
CHAPTER THIRTY	293
CHAPTER THIRTY-ONE	303
CHAPTER THIRTY-TWO	315
ABOUT THE AUTHOR	329

ACKNOWLEDGMENTS

I would like to thank Mrs. Wright, my grandparents, James LeDoux, Alan Heathcock, and my friends in the critique group, for encouraging and helping me along the way to accomplishing my dream of writing a book.

Even a man who is pure of heart
And says his prayers by night
May become a wolf
When the wolfsbane blooms
And the autumn moon is bright.

PROLOGUE

"Can you ground a werewolf?" Grady wondered, crossing his arms with a huff. He sighed, considering the problem of grounding a twenty-five year old with a job even without the werewolf issue. "I'm going to ground her somehow."

Camped out in his truck with the heat on high, he watched his breath puff out in thin streams of fog. He'd been sitting there for an hour and the cab still hadn't warmed up. First, he'd watched her take off into the night through a hole in his fence. Now his heater wasn't working.

He smacked at the wiper controls again and watched the blades lurch across the windshield. They left wet streaks in their wake, blurring his view. Not that he had much to look at. The clearing where he'd parked was bare, covered in a thick layer of undisturbed snow. It looked like the surface of the moon. "No more fresh meat. Nope. She's getting dry kibble. Stale, dry kibble. That can be part of her punishment. Seems fair."

The actual moon hung overhead, full and bright, giving the snowy landscape an eerie lunar glow. It should have been pretty, had he been in the mood to appreciate it. He glanced down at the radio, saw the time, and sighed. AJ had yet to arrive, and it had gone from late to early. Not that he'd blame her if she went back to sleep. Part of him was ready to drive home and leave his escape artist out in the wild for the night too. Maybe if he stopped chasing her every time she ran off, she'd learn to stay inside. The late night games of hide and seek were getting old.

Tempting as the thought was, he knew he couldn't leave her. Another swipe of the wipers and a glance at the thick, steady snowfall sealed the deal. He could picture her somewhere curled up, cold and alone. Instead of reaching for the gear stick, he settled back against the worn bench seat. The hard part wasn't deciding to stay, but finding a comfortable position that didn't leave his knees jammed under the steering column.

"Definitely grounded," he said and tipped his head back against the headrest.

He waited another half hour, watching the minutes tick by and sipping coffee from his thermos. Unable, unwilling, to wait another full hour for AJ, he reached for his phone. Of course the second he managed to grab it with his gloved fingers, he glanced up just in time to get blinded by a pair of high beams.

Dropping the phone and blinking spots out of his eyes, he cranked down the driver side window and offered a wave as the other vehicle pulled up alongside.

"Grady," AJ said and leaned out her own window with a toothy grin. "We've got to stop meeting like this."

"I wasn't sure you were going to make it. I'm really sorry about that – the time – and this whole thing." He sank lower in his seat and scratched at his head. He felt like a teenager caught sneaking into the liquor cabinet. "Thanks for coming to help. Again."

"Eh, it's not like I was doing anything important besides, you know, sleeping and staying out of the storm. Sorry it took me so long. I may have fallen back asleep after you called. Until I realized this wasn't actually a very realistic dream."

He nodded and stretched across the seat to snag the straps of his headlamps. "Understandable. I brought stuff for the party, did you?"

"No, I forgot," she said and shoved the furry front of her trapper hat back. Enough for him to see her eyes glaring at him. "Of course I did. What am I, new? They just need to be loaded and we're good to go. I don't suppose you know where my buddy has gone?"

With a shrug, he gestured at the far tree-line. "She always goes the same place, right at the edge of town. You'd think she'd have learned to change it up just to annoy me more."

"That makes sense, actually. She's established territory." AJ grinned again and draped her arm over the door. "You do know she doesn't do this to piss you off, right?"

"Says you. From where I'm sitting this feels planned out." He rolled his eyes. "Territory. How can she have territory? She's not even – I mean…"

"I just call it what it is. Wolves are territorial and she's a wolf. I'm sure she's got a nice patch of land all marked out. It's instinctual."

"Lovely," he said with a frown. "Well, how about we go find her and drag her furry butt back to *my* territory. You can explain this whole instinct thing to me later. As much as I'd love to wait at home for her to show up, it probably would make me a bad guardian to leave her out here."

"I'm sure a good, old fashioned guilt trip will work." She pointed a finger to the sky and whirled it in a circle. "I'll pull around so we can use the spotlights, at least for a bit. Then we can get this party started."

Down to business then, he thought and sighed. Just when the truck was starting to feel warm.

He shoved open the door and made peace with the fact he was in for a long, cold night. Glaring at the snow didn't make the situation better, but it made him feel more in control. He hopped out and landed with a scrunch in the knee-deep, icy mush. Fat flakes were still streaming down. Some landed on his upturned face and melted away, trickling into his beard. It wouldn't be protecting his face so well when it froze.

Thoughts of murder popped into his head again. He shoved his hands into his pockets and watched AJ jump out of her Jeep. Like always, he couldn't think of a single damn thing to say. With a name like Grady Sullivan he'd thought he might inherit more than traces of red in his blonde hair. It seemed the oft-lauded luck of the Irish had been exaggerated, as well as the charm. He didn't feel all that lucky or charming as he stood there. Perhaps the luck of his kinsmen was only granted to those born on the shamrock shores of the Motherland.

A howl sounded in the distance, deep and mournful. It sent a shiver racing down his spine that had little to do with the cold seeping through the layers of his clothing. He looked toward the woods and saw nothing beyond shadows and the tops of the trees. They were surrounded by forest, save for the narrow access road.

The wolf howled again.

"Hey."

He jerked around and saw AJ standing with a hip cocked at the opened back of her Jeep. "You can think deep thoughts when we're out of the woods," she said and waved him over. "You remember how these work, yeah?"

The sight of the ballistic needles made him gulp. They could have been comical looking with the pink tufts of fake feather on their tails. The hypodermic needles on the business ends, however, were anything but funny. Even knowing they weren't meant for him, he still had to fight back a rush of nausea. "Hard to forget," he said. "But so I'm clear. The pointy end goes in first?"

"Don't be a smart-ass."

"Yes, Ma'am." He saluted her and tried to get his half frozen face to return her smile. "Sorry, again. I did mention that I'm sorry to drag you out here?"

"Once or twice, and I think I told you repeatedly it's no trouble. I'm happy to help and glad you called." She glanced at him. "I'm dying to hear what happened this time. I thought you had it "all figured out" after the great tunneling incident."

"I didn't exactly have time to stick around and play Sherlock, Watson." He shuddered as he watched her load a dart into one of the rifles. Even with heavy gloves on she appeared so at ease. "I'm, uh, more worried about the trouble she could get in. And I'd really like to avoid having to explain another torn up deer carcass strewn around my yard. Mr. Reimann stares at me like I'm a serial killer or something."

"It's kind of sweet," she said and clicked the safety switch. The loaded rifle was then thrust into his hands. "Not you maybe being a serial killer, but — Ike brings me things all the time. They're gifts. It means she likes you."

"Would that be more instinct?" he asked, slinging the rifle over his shoulder. "There's kind of a big difference in your dog bringing you dead ground squirrels and me having a deer head on my back porch."

She hummed and went about her business, loading another dart into her rifle. They looked so real. Not like the plastic, toy-like, tranquilizer rifles he'd seen in movies and various nature shows. These weren't toys and the weight of them in his hands always reminded him how real the potential danger was.

"You sure you got the right dosage of Telazazzle in these?"

"Telazol," she corrected, like she had every time he butchered the name. "Yes, I'm sure. You keep asking and I'm starting to wonder if you think I'm bad at my job."

"No." He shook his head. "I know you're the best. That's why I'm so grateful for your help, and trust you with her."

"Uh-huh, and it has nothing to do with me being in on the secret?"

"Come on, AJ, just take the compliment."

"Fine. I'm awesome, thank you for saying so." She slammed the hatch closed, a smirk appearing when he flinched at the sound. "Jumpy tonight?"

He retaliated by flicking on the headlamp secured to his head. His chapped lips stretched into a genuine smile when she squeaked and shied away from the blast of light.

"Jerk." She blinked at him for a few seconds, then scowled.

"Can we go now?" he asked, holding out the other lamp for her. "My socks are getting wet."

"Poor baby." She fixed her lamp over the fuzzy front of her hat. "Do I get hazard pay for this? And I don't mean for finding her, I mean for working with you."

He followed her around to the front of the vehicle, waiting while she flipped on the rack of spotlights mounted over her windshield. She joined him and they both paused, staring at the illuminated tree line.

The fine hairs at the back of his neck and along his arms stood on end. He found himself grateful AJ needed a moment as well. To solidify a plan in her head, perhaps. He needed the moment to dig deep for his courage. Once they left the relative safety of the clearing he would need all the false bravado he could summon. They may have looked the part of the hunter, but he knew better. So did she. On that night in particular, once they crossed the line into the forest, they would be playing the role of prey.

Another howl broke the uneasy silence and he inched closer to AJ. "Do you think - could it be depression? She's been distant, moodier. Even for her."

"I'm not exactly an expert in that area," AJ said. "She is traumatized, Grady, and wolves... wolves are not solitary animals. They have packs and intricate family structures. She's cooped up and alone with her memories. That would make anyone depressed."

"I promised not to let her run free. Something could happen again." He flexed his hands around the rifle, but couldn't look her in the eye. Just because she knew didn't make it any easier to face. "I feel like I'm mistreating her. I tell myself it's for her own good, and I promised. I'm trying to keep her safe."

"I know you're doing the best you can. You don't have to explain to me."

He peeked over at her and she offered a half-smile. "Wolves are predators. It's in their nature to run and chase things. It's in her nature. She's not a house dog. We can't blame her for being depressed and angry and acting out because she wants to do what comes naturally."

"I guess I was really hoping she'd outgrow this behavior," he mumbled and kicked the snow. "Her mother was never like this. Not that I can remember."

"You never talk about her," AJ said after a beat.

"Some things are still too hard to talk about."

"That's alright, we'll focus on the present. Let's go get her before we all get frostbite." She gestured with the muzzle of her rifle. "After you?"

"I'm pretty sure I'm supposed to insist the lady go first. I'll let it slide, but you're on point next time. Fair is fair. Equality and all that."

"Can't we both hope that there won't be a next time?"

He decided not to comment, and instead took that first tentative step forward. There were marks in the snow, tracks. Big paw prints that couldn't be mistaken for anything else. He followed them up a short incline. At the top, a tree lay fallen across the ridge. They were both soaked and out of breath by the time they reached it.

AJ stayed close behind him. So close that when he stopped to scan ahead, she ran right into his back. He started to laugh, but choked it back.

Deeper and deeper they crept. Their progress often slowed when they got caught up on limbs of dead trees or tangled in the branches of bushes buried by snow.

"Cooper's okay?" AJ whispered as they halted again. He grunted, bending to untangle his foot from whatever bit of plant life that snared him. "I forgot to ask and..."

"Cooper's fine," he said, giving his boot a firm shake as he high-stepped away. "He thinks she's amazing. Which I suppose is a side-effect of raising them together. He was worried. I had to threaten to ground him from his comics to get him to stay behind." Thinking of his son, he scrubbed at his forehead. Maybe those Irish-luck genes skipped a generation. "He scares me sometimes. It's like he thinks he's invincible."

"Were you really that different when you were his age? He's a teenager." She winked at him when he turned back to her. "And brave like his father."

He hoped his frozen beard would hide most of his blush. "Well, when you put it that way."

A twig snapped nearby, the sound echoing around them. He froze mid-step, his boot hovering just above the ground. AJ caught him as he swayed. She clung to the crook of his elbow with one hand and her rifle with the other.

"To the left," he said, out of habit more than necessity. "It could be a deer, maybe?"

She shot him a skeptical look. "Right, you want to bet on that one? Bait or shooter, tough guy?"

He shook his head, chest tightening at the thought of her offering herself as a lure. "I'm bait. I'm always bait. She's my responsibility and you're... the better shot."

"How nice of you to admit," she said and dropped her hold on his arm. "Don't get so close this time, please. Leave the heroics for Cooper's super heroes."

"She'll run, she always runs." After he said it, he crossed himself and looked up at the sky. Just in case. *Please, let her run like always.*

"There's that instinct rearing its head again. You, of all people, should know better than to assume. Especially with her. So be careful, okay?"

"I'll be careful if you are." He stayed still and stared straight ahead, offered a slight nod when she patted his shoulder.

"Better be," she said from behind him. "You still owe me a beer for last time. Now you owe me two. Not cheap ones, either."

He couldn't watch her go, it messed with his head. Made his gut feel like it was full of rocks. He listened though. Heard her clothes rustling, the odd crunch of snow under her feet, tree limbs snapping as she pushed past. If he could hear all of that, they had no chance of surprise. Not that they ever did.

Then he felt it, the uncomfortable sick feeling that came from knowing you were being watched. He held his breath and turned, heart pounding loud in his ears. The wolf would be able to see him, hear him, smell him. No matter what he tried she would know where he was. It made him feel insignificant, helpless.

"Marco?" he called out, and didn't recognize the croak of his own voice. They'd played the game often when she was young. He hoped the memory might distract her. "Marco?"

He inched his way in the opposite direction his body wanted to flee, moving toward danger, not away from it. "Marco?"

It didn't take him long to draw her out of hiding.

Two gold eyes, glowing in the moonlight, peered at him from the shadows. A massive outline detached from the dark, the color of her fur blending with the night. She slunk toward him with a grace more like a big cat. Her hackles raised, fur bristling along the ridge of her back and neck. She growled.

He trembled at the rumbled warning and felt his toes curl against the sodden material of his socks. Too late to run. "Polo?"

Fangs gleamed as her lip curled up, showing him the threat wasn't idle.

"Easy." He slung his rifle onto a shoulder. Every bit her hostage, he raised his hands. "Easy."

Pointed ears flicked back and forth and the growls petered out as her lip dropped back over her teeth. She stared at him and cocked her head to the side.

"That's it." He smiled, wondering if maybe he and AJ had both been wrong. This time, maybe they could all go home without a fuss. "Do you want to go home? Get out of the cold?"

She sat with a small huff, never once looking away. Those gold eyes bored into him and he swore he saw annoyance. He heard her sniff, and then that big head whipped around with surprising speed. Her long nose pointed in the direction AJ had gone and the growling returned. She hunched, ready to launch.

Before he'd stopped to put together any sort of plan the rifle was back in his hands. He pressed his cheek to the stock and tried to aim for the haunches. "No!"

She tipped her head his direction again, stood from her crouch and shook. Semi-warm, wet-dog smelling droplets of melted snow hit his face. After she seemed satisfied with drenching him she took a step forward, ears pricked.

AJ's rifle went off with a soft pop. There was no yelp to accompany the strike of the dart. The wolf jerked to the side, ears flat back against her skull, and snarled.

"Grady?"

"Cut that out," he told the wolf and swallowed at the baleful look he received in return. Animals should not have human expressions, but sometimes he knew better. He licked at his lips and cleared his throat. "I'm good, AJ. You got her. She's not down yet."

The wolf twisted and sniffed at the neon pink tuft peeking out of her fur. Then she snorted, like their puny needle attack offended her. Raising her snout she let out another howl. The deep timbre bounced off the trees and rattled him, the sound reverberating through his body.

AJ came at a run, stumbling and crashing through the underbrush like a panicked elk. "What did I say? Too close. Back off."

"It's alright. She's — we're alright," he said, watching the wolf sway. Her long legs wobbled as she staggered away, she weaved like a drunk attempting to stay upright. "She's not going to get far."

"I'm not going to be able to drive back in here. I'll go get the sled and we'll pull her out." AJ grabbed his arm and squeezed.

"I'm fine," he said and handed her the rifle. "We'll be fine here."

Her jaw worked back and forth, but she didn't say anything.

"AJ, I promise, we'll be here when you get back."

The wolf collapsed with a low whine, back legs going first, followed by the front. She kicked and struggled for a few moments, making a wolfy snow angel. She gave up with a sigh and lay still on her side.

He eased next to her, mindful of the beam of his headlamp. She whined and tossed her head when he took a knee beside her.

"You are such a pain in the ass." He stroked a hand down her back, flattening the fur still standing up.

Her tail swished in an almost wag and she whimpered. A pathetic sound for such a noble beast.

"I'm sorry, you know," he said and scratched behind one of her ears. "But I swear you're grounded."

CHAPTER ONE

Harper

Harper woke to the taste of dirt in her mouth. She groaned, moved strands of greasy dark hair out of her face, and cracked an eye open. Through the bars of the cage she saw the worn boxes filling the basement, some placed in haphazard towers as high as the few dirty half-windows. Even with the makeshift bricking, sunlight filtered through the cracks. She saw dust dancing around in the shafts of light, the smell blending with undertones of dirt and mildew. Her nose wrinkled seconds before she sneezed. A headache formed behind her sensitive eyes and her ears rang.

With a grunt, she dragged the moist blanket over her naked body, all the way over her head. The bare mattress under her cheek was damp with drool, but her head hurt too much for her to move away.

Her blanket cocoon wasn't much better. It was darker and the blanket felt nice on her overheated skin, but she couldn't escape the sounds. Every creak in the house, the skittering of rodent nails against the concrete floor, even the distant sounds of the television in the living room. Each added another percussive splash to the steady pounding in her head. Cooper called the cage her Fortress of Solitude, like Superman. She wasn't feeling superhuman at the moment.

Her cellphone went off just as she started to drift back to sleep. She growled and poked her head out of the top of the blanket. On the other side of the heavy bars she saw the little device, lit up and blaring "Hungry like the Wolf."

"Cooper." Annoyance flared with the headache. He thought he was funny. She huffed and reached to grasp the bars, pulling herself and the mattress across the floor. "Har, har, it's a wolf joke."

She licked at her lips, winced at the sour taste in her mouth, and slapped a hand down on the scratched phone. Not wanting loud noises near her ears, she set the phone to speaker and glared at it. "What?"

"You're late," Grady said, gruff voice tinny through the phone.

"I'm not going." She laid her head down on her arm and growled. "I have… Ebola. Yeah. Ebola."

"Harper."

"Uncle."

"Any memory of last night?"

"No," she said with a whine, and rubbed at her aching jaw. "Just the usual hangover. I didn't – "

"You didn't hurt anyone. Or anything, aside from my fence." He sighed and she could picture him glaring out the window of the bar. She didn't know why he was so attached to the stupid, flimsy fence anyway. "You'll be fixing that later. Right now you're going to your appointment."

"Fine," she said. "But when my head explodes, it's going to be your fault."

"Don't be so dramatic."

"Don't be so demanding." She pulled the blanket back over her head. "Forget the Ebola. There's an alien trying to hatch out of my skull."

"I wish it the best of luck, considering how hard your head is."

"Hey!"

"Get a move on, Harp. I know it sucks, but these appointments are important. They could –"

"Save my life, I know. I'll see you at work." She cut the call before he could say anything else. Something gentle or caring. Or worried. He did like to worry. Satisfied with having limited the amount of sap in her morning, she looked up at the wall. The key to the cage hung from the nail, within her reach if she stood.

"I hate this day already."

***

Foul mood cemented, Harper slammed out the front door with a scowl. The crisp mountain air ached in her lungs at the first intake. Some people loved it. Tourists liked to talk about it. Like the people who lived in Montana year round didn't know the air was clean. The Californians, in particular, raved about the fresh air. She liked it well enough, except for that first lungful the morning after a full moon. It didn't make her hangover feel any better.

Hands on her hips, she tilted her head back, stretching the kinks out of her back. Vertebrae crackled and popped from her neck to her tailbone. She looked down the street toward town. Their house sat right at the base of Mooneye Mountain, the town of Fincher sprawled out below.

The grocery store, strip mall, Pronghorn hotel, all were where they'd

PURE OF HEART

been the day before. So at least she knew she hadn't gone on a rampage and burned it all down. Her lip curled at the sight of Mooneye Lodge, still standing. That one she wouldn't have felt bad for ripping down with her bare paws.

Her nose twitched, the smell of cat and aftershave burning her sinuses. She spotted Mr. Reimann stepping out of his house. He had his Elmer Fudd hat perched high on his bald head and a snow shovel over his shoulder. He paused halfway down the steps from his porch and stared right at her.

She wondered if the wolf had kept him up. If he'd been tucked into his bed with the light on and heard her howling in the woods. He'd bellowed at Grady more than once over the disgusting messes sometimes left in their yard. Okay, and his, but just that one time. He'd never mentioned the howling though. Or made a noise complaint.

It wasn't like she could help it. The part of her she kept hidden was proud of the gifts it brought the family. Not that Mr. Reimann would care about the why behind the messes. Just about his neighbor's niece turning into a giant wolf when the moon was full. He'd care about that.

"Probably already has a pitchfork," she muttered, but waved anyway. In as sarcastic a manner as she could, of course. He ignored her and began shoveling.

The scrape of the shovel against the concrete irritated her the same way Grady's ancient vacuum cleaner did. She shuddered and fled down the sidewalk.

Running in snow boots wasn't ideal, but it did give her muscles a chance to stretch. The endorphin rush wasn't bad either. By the time she made it down the hill to Black Bear Coffee she almost smiled. Then she saw the bear in a Santa suit painted on the glass door.

She rolled her eyes and shoved the door open, wondering when the cutesy Christmas stuff would disappear. All the fake cheer gave her a stomach ache. Preoccupied with Grinch-y thoughts, she missed Logan walking toward her.

They collided with a thunk, her forehead connecting with his chin.

She shrieked as the sting of scalding liquid soaked through her thin shirt.

"Harper!" he yelped.

"Yeah, that's me." She groaned and held out her shirt to check the damage. "Walk much?"

Blue eyes looked at the squashed paper cup and then back at her. "Uh. I'm really sorry, Harper. I didn't see you." His best sheepish smile and puppy dog expression appeared. If only he knew it irritated her further. "I'll buy your coffee, okay? To make up for it."

She huffed. "No, thanks. I think I want to keep some distance between us when you're carrying hot beverages."

"Come on, Harper. It was an accident. Besides, in section three of the best friends' contract it says I'm supposed to buy you nice things when I do something dumb."

She shook a coffee dripping finger in his face. "You need to stop quoting something we wrote in crayon. Especially in public."

"Colored pencil," he corrected and tried to dab at the stain setting into the red fabric of her shirt.

"Whatever." She smacked his hand away and glared at him. "Stop it, you're making it worse. What distracted you anyway?"

"Nothing," he said, backing away and blushing.

"Marissa?"

"Harpy." He groaned, shaking his head.

She screwed up her face at the unfortunate nickname. "Are we eight? Did I get stuck in some sort of time vortex?" She grabbed her chest and sighed with mock relief. "Nope. Those are still here. Definitely not eight."

He wrinkled his nose. "Cut it out. You're in a mood today."

"I think it's a side-effect of being doused in coffee instead of drinking it. Contact high? Sugar rush through osmosis?" She glanced at herself again. "Do I even want to know what that was? I smell like I fell into Wonka's chocolate river."

"It's a double-shot chocolate –"

"Never mind. Why don't you ask for her number already?"

"Who?" He ducked his head, floppy brown hair falling into his eyes.

Her lip curled into a smirk. "Really? Look, if you don't man up I'm going to have to do that thing I swore I would never, ever do again."

"Skinny dip?"

She slapped his shoulder. "Meddle in your love life."

"No, no. Harper, don't even think about it."

"Too late. What's your deal?"

"Maybe I-" he paused and scuffled the toe of a shoe on the checkered linoleum. "Maybe I've got somebody else in mind."

She sized up every woman under the age of sixty in the small room. "Somehow I doubt you're picking up retirees. When I figure out who it is I'm only going to torment you more. Because I care, and you're keeping it secret. You know how I adore a good love triangle."

"You hate soap operas."

"Exactly," she said and nodded, lips pursed. "Imagine what I would do to you if you made me live one. Now, is there any chance we could sit down and discuss whatever it is you desperately needed to talk to me about? Since we're both here and I'm already late, why not?"

He stared at her for a long moment, squinting one eye. "For a smart person you're really dumb sometimes."

"Well now that you've buttered me up." She flapped her shirt with a grimace, skin sticky underneath. "Or maybe you marinated me."

"Just sit down, will you? I'll get your coffee and I promise not to spill a drop. Black, right?"

She nodded and slid into the nearest dark green booth. "And a huckleberry bar!"

"Yeah, yeah," he said, waving.

Behind the counter, Marissa, who'd been eyeballing them the whole time, smiled at her. She was cute in that girl-next-door kind of way, the perfect complement to Logan's awkward boy-next-door. Except she wouldn't be the type to make the first move, and Logan was far too nervous around girls to ever stutter a request for her number.

Harper turned away first, feigning boredom. The usual morning crowd filled the shop, giving her plenty to look at. Older couples, mostly, sharing the local paper and enjoying a good cup of coffee. She didn't want to watch them either, but the various bear pictures that made up the décor were even more dull.

Then again, bear pictures didn't talk about her.

Her ears picked up the hushed conversations from the patrons around her.

"She seems calm now. I wonder if Grady got her some help."

"You didn't see her a couple nights ago. Tossed Ken out on his rear with one hand."

"Ken Southard? You're making that up. He's twice her size."

"I'm not. He swatted her on the backside and she knocked the whole table over to get at him. Sheriff got called out again."

"That temper of hers is going to get her in hot water sooner or later. Hot enough Grady won't be able to fix it."

She sighed through her nose, rubbing at the corner of her eye as it twitched. Somehow tossing a guy out of the bar for playing grab ass made her the villain. That made sense. Not.

Logan sidled up to the booth and handed her a massive cup of coffee and napkin wrapped breakfast bar. She smiled. "Well?"

"No well. I told you, Marissa's nice, but I've got someone else in mind."

"Is she out of your league or something?"

"Thanks a lot," he said, flopping down opposite her with his own fresh cup.

She sighed. "I didn't mean to imply anything. What I'm trying to say is if you like this mystery woman you should tell her."

He rolled his cup between his hands. "Yeah, and if she doesn't react in a positive way, then what?"

"Then you move on and find somebody who deserves your attention." She nibbled at the corner of her bar, frowning as she chewed.

Logan rubbed at the back of his neck, face red, eyes focused on his coffee.

"Is this what you wanted to talk to me about?" she asked.

"Kind of. I — " He sucked in a noisy breath. "Harper, I wanted to ask if you – I'd like to take you out to dinner."

The huckleberry bar bounced on the table. She swallowed, hard, trying not to scream "no" at the top of her lungs. "Logan, I don't think that's a good idea."

His fingers tapped out an odd rhythm on the Formica tabletop. "Look, I know you haven't dated since Ben died."

No, don't say his name. Don't. She closed her eyes and shook her head. Her stomach roiled, muscles twisting. A heaviness fell on her back and chills struck her side. She knew what she'd find if she looked.

Ben sat beside her, grinning at her with his bloodstained teeth, his throat torn open.

"I can't," she said. "I can't. We're best friends. You've been my best friend for years. I'm not going to risk that. I'm really… flattered, but it's not a good idea."

Logan ran a hand through his hair and puffed up his cheeks before expelling a long sigh. "Why not? Why can't we try? I know I'm not him and you're still – he was your first love, I get it. I'm not trying to replace him or anything. But you said it. We're already best friends, we hang out all the time. Nothing really has to change."

We can't "try" because I will "try" to kill you too. Try and succeed. She shivered and glanced again at Ben. Logan would be the same. He'd want the same things that had gotten Ben killed. The hand holding, cuddles, kisses, and the… other things. "We don't hang out all the time."

"Not as much, but we used to. We used to be inseparable, remember? Until Ben's accident. I know it's awful, and I'm so sorry, but Harper, you're so sad and I know you're lonely."

"It wouldn't be like it used to," she said and shook her head. "It wouldn't." *Not when you're trying to date a werewolf.* "Logan, we wouldn't work as a couple. Trust me. Being friends with me is hard enough. You don't want me as a girlfriend."

He reached over and squeezed her hand. "How do you know? If it doesn't work out, it doesn't work out. No big deal. We'd still be friends, I promise. What harm could come from trying?"

"You know better. Maybe it wouldn't totally destroy our friendship, but it would strain it if we broke up. I don't want to risk it."

"Just one date, and if it doesn't feel right, I won't bother you about it again."

It hurt to disappoint him, but she'd rather hurt his feeling than rip his throat out. "I'm sorry, Logan. No. You're a great guy and some day you're going to make the right girl over the moon happy. I'm not that girl."

PURE OF HEART

His hopeful smile fell, he let go of her hand. She slipped out of the booth, clutching her coffee and breakfast, wincing at him. "I'm sorry, I really am. I have to go. I'm late."

"Yeah. Sure," he said, looking out the window.

***

It didn't take her long to speed-walk through the heart of Fincher. AJ's house, which doubled as her vet clinic, sat just to the side of the largest subdivision in the valley. Harper was glad to turn the corner off the main street and see the blue, dog-shaped sign. "Dr. Bell's Veterinary Clinic" it boasted in big white letters. She'd survived another trek through touristville. Everything in Fincher was bright, gaudy. She'd about had it with the Christmas barf all over town. AJ's bore no such trappings. The dark blue home was soothing to look at, free of lights and wreaths and weird plastic Santas, snowmen, or reindeer.

On her first step up the slanted sidewalk leading to the clinic door, her feet went out from under her. She caught herself, slapping both hands down on the railing on either side of the walkway. The rings on her hands clanged against the cold metal and she thought her teeth might have clicked together like a cartoon. She managed not to take her frustration to the next level by stomping around and throwing a Yosemite Sam type fit.

Teeth clenched, she held on for dear life and crept toward the door again. She may have looked like an old woman going about it that way, but she was an upright old woman. That would have to do.

"AJ, are you trying to get yourself sued?" she called as she threw open the door. "You have ice melt, what are you hoarding it for? The Snowman Apocalypse?"

"Ahem."

Harper turned toward the throat-clearer, scarf still half unwrapped. "Trish."

"Harper." Trish smiled in that frightening, tight manner of hers.

It always meant the same thing. Game on. "Fresh bleach job?"

"Fresh face job?"

"How nice of you to notice," she said, patting her cheeks. "Where's AJ?"

"For a social call? Oh, no, another appointment. Are you aware Dr. Bell is a veterinarian?"

"Are you aware that there's a puddle of piss on the good doctor's hardwood floor two feet in front of your desk?" She pointed, making a circle with her finger to indicate the size of the wet spot. Exaggerated, because she liked to see Trish's eyes bulge. "Clean up on aisle bitch."

Trish smiled, teeth gleaming in the fluorescent light. Her real smile. Point, Harper. "Dr. Bell is busy."

"Come on, Trish. I'm here for my rabies shot," she said with a pout.

"Very important. I saw what happened to Old Yeller."

"You're ridiculous."

"And you love it." Grinning wide, she gestured toward the back offices. "Really though, where is she? I'm supposed to be helping out."

"Out back with Freckles." Trish rolled her eyes so hard the action could have been seen from space. "Try not to make a mess today, okay? And stay away from the cats. It took us an hour to coax Mittens out from under AJ's sofa."

Her grin fell into a frown as she looked out the window facing the barn and paddock outside. "Freckles... the horse?"

Trish nodded, hiding another cheeky grin behind a fake'n baked tanned hand.

"Perfect."

Game, Trish.

***

Snow had started falling in the short time Harper had been inside, thin flakes that melted away as soon as they landed. She groaned as she caught the scent of butterscotch, blended with the heavier odor of horse. Tracking the smell was easy enough. She stopped short when she saw AJ. Out in the paddock where Trish had said. With a giant horse. Gray and black and speckled, he towered over the petite woman.

AJ looked up, flicked her long coffee-black hair over her shoulder and raised a hand in a wave. "Harper! You're late, but at least you made it, and fully clothed."

"That never gets old for you, does it?" She slunk toward the paddock fence and froze when Freckles turned to stare at her. His nostrils flared and she felt herself mimic the action.

"Nope, 'fraid not." AJ grinned, unperturbed by the staring contest going on. "Come on in."

"Thanks, but I think I'll stay here."

"I insist."

She shook her head, without looking away from wide, horsey-brown eyes, and crossed her arms over her chest. "I politely decline."

"Guess it's going to be a 'sorry Charlie' type day for you. Get in here."

Kicking at the snow, Harper gripped the upper bar of the old gray, wooden fence and started to climb. "Horses don't like me. They're mean. They bite and run away even when I try to give them treats."

AJ shrugged and turned around to pet Freckle's dark muzzle when he nudged her shoulder. "You'll just have to work harder to win him over with that sweet personality of yours. Freckles might be sympathetic if you tell him about the tests I'm going to run on you later."

Harper narrowed her eyes, one leg hanging in the air over the beam. "Every time, Jay?"

"Sorry, Charlie." AJ flashed the worst innocent smile ever.

"How much blood do you need, woman?" Resigned to her fate, she dropped into the snow in the danger zone. "Are you running some sort of underground wolf blood operation I should know about?"

"Come here, you." AJ reached for her, gloved hand out, palm up. "I'm a scientist, I'm studying. Studying means research, research means samples. You happen to be what I'm studying, which means to do research, I need samples, from you, so I can work."

Ignoring her outstretched hand, Harper inched toward her friend and the horse. "And people say I'm a smart-ass."

"People say a lot of things, but that one's true."

"He's already scared," Harper pointed out. Freckles snorted, as though in agreement.

"He probably smells predator, as I'm sure part of you smells prey," AJ said. "He needs to know you're not going to eat him."

"Oh, is that all?" Deciding to stay clear of the toothy end of the horse, she stopped out of Freckles reach and held her hand up over her nose. She wouldn't tell AJ, but there was a smell coming from the twitchy animal other than plain horse odor. Something sour and sharp. Fear. Her mouth watered even as her stomach twisted in revulsion. "Hello, non-prey prey animal," she said with all the fake bravado she had. "I promise I have no desire to eat you. Not even if you were smothered in barbecue sauce."

"Harper!"

"What?" She held up her hands and stepped back, away from AJ's reproachful glower. "I'm just doin-"

Freckles' hooves slammed into her ribs, and she somersaulted through the air. She hit the fence, what little breath left in her lungs exploding out of her mouth at impact. The boards cracked and splintered beneath her and she crashed into the snow.

Everything went still.

"Harper?"

"Ow," she said, fighting both nausea and strong murderous urges. When she opened her eyes, she sucked in a deep breath, despite the pain in her ribs. Her vision sharpened, like a flicked switch had taken her from regular to high-definition.

"Harper! Are you okay?"

She twisted to check her arms for breaks and wiggled her hips to make sure she had sensation in her legs. When everything checked out she sat up with a low groan. "Nothing's broken, I'm alive. Keep that asshole over there and tell him he hits like a girl."

AJ nodded, hands clamped on Freckles' face. The big baby leaned all his weight onto tiny AJ, hiding his face in her chest. "Are you sure you're alright? Sweets, that could have killed you."

"I'm fine. Promise, promise." Harper shook her head again. She struggled back to her feet and glared at the horse.

"Your eyes!" AJ gasped. "I need to – how long does that last again?"

"I haven't exactly timed it," she said, blinking to adjust to her super vision. Seeing the freckles dusted across AJ's cheekbones and the indentation of her teeth where she'd chewed her lip was weird. She closed her eyes again. "I'm reconsidering that whole horses are friends not food thing."

Freckles whinnied and stamped his feet.

Laughing at her.

Stupid horse.

***

Harper sat on an examination table in the back of the clinic. Away from prying human eyes. The cats in the kennels across from her, however, had no problem staring. She held tight to the rolled lip of the stainless steel table and fought to hold back a growl. Her lip curled as one fluffy white cat hunched up and yowled at her.

"This is absolutely fascinating," AJ said, poking and prodding at Harper's tender rib-cage. "Minimal swelling, the bruise is already fading. At this rate, in an hour it'll be like it never happened." She swatted Harper's knee and glanced up from her too close examination. "Stop antagonizing my patients."

"She started it." Looking away proved difficult. The cat hissed and slashed at the cage door. "See?" She huffed when AJ pinched her stomach. "Are all your patients so aggressive?"

"Some more than others," AJ said, back to pressing at Harper's ribs. "I don't think anything's broken. Or at least not anymore. I want to do an X-Ray, see if there are any cracks and track the mending. Can anything stop you? I should take pictures."

"Mm, yeah, it's all very cool and sciency. Egghead. I regenerate or heal or whatever. I'm an X-Men, man – woman… Thing." She leaned away from AJ's cold fingers. "Can you put my shirt down now?"

"Sweets, you're one of a kind. I need to know about this, about you. It could save your life someday."

"Do you see an angry mob in my future? You and Grady keep talking about saving my life."

AJ shook her head and dropped the shirt. "Let's not think about it. We worry, and we'll leave it at that. I'm going to take your temperature and draw some blood."

"Goody," Harper said, eyeing the thermometer. "That's yours, right? From upstairs? Not the one you – with the animals in the…" she gestured.

"Please." AJ waved the instrument back and forth. "You think I'd do that to you?"

PURE OF HEART

Harper opened her mouth to retort and AJ struck, sticking the device under her tongue with scary accuracy.

"There. See? Not so bad," she said with a smirk. She wrapped a tube around Harper's arm while they waited for a reading. Then picked up a needle attached to a vial. "Okay, little prick."

The thermometer beeped as AJ plunged the needle home. Harper used her un-occupied hand to free her mouth and squinted at the readout. "I can never tell if you're calling me a little prick or warning me."

AJ smiled. "I'll leave that up to you."

"How considerate."

"What's it say?"

"One hundred and three." Harper shivered as AJ pulled the needle from her arm, not bothering with putting a cotton swab against the small wound. It would stop bleeding in seconds.

"Higher than normal. Do you feel alright?"

"I feel like I got kicked by a psycho horse and stabbed with a needle."

"Harper."

"It's normal. It goes up when I'm injured, and the night before and day of the full moon. It'll go back down." Leaning back on the palms of her hands, she stared up at the lights and kicked her feet.

"Do you mind staying here until it does? I'd like to track that too. And keep an eye on you."

Harper shrugged. "Why not."

"Don't sound so excited," AJ said, grinning when Harper sighed. She stepped close and untangled the stethoscope from around her neck. "Consider it a girls' day."

"This is the worst spa ever."

"So anybody special to talk about?"

"Subtle." Harper stiffened and arched her neck away from AJ. She thought about Logan and winced. Over AJ's shoulder she saw Ben again, standing by the cats. His shirt hung in tatters from his shoulders, a gaping hole in the chest exposing shredded flesh. He grinned at her, blood dribbling between his teeth and down his chin.

"Hey, I'm just asking. It's this thing called girl-talk. Humor me."

"There's nobody. There hasn't been since Ben." She snapped her mouth closed, tightening her jaw. "Never mind. It wouldn't matter if there was, and you know that."

"Breathe deep for me," AJ said. She listened, head cocked to the side as Harper complied. "Harp, I know it's difficult, but you're human. You're human and something more. Humans crave company and there's also a part of you that's a pack animal. It's not bad for you to want companionship, it's healthy."

"That's not – I have a –" Harper choked and then all but spat the word.

"Pack. You, Grady, Coop… Logan." *If we're even still friends.* She glanced at Ben again and shuddered. "I've dated, remember how that ended? It's not a good idea. I won't risk it again. I'm not normal. I'm dangerous."

"Harper." AJ dropped the stethoscope and leaned in, bracing her palms on either side of Harper's hips. "It was an accident."

"It was murder, and it wouldn't have happened if I was normal."

"You can't give up," AJ said. She straightened, pulling a penlight from her pocket. "You'll learn to control it, and then what? Life is for the living."

Harper fixed her face into a blank mask and watched the light move back and forth. "Learning to control it now won't change what happened before."

"Nothing will. But the past is the past, we live today and dream for tomorrow."

She snorted. "Thanks, Dr. Phil."

"Maybe, Sweets." AJ smiled and tugged at the end of Harper's braid. "Maybe you haven't met the right person. Someone both parts of you accepts. Someone you can trust."

"Because that's simple. What category do I put werewolfism under on my online dating profile?"

"First and foremost, it would probably help if you let your walls down a bit." AJ raised a hand, thumb and forefinger close together. "Just shy of impenetrable should do."

"I want to be normal," she said, gaze falling back to the corner where Ben had been standing. "I want a normal life. It's just not possible."

AJ clicked the light off. "I thought you never backed down from a challenge."

"Sometimes people are meant to be alone. That's not a challenge, it's a fact."

"Normal is boring, Harper." AJ said with a small smile. "You're special, that's all, and it's beautiful."

"I thought the argument was that everyone is special?"

"Oh." AJ picked up the chart at the end of the table and scribbled notes. "So you are normal then?"

"I hate it when you do that." Harper rolled her eyes and offered a weak grin when she caught AJ's smirk. Her chest ached, and it had nothing to do with the healing contusion.

"When I win an argument?"

"No, when you steal my thunder."

"I see," AJ said. "Ever the sore loser. Let's get an X-Ray. We'll tell Trish we're testing the equipment. I promise I'll let you go in time to get to work."

Harper craned her neck to try and see her file, catching a glimpse of a photo. A black wolf mid-stride, almost posing for the picture. "You keep that locked up, right?"

"Your file?" AJ shot her an incredulous look. "I promise it's safe. Nobody is ever going to be interested in digging through my files. Trust me."

"You I trust, it's everyone else I worry about."

"Well, I don't think you need to worry about Trish stumbling over it and trying to go all werewolf hunter."

The mental image of Trish dressed up in a duster with a wide-brim hat and holding a revolver loaded with silver bullets made her choke back a laugh. "No, I don't think Trish is someone to worry about. But if she told someone else what she'd found, like Holt, that would be bad."

"Holt's an idiot," AJ said and pressed Harper down onto the table. "You don't need to worry about him. He may hunt everything he can get a tag for, but I don't think you're in danger. I'm going to take some pictures, real quick. Then we'll get back to the dating discussion. Speaking of dating, and Holt, please don't date him."

"AJ." Harper groaned and squirmed on the table. "Gross."

CHAPTER TWO

Run.

The thought and accompanying urge buzzed through Harper's body. She groaned, turned onto her side and folded her pillow over her head. "Five more minutes."

Her feet twitched, stirring the blankets.

Run.

"Yell all you want. You're not the boss of me."

She felt the familiar pressure of a budding cramp low in her calf. Gritting her teeth, she pulled the pillow harder against her ear. One eyelid joined the twitching party, along with her feet and hands. "I don't negotiate with terrorists. Do your worst."

Determined to get five extra minutes of lounge time, she continued to ignore it all. Even when the muscles in her thighs began to flex and relax.

It went away, all of the twitching, as quickly as it arrived. Thinking she'd won, she smirked and nestled deeper into her mattress.

Then the calf cramp returned with a vengeance.

She yelped and rolled as agony ripped through her leg. Her quick reflexes saved her from face planting as she toppled over the side of the bed onto the floor. She slapped a hand against the carpet, elbow stinging from the awkward landing, the side of her face smushed against the rug. "Alright, I'm up."

She grabbed the toes of her stricken leg and pulled back as hard as she dared. The sensation bled away, replaced by a dull throbbing.

If she'd had a tail at that moment, it would have been wagging.

"This is ridiculous," she muttered with a wince. "I'm my own demanding pet."

***

Harper hopped forward through the fresh snow in the backyard. She told herself her bigger steps were to keep her socks from getting wet, and had nothing to do with mounting excitement. All her reasoning fell away as she neared the fence. She could see the gaping hole where she had crashed through to escape, made a note to fix it later, and grabbed the top, hauling herself over in one fluid motion.

On the other side she stood up and stretched, took in the view. It always felt a bit like surveying her kingdom. She realized the thought was absurd, but she couldn't deny the brush of pride, looking over this patch of Earth. Her territory. The wolf in her relished the idea. Every log she vaulted over, every stream, rock, tree, and bush, all of it was hers.

She bounced twice on the balls of her feet, then took off for the trees. Her legs flashed out in front of her, toes digging into her shoes and the ground beneath, hurtling her forward. It felt right; she belonged here, running through the quiet forest in the gray pre-dawn. She ran faster, leapt higher, grinned even when she lost her footing and splashed through thin ice into half-frozen puddles. As she cleared a fallen tree, a whoop escaped her throat, spurring her on.

Her ears pricked, as she listened hard for an answer to her call.

She felt an uncomfortable sensation, a sharp tug in her gut that had nothing to do with physical exertion. The fresh wave of excitement that followed caused her to trip, left her jittery like she'd had too much coffee. An even stronger urge to howl made her chest ache.

She grit her teeth against the feeling and ran harder. Whatever the wolf was up to this time she could ignore. They were out for a run, not to hunt down some animal or whatever else might have it excited.

Five miles went by in a blur. Her destination loomed ahead, sooner than she would have liked. She could see the cairns she'd constructed, stone towers standing side by side like sentinels. Her heart climbed higher into her throat at the sight of them, covered in snow, standing in a clearing with more flakes trickling down from the trees. They beckoned her forward. Her stride slowed, her body reacting out of habit.

She stumbled the last few steps on numb feet. "Hi, Mama," she whispered and dropped to her knees before the somber monuments. "Dad, Ben, Naomi." Ben sat beside his cairn, covered in blood, neck ripped open, grinning like a fool.

The lump in her throat rode up and down as she swallowed. She shook her head and dug trembling fingers into the snow on either side of her legs. "I'm sorry I don't have flowers. It's kind of cold for wild ones. I'll pick some up later and bring them tomorrow."

She pressed on, and told them about how things had been. Recounted the story of Freckles the horse, and the drama with Logan.

Out of the corner of her eye, she saw the sun coming up over the lake.

She turned to watch. A small breeze picked up, tossing the damp hair that had escaped her bobby pin. She smiled and pushed her bangs back.

"Good morning to you too," she said. "I miss you guys."

Once the sun had fully risen, Harper forced herself to get up and go back. Returning home felt like trudging through waist deep sludge wearing ankle weights. Everything, every cell and fiber in her body, resisted. The wolf pressed against her, urging her to go the opposite direction, deeper into the woods, further from civilization and the pain and loneliness she couldn't fix.

Her muscles strained with each step. Steam came off her body, her joints ached. She lurched forward. And stopped.

She groaned. Her body swayed backwards, feet planted in slush. "Come on, Grady will kill me if I disappear into the woods again. There's nothing here but gravestones."

Another small step forward, and another, until her slow creep turned into a rough jog. Each step sent a jolt of pain through her legs.

She stretched her stride when she felt things loosen. Driving her feet hard into the snow, she leapt over the last log laying over her path before the trail home. The last mile marker. Soon she'd be able to see the ugly yellow paint of the house.

She caught the hint of an odor that didn't belong, and her feet ceased all forward motion so suddenly her upper body rocked forward, and she slid. A thin current zapped down her spine, the wolf raising hackles it didn't have. She caught the scent again, no longer faint but growing stronger. Compelled to face the intruder, she turned, every muscle stiff, ready for a fight. Her vision sharpened and a warning growl gurgled in the back of her throat.

Behind her a gray and white dog with mismatched eyes stood on the trail. He raised his hackles and growled back, lip curled and teeth on display.

"Luka," she said through clenched teeth. She didn't need to see the name etched on his ID tag to recognize him. Only one person in Fincher owned a Malamute. He'd been in AJ's before too, and she hoped he wasn't still angry about the neutering business. "Does Trevor know you've gone for a stroll?"

He stepped toward her, head low, tail out straight behind him.

An aggressive stance, a challenge.

She felt itching along her gums and shook her head. The wolf pushed so hard her head swam, she held up her hands. "Hold on, just — " She sucked in a deep breath and closed her eyes when a knuckle cracked and one of her fingers snapped. "Wait, wait."

Dizzy and already tired she opened her eyes in time to see Luka lunging straight at her face, jaws gaping.

She caught him by the throat with one hand, and sidestepped. Her other hand followed him down, slapping the side of his head. They crashed together onto the forest floor, with her perched on his ribs. Her fingers closed around his throat as she leaned down, unperturbed by his snapping teeth. His legs kicked out, searching for leverage, but she settled her weight and pressed his face harder into the cold ground.

He licked his lips and whined.

It would be easy to kill him. She flexed her fingers and another knuckle wrenched itself out of place. He'd challenged her in her territory. If she let him live, he might come back and try again. Better to take his throat and extinguish the threat once and for all.

"No," she said, words garbled through a mouthful of canines. "No."

He whined repeatedly, ears flattened back against his skull. Her grip tightened. Anger sat, a hot and heavy stone in her gut. Luka let out a strangled yelp, his ribs expanding under her as he struggled to breathe. She gripped harder, watching him panic. Another growl warmed her throat and she dug deeper into his downy white fur. He mewled, a pathetic sound. A little harder, hold on a little longer and he would stop struggling forever.

"No!"

She gasped and released him, sat back on her heels, moving away from his face. She looked at her hands, horrified, and saw tufts of hair trapped between her fingers. He raised his head and turned to look at her. The acrid stink of his fear and the heavier, muskier scent of wet dog burned her nose. Tears blurred her vision as she looked at him, panting and trembling.

Vulnerable.

"God, I'm sorry. I'm sorry." She slid off of him and stood. He rolled over and staggered to his feet, tail tucked and body hunched. When she reached for him, he recoiled.

"It's okay, it's okay, buddy, I'm sorry," she said as her teeth receded. He wagged his tail once and allowed her to pet his head. "Sorry."

He leaned into her hand when she scratched behind one ear. "Go on home."

She didn't have to tell him twice. As soon as her hand left his fur he slunk around her and trotted back the way he'd come. Pausing once to glance back and wag his tail hesitantly.

"We're good."

The second he was out of sight she dropped her chin to her chest. Her eyesight dimmed after a few deep breaths and she turned to once again force her leaden feet to carry her home.

***

She didn't stop to clamber over the fence covertly. All she wanted was to get inside and take a long, scalding shower. She jumped once in range, hooked her fingers over the top of the wood. The fence swayed and wobbled under the abuse. She pressed her feet against the boards and shoved.

In the back of her mind, she knew it was risky. If the neighbor caught her again, she'd have to come up with another excuse for the acrobatics. But she didn't smell him, so she thought she'd made it free and clear.

Her landing lacked any grace. She hit the ground and rolled, kicking up powder.

The scent of honey whiskey, peat and pine brushed against her nose midway through her somersault.

"I give it a three point five," Grady said. He stood on the back porch, both hands on his hips. The smile he wore made her feel like she ought to copy Luka's earlier repentant stance. Tail between her legs. If she'd had a tail to tuck. "You've got to stick the landing."

"Uh..." She pointed back at the fence, mouth flapping as she chased an explanation.

"Don't even try. Not even you can come up with a passable excuse for parkouring your way over my fence. Which you will be fixing later, again."

"Right." She cleared her throat and stood, swatting at any clinging snow or other woodland debris.

"Cooper's awake. Said you were making pancakes." His grin turned devilish. He opened the back door and made a grand gesture for her to go inside. "Madame, the stove awaits."

She skittered around him, wet shoes squeaking against the floor. She felt him glowering at the back of her head. "I'll mop up before I go out."

"You think?"

"I don't suppose I have time for a — "

"Nope. You promised. Pancakes. Coffee."

She groaned and marched into the kitchen with all the enthusiasm of a prisoner on their way to the gallows. "Coffee first?"

"That's my girl," he said and settled himself at the kitchen table.

"I'm sorry about the — "

"Uh-uh." He held up a finger and then pointed it at the modest coffee maker. "Brew."

"You're not even going to let me apologize?"

"Nope."

Fuming, she dumped grounds into the filter. For a brief moment she considered revenge. She could switch his coffee to decaf, but she abandoned the plan. They could all be awful in the morning, but Grady without caffeine was like a bear trapped in a mini-van.

Once the pot started to burble she turned to the cupboard and dug out the pancake mix. "Sometimes I feel like a maid or something."

He snorted, face obscured by the paper. Save for his forehead and the eyebrow she could see arching. "If that were true, I would have fired you already. Have you seen your room?"

"Have you seen yours? I can smell it, even down here." She smiled, attempting innocence. He dipped the paper to glare at her. "Right. Less smartassing, coffee's done."

"So," he said after she set a warm mug in his waiting hands. "What happened to you this morning?"

She looked down at her damp clothes and the gaping hole in her shirt. "That's two shirts in two days. My luck sucks."

"Your avoidance tactics are as bad as your luck. Did you get in a fight with a tree?" he asked, setting his mug down after taking a sip.

Her eyes rolled. "Yes, Grady, a Spruce. Leave the sarcasm to the professionals, please."

"I must be rusty."

"Or old."

"Harper." He reached out as if to strangle her, then changed his mind and grabbed his coffee again. "What happened?"

She shrugged. "I had a run in with Trevor's dog. That's all. Nothing out of the ordinary."

"You didn't hurt him, did you?"

"Oops. Think he'll notice his dog is missing?"

Grady's cup clattered on the table.

"Joke, Grady. Joke. I didn't hurt the puppy." *Almost did*, but he didn't need to know that. "Speaking of puppies, where is young master Cooper?"

"Cleaning his room. Which I assume you had something to do with. God knows I can't get him to do it unless I threaten to ground him for life."

"You need better material." She shook her head and flopped a finished pancake onto the stack she'd been building. "I told him I'd play Warrior of Duty or something if he did his chores. I find positive reinforcement works best."

"For him or you?"

She waved the spatula at him. "Don't be an ass."

"Because that's your job? We could talk about last night at work instead?"

"That sounds suspiciously like you being an ass."

"It's called being a concerned uncle," he said, grinning.

"Holt happened. What's there to talk about? Same Holt, different night. Didn't we already cover this?"

"I don't know, Harp. You tell me. These incidents with him seem to be happening more frequently."

"He's got his..." she held up her free hand for finger quotes. "'Sights' on me. Guess he got tired of chasing the tourists. I keep telling him no, but he won't take a hint. Laughs it off like I'm playing a game." She flipped a pancake, spattering the stove with batter. "It's worse when he's drunk."

"Can you explain why I'm not allowed to break his fingers?" Grady asked.

"Break his fingers? Are we running a mob?"

"Knee capping would be more mob style." He tossed the paper aside and pushed his mug away. "It only takes one time. If you're exposed — "

She clicked off the stove with more force than necessary and rubbed the back of her neck. "Don't talk to me like I don't know the risks to all of us. I'm the monster here. The one with blood on her teeth. I'm the one they'll kill or, I don't know, ship to Area 51, or whatever."

"That's not going to happen. That's not what I meant."

"Isn't it?"

"No. I meant we should develop a game plan. See if together we can come up with a way to get some distance between you two." He stood up, but she shot him a sideways glance so he didn't approach. "Harper, you're not — I know this is hard. It's hard on all of us. But you are not a monster. Your parents weren't monsters either."

"Well they're not here," she said with unintended bitterness. "I'm alone, and I don't know how to do this. There's nobody to show me how this works."

"We'll figure it out. You're already so much better."

"Am I? I'm still in a cage every full moon. Still locking myself in the freezer at work, because if I lose my temper I could kill someone. Maybe we need to stop kidding ourselves."

"Harp."

"No." She slapped the spatula down on the stove. "I'm done. Thanks for the talk. I'll handle Holt. I need to learn to control myself without going furry and fanged. I'll keep my dirty secret. Right now I'm going to get Coop, so you two can have a nice, normal parent-child conversation over breakfast." On the way out of the kitchen she snagged the truck keys. "I'm going to the store. Add whatever you want to the list."

She left the room before he could say anything else, her hands scrubbing her eyes.

***

"Perfect. Fabulous." Harper huffed and glared out the window of Grady's truck. Snow. Again. Big flakes that would stick and make everything slick.

She reached across the seat for her leather jacket. The sound of a squeal outside the window startled her. People were walking by on the sidewalk, sipping from paper cups, and laughing at the snowmen the townies had constructed. Festive and cute, another draw for the tourists and their money. The squeal had come from a little boy she didn't recognize. He was so overdressed for the snow, she thought he might bounce like a ball if he fell. Another squeal escaped his wide open mouth. He pointed up at the snow and flailed his mittened hands. His parents smiled and waited while he bounced in place and stuck his tongue out to catch a flake.

They had to be from someplace warm, sunny. That reaction didn't come from people used to this.

He managed to catch one and squealed again with childish delight. His father bent down and scooped him up, swung him up onto his shoulders. His mother grinned and tugged on one tiny foot. They continued on their way, laughing.

She watched them go, a familiar pang in her chest. Puffing up her cheeks, she let her held breath out in one big whoosh. "Get the groceries. Go home."

The truck door creaked open. She rolled her eyes and flapped it a couple of times. "And add something to fix that noise before I break the door off."

Hands wedged deep in her pockets and head bowed she stalked down the sidewalk, the argument with Grady fresh in her mind. She knew he meant well, but the more she thought about Holt and the wolf, the angrier she got. Conversations like that only served as a reminder of how different she was.

"Look, there's Harper," she heard someone say and shuffled her feet faster. Not fast enough to outrun wolf hearing. "Poor dear, she had another episode last night. Did you hear? She's got quite the temper."

"Holt's such a sweet boy, he really should aim higher."

Her phone went off in her pocket. She hadn't noticed she'd stopped, and blinked a couple of times to refocus. With a sideways glare at the two gossiping ladies, she growled and dug into her jeans. A text from Logan greeted her.

Movie l8r?

He'd added a smiley face. She felt an urge to punch the smile right off the screen.

I promised Cooper video games, she sent back. With a shake of her head, she started walking again, boots crunching on snow and ice melt.

A ding got her attention again. She wondered how much trouble she'd get in if she tossed the device into the nearest garbage can.

Tmrw? Il swtn teh deal. Dnnr & movie.

She laughed, thrilled her rejection hadn't disturbed their friendship, as she tapped out a response. *Warm beer and microwave pizza. How could I refuse? I pick the movie.*

Thinking the conversation over, she squished the phone back into her pocket.

It went off again.

PURE OF HEART

"Logan, I'm not in the mood for text bombing," she said with a groan and raised it back up.

I mnt a rstrant and movie theater.

Her breath got trapped somewhere between her lungs and her mouth. She read the text again, just in case, and slowed her stride.

As friends, she typed back, afraid to breathe as she hit the send button.

She stared hard, waiting for a quick reply, chewing on her bottom lip. There would be no going back from this if he pushed. She didn't want to hurt his feelings, but she didn't want to date him. Wouldn't do that to him. He'd been her best friend for years. Uncomplicated, safe. She could rely on him. Or so she'd thought.

Her text tone pinged; she ducked her head and went to open the message. Dread heavy in her gut.

Before she could read it, her phone was stripped away. It clattered to the sidewalk as she ran nose first into something solid and warm. She reeled backwards, more out of surprise than from the force of impact. Books joined her phone on the ground, flopping at her feet and off the sidewalk into the muddy snow gathered in the gutter. In her shock she didn't try to break her fall. She hit the sidewalk, flat on her backside.

Across from her, the person she'd failed to bulldoze mirrored her position, gaping over at her.

"I'm so sorry!"

The smell hit her next, just as sudden as the crash. Coconut, a hint of vanilla. Her mouth snapped closed, teeth clicking together with her own apology trapped behind them. Wide blue eyes stared at her, peeking over the top of a pale hand.

She tried again to apologize for being a total klutzy jerk, but her mouth refused to cooperate. Each breath brought more of the new scent to her and it felt like her sinuses had taken over. She scrambled to her feet, reached for the closest book. The other woman stood as well, hands brushing at the skirt of a very red dress. Who wore a pretty dress and heels in snow? At least she also had a warm-looking coat on over the top. She stooped and picked up the remaining books and Harper's phone. She held it out with a tentative smile.

"Are you alright? I really am so sorry. I know better than to read and walk. "

I've become a mute, Harper thought. She struggled to get her lips to form words. Any words. A half strangled mewl came out.

Then it bubbled up in the back of her mind. Stronger than usual. The cool confidence and instincts of the wolf. Her face went numb first, then the feeling swept down her neck and through her body. She didn't even have the chance to panic. No warning. Her body froze, books clasped tightly in a white-knuckled grip.

She tried to give them back to their owner. Nothing happened. She tried to lick her teeth to check them, and that didn't work either. Her eyesight remained dull by some miracle. So at least she wasn't looking at the poor woman with freakish gold eyes.

"Um." The woman shifted and seemed to shrink into herself. "I'm Emerson, by the way."

And I'm paralyzed. Harper tried not to panic as she fought to bring even the smallest of muscles under her control. Panicking wouldn't do any good.

"Harper," she heard herself say. Her voice sounded rougher than usual, like she'd just woken up. She felt her mouth moving. Felt everything from the dampness of her jeans to the slick covers of the books in her hands. But she wasn't the one speaking. The shock of having the wolf speak through her made her head swim again.

"That's your name? Really?" Emerson said with a shy, pleased grin. Harper's stomach twisted. "To Kill a Mockingbird?"

Harper's head cocked to the side and Emerson's smile faded.

"The author? Harper Lee? I'm named after an author too. Ralph Waldo Emerson?"

Harper stared, like a lunatic. Her hands clenched so hard at the book covers she thought they might break. That would go over well.

Give me back my body! She thought and tried to force herself, human Harper, back to the forefront. The wolf didn't seem to have any problem keeping itself dominant. It inhaled deeply, like a total freak, and leaned forward, wanting more of the scent.

"This isn't how I intended to make acquaintances," Emerson said. She tucked a strand of bright blonde hair behind an ear and ducked her head. "I thought it might go... differently. I hope you're not mad I ran into you. I'll take my books and get out of your hair."

She reached out and Harper looked down at the books in her hands. Titles and authors she didn't recognize gleamed back at her. French, Harper realized. They were in French. The wolf seemed confused and hesitant to relinquish them.

It's not like you read French, Harper told her other self in annoyance. *You don't even read.*

"Emerson," the wolf said in that scratchy voice. It made a soft rumbling sound. One Harper didn't know she was capable of as a human.

"That's me," Emerson said. She nodded, her small smile appearing again. "Trade you?"

Control slammed back into Harper. So hard she swayed on her feet. She gulped in a breath, like she'd been underwater. Her shaking fingers brushed Emerson's as she reached out. Goosebumps erupted down her arm. She snatched the phone and pressed the books back into Emerson's arms.

"Sorry," she said and then escaped as fast as she could.

She ducked into the first alley she came to. Pressed up against the scratchy brick wall, she stared up at the sky and drew in breath after breath.

"What just happened? What the hell just — " she cut herself off with a groan and pressed the heels of her hands against her eyes. "What's happening to me?"

CHAPTER THREE

"AJ!" Harper threw open the truck door and launched herself into the snow. Her feet slipped in the fresh powder, hands digging for handholds. She left the door hanging open as she scrambled forward. A voice in the back of her head – one that sounded an awful lot like Grady – squawked in offense. She didn't care. Not when she could see her friend bent over the broken section of fence. The sight of her and the smell of butterscotch meant home base. She just had to get there before things went wrong again. Then it would all be okay.

"AJ!" She ran as fast as possible in the slick, shifting snow. The wolf tugged at her, wanting to go back to town. It had zero interest in AJ, or even the two dogs playing nearby. Its single-mindedness frightened her and made gaining traction even harder as it fought her.

Ike broke away from his playmate and came bounding toward her like a black and white rabbit. He ducked under the lowest rung of the fence and streaked straight for her. The wolf didn't care, and that sent a shiver tap dancing down her spine.

AJ stood and swept her hair out of her face. "Harper?"

She blew right past Ike, ignoring his yips and whines for attention. Once sanity returned, she'd make it up to him. For the moment she had to be locked on target like a homing missile. She knew if she lost focus for a second she'd be on her way back to town to stalk Emerson.

AJ's smile faltered.

Harper vaulted the fence, unable to stop now. Her mind had conjured up terrifying images of blood, shredded flesh and dead blue eyes. Images that felt too much like a hazy and disjointed memory.

AJ's eyes widened, she stumbled back a step. "Harper, wait, wait, Harper!" She shrieked as they collided and toppled backwards. Snow flew up around them and coated them both. The dogs stopped barking, as though holding their breath for the explosive reaction.

"Thank God I found you," Harper said. She pinned AJ's shoulder to the ground by resting her aching head on it. "I made it. I made it."

"Ow, ow, ow." AJ groaned and shoved upwards. "Harper, you big puppy. What the hell?"

"You have to help me!" The squirming under her stopped.

AJ blinked melting snow out of her eyes and frowned. "What?"

"Something happened. Bad. I need you to knock me out, or lock me up. Maybe both, just do something!"

"Before I launch completely into panic mode…" AJ said, sitting up on her elbows and blowing at the hair draped over half her face. Harper let her, but didn't move from her position on AJ's legs. She couldn't risk losing contact with her tether to humanity. Letting go would be a very bad, no good idea. "Would this be a hospital visit required emergency? Or did you eat raw steak again?"

"This isn't a cow craving." Her growl sounded more human than wolf. Progress. AJ slowed the wolf possession. "This is serious. You have to stop me."

"Stop you from what?" AJ squinted and wrinkled her nose. "What the hell is going on?"

Oh, the usual. Panic over the threat of someone's death and a psychotic mythical creature trying to tear its way out of my skin. She grabbed handfuls of AJ's coat and gave her a solid shake. "Someone is going to die. I can't again Jay, not again."

AJ's already pale face went even whiter. "What? Who?"

Harper tightened her grip, gulping down her fear. Her eyes welled up and her breathing grew ragged. She whimpered again. "It took control of me. Or I lost it. It doesn't matter. You've got to stop it, me. Please. Please don't let – don't let me change. I don't want to kill her."

A light bulb might as well have appeared over AJ's head. She cupped Harper's cheeks in her chilly hands. When she spoke again her tone changed, all traces of fear gone. Her voice was low and gentle, a little above a whisper. Just like when she talked to animals in the clinic when they freaked out. "Breathe, Harper. Focus and breathe. I can't carry you inside if you pass out. Come on now, it's alright."

"I thought I would kill her," she said, wheezing like an asthmatic. "I'm so scared."

"You're not going to kill anyone, Sweets." AJ smiled, but with wolf vision Harper saw the strain there. Because they both knew better – knew how easy it would be. It had happened already. The wolf had proven it had no issue tearing someone to pieces, no matter who they were, or how its human half felt about them. "Harper, look at me. It's not going to happen.

That was years ago. Let's get you inside and warmed up. Then we can figure this out."

She let AJ stand, but sank back into the snow on her knees. Her legs felt too heavy to move again. Ike wiggled over and slobbered on her face. She grabbed hold of his fluffy neck and looked up at a blurry AJ. Her lips trembled around a single desperate word, heavy on her tongue. "Help."

***

Harper leaned against AJ all the way inside. Not because she couldn't walk on her own. It made her feel better to hold onto her friend. The muscles in her forearms trembled and her knees shook, but AJ wouldn't let her fall.

Or run back to town.

The cushions on the couch embraced her with a sigh-like noise when she sat down. She relaxed into the comfort and tipped her head back with a groan.

"Right then," AJ said and pointed at Ike and the Kurtz's dog. Philippe, if she remembered right. Stupid name. "You two sit and stay. Harper, hang tight, I'll be right back."

Too tired to respond with her usual snark, she nodded and watched AJ slip through the door to the other side of the house. She didn't have to strain her ears to hear the conversation with Trish. AJ's voice was low and soothing compared to Trish's high pitched response.

Ike and Philippe turned toward her with matching dopey expressions. She made eye contact, signaling they no longer had to sit and stay. Ike hopped onto the couch beside her, worming his way under her arm. Philippe remained cautious, sniffing her direction.

She felt a tickle of vague curiosity from her other half. They hadn't met the big golden retriever before. Not up close anyway. "It's okay," she said.

He scrunched himself down into a submissive position and tapped his tail against the rug.

"It's okay, Phil. We can be friends." She held out a hand for him to sniff. "For a big guy you're kind of a scaredy cat."

Past the initial interest, the wolf didn't seem all that concerned with the retriever. It went right back to pining. Philippe scooted across the floor, still hunched up as small as possible, and balanced his giant head on her knee.

"See? I don't bite. We're kind of like cousins," she told him and scratched at his ears. "Very distant cousins."

Both dogs wagged their tails. Ike bumped his freezing nose against her chin and then blew kibble-scented doggie breath in her face. "Thanks, Ike. I don't suppose either of you know what's going on with me?"

Ike whined and Philippe sneezed.

"Thanks a lot. That clears it right up."

"Trish is gone," AJ said as she stepped back into the room. She leaned back against the door with a long sigh. "You have my full attention, and we won't have to whisper."

AJ removed Harper's shoes and wet socks, unfurled a blanket and tucked it around her. It made her feel like a kid who had stayed out in the snow too long. "Gee, Mom, can I have some milk and cookies too?"

AJ smirked and ruffled Harper's damp hair. "That's better, you sound like you again. How about some hot chocolate instead?" She didn't wait for an answer.

Harper took a couple of breaths with her nose pressed against the blanket. Weird and creepy, but it helped. AJ's scent saturated the fleece — an odd, but pleasant combination of sawdust, butterscotch, dog and... something flowery she couldn't identify. It didn't matter though, to her it meant AJ.

Safe, she thought and took in another lungful. *Safe*.

Lowering the blanket, she peered around. AJ's various certificates hung above the glossy desk in the corner. The framed newspaper article about AJ and her research hung there too. She'd caused such gossip in town when she moved in, spending her free time in the woods with wolves for company.

Little did she know a very different kind of wolf lived nearby. The chair Harper had gouged with her claws remained in the living room. Harper smirked, remembering the morning AJ had discovered her secret. It had been frightening and embarrassing at the time. Now she had to keep from chuckling. What a sight they must have made. Her in a blind panic, ready to run out of the house butt naked to escape, and AJ not much better, in her shock.

"Now that you're nice and calm," AJ said, spooking Harper from her memories. "You want to tell me what happened?" She sat down on the coffee table and unlaced her boots. "From the beginning, please."

"Once upon a time there was a werewolf named Harper."

AJ shook her head, tossing her first boot toward the back door. She rolled Guinness brown eyes and sighed. "Not that far back. Try again."

"Sorry. In the beginning Grady said thou shalt get groceries."

"Harper." AJ chucked the other boot and reached over to pinch Harper's calf. "Skip the sarcasm, you don't need to be all tough. Just tell me what happened."

"I ran into someone new."

"Better. Okay, then what?"

"I was paralyzed. My whole body went numb." Her back stiffened and she squeezed Ike. She hoped talking about it wouldn't bring about a relapse. To make sure she wiggled her fingers. They moved and she let herself breathe. "It happened so fast. Logan was texting me one second and the next I'd run into this chick."

The tea-pot interrupted with a shrill whistle. She winced at the sound. AJ held up a finger. "Hold that thought."

She came back from the kitchen with two steaming mugs, but paused with one outstretched. "Oh," she said, frowning. "Can you even have chocolate? I've never asked and didn't think about it."

Harper snagged the mug, managing not to spill any of the sweet smelling beverage. She didn't need to ruin another shirt. "Really? Yes, I can have chocolate. I may be part wolf, but I'm still female. Chocolate is essential."

To prove her point she took a long, scalding slurp.

AJ sat back on the coffee table and gestured with her own mug. "Continue then. You ran into a new chick…"

"Emerson." She closed her mouth so hard her teeth clicked together. The name alone stirred the wolf. A surge of images accompanied the name. So vivid, almost like she'd teleported into the room. A whine threatened to escape her throat. She drowned it with a mouthful of cocoa.

"Emerson? Interesting name," AJ said. That damned eyebrow of hers arched up again. "You ran into her and then what?"

"I smelled her." She screwed up her face. "God that sounds perverted. I didn't sniff her or anything. I caught her scent."

AJ chuckled. "I imagine you have a whole catalogue of smells stored in your brain. Though I'm not sure how you have room with all those Harperisms."

"You smell like butterscotch, mostly. Or it translates to butterscotch to me. There's hints of dog, sawdust and some sort of flower."

"That does not sound appealing."

"No, it's not bad. It's hard to explain. It's just you. It means AJ in my head. Cooper's kind of stinky, like grass, feet, and cinnamon. Trust me, you smell way better than a teenage boy."

"Good to know," AJ said. "What does Emerson smell like?"

The absurdity of their conversation hit her and she choked on her cocoa. "This is the stupidest thing we've ever talked about. Coconuts and vanilla. She's teeth achingly sweet."

"I think I'm mostly relieved she doesn't smell like steak. What happened after you caught the scent?"

"I couldn't talk. I tried, but my mouth didn't work and it got worse from there. I – my –"

"Your wolf?"

She sighed and pinched the bridge of her nose. "My wolf decided to take a test drive. I felt her like I do when I change. Her consciousness or whatever you want to call it, that's always there. When I change it's stronger, I feel more of her. It kind of bubbles up, tickles the back of my head." She paused, wondering if talking about it would make it happen. When nothing changed, she continued. "So that happened and I got trapped. I could see and hear everything but I wasn't driving my body any longer."

"And what did she do when she had the keys?"

"Stared," Harper mumbled, remembering the feeling. Like she'd found something miraculous, amazing. But she couldn't think of a single thing about Emerson that was a reason for that reaction. "I stared at her, like a total creeper. I said my name, repeated her name once she told me. In complete Tarzan mode, by the way. Then bam, I was back in charge."

"Just like that?"

"Just like that. It gave me vertigo." She swallowed the last of her drink, hoping to dilute the bad taste in her mouth. If the wolf ruined the taste of chocolate for her, things would get ugly. "I had to get out of there before something else happened. I could have killed her."

AJ set her mug aside, reaching over to take Harper's hand. "If you wanted to kill her you would have."

"I didn't want to kill Ben," she said through clenched teeth and jerked her hand away. "That happened anyway."

"Did you feel threatened, territorial, or see her as prey at any point?"

"No." She slumped, pressing her hands against her eyes. "Not even a little. The wolf was fixated, fascinated. Human me was afraid. I still am."

"You know animals are really good judges of character." AJ pointed at Philippe. "Look how quickly he's taken to you. And wolves are even better at discerning friend from foe. They know the second they see you. Maybe you liked her."

Harper scoffed and lowered her hands. "Jay, Ike practically has fits when he meets anyone. This was not like that. It wasn't giddy, puppy-like excitement. It was more like the wolf recognized her. That's never happened before." An expression passed over AJ's face too briefly for Harper to decipher. She narrowed her eyes and leaned forward. "What?"

"Nothing." AJ sat back, stared into her mug. "That doesn't sound like hunting or territorial behavior."

"No, nuh-uh, what were you going to say? I'm freaking out here. I could seriously hurt her, and I don't even know her."

"I don't —" AJ ran a hand through her hair. "I'm not an expert on werewolves. Nobody really is. I know wolves, *Canis Lupus*, not the *Faoladh*. All I know about you has come from you, Grady, and questionable internet resources." She fidgeted. "I don't want to speculate, I could be wrong."

"What if you're not? What if you're not, and you could stop something horrible from happening?"

"You're not going to hurt her. Of that I'm sure." AJ smiled, but it wasn't the familiar broad grin. She looked tired and...

Worried.

"AJ."

PURE OF HEART

"Let me do some digging before I offer a theory, okay?"

"No," she said. "Not okay. How could this be okay? What if I run into her again?"

"You and the wolf are the same being. I know you don't like to think of it that way, but it's true," AJ replied. "One doesn't exist without the other. If you don't want to hurt Emerson, you won't."

"But I didn't want to hurt Ben." She glanced over at him, sitting right next to her on the couch. The firelight made the blood in his throat look fresh. "I didn't want to kill him and he ended up dead."

"This isn't anything like what happened with Ben. Not if what you told me about your relationship with him is true." AJ shooed Ike away, folded herself in beside Harper, and looped an arm over her shoulders. "The next full moon isn't for a few weeks. If something happens again before then come get me and we'll figure something out. I'll hide you in the barn if need be."

"If I lose control again I won't be able to call for help. I'm still scared."

"I know, Sweets. It'll be okay, I promise."

Harper turned to her and tried to smile. "Promise promise?"

AJ nodded. "Yup. Here's what we're going to do. I'm going to give you some tranq's to take home. Just in case. You take today off work. Grady can call me if he wants to whine about it. I'll even write you a doctor's note."

"Excused from work due to wolfy issues?"

"Excused from work due to extenuating circumstances. Doctor speak for mind your own damn business."

Harper leaned against AJ. "You're a really good friend, you know that?"

"I'm such a good friend that I'll shoot you in the ass with another tranq dart if I have to."

With a laugh Harper closed her eyes and tilted her head back against the couch. "Thanks."

CHAPTER FOUR

It didn't occur to her until she got home that she'd never checked her last message from Logan. She leaned her forehead against the front door and pried her phone from her pocket. Not one, but three texts awaited her.

I was hping mayb we cld try it. A date, u know. No smiley face. She groaned.

If u dnt wnt 2 its cool. I ms spnding x w u as frnds.

"I hate text spelling." She knocked her head against the door and opened the next one.

Ur mad arnt u. Sorry. 4get I said nething.

"Why, why, why," she said, knocking her head to punctuate each word. Now her head hurt again.

The front door opened, and she fell forward right into Grady. He caught her by the biceps before she could slide onto the floor. "Harper? What are you doing knocking and talking to yourself?"

"You didn't lock the door."

"Don't tell Coop."

She shrugged. "What's one more secret in this family?"

He ducked, trying to see her face. She kept looking beyond him, focused on the staircase. A boiling hot shower sounded like the best idea ever. Maybe if she got lucky it would turn her into goo and she could disappear down the drain.

"AJ called."

"Oh?"

"She said you were feeling off. Are you sick?"

"I'm always sick. I have werewolfism – itis – syndrome. Can I take a shower or were you planning on keeping me outside?" She raised her chin, daring him. "Do I have to huff and puff?"

"Harper."

"I'm tired. I had a not so fabulous day. I want to take a shower and go to bed. Not play twenty stupid questions on the doorstep."

"What happened?" he asked, but also let her in. "Talk to me."

Halfway to the stairs and her precious alone time she whirled around. Her vision flickered and Grady recoiled. Her lips twisted into a harsh smirk at his startled expression. "Afraid of the big bad wolf?"

"No." He continued to follow her up the stairs.

"I am," she said and darted into the bathroom, slamming the door on his wounded look. "We can talk later. I need some space."

"Do you want me to call AJ?"

"I want you to go away." She tucked a towel over the mirror and turned the shower on. For a moment she stood still, watching the water pound down against the tub, her ears trained on the door. Over the hiss of the spray she heard him swear, once and then again. His footsteps faded away and she sagged against the towel rack in relief.

The first sob caught her by surprise. She didn't know she'd been crying. The second sent her to the ground when her knees gave out. By the third she'd curled up next to the cool side of the tub. She pressed one hand to her mouth and clutched slick porcelain with the other.

Those eyes, blue like the glacier lakes, popped up in her mind again.

She cried harder when she smelled coconuts.

***

When she emerged from the steam filled bathroom, her eyes were puffy and her throat felt sore. But it didn't matter because she also felt human again. As human as she could be with the constant presence of the wolf in her head.

She'd drowned out the smell of Emerson with some effort. It had taken her entire bottle of body wash and washing her hair four times, but she'd done it.

She stepped in to the living room, unsurprised to find Grady waiting. He sat in his overstuffed recliner, head in his hands, and guilt swamped her.

She cleared her throat. "Where's Coop?"

Grady looked up and she frowned, reaching for her neck. She sounded like she smoked four packs a day.

"He should be back soon. Said something about you promising to play video games?"

She nodded and leaned against the wall. "I'm sorry about before. I was being a jerk."

He smiled and scrubbed his hands over his hair. "That word gets used a lot around here?"

"Jerk?"

"No. Sorry."

"I guess we all have a lot to be sorry for."

"Not as much as we think. You don't have to apologize for wanting space."

"I'm still sorry," she said, taking a seat on the couch near him, but not close enough for him to touch her. Her skin still felt raw from the vicious scrubbing, despite the layers of lotion she'd applied. "I shouldn't have snapped at you."

"I shouldn't have pushed you."

"Is that another way to say sorry?" She shot him a tentative smile.

"You want to know what I'm not sorry about?"

"Absolutely," she said and tangled her hands together in her lap.

"I'm not sorry you're here," he said with a more genuine smile. "I'm not sorry I flew out to Anchorage to get you. I'm not sorry Cooper got to grow up with you. You can be a pain, but I love you. We all do, and nothing is going to change that. No matter how grumpy we can be with each other. I've never been sorry to have you in our lives. You could rip down my whole fence and I'd still love you."

She laughed, or tried. "Should have put in a metal one instead."

"Eh." He shrugged. "You'd just dig holes to get under it. Maybe one of those invisible ones that would shock you if you ran over it?"

"Think you could get the collar on me?"

"After AJ knocked you out, hell yes. You're like a big teddy bear with Telazazzle in your system."

"Telazol," she corrected with a roll of her eyes. He grinned and she laughed again. "You're insane."

"It runs in the family."

"Certainly explains Cooper."

"He's more like his mother. The good looks and sparkling sense of humor are from me."

"Wow." She dropped her head back against the couch, still grinning.

"You know you're just like her. Sometimes it's uncanny," he said after a comfortable silence.

"Like Naomi?"

"No." He shook his head and that wistful smile came back. It made her stomach knot up. "Cassidy. You are so like your mother."

"Thank you," she said. "I miss her."

"I do too." He looked at the picture sitting on the mantle. An old family photo taken the year Grady had visited them in Anchorage for Christmas. They were all there, minus Cooper, who hadn't been born yet. Her parents, grandparents, Grady and Naomi. Grady sat in the middle, beaming at the camera with a squishy, pink baby Harper in his lap.

"You know, you should ask AJ out."

Grady coughed and turned back to her, both eyebrows at his hairline. "And from left field, it's Harper Cahill!"

"I'm serious." She tossed a throw pillow at him. "She wants you to."

"What are you Cupid now?"

"No, and I'm also not blind or stupid. You like her, she likes you. It's kind of annoying watching you two make googly eyes at each other all the time."

"Not that it's any of your business, but I'm working up to it."

"For how long now?" She grinned when he blushed. "So cute."

"Shut it."

"Dad? Dad!" Cooper yelled as the front door collided with the wall. "Is Harper back yet?"

"We're in here and I promise I'll burn every comic book you own if you put a hole in my entry way. What did I say about the door?" Grady shook his head in Harper's direction. Cooper's blond head appeared around the corner, blue eyes wide with fear of burned comics.

"You said not to throw it open."

"I did. I also said, many times, to lock it behind you."

"Right."

"You were saying something about positive reinforcement?" Grady waved a hand. "How can I positively reinforce him, or you, if neither of you ever do what I ask?"

"Like this," she said and stood. When Cooper came back, she jumped on him. "Good boy! Such a good boy locking the front door! Who's a good boy?"

"Harper!" Cooper shoved her away. "Why are you crazier than normal?"

"You're not a good boy?" She pouted at him. "But good boys get treats."

His scowl vanished. "Treats?"

She smiled over at Grady and nudged Cooper. "Something came up when I was headed to the store. However, I happen to know there's a candy bar hidden in the cookie jar."

"Score!" He bounded off, ignoring Grady's protest.

"I was saving that!"

She tapped the side of her nose with a triumphant smirk. "You can't have secret stashes with me around."

He grunted and crossed his arms over his chest. "You didn't make it to the store?"

"There was an... incident." She flopped back onto the couch and pulled a throw pillow over to hug against her chest. "I didn't do – it wasn't a Holt incident. Nobody noticed anything either. I'm safe for now."

"AJ didn't say anything, I'm assuming this incident has something to do with your visit with her? You don't have to tell me, but maybe I can help?"

She sighed and toyed with a loose thread on the pillow. "My wolf took over for a couple of minutes. Full body. It's never done that before." When she glanced up Grady's face had gone pale. "I didn't hurt anybody," she added before he had a heart attack. "It was – I don't know what it was. An out of body experience for damn sure. Did Mom or Pops ever mention anything like that happening to them?"

"Your mom didn't talk much about wolf things. Neither did your pops. I'm not a wolf so I didn't need to be in the know. Are you okay?"

"I'm afraid it could happen again and it might be worse next time. It could have been way worse."

"Do you have any idea what triggered it?"

Coconuts. She looked up at the ceiling, felt heat blossoming across her cheeks. "Uh, a girl."

"A girl? Like a little girl?"

She made a face at him. "No, my age. Someone new in town. She said her name's Emerson. Does that sound familiar to you? I swear I recognized her."

"Not in the slightest, I think I'd recognize that name. So somehow this Emerson triggered the wolf?"

"I ran into her, or she ran into me. It all happened so fast. I was in control and then I wasn't."

Grady stammered, no clear words escaping. He was staring openly at her. His jaw worked like his words needed to be chewed into bite size pieces first. "Did, uh, what... hmm. Were you angry because of the collision or something?"

"No. Not angry at all. The wolf was fixated. The rest of me was terrified I was going to rip her throat out. I don't know how to explain it to you." She shook her head and huffed. Why did everything have to be so difficult? "Usually I feel like I'm searching for something. I always figured I was looking for other wolves. This morning there was a stronger pull, then I met Emerson and now it's almost constant."

"You think she's another wolf?"

"I don't think so. This is something else."

"And it's worse?"

"I'd say I'm now off the weird behavior scale, and that's not better." She nodded to herself, then recoiled when Grady's face came in and out of sharp focus. "What the – um, you need to trim those nose hairs. There are things I don't need to see."

"That's a pretty strong reaction," he said, rubbing his nose.

"AJ acted like she might have a suspicion about what's going on. But she wouldn't tell me. You have any ideas?"

He shook his head. "Not really. Anything else happen?"

She hesitated to mention it, but the desire to have any sort of clue won out. "When I gave her back her stuff my hand tingled."

"Tingled?"

"Pins and needles, like it had fallen asleep. I got goosebumps too."

"Sounds like a crush."

"It does not!" She gaped at him. "Seriously? What kind of crushes do you have? A crush? This is serious."

"Hey, I'm just spitballing." He held up his hands. "Did you get butterflies too?"

"This is why I go to AJ when I have problems."

"Who does Harper have a crush on?" Cooper asked, sauntering back in to the room. An empty candy wrapper hung from his pocket. He took a big bite of the sandwich in his hands.

"See what you've started?" She turned her glare on Cooper. "I do not have a crush, I have a werewolf and you shouldn't eavesdrop."

"What are you doing?" Grady asked, pointing at the half-eaten sandwich. "I'm making dinner soon."

"Ooh, undercooked ravioli." Cooper took another giant bite and shrugged. "I was hungry," he said around a mouthful.

"Ugh, gross." She wrinkled her nose. "More things I don't need to see. Ever."

He swallowed and jerked his thumb back toward the front of the house. "So I don't know if you two care, but there's a hot girl and some dude coming toward the door."

Oh no. Her stomach turned over and a familiar jittery excitement took hold of her limbs. "Short, blonde, red dress?"

"Yeah, how'd you…"

Her body lurched off the couch. She couldn't feel her legs, but they continued to move, limp, trying to find grip on the hardwood. The wolf came screaming to the forefront of her mind, vying for control. It didn't have a good grasp on moving her body, yet, but that didn't stop it from trying. "Grady, stop me!"

She felt her nails elongate and her toes dig into the floor. Then she was swaying like a drunk toward the front door. She tried to keep her balance, flailing her arms. "You've got to be kidding me."

"What's wrong with Harper?"

"Nothing to worry about, Coop." She squeaked when she felt Grady come up behind her. Strong arms closed around her waist and tugged.

"She'll be fine," Grady said, sounding way more sure than she thought he should. "It's a wolf thing, but we've got it under control."

Nothing to see here, she thought. Grady tried to yank her back and her hands shot out to grab at the wall. Her fingernails sank into the drywall and she couldn't hold back a growl.

"God, I'm sorry," she said through gritted teeth. Her fingers refused to relinquish their grasp. "Put me in the basement."

"If I could get you off the wall I would!"

He pulled and her hands slid along the wall, digging several deep tears.

PURE OF HEART

"I can fix that," she said, wincing.

Another pull and they toppled backwards. Cooper stood beside them, watching the show with his phone in hand.

"This is priceless," he said, grinning from ear to ear. "Too bad I can't show anyone."

A light knock at the door quieted the whole room, and then she lunged forward, slipping from Grady's grasp.

"Harper!" He grabbed her around the middle again and dragged her to her feet.

She whined and leaned all of her weight in the direction of the door. *Coconuts. Emerson. Right there. She was right there.*

Her feet left the floor. Grady grunted in her ear and turned them around, toward the hall and the basement door. One of her feet snapped back and up, heel connecting solidly with his groin. He let out a mewling sound and together they hit the floor again.

"Dad?"

Oh, now Cooper would be concerned. She squirmed out from under Grady, bounced off a wall, and headed back toward Emerson on her hands and knees.

"Get Harper," Grady said in higher than normal pitch. He rolled onto his back, cupping his tender bits with one hand and pointing with the other.

"She bites!"

"Just help!"

"Cooper, do something!" She said, wanting to shout and be quiet at the same time.

"Banzai!" Cooper whisper-bellowed and launched his attack. An impressive flying tackle she hadn't expected. He hit her dead in the chest and they went sliding into the kitchen.

Her hand bunched up into a fist as Cooper sat up, hair as crazy as his grin.

"I got her!"

"Cooper, punch!" She shouted in warning.

"What?" He ducked the wrong way, smashing his own face into her fist.

She socked him pretty good for being under the control of a wolf who didn't know how to punch. Pain flared through her abused knuckles and Cooper dropped to the side.

He sat up, cradling half his face. One blue eye narrowed at her. "You hit me!"

"I tried to warn you!"

"I expected your right hand," he whined.

"I'm left handed!"

Grady stumbled, bow legged, into the room. "Enough. The kid gloves are coming off."

She growled and felt a tingle ripple down her spine. Two of her fingers cricked out of place. "Grady, hurry, it's trying to shift."

"Coop grab her shoulders, watch the teeth."

"Easy for you to say, both your eyes work."

"Don't even try to compare war wounds with me."

They tackled her at the same time. Her head bounced off the linoleum, ears ringing with the impact. That didn't stop her body from fighting back. The best she could do was shout warnings.

"Grady, foot!"

"If you kick me in the balls again, I swear…"

"Cooper, duck!"

"Ow!"

"I'm left handed, left!"

Somehow they managed to pin her down on her stomach. She growled and snarled and bucked, but they held on.

"Is the hot girl the mail lady or something? Or is it the dude?"

"Never mind, Cooper, just help."

Harper groaned, laid her cheek against the cool floor and blew her sweaty bangs out of her eyes. "Just hogtie me and throw me down the stairs."

Grady tied her wrists and ankles together with dishtowels. Then he and Cooper dragged her along the floor to the basement door. She could hear her skin squeaking as it slid. The urge to howl grew so strong she bit down on her lip until it bled. She whimpered instead.

"Alright," Grady said, panting and wiping sweat off his forehead. He propped her up against the wall at the top of the basement steps. "I'll be right back to let you out."

"Sorry, again," she mumbled. "I'll fix the wall."

"We'll talk about it when I get back."

He closed the door after one last stern look. She pressed her ear against the wood. Emerson's voice, light and cheerful, came through loud and clear. She whined again and her bound hands reached up to scratch at the door. Another howl threatened to escape, stuck in her chest like a painful hiccup. She felt wave after wave of nausea and something an awful lot like despair. Her shoulders slumped, but her hands kept up their pitiful scratching motions.

She turned her focus inward and tried to get a reading on the wolf. The loneliness and desperation grew stronger. Tears pricked at her eyes.

Perhaps the wolf had been alone too long, and gone insane.

She'd finally lost her mind.

CHAPTER FIVE

Emerson

Bigger. Because size mattered. Or did it? Smaller fit better in her hand. She liked being able to curl her fingers all the way around it. Then again bigger had more heft and felt fantastic in her grasp. It gave her a sense of control, and made her feel like she could take on anything.

Maybe she'd be better off asking her brother's opinion. He had more experience.

Emerson frowned and looked from one wrench to the next. If she went home with the wrong one Oscar would be upset. After the speech she'd delivered about her gender not being a handicap, he'd tease her too.

She could figure it out. It wasn't *that* big a decision. Sure she didn't know what half of the tools on the shelves did, but that didn't mean she couldn't learn. Or do something as simple as pick up the items on Oscar's shopping list. She knew the difference between a wrench and a screwdriver.

The bigger wrench still felt better. She chewed on her bottom lip and twisted both tools around. It was heavier and strained her wrist, but felt like she imagined it should. In a pinch she could use it for self-defense. Bonus.

Her phone blared. She dropped the larger wrench and winced as it clattered on the floor. A blush burned her cheeks at the noise she'd made and attention she'd drawn. The guy working the lone register leaned out to peer down the aisle at her. She ignored him, and the wrench, in favor of answering the call.

"*Mère de putain enfer*," she swore as she opened her bag and reached inside. Her fingers fumbled around the depths, seeking the smooth contours of her cell. Instead, she found something wooly. Not something she could recall stuffing in there earlier. She kept her eyes trained on the wall of wrenches before her, not wanting to seem completely scattered. Her curiosity about the mystery item would have to wait.

Just until Oscar could clear up the size matter for her.

She snagged her phone and tracked her thumb across the screen without looking, so she could smile and wave the smaller wrench at the nosey cashier. "Oscar, you need to be more specific in the future. What size wrench did you want?"

"Emerson?"

"Mother?" She frowned again. "You're calling early. Is everything okay?"

"No, everything is not okay. My daughter went gallivanting off into the wilderness."

She rolled her eyes. "I'd hardly call it gallivanting. I drove to Montana. There hasn't been any swashbuckling either. Why do you sound like you're driving through a tunnel?"

"What?"

When she pulled her phone away from her ear to check the sound settings, she discovered the issue. Her mother wasn't driving through a tunnel. She'd put the phone to her ear upside down. "Never mind."

"Emerson, tell me you're done with this little rebellion, and are coming home. You have to have had your fill of nostalgia by now. Come back where you belong."

New tactic for the same argument they'd been having for weeks. "Did you think calling earlier in the day would change my mind?" She sighed. "I know this doesn't make sense to you, but I like it here. It's charming."

"Charming?" Her mother laughed in that haughty manner of hers. The same sarcastic, snobby laugh she used at dinner parties. "How could that hick town possibly be charming? You're a young lady. You have no business being up there."

"What exactly is going to happen? Oscar's with me. I haven't developed an addiction to cheap beer or cigarettes. Nor do I intend to. Honestly, I'm more worried about us corrupting the town instead of vice versa."

"I'm concerned about the... local wildlife."

She wrinkled her nose and took another surreptitious glance at the cashier. He had a full mountain-man beard and a ratty ponytail. It also seemed he'd grown tired of staring at her legs and gone back to his magazine. As she watched, he grabbed an empty bottle nearby and spit something brown and slimy into it. She pulled a face and redirected her attention to safer things. Wrenches. Wrenches were safe and doubled as bludgeoning tools. "Still not pregnant, Mother. I think you can cross that concern off your list for awhile. The wildlife is... interesting so far, but I think I'll wait for something more domesticated to cross my path."

Her mother coughed. "Yes, well... You left behind dear Gabriel. I

PURE OF HEART

doubt you will find anything of his caliber in the wilderness."

"Gabriel left me, if you recall." Because she found his sister more interesting, but her mother didn't need to know that. "Why are we having this conversation? I'm in a store. Oscar and I are both fine. I'll be fine after Oz leaves too. I can manage on my own."

The silence stretched. She sighed again. "Mother?"

"I'm worried about you. You're my daughter."

"That's fine and I understand. It must be strange not to have me at home." *Where I can always be at your beck and call. Emerson, wear this dress, we're having a party. Emerson, get your things we're going to the clubhouse. Emerson, this is Mr. Cavanaugh and his son Blake, isn't he a handsome young man?* She shuddered at the memories. "You're welcome to come and visit. Once I have things fixed up, of course."

"Fixed up? Your father told me your grandfather didn't leave that place in shambles."

"No, it's nothing like that," she said and winced at the half-lie. Not in shambles, exactly. "I just want it to be perfect, put my own spin on things, before you see it. I'd like you to be proud of the work I've done here."

"Honey."

Familiar with both the tone and word choice, she hastened to cut off the next part. "I'm kind of in the middle of some business right now. Can we talk more at the usual time tonight? Thanks. Love you!"

She hung up with a groan. There'd be hell to pay for that later. She went to put her phone back in her bag and frowned at the fuzzy stowaway. This time she grabbed the soft fabric lurking inside and pulled it free. A red scarf filled her palm. Not one of hers.

"Where did you come from?" she wondered, rubbing it between her thumb and forefinger. Her eyes widened as she realized she knew where it came from. The woman with striking green eyes and dark hair that she'd run into. She'd been wearing a leather jacket and a long red scarf. Harper, she'd said her name was.

Great, the whole town would think she was a thief. That'd go over well.

"Hey, that's Harper's!"

She jerked around and saw a guy staring at her, pointing at the scarf. He couldn't have been much older than her, with his barely-there beard and a youthful roundness lingering in his cheeks. *Much less frightening than the tar-spitting bearded man at the register*, she thought. Until he stepped close and towered over her, then he jumped up a few points in the frightening category.

She wanted to step back to reclaim her space, but changed her mind. The documentaries always said to stand your ground, because if you ran, the beast would see you as prey. She raised her chin and stared up at him. "How do you know? It could be mine."

"It's not. Her aunt made it for her for Christmas," he said. His blue eyes tracked down and back up her body. "Why do you have Harper's scarf?"

Small wrench in one hand and the scarf in the other, she crossed her arms over her chest.

I mugged her for it. She wrinkled her nose. Sarcasm probably wasn't the best course of action. "I ran into her outside and must have picked it up by accident."

She arched an eyebrow, daring him to contradict her.

"You ran into Harper? And you're in one piece?"

Manners be damned, she leaned forward and asked in a stage whisper. "Is she a serial killer? Would she have chopped me up into tiny bits?"

"You're clearly not from around here," he said with a shake of his head.

"And you're very observant."

"Look." He sighed and tousled his already messy hair. "I'll just give it back to her. No harm done."

Annoyed, she closed her hand around the fabric and shook her head. "You know, I think I should do it. It's my fault, and I should be the one to make it right." It could be an adventure. One not involving tools she knew nothing about. That's what would happen in books. The heroine would return the scarf to the stranger with the wild eyes, and they'd be best friends. Very Anne of Green Gables, Harper could be her Diana. Bosom buddies to the end. "Since you know her so well, perhaps you could tell me where I could return it?"

He faltered, his Adam's apple bobbing around a swallow. "Uh, that's not a great idea."

"Because she's a serial killer?"

"Because she's Harper," he said, grimacing. "Trust me, it's better to let me do it."

"Trust you?" She scoffed and shook her head. "I don't even know you. How do I know you're not trying to steal it?"

"Because that doesn't make any sense," he stammered.

"Neither does a strange man approaching a strange woman in a hardware store to argue over a scarf." She smiled. He did seem sweet, in a puppy-dog way. She decided to throw him a bone. "I'm Emerson, by the way. Emerson Grey. That's how normal people greet one another."

She tucked the scarf back into her bag and held out her hand. His mouth opened and closed a few times, but then he sighed and grabbed her hand.

"Logan."

"It's nice to meet you," she said and pulled back from his clammy grasp. "I seem to have accidentally purloined your friend's scarf. Would you know where I could find her to give it back?"

Her mother was so worried about the "wildlife" in Fincher. She appraised the nervous man-boy in front of her and had to stifle a laugh. They didn't get less gritty than Logan. He appeared so confused by what had just happened. She could almost see the wheels turning in his head as he tried to pinpoint where the conversation had gone awry.

The frat boys at college had been ten times as dangerous. She sighed and tapped the toe of one Louboutin against the shiny floor. "Well?"

"I – uh. But Harper..."

"She seemed nice, if a little shy."

He tilted his head back and rubbed at the back of his neck. "Oh boy."

"Loogie!" A deep masculine voice bellowed.

She leaned to the side to see the new arrival, and noticed Logan sag as if he'd been sapped of all energy. The new guy approached with a wide smile, showing off a matching set of dimples.

"Stop calling me that," Logan muttered.

"Hi there, I'm Holt," said the new guy. He slapped a hand against Logan's shoulder. She saw his fingers tighten enough to make the boy squirm. "Is this guy bothering you?"

He had curls like a Jonas Brother and bronzy brown eyes. A giant step up from grizzly cashier man and Logan the puppy. He could have been someone she'd met at college with his preppy shirt, fitted jeans, expensive shoes, and gorgeous watch. What she found more interesting was the way Logan slanted his body away like Satan himself had walked up.

She frowned at both of them. "No, not at all. Do you work here, Holt?"

"Me?" He laughed, showing off a dazzling white smile. "No. My dad owns the lodge."

Ah, so you don't work and live off your parent's wealth. She quirked an eyebrow. Not that she had any room to think ill of him for that.

He leaned around Logan and stretched his arm out to rest a palm on the wrench wall. "And who might you be? I haven't seen you around."

She felt her nose twitch at the overwhelming smell of his cologne. "Emerson."

"Cool name."

"Thank you." She raised her chin to see Logan over Holt's wide shoulders and smiled at him. He winced.

"Where are you from?" Holt asked, raising his arm to block Logan from view.

She narrowed her eyes at his dominant posturing. "Atherton."

Both boys squinted at her, and made brief eye contact with each other. Apparently they could be civil if they were both confused. She wondered how often that happened.

"It's in California."

"Oh." Holt smiled again, wider this time. He did the same full body scan Logan had, but took his time. "What brings you all the way out to bumfuck

Fincher?"

Her mother would hate him. So would Oscar. A swearing Neanderthal of a man who dressed like a suave gentleman, she could already hear the horror in her mother's tone.

That could be fun.

"I'm tracking Sasquatch."

Holt pulled back, almost knocking his head into Logan. "For real?"

"No." She thought he might be put off after that. Most of her dates didn't like her sense of humor, or maybe just didn't expect it. Holt grinned again after a second and resumed his casual stance.

Logan coughed and she tore her gaze away from his handsome friend with a small laugh. "I'm sorry, but I was having a conversation with Logan and…"

"He doesn't mind me butting in. Do you?" He shot a glance at the smaller boy and smirked.

"Find a cliff, Dolt." Logan glared, then turned to walk away.

"That's a good one, loser, thanks for playing." Holt raised a hand in a dismissive wave, still focused on her. "See, we're friends, we joke around. So, Emerson, what's the real reason you're here?"

Finding Neanderthal repellent. "I inherited the bookstore. It belonged to my grandparents."

"We have a bookstore?"

She rolled her eyes. He laughed and touched her wrist.

"I'm kidding. The Grey's place, right? What's it called again?"

"Early Bird Books."

"I'm sorry for your loss," he said with a touch of sincerity. "They were nice. You up here on your own?"

"No." She took a harder look at him, trying to read behind his eyes. Now that Logan had left, he seemed more relaxed and less territorial. She ran a hand through her hair. "My brother came up with me to help me get settled."

"You must have just arrived. Haven't seen any new people around, and I usually notice."

I bet you do. The ones with breasts anyway. She wiggled the wrench. "Between moving in and working on the house we haven't been out much."

"That's a shame. The town is really beautiful this time of year. I'd be happy to show you around. I'm a pretty awesome tour guide."

Her eyebrow arched up again. "I'm pretty busy."

"Too busy to have a drink with a nice guy and check out the place you moved to?"

"I've only known you for half a second. Not sure I'd be willing to call you nice yet."

"Well if you let me take you out, I could change your mind. Over a

PURE OF HEART

drink you'd get to know me for a whole minute." He shrugged. "Fincher's pretty small. We'll see each other anyway. Why not let me speed up the whole new girl meets new people process?"

"That's kind of you," she said and offered him a small smile. He returned it, dimples reappearing. "But I really don't have the time right now."

He nodded, stuffed his hands into his pockets and then inclined his head toward the wrench. "That's a pretty lightweight wrench."

She was starting to get the impression Mr. Holt had never been turned down before. "My sink did its best Old Faithful impression this morning."

"You're going to use that to fix plumbing?"

With a frown, she looked down at the bigger wrench still on the floor. Bigger was better, she knew it. She cleared her throat. "I'm sure this one would do just fine. Maybe it will be useful in fixing the dryer as well."

He chuckled. "Do you even know what you're doing?"

"Are you suggesting because I'm a woman I can't fix my own house? I'll have you know –"

"Easy!" He held his hands up. "I was going to suggest you let me take a look."

"You don't give up do you?" She shook her head. He could backtrack all he wanted, but he was still implying she needed a man to help her. Poor little woman couldn't fend for herself. She glared at him. "I'm not comfortable having a strange man in my house."

"But I'm not a stranger anymore. Not really." He jerked his head toward the back of the store. "Mark, the plumber, he's a stranger. You'd let him in to fix your plumbing over a nice guy you've known for longer than two seconds now?"

"I think my brother and I will be fine without you or Mark," she said.

"I could take a look at your dryer too," he added. "I mean, if you wanted to not have to use the laundromat anymore. That place is pretty sketchy, and there're a lot of strange people in there."

She almost snorted. The laundromat would be a step up from the clothesline in the back yard. Her sheets were half frozen, hanging from the sad line like a row of captured ghosts.

"I promise to be an absolute gentleman. Won't even ask for your number," he said with a wink. "And your brother will be there, right? Let me prove not all strangers are bad news. There are lots of nice people here in Fincher, I'm just one of 'em. We like to be good neighbors."

"A plate of cookies would have sufficed," she mumbled. Oscar would have a great time with this. "Fine, I'll accept your offer, but you should know I have mace, and I'm not afraid to use it."

"Best behavior," Holt said with a grin. "Cross my heart."

***

Holt followed her Prius back up the hill in his monstrous long-bed truck. She kept glancing in the rearview mirror as they crept along the icy streets. It hadn't escaped her that he would now know where she lived. He didn't seem dangerous, just a touch aggressive. Not anything she hadn't dealt with before. She convinced herself he would come in handy after Oscar left. Not that she couldn't handle her own business, but some items were too heavy for her to lift. Having some brawn around might be helpful.

She pulled into the gravel driveway in front of her grandparent's, now her, cabin and cut the near silent engine. Behind her Holt's truck continued its diesel rumble. She gripped the steering wheel and waited for him to turn it off before exiting her warm car.

The low growl had just died when the front door opened. Oscar appeared on the front step, already glaring, with his hands on his hips.

Emerson winced and scooted out of her car. "I got the stuff," she called out and held up the plastic bag with a sheepish grin.

Oscar didn't bother with a coat. He marched right out into the snow in his slippers, striped pajama pants, and faded Stanford t-shirt. His blue eyes zeroed in on the truck behind them as he stopped beside her open car door. "We've been here a week," he said and spared her a glance. "You're already bringing home strays?"

She reached over and patted his chest. "He wouldn't take no for an answer. Seemed really keen to help us."

"Oh, I bet he was keen on something."

"Oz, save the protective big brother routine for someone who actually poses a threat," she said. He didn't respond so she poked him in the ribs. "I mean it. He's harmless."

Holt chose that moment to hop out of the truck and Oscar stood up straighter. "Harmless? He's a gorilla. We're not in Atherton anymore, Dorothy."

"Yes, I realized that when the sink exploded this morning. Can you imagine Mother's response if that had happened at home?" She nudged him and grinned when he chuckled.

"That high pitched squeal?" He returned the grin. "Yours is similar."

"I did not squeal!"

"You did, and had I not been rushing to your aid I would have stopped to get it on video."

Her laughter faded into a sigh. "See if I make you breakfast tomorrow after that comment."

Holt approached wearing his wide grin, hands deep in the pockets of a heavy wool peacoat. "Hi, you must be the brother. I'm Holt."

"Oscar."

She cleared her throat and stepped on Oscar's foot with a light pressure. Not for the sake of his toes so much as his favorite UGG slippers. She'd given them to him for his birthday and would never hear the end of it if she left a mark on them.

He grunted, glared at her, and then held out his hand. "Emerson tells me you've come to help out?"

Holt grabbed his hand and she could see the tendons in Oscar's forearm as he squeezed. She rolled her eyes.

Boys.

"Yeah, she mentioned the sink and dryer. I'm not an expert, but I thought another set of hands couldn't hurt."

"How nice of you to offer," Oscar said from the corner of his mouth.

"Just being neighborly."

"*Pour l'amour du Christ.*" She cleared her throat and smiled at both of them. "Why don't we go inside and discuss it? You know, where it's warm?"

Both men shrugged, but Oscar continued to scowl at Holt who pretended to be oblivious.

"Was that French or something?" Holt asked, his eyes taking another tour of her body.

She nodded, a blush warming her chilled cheeks. Oscar crossed his arms.

Holt grinned even wider. "That's fucking cool."

"Yeah, he's not a giant monkey at all." She heard Oscar say as he tugged her after him toward the house.

***

"Wow, what did you do?" Holt asked, tucked under her sink. He'd stripped down to his jeans and a spotless white undershirt. Emerson cocked her head as she took in the sight. A monkey maybe, but a well-developed monkey nonetheless. He came back out of the cupboard holding some sort of plastic tube. "The whole thing is a disaster. The pipe is cracked."

"Is it?" She leaned against the counter and wrinkled her nose. "We hadn't noticed."

Oscar snorted.

Holt set aside the piece and ran both hands over his face. "I'm sorry, Emmy, but I don't think I can fix this."

"What a surprise," Oscar grumbled.

She ignored him, full attention on the man sitting on her kitchen floor. "We've known each other long enough for you to give me a pet name?"

"Two hours," Holt said, checking his watch. "Yup."

"I wonder what his timetable looks like for getting under your skirt," Oscar whispered.

"Shut up," she said and swatted at his shoulder. "Thanks for trying anyway, Holt. We appreciate you fixing what you could."

All he'd done was tighten something on the faucet, but she'd take what she could get. At least her wrench purchase had come in handy.

"Sure." He stood up and wiped imaginary grime off his jeans. "Anything else you need while I'm here? I could move some boxes or take a look at the dryer."

The list in her purse of things to be done said yes. Oscar beat her to it.

"No, thanks. I think we can handle the rest."

Then it occurred to her. Holt knew everyone in the small town. She held up a finger and stepped out of the kitchen into the modest dining area. Her cat, Mr. Darcy, sat on the table, right on top of her purse, as though he knew she'd be headed for it and wanted to help Oscar cut her time with Holt short. He stared at her, unblinking, tail twitching. She tried to wave him away, but he meowed in response and stayed put.

"Holding my bag hostage will not help the situation," she told him and scooped him up. He yowled and squirmed against her chest.

"What's that?" Holt called from the kitchen.

"Satan," Oscar replied.

"My cat," Emerson said with a huff. Mr. Darcy succeeded in pushing away and dropped to the floor. He scurried off, chocolate colored tail high in the air, no doubt on his way to knock more books off her shelves in retaliation. With a sigh, she reached into her bag and pulled out Harper's scarf. The vibrant color almost had a sheen in the fading natural light. She rubbed the material between her fingers again. "Holt, I don't suppose you'd know where I could find a woman named Harper, would you?"

She re-entered the kitchen in time to see Holt smack the top of his head on the cupboard. Oscar sniggered and she rolled her lips together to keep from joining him. "That's quite the reaction. Why does everyone act like she's the boogeyman?"

"Harper? Harper Cahill?" Holt asked, hand cupping what would surely become one hell of a goose-egg.

"Is there more than one Harper in Fincher?"

He shook his head. "No. What do you want with her?"

Oscar pointed at the scarf. "What did you do now?"

She shrugged and handed it to him. "I literally ran into her today and accidentally picked that up. I'd like to give it back."

Holt stared at the scarf like it might turn into a snake and bite him. "You ran into Harper? She came out in the sun?"

"First she's a serial killer, now a vampire," she said and rolled her eyes. "What is it with her?"

"Leave it to you to run into the local mystery monster," Oscar said. He held out the scarf. "Take it back before I'm cursed to become her next victim."

"I can't believe you lived to tell the tale." Holt frowned. "She's kind of, well, she's Harper. You don't want to mess with her. Or any of that bunch.

They're weird."

Oscar fake gasped. "There's a weird bunch of people in this town?"

She whipped the scarf at him, grinning when he shied away. "Stop it. Weird how?"

Holt shrugged. "They're just... weird. Harper especially."

The bitterness in his tone suggested a deeper story. One she had an idea she knew. Perhaps he had been turned down before. "So you don't know where she lives or works?"

"Why don't you give it to me? I'll get it back to her."

Oscar ran a hand over his short blond hair and shot her a look. "Emerson."

Curiouser and curiouser, she thought, and shook her head at him. No way she'd be letting go of a story this good. She smiled at Holt, trying to appear as sweet as possible. "Oh, no I – You know I feel so bad about knocking her down. She took off like I'd scared her. I'd like to make amends. Logan said the scarf was a Christmas gift, I'm sure it holds some sentimental value."

"You scared Harper?" Holt snorted. "Right."

She pouted, cocked her hip and looked up at the ceiling. "I guess if you don't want to help me…"

"No," he said and scrambled to his feet. "I'll help, sure. I mean, if you want to brave the lion's den – I can't let you do it alone. They might eat you."

"Now they're cannibals?" she said, amused. "That's an interesting rap sheet."

Oscar widened his eyes at her and shook his head in tiny, sneaky, motions. Much like he did at home to keep her from starting a brawl with their mother.

"You don't know them, Emmy," Holt said.

She scowled at the return of the pet name. Her daddy got away with calling her that, but nobody else did. Not even Oscar. "Do they live close by? I'm curious to meet this mysterious family."

"Emerson," Oscar warned again.

"One street over, actually." Holt scratched the back of his neck and peered out the window. "She'll be going to work soon, I think. We might be able to catch her."

"You know her work schedule?" She tilted her head with a knowing smirk.

He blushed. "I've known her since we were kids. Small town, small social circles. It's hard not to know everybody's business."

And a beauty like Harper, she bet he knew more than her work schedule. "We should go now then."

"Well if you're going, I'm going," Oscar said. "God knows who you'll bring home next if I don't," he added under his breath.

"So, Holt, will you take us?" she asked and held out a hand to help him off the floor.

He looked up at her like she'd just asked him to slay a dragon. "Sure."

CHAPTER SIX

Oscar had to change into proper 'meet the neighbors' attire. Which left Emerson to entertain their guest. She didn't mind at first, Holt scooped up Mr. Darcy and rambled about Fincher. Perhaps to keep himself from being nervous about visiting the mysterious Harper.

But as Oscar took his sweet time getting ready, she found Holt's conversation skills were about as well developed as his talent for charming animals. The cat hated him, yowling and growling every time Holt's hand touched him. Holt didn't notice and continued to wrestle the twisting ball of hissing fur and slashing claws. He didn't say anything about it, or the fact his hands looked like someone had gone at him with a staple gun.

She managed to keep her eyes from widening, barely, but couldn't stop wincing with every strike of Mr. Darcy's paw. Meanwhile, Holt continued to go on about the various outdoor activities "they" would have to engage in when the weather warmed up.

"And there are so many mountain bike trails. I prefer four wheelers, but you might like biking more," he said. Mr. Darcy attempted escape, but ended up squished once more against Holt's broad chest. "Your cat is awesome. Really playful."

He smiled and she smile-winced back. "You definitely bring out the… feisty side of him."

"Okay, I think I'm good now," Oscar said, still finger tousling his hair as he came down the stairs.

Holt's eyebrows drew together and Mr. Darcy took the opening to free himself. He landed on the floor with a loud thud and ran under the nearest sofa with one last growling wail.

Emerson raised an eyebrow, and had to stifle the urge to giggle at Holt's bewildered expression. Her dear fashion concerned brother had chosen his favorite "simple" ensemble, a pair of gray pinstripe trousers and a dark navy cashmere sweater with the collar of a crisp white button up peeking over the neck. To Holt it probably looked like they were headed to the Country Club, not off to face down the scariest people in all of Fincher.

Holt still looked mystified as he followed Oscar out the front door. He kept stealing glances and scrunching up his face.

"Hey, not that I care or anything, because I totally don't, but –" He licked his lips and leaned closer to her ear. "Is your brother gay?"

She couldn't stop her laughter that time, but kept it quiet. "Not at all. He just likes clothes. Would it bother you if he was?"

He was quick to hide his grimace, but not quick enough. She frowned.

"No, no that would be cool with me. I just wondered."

"Oh." She nodded and smiled tightly before moving away.

They piled into Holt's truck after a short squabble over who would ride where. She ended up squished in between Holt's thick side and Oscar's leaner, pointier one.

"Oscar, your elbow," she said, struggling to squirm away.

"Sorry." He leaned tighter against the passenger window.

She slipped closer to him, despite the elbow. As warm as Holt was, something had to be done about his overdose of cologne.

"You know you could have taken the back seat," Holt commented.

Oscar glowered out the windshield. "I get carsick. Why didn't you ask Emerson to ride in the back?"

"Ladies ride in the front." Holt smirked.

Emerson turned her head up to her brother and winked. "How gentlemanly."

"Alert the media, the apes have learned how to woo women," Oscar mumbled.

She dug her own elbow into him and smiled at Holt.

They went around a corner and started up a short hill. Holt's truck engine roared a bit louder, but they didn't slip and slide. For that she was grateful. Her beloved Prius didn't appreciate the snow and ice much.

The mountain loomed over them and she took a moment to appreciate the beauty of it. "What's the name of this mountain again?"

"Mooneye," Holt said and grinned over at her. "In the spring you'll have to let me take you up four-wheeling. The view's almost as pretty as you are."

Oscar groaned.

She elbowed him again. "Thank you, you're very sweet to say so." But no, she would not be climbing on the back of a mud encrusted ATV with him.

"Harper's house is right at the base," Holt said, pointing.

She'd expected to see a house like one would picture existing in a horror novel. Not a faded yellow postcard-worthy two-story. It even had a white picket fence surrounding the front porch and a chimney spewing smoke. A green, white, and orange flag hung off a support post. An Irish flag. Strange, but she'd take it as another sign of normalcy. No black cats. No broken shutters flapping in the wind. Nothing seemed sinister, but the lack of horror stereotypes could be camouflage. After all, successful serial killers, like Ted Bundy or the fictional Dexter Morgan, had a normal guy façade they hid behind.

An old pickup sat in the gravel driveway at the side of the house. She hoped that meant they'd made it before Harper left for work.

Holt pulled in behind it. "You have arrived."

She and Oscar leaned forward to search for signs of anything spooky beyond the endearing qualities they'd noticed on approach.

"Yes, I can see why everyone would think serial killer just looking at the place," she said.

"My God, the hummingbird feeder practically screams it," Oscar agreed.

Holt leaned back and dropped his hands from the steering wheel. "Just be careful. I promise not to tell anyone if you run."

"Are you not getting out?" she asked.

He shook his head. "Nah, I got into it with Harper the other day. Don't really want a repeat."

Oscar shoved open the passenger door, slid to the ground, and held his hands out for Emerson. "How gentlemanly," he said.

She accepted his help despite the jab, stumbling for a second as her heels dug into the loose gravel. "Leave it alone, Oz."

With her hand clutching at the crook of his arm they hobbled up the driveway.

"Really, Dorothy, I think you've got yourself a keeper there."

"He's nice," she said and squeezed his arm. "Simple, but sweet."

"Well, he does have good taste in watches at least. Did you see it? Beautiful. Now if you could only teach him not to marinate himself in Axe and moonshine."

She laughed and bumped him. "He does not smell like moonshine."

"How would you know? But he does smell like he bathes in Axe. I think it's leaking from his pores."

The wooden porch steps creaked under her heels. Her good humor evaporated. She swallowed mounting trepidation and straightened her posture. Harper had not seemed pleased earlier, and she hoped she'd calmed since then.

And wasn't a vampire.

"You alright?" Oscar asked.

"If they turn out to be cannibals, I'm serving you as an *apéritif* and running away."

"Like you'd get far in those heels."

The front door, with a wreath hanging on it, stood before them white and pristine. She bit her lip and glanced at the windows, but all the curtains were drawn.

"Knock twice and then wait?" She looked to Oscar for guidance. "That's polite, right?"

"No, ring the doorbell. That's not rude, it's what it's there for."

She stretched a finger toward the button, but hesitated. Her finger curled back toward her palm. "What if no one answers?"

She thought she heard a crash inside the house and frowned over at Oscar. He drew his eyebrows together and cocked his head. Another bang sounded, followed by voices and a yelp.

"Okay, so maybe they're weird," Oscar said.

"*Mon Dieu*, weird people in a small town. How unheard of," she said and rapped on the door. With a polite smile in place she clasped her hands and settled in to wait.

More muffled sounds came to her ears. Her smile slipped back into a frown. She couldn't make out any clear words, but she heard what she imagined was a heated conversation.

Then footsteps.

She straightened back up, ran her fingers through her hair and smiled again. "Time to meet the Fincher cannibals," she said from the corner of her mouth.

Oscar huffed.

The door opened, but not all the way. A large man with a strawberry-blond beard and narrowed blue eyes filled the space. He looked pale, a bit frazzled. She wondered what they had just interrupted. A fresh murder, perhaps, though he didn't have any blood on him.

"Can I help you?"

"Yes, hi," she said, or maybe squeaked. She held out her hand. "I'm Emerson, this is my brother Oscar. I'm sorry to bother you and I know this is going to sound strange but I literally ran into your daughter."

He shook his head, square jaw clenching. "Niece. Harper."

She bobbed her head in a short nod. "Niece, right. Um, I accidentally picked up something of hers when we collided. I'd like to return it."

They stared for a minute. He squinted at her like he was trying to figure something out. She felt Oscar shift next to her, but kept her smile frozen in place and hand outstretched.

"Grady Sullivan," he said. His hand dwarfed hers when he shook it, rough and quick, like he didn't want to touch her. Oscar didn't offer his hand and Mr. Sullivan didn't reach for it. "It's nice to meet you, but Harper's not here."

"Oh." She tried to cover her disappointment with a shrug. "I can come back later. I just live a street over."

His eyes went wide. "No!"

Oscar jumped and she nearly shrieked in response.

"I mean, sorry," Mr. Sullivan said with a sigh. "I mean no, that's not necessary. I can give it to her." He held his hand out. "Thanks for bringing it back."

The 'but' she wanted to say died on her tongue when Oscar elbowed her. Mr. Sullivan's eyes darted back and forth, then fixed on something to the side. She turned to see what had caught his attention and saw Holt in the truck. Holt raised a hand in an abbreviated wave.

Oscar nudged her again.

"Oh, um, please tell her I'm so sorry for taking off with it." She dug the scarf from her purse and handed it to him. It almost made her sad to feel it slipping out of her fingers.

"I'll let her know. Thanks again."

He closed the door in their faces. She almost knocked again.

"Now that was rude," Oscar said.

With a shake of her head she pulled him with her off the porch, all but stomping. The feeling of something watching her gave her pause. She hesitated half way back to the truck and Oscar almost ran her over.

"What is it?" he asked.

She stared over her shoulder. For half a second she thought she saw movement in one of the basement half-windows. A basement could be creepy.

Holt rolled down his window and called out to them. "You made it. Congratulations."

"They're not that bad," she lied. "Harper wasn't there."

"Huh, she must've gone out for a run. That girl's nuts. She's always out in the woods, even if the weather is shitty."

"And how would you know?" Oscar asked.

"She ran cross country in school. Pretty good too, won some trophies. And I know about the woods because it's a small town. Remember? People talk."

She used her hand to shield her eyes from the fading rays of the sun and looked out over the forest. It pressed right up against the back fence. A person could get lost in there. She could see the appeal. "Maybe that's where they hide the bodies."

Holt grinned. "Maybe. So how about that drink?"

"You said you wouldn't ask again," she said before Oscar could add his input.

"No, I said I wouldn't ask for your number and I'm not. One drink. Both of you. Maybe we'll run into Harper at work."

"She does sound more intriguing than Holt," Oscar muttered. "Then again, a rock would be more intriguing."

"One drink," she said and held up one finger. "I mean it. One, and tomorrow night, we've got things to do tonight."

"You got it."

Oscar opened the passenger door for her and helped her up into the warm cab. They rumbled back down the snowy street. She thought of sagebrush green eyes and turned her head to look behind her.

More intriguing indeed.

***

The bookstore hadn't been visited overnight by magical fairies. Books were still stacked on the floor in leaning towers. The shelves were still stuffed to the brim. Dust covered every surface. The computer said it was still installing updates from the day before. Emerson sighed and set the cat carrier on the front desk. "One thing, Mr. Darcy. I just want one thing to go right."

He made his usual cackle-purr noise and pawed at the grate. She opened it with a roll of her eyes. "I won't complain if you use your fur to clean up some of the dust. Just try not to add to the mess, okay?"

She smiled as he stretched before darting off, probably to look for mice. A horrible thought, but as long as he didn't bring a carcass back to show her, she didn't care about his mousing. At least they would be one less thing for her to worry about.

Her eyes drifted, away from the back office where her cat had disappeared, to the shelves.

"Best to start there," she muttered and deposited her bag on the desk. Glasses on and hair tied back, she set her shoulders and marched for the nearest bookcase. "Right."

One tiny problem. She huffed and stared up at the top shelf, just beyond her reach. Even though she wore four-inch heels. Sometimes it felt like the universe conspired against her. Not about to be defeated by an inanimate object she tried to stand on the bottom shelf. The overburdened case swayed. She clung to the top and closed her eyes, waiting for it to stop.

On her tiptoes, she craned her neck and peered over the lip of the shelf. A thick layer of dust covered almost everything, making the titles impossible to read.

Her eyes widened when she felt the first tickle in her nose. Not able to fend it off after the initial warning, she sneezed and shoved forward. It had a spectacular effect on her already precarious position.

The bookcase groaned, wobbled forward and then back as she held on and tried not to scream. It toppled back, taking her along for the ride. The top edge smacked into the wall and she let go, landing on her back. Dust and books flew off the shelves straight at her face. She squealed and raised her hands in defense. Books thunked against her and a thick cloud coated her. She wheezed, coughed, sneezed again and rolled away before the whole thing collapsed and killed her.

"*Ta mere est une pute*," she swore. Not that the bookcase would care what she thought of its mother. Still. "I'm sorry, your mother is not a whore. She's a tree."

A quick check revealed minimal damage to her legs. One small cut on her knee, and a few spectacular bruises. It still stung, even if it was small. She hissed out a breath and considered kicking the bookcase in retaliation. At least she hadn't put a hole in her dress.

Her phone rang.

With another vicious stream of French she hobbled toward the desk and her purse. She took a deep breath before answering the call, seeing her father's face on the screen.

"Daddy?"

"Emmy!"

She smiled, despite the ache in her leg, and swiped at the dust clinging to her clothes and face. "It's so good to hear from you."

"How's my girl? You sound a little out of breath."

"It's nothing, I was just –" she turned to glare at the mess. "Cleaning up. Mother called you, didn't she?"

"Guilty. But I was planning on calling to see how you're settling in anyway."

"I'm good. It's changed a lot from what I remember, but I like it here. I know she wants me to come home." She shook her head and sighed in chorus with him. The similar reaction made her smile again. She could always trust him to understand. "I'm not going to though."

"She's trying, Emmy. You're her little girl and she worries about you being off by yourself."

"I'm not a child anymore," she said, gently. "All grown up, graduated from college and everything."

"I know, and I'm proud, Stanford graduate. We both are. It's just going to take her a little longer to adjust. We both remember you running around the house in a princess outfit terrorizing Oscar."

She rolled her eyes and turned to look out the front windows. "I think I'd prefer you to hold on to a less embarrassing memory."

"So how's the shop?" He asked after a longer pause. "And the house?"

"I think Papa lost interest in… everything, after Nana passed." She touched her fingers to the dirty glass and added one more thing to her lengthening list of chores. "It's pretty messy, but I can handle it. I should be ready to re-open in a couple of months."

"A couple of months?"

"I'm going to restructure some things, paint, put in new furniture. Add some new life and a touch of Emerson to the place. It's mine now anyway."

"Sounds great. Is your brother helping?"

She nodded and then remembered he couldn't see her. "Yes, he's out on a breakfast run right now. He's going to take a look at the ledgers when he gets back. Teach me how to run the place. I think he just wants to spy on me."

"That's what brothers are for. Looking out for his sister is as ingrained as tormenting you."

He said something else, but she didn't hear him. Her attention was caught by a lone figure walking through town.

Harper, in that leather jacket again, scarf once more wrapped around her neck. She had her head tucked down, long strands of near black hair flowing behind her.

"Emerson?"

"Huh?" She shook her head, blinked twice and Harper was gone. Maybe she'd imagined the whole thing. "Sorry, Daddy. What was that?"

"I asked if you've made any new friends? Met anyone interesting up there in Hicktown, as your mother so affectionately calls it?"

"Maybe. There are a couple of characters I'm interested in getting to know. Might be something of a town mystery to unravel too."

"Sounds exciting."

"You know me," she said and turned back to the mess on the floor. "I love a good puzzle."

"You're good at them too. Be careful, alright? And email me about this mystery, I want to hear all about it."

"I will. Love you."

"I love you, Emmy. Bye."

She hung up the phone and jumped as something else crashed to the floor. Mr. Darcy yowled and darted toward her legs, leaving behind the tower of books he'd knocked over. With a groan, she scooped him up and set him on the desk. "So step stool needs to be added to the list under new dryer. Right after I buy a new bookstore."

***

Oscar stepped back in as she finished sweeping up.

"There's only one coffee shop in the whole town," he said. He swiped at the top of his head, flinging melted snow off his hair. "Also, in case you missed it, it's snowing again."

"It snows in New York too, Oz." She clutched at the broom handle with both hands and looked to the ceiling. Any minute now…

"Yeah, it does. But it doesn't snow like this in Atherton. You're going to need a new wardrobe." He paused and she heard him take in a long breath. "Holy book hating tornado, what happened?"

She rubbed the side of her neck and winced. "I sort of knocked over a shelf."

"Sort of? It looks like Godzilla visited while I was gone." He stomped over. "Are you hurt?"

"Just a scratch," she said and held out her leg for him to see. "Not bad. Not as bad as the mess."

"How did you manage to knock over a huge shelf?"

Her face went hot. "Um, I was reaching for the top."

He laughed. "Aw, my poor Hobbit sister. Those stilts probably didn't help at all."

"I am not that short," she said with all the indignation she could muster.

"You're freakishly tall for a Hobbit, especially in those heels, but that's not saying much."

She whacked him in the chest and leaned back, pouting. "These are Tabitha Simmons, and I'm not a hairy Hobbit."

"No, of course not. You're a very well groomed Hobbit." He smirked and jumped away when she took another swipe at him. "I was unaware they had waxing salons in Hobbiton."

"Thanks for making me feel better," she said with a glare. "Can you help me put the shelf back up?"

"Did you bring a change of clothes?" He put his hands on his hips and took in the leaning shelf. "You're not lifting anything in that outfit. I can hear the whining now. Oscar, my Tabitha Simmons!"

She fidgeted with her glasses. "I have some running clothes in the trunk," she mumbled.

"What?"

"I said I have a change of clothes in the trunk." She sighed and pushed her glasses up on top of her head. "But what if someone comes in?"

He raised both arms and spun in a small circle. "What if someone comes in? Have you seen this place? Besides, it's been closed for months."

But Holt knew where she'd be. She wouldn't put it past him to drop by to remind her about their drink scheduled for that evening. "Someone might come by."

"The monkey?" Oscar made a face. "Why did you have to agree to go out with him? And include me?"

She raised an eyebrow. "You want me to go alone with him?"

"No. Damn it."

"He's not that bad, Oz," she said, shoving him.

"You mean his muscles aren't bad."

"Well if we're going to list his more attractive qualities…" She grinned at Oscars pinched expression. "He's sweet, Oscar. I'm not saying I want to elope, but why shouldn't I have some fun?"

"I'm thinking dating someone you just met in a new town might be going a bit fast. You don't know anything about him."

"I'm not dating him," she said with a shake of her head. "Not yet, anyway."

Oscar groaned.

"It's one drink. It'll help that not knowing him thing. If he's awful, I'll cut things off before they start." She laughed as Oscar fake gagged. "And you'll be here to point out all his flaws."

"For now, but I'm leaving at the end of the week."

"Stop worrying, you'll get wrinkles and gray hair."

His eyes widened and a hand went automatically up to his full head of hair. "Don't even joke about that."

She rolled her eyes. "And people think I'm vain."

He continued to stroke his hair, like it needed to be consoled. "You just have this habit of stirring up trouble."

"What happened with Gabriel could hardly be called trouble," she said. "He asked what was wrong, and I told him."

"Interesting you jump to that immediately. Did you have to tell him he was boring?"

"I was being honest. He was. He couldn't hold a conversation." She crossed her arms. "The only reason he wanted to be involved with me was the family name. I made an excellent accessory for his arm."

"You didn't have to break up with him quite so publicly. A shouting match in his driveway was dramatic, even for you."

"The only trouble I caused was with our mother. I embarrassed her and disappointed her, but that's par for the course. Are you taking her side?" Her heart seemed to stutter in her chest, and a lump took up residence in her throat.

"No. You know better." He reached out and gave her a gentle shove. "But you can't deny there was a bit of trouble involved. What about the shenanigans with his sister?"

"I can't be held responsible for other people's assumptions," she said with a shrug. "There were no shenanigans, I told you, we were just friends. Shiloh is interesting and adventurous, like me. Of course I wanted to spend more time with her than her idiot brother."

"Trouble," he said and pointed at her. "That's what I'm talking about. Gabriel was talking about marrying you, and you were trying your damndest to get him to dump you."

"Well, I didn't want to dump him. You know how she gets when I break up with the suitors she throws at me. It's easier if they take most of the blame."

Most of, but not all, she slumped at the thought. Her plan had flaws. "It felt like an arranged marriage. Some deal our parents cooked up."

Oscar's expression softened, and he held his hands out. "We thought you liked him. Honest to God."

"I did, at first. But then I realized how fake he was, and I just couldn't."

Everything was a lie, a show, and I hated it. I'm not meant to be someone's trophy wife."

"And Holt's nothing like that?"

"I don't know," she said, and kicked the bookshelf. "But he seems more genuine. Is it really so awful to want someone honest?"

"Not at all." He wrapped an arm around her and kissed the top of her head. "I just want you to be careful, that's all. You get attached pretty quick and easy."

"I'm a romantic, I can't help it."

"Yeah, I know. Trouble." With a grin he tousled her hair and pointed at the front door. "Go get those clothes, let's fix this mess of yours before we go making a new one."

"If only a change of clothes made all messes easier to fix."

CHAPTER SEVEN

Harper

Full bar. Full tables. Full room. Harper winced and rubbed slow circles against her temples. The headache had started at the back of her head. Then it got ambitious and the pressure moved to her face, down through her shoulders. Her nose hurt, and she had her jaw clenched so tight she thought it might break.

They were so loud, even over the thump of Grady's Shamrock playlist. The symphony of a crowded bar battered her senses. Glasses clinked and boots stomped, chairs scraped and clattered. Booze splattered on tables, slopped onto the floor. One idiot in the back kept braying like a donkey. It blended with the pig snorts coming from his table-mate. Those sounds only punctuated the never-ending drone of conversation. Her ears were buzzing like an over-driven speaker in a car.

That was just the sound. Then there were the smells on top of it, or maybe lurking below, layered on the floor like a noxious mist she couldn't see. Perfume, body wash, body odor, cologne, alcohol, laundry detergent. Smells from outside too — wet clothing and hair, fresh snow, stale cigarettes.

"You okay?" Grady half-shouted in her ear.

"What?" She jerked away and narrowed her eyes. "Peachy."

He grinned at her. "Busy night."

"Yeah. God bless the tourists," she said through her teeth. The regulars, townies, she didn't mind so much. They knew her rules and followed them with little argument. But the tourists didn't give a damn. They'd grab her ass if they felt like it, or lurch out of the bar too drunk to stand, let alone drive. "Stop grinning at me like that."

"Come on, Harp. Fincher needs the money these guys bring in. Not to mention we need it."

"You sound like the obnoxious mayor in Jaws, do you know that?" An apt comparison, if she did say so herself. After all, there was a monster waiting below her skin that would love a tasty tourist snack. She wondered if any of them sensed the presence of a predator in their midst. If they ever paused for a moment because they felt vulnerable or felt her eyes tracking them.

"You sound like a snob," Grady said, grin never faltering.

"I'm not." She glowered at the crowd. They were just so loud. It made things harder to control when she couldn't focus, and she couldn't afford to lose control again. Not after the Emerson incident. A hole in the wall or fence she could repair. A hole in someone's throat was much harder to fix, even with her considerable drywall skills. "I don't like crowds."

"You like the tips though." He leaned in toward her ear. "You sure you're okay? Do you need to go home?"

She shook her head. "No. I'll get over it. Just a headache."

"Alright, I'm going back to the office, holler if you need me."

With a low growl she scratched the side of her nose and bent back to her previous task. A ring of liquor had dried on Grady's prized granite bar. She wanted to get it off before closing time. Before Grady noticed it and raised hell.

"Harper?"

"At your service," she said and forced her lips into some semblance of a smile.

Scott Langan gave her a two fingered salute and took his customary seat. He took his filthy fishing cap off and ran a gnarled hand over his bald head. "You okay, kid?"

She nodded and gestured to ask if he wanted a drink. Of course he did. He ordered the same thing every night. She always asked though, hoping one day he'd wave her off and order a burger instead of a whiskey and coke.

Ben sat next to him, a glass of something suspiciously blood-red in his hands. He raised the glass at her in a toast and took a swig. The liquid rushed out the hole in his neck, splashing down his destroyed chest.

Scott grinned when she slid the drink over to his reaching hands. "Harper, you are my most favorite person."

"Flattered," she said, wincing as she watched him take a hearty gulp. He let out an exaggerated "ahh."

"It's perfect, like always."

"Good to know I can do something right." She went back to wiping the bar, unable to watch anymore. He looked too much like Ben. They had the same kind brown eyes and full grin. It hurt to watch him drown himself in the booze she provided.

PURE OF HEART

"Harper!"

She sighed through her nose, which offered brief relief right up until she inhaled. The near toxic *eau de people* hit her all over again. Logan approached the bar with an empty pitcher dangling from each hand.

He smiled at her, trying too hard to be as smooth as the charming men on TV no doubt. She wanted to groan or maybe shake him until his brain rattled back into place. What did she have to do to convince him she wasn't being shy or afraid for no reason? If she ripped out his liver, he'd probably grin and insist they were still perfect for each other. He had the persistent part down, she'd give him that.

"Table two is ready for more."

"Two Freddy's, right?" She grabbed the pitchers and whirled toward the taps.

"Yeah. Hey, you're looking a little paler than normal." He leaned his elbows against the bar and peered at her. "Headache?"

"I was just about to say something," Scott chimed in.

"Okay, Doctors, thank you for the un-asked for evaluations." She glared at both of them as she refilled one pitcher. The skunky scent did not help. "Can we not play what's wrong with Harper today? Thanks."

"Come on," Logan said. "We're just concerned friends. No need for sarcasm."

"It's my default setting." She shoved the pitchers at Logan and smiled with faux sweetness when beer splashed on him. "Oops, clumsy me."

He dipped his chin to take in the considerable wet spot on his shirt. "What did I do to deserve that?" He cast a glance Scott's way, but Scott was quick to busy himself slurping his drink. "Some help you are."

"I'll get you a drink later. Fair is fair." She jerked her head toward the table missing their beer. "Go on. Better hurry before they start chanting beer and slamming their cups on the table again."

He staggered away, weaving through tables and chairs with the pitchers held high. She shook her head before going back to the stubborn stain.

"At the risk of earning your wrath," Scott said, moments later. "I think I have some headache stuff in my car."

"Thanks, that's sweet of you to offer, really. But I'm okay." He didn't need to know she'd already taken a prescription pill before coming to work. Nor did he need to know she was considering doubling the dose. One didn't cut it anymore. The wolf had taken a page from Logan's book and begun to practice its persistence. Just what she needed.

"You sure? I mean, it's just out in my glove box," he said, jerking his thumb toward the parking lot.

"Positive. Just as I'm positive you're giving me the keys to your truck anyway." She huffed and bent closer to the bar, rubbing the damp towel harder. "You know the rules."

"Aw, Harp…"

She stopped and peered up at him, then looked pointedly at his empty glass. "I mean it. Rule number one: more than one, no driving. Besides the walk home should give you time to mask your whiskey breath with a mint or five."

He squinted at her. "Will you be insisting the rest of these fine people walk to their hotels or rentals?"

"I'll be insisting you abide by my rules because you're my friend and I care about you." She snatched up his glass. "Or I could end this argument right now, and cut you off."

"Who's arguing? I thought we were having a pleasant discussion about the perils of drinking and driving?"

"Mr. Langan," she said, lowering her voice. "Ben would want you to be safe. I'm trying to take care of you for him. The best I can, anyway."

"Scott," he corrected. "Please don't call me Mr. Langan, Harper. And it's not fair for you to bring him up like that."

"Lots of things aren't fair," she said, swallowing. "Keys for the next drink."

He sighed and reached into the breast pocket of his flannel shirt. "Hard ass."

"That's Har-per. Ass is my middle name." She pointed at the name plate fixed to her black vest. Her pointer finger traced over the stenciled letters, in case he had trouble spelling it out. "Har. Per."

"I should have said smart ass."

"You should have said thank you," she said and swapped his keys for a fresh drink.

"Thank you."

"Say it right."

He grinned again, looking more like the man she remembered and less like the shell he'd become. "Bless you, Lassie."

She smirked at the inside joke she hoped he'd never be privy to. "Was that so bad? You're welcome."

His reply was cut short when the door opened and the bar erupted in a chorus of hellos. Holt walked in like he owned the place, exchanging high fives and grinning from ear to ear. Mr. Popularity, strutting his stuff like he had in High School. Too bad nobody informed him being Big Man on Campus in Fincher wasn't much of an achievement.

Oh wait. She had, multiple times.

She frowned and raised an eyebrow at Scott, who shrugged.

Holt joined a table, pulling out a chair and straddling it. He started some sort of tale. A hunting story, if she read his hand signals and pantomiming correctly. His audience ate it up, of course.

"Holt the mighty hunter," she mumbled and shuddered. She'd been to

PURE OF HEART

the lodge once, and seen all of his trophies. Animals stuffed and posed, mounted on the walls. The image of the snarling wolf's head over the fireplace stayed with her. "He needs new material."

"Or a girlfriend," Scott said.

"How about an actual life?" she wondered aloud. They shared a grin. "They sell those at the mall, right?"

"Harper!"

"How many times are people going to shout my name tonight?" She pursed her lips and Scott chuckled into his drink. "At this rate, I'll never get to be the mysterious bartender with no name."

Holt sauntered over to the bar and she straightened up. If he wanted to fight again, she was game. A public arena made it more fun. Then she could humiliate him in front of his friends. Worth the gossip that would follow her for the next few days. Or years.

He leaned right into her space, ignoring Scott, who glared at him when their elbows bumped and nearly spilled his drink. She took one look at his white teeth and dark eyes and thought of sharks again. *Dun, dun,* she thought and wrinkled her nose.

"Harper Cahill. You're looking plaid as ever."

Her father's faded plaid shirt, one of the few things she had left of his. Holt didn't know that, and she didn't see the point in mentioning it. So instead she batted her eyelashes. "You say the sweetest things. It's like a banshee wailing in my ears."

"Why do you have to have a comeback for everything? All I ever wanted was to make you happy, you know? We could have been good together."

"Oh, you're the key to my happiness?" She gasped, covered her mouth with her fingers and widened her eyes. "If only I'd known. I've been so blind."

"Well, too late now," he said and puffed himself up. "I've moved on and you've missed your chance."

"I'll cry about it later." She smiled sweetly. "That poor girl. It's so tragic."

"I just wanted to let you know, okay?" He sighed and shrugged. His wounded puppy look was not as good as Logan's. "I didn't want to start a sarcasm battle or anything. Alright?"

"That's good, because you wouldn't make it past round one," she said.

"Thought you'd like to know I did what you suggested. And hey, maybe you were right anyway."

The door opened again and the smell hit her with such force she wobbled.

Coconuts. Her favorite, once upon a time.

Coconuts, vanilla and some a new spicy orange-like scent that made her want to sneeze. Not Holt. Holt smelled like leather and moss. No, it wasn't him. She wrinkled her nose and tried not to panic. It didn't matter who the other smell belonged to because coconut meant one thing.

Emerson.

Another dress, dark blue, played up the brilliant icy color of those ridiculous eyes. Pale legs almost glowed in the dim lighting. She could see the definition of her calves, no doubt thanks to the heels on her feet. She smiled and ran a hand through her wavy blonde hair, bit down on the corner of her mouth. When she took off her coat, revealing her bare shoulders, Harper almost fell over.

"Jesus H. God." Her stomach lurched. She groaned, clamped her hands down on the bar and looked to the ceiling. "Why do you hate me?"

"Probably because of your mouth," Scott said. "What's the matter?"

"Emerson, Oscar! Over here!" Holt waved, and then smirked like the smug bastard he was.

Harper's eyes widened. *No, not Emerson.* She growled and smacked a hand over her mouth to keep it inside.

The owner of the spicy scent came next, shaking snow off his long black coat. He eyed his surroundings with a puzzled expression and then shrugged. "Emerson, give that to me," he said and reached for her coat. "I'll find some place to hang it up."

She couldn't help but lean forward and take a deeper breath. It took her a few to isolate the scents she wanted. Her head swam, but she had to know who this Oscar guy was. Right that second, before she broke the bar under her hands. Relief flooded her as she caught a shared note in both scents. Not something she could put a name on, but a similarity.

Relatives, she thought. *Too young to be Emerson's father, so a brother most likely.*

But that didn't mean Holt wasn't… competition.

She cleared her throat and covered her mouth again, hiding a snarl and another furious growl.

"You know I really meant it," Holt said. "That plaid does look good on you. Brings out the green in your eyes."

She narrowed said eyes. He'd put emphasis on green — *Green as in jealousy?*

Oh, she was going to kill him.

Her teeth bit into her own palm. Blood welled and wet her lips. She had no right to be jealous. No reason, and yet she shook with it. The urge to reach over the bar and drag Holt across by his hair made her muscles quake.

Mine.

The thought came from nowhere, amplified and echoing in her head as though it had been shouted.

Mother douchetitty. Not yours, freakshow. Not ours. She dropped her hand

PURE OF HEART

from her mouth, quick to cover it until the bleeding teeth marks healed. "Did I get hit on the head last full moon?"

"What did you say?" Scott asked. He cocked his head. "You don't look good. You sure you're okay?"

"I'm fine," she snapped, avoiding looking at Ben, who continued to spill his bloody cocktail from his throat. He grinned at her with bloody teeth.

"Hello Holt, good to see you again," Emerson said, approaching the bar with her brother right behind her. He grimaced down at her, and Harper wondered if he already disliked Holt.

Smart man.

"And hello to you too, Harper." That bright grin lit up the room, or lit up Harper's view of it anyway.

"Hi," she said stiffly. "Thanks for bringing my scarf back."

"Of course!" She sat on the bar stool Holt pulled out for her and pointed over her shoulder. "That's my brother, Oscar." He waved, looking bored. "Holt told us you're quite the bartender."

The look on Holt's face told her he'd said no such thing.

"Did he now?" The grin she aimed at Holt would have been terrifying if she'd had her wolf teeth in place. More of a sneer than an appreciative smile. It made him squirm, much to her satisfaction. "How... kind."

Oscar sat on the other side of Emerson and leaned back to look at the shelves behind Harper. "I haven't been in a pub since college."

Harper felt the corner of one eye starting to twitch. "This isn't just a pub, it's an Irish pub. As authentic as can be."

"So you are Irish?" Emerson smiled again. "I saw the flag outside your house."

"I'm half. My Uncle, he owns this place, he's full blown pot o' gold Irish." She sighed and threw the rag she'd been scrubbing the counter with over one shoulder. "So what can I get for you?"

"What would you recommend?"

I'd recommend you leave now. There's volcanic activity in my bloodstream. I'm about to go Mount Doom. She tried to turn her wince into a smile and shrugged. "Guinness is the favorite around here. We also have Harp, Kilkenny, and Murphy's if you don't want a milkshake beer. Or there's the usual bar flavors if you're not feeling curious."

Emerson was too close now. Every breath Harper drew in was laced with coconut. She waited for the numbness, or tingling, anything out of the ordinary. Werewolf behavior.

Scott eyeballed her over his drink, one eye squinted. Holt couldn't grin any wider without his head breaking open. Emerson had her chin in one dainty palm as she listened with rapt attention.

Oscar. Harper refocused her attention on him. So far he was the only one of the bunch that didn't make her want to run screaming from the room. He was scrutinizing the bar and ignoring her.

Perfect.

She licked her teeth and tried to sound normal. "If you're hungry the corned beef on soda bread is pretty good. Or, again, there's the usual — burgers, nachos, that sort of thing. I can get you a menu?"

"Ah, no, but maybe next time," Oscar said, turning back to her. He smiled a half-smile. Not at all like Emerson's, more cheeky and secretive.

"We ate already," Emerson said, sounding sorry. "But next time I'd love to try something Irish. That sounds adventurous."

Oscar jerked around and narrowed his eyes at the crown of Emerson's head. "Or like trouble."

"Try a Guinness, Oscar, you'll love it." Holt reached around Emerson to slap Oscar on the back. It earned him a harsh glare. A glare that grew more pointed when Holt's arm stayed around his sister. "Or not."

"I've had Guinness before, believe it or not. I'd love a Harp, please."

"Sure." She steeled herself and turned to Emerson. "For you?"

"I'll try the Guinness, since you recommended it."

Be still my jackhammering heart.

Holt frowned when Emerson looked over her shoulder at the rest of the bar.

"Where's the men's room?" Oscar asked, blue eyes pingponging between Holt and Harper.

"It's marked Lads," Harper said and pointed toward the far corner. She felt drawn back to Holt, stared hard at him. It reminded her of the stare down she'd had with Luka. Territorial. The wolf surged, its anger and power making her hands tremble.

"Hey Harper, when you're finished with their order can I get a refill?" Scott cut in, looking sheepish as he wiggled his glass. The half melted ice cubes rattled, and she wanted to snatch it from him to make it stop.

She busied her hands, to keep her brain occupied and to keep from punching Holt in the nose. He wouldn't stop grinning. She hated that he'd clearly brought Emerson to the bar to make her jealous, and it worked. Not in the way he intended, she was sure, but that knowledge didn't help much. She hated that her skin burned, and she couldn't seem to stop growling. Mostly she hated that every time she glanced at Emerson a jolt went through her.

"So, Harper, how long have you lived in Fincher?"

That damn voice. She shivered and kept her eyes glued to what her hands were doing.

"Don't distract her, Emmy, she's using all her brain power on making drinks," Holt joked.

Holt.

Holt with Emerson.

PURE OF HEART

Holt was touching Emerson. He had his stupid arm around her slender shoulders. He was making fun of her and touching Emerson and...

"Harper, you didn't ask me what I wanted," he said. She snapped her eyes back up to his face and her vision shifted. *Don't do it. Do not reach over and yank off one of his eyebrows. Or an ear.*

You sir, she wanted to say, *are the sombrero of asshats.* Instead she said, "Sorry, what can I get you?"

He grinned and she tensed, ready for his usual sloppy innuendo.

"Your mom?"

The pint glass broke. She'd picked it up and then her fist clenched and it exploded. Shards dug into her skin and landed all over the counter. Blood ran down her arm, slick and hot, dripping everywhere. She watched it with some fascination. Her stomach rolled at the smell. Blood and coconut and whiskey all mixed together.

"Oh geeze, Harper," Scott said, bending forward to see.

"Get her a towel!" Emerson covered her mouth, eyes wide.

"Harper!" Logan called, hustling toward the bar with another empty pitcher.

The bones in her hand snapped, one by one. She snarled and smacked it down, cracking more glass beneath it and smearing red all over. "What did you just say?"

When Holt didn't reply, she grabbed a handful of his shirt and felt a thrill run through her at his small squeak of pain. She yanked him forward, half over the bar, and leaned down so they were eye level. Her lip curled up on the left side and she heard more bones crunching in her chest. On the hand clenching at Holt's shirt her mother's wedding band gleamed in the low light.

"Say it again," she said, voice shaking with every syllable.

CHAPTER EIGHT

"Harper!" She ignored the frightened call and tightened her fist around a wad of Holt's shirt. "What did you say?"

He grabbed at her wrist and squeezed. She felt the pressure but no pain. Everything outside his face faded to a ring of hazy black. His eyes first widened and then narrowed, dark eyebrows gathered together. He glared and she snarled back.

"Your mom," he said through his teeth. "It was a joke, Harper. God."

"You don't talk about my mom." She flexed and his head dipped, almost hitting the bar top. Her muscles quivered with the strain of resisting the impulse to bash his head in. "You ever say something like that again and I'll rip out your tongue and wear it as a tie."

His eyes widened again, pupils dilated, and his face turned an interesting shade of red. She adjusted her grip until her knuckles pressed against his throat.

"Bitch," he said, low enough only she could hear.

Dizzy, nauseous, and trembling she tugged again. "That's right, I'm a bitch and you don't speak my language. Asshole's a different dialect, so don't bother trying again. In fact don't speak to me again. Don't even look at me. I promise you won't live to regret it."

She pulled away, but Holt didn't release her wrist. His thick fingers squeezed again, harder, and he pulled her back toward him.

Heat blossomed in her chest and the black ring around her vision narrowed. The smell of coconuts clashed with everything else and she found it hard to breathe. "Let go of me."

He narrowed his eyes.

"Let go of me, right now." She heard and felt something click in the back of her mouth. The pressure in her head escalated to unbearable levels.

"Hey, what the hell?" Logan yelled. He came up right next to her and clasped his hand over Holt's. "Holt, let her go!"

"Stay out of it, Loogie. Like she's going to fall for that pathetic hero routine."

"Screw you, Dolt."

"Holt, I'm warning you," Harper said.

"Holt, let her go. Please." It was Emerson's voice that time, and a pale hand came into Harper's field of vision. It landed on Holt's shoulder, pretty French tipped fingernails digging into soft fabric.

The wolf snarled.

"She started it," Holt said.

"I'm about to finish it too," she replied and clenched her still bleeding fist. Holt's shirt and hand were smeared with red and she thought it would be perfectly fair if she spilled a little of his.

She heard the rest of the bar noticing the altercation. Couldn't tune out the whispers after the first of many reached her ears.

"What's happening up there?"

"There she goes again. Another night, another tantrum."

"Poor Holt. He should stay away from that girl."

Poor Holt, it was always poor Holt. The Fincher Favorite could do no wrong. They always rallied to his defense. She'd always be the weird one, dangerous, and with the temper that flared for no good reason.

"Look, dick utensil," she said, leaning closer. "I don't care about you dragging little miss bright eyes in here. I think it's disgusting, but I don't care if you screw her and half the town at the same time. Get it through your Cro-Magnon skull. I don't like you. I'm not sleeping with you, and trying to make me jealous isn't going to change that."

"Get over yourself," he said. "If I wanted you that bad I'd already have the notch in my bedpost."

"Isn't he a charmer," she said to Emerson. "Do yourself a favor and get checked. God knows what diseases he's riddled with."

"Excuse me!" Emerson stood, stool legs screeching against the floor. A deep blush colored her cheeks, and tears gleamed. She snatched up her purse and shook her head. "Are you two really this juvenile?"

Another hand joined in. Thick fingers wrapped around the back of Holt's neck, flexed in warning. Scott spoke up, and even though his words were a bit slurred, his tone had enough rumble in it to make Holt pale and Harper shiver. "Holt, I don't care whose son you are, let her go right now. Let her go or I'll bust that pretty face of yours on the bar."

Holt's grip loosened and she jerked her hand back to her chest. They continued to glare at each other.

Scott shoved at Holt's neck then let go. "Be a gentleman. Mind the rules."

The rules. Her rules. The bar rules that were different from her own personal set.

She was dangerously close to breaking her first commandment.

Thou shalt not wolf out.

"Emerson," Holt said, working his jaw and reaching for Emerson's hand. She backed away from him and then turned.

"Oscar!"

"What is going on?" Oscar rejoined the party. He stood a few steps away, arms crossed over his chest. He spared Harper a swift glance and his expression hardened. "Emerson, come on, we're leaving." He pulled out a wallet and tossed some bills onto the bar, even though they hadn't so much as seen their drinks. "I hope you two are very happy together," he said with a sneer directed at Holt.

Neither spared a backwards glance as they hurried off. Harper heard Emerson huff and Oscar whispering an "I told you so."

"You ruin everything," Holt said. He knocked over his stool, stood, and raced toward the door. "Emerson, wait!"

A whine escaped Harper's clenched teeth. Her stomach twisted and she gagged, close to puking all over.

"Harp, you okay?" Logan put his arm over her shoulders and an unpleasant sensation ripped through her. Like she'd been dunked in boiling water. "Jesus, you're burning up."

She knocked his arm off and darted for the kitchen. Logan and Scott called after her, but she ignored them. The freezer, she had to get to the freezer. Neither cook commented as she stumbled past, clutching her abdomen. The muscles shifted under her trembling fingertips.

Her skin prickled with heat, her forehead felt damp. She yanked open the heavy door and slammed it shut behind her. Steam rose off her arms, sweat chilled across her collarbones. She moved further into the room and took a seat on the floor in the farthest corner. Her gums itched, so she rubbed at her jaw and tried to think of something boring. But every time she closed her eyes she saw Holt, Holt and Emerson. A growl vibrated in her chest and a puny human canine elongated. Her hands shook as her vision sharpened.

"Don't do this," she said and closed her eyes tight. "Not now."

More teeth were replaced, coming in quicker and quicker. She huddled deeper into her corner, drew her knees to her chest and focused on breathing. Slow breaths that made her lungs ache. With her forehead pressed into her arms, she searched for a memory to hide in.

She pictured her father's office. The big, plush leather chair, the imposing desk cluttered with papers and gnawed pens. She remembered the scent of coffee, leather and polish, books, and something that registered as "home". Another breath and she almost felt the tickle of carpet under bare feet, the smooth black leather of the chair under her body.

Her heart rate slowed, still loud in her ears but better. She counted the beats until the itch in her mouth diminished, until another set of pops reverberated through her skull. When she ran her tongue along her teeth, she found nothing but the familiar contours of short human ones. The pressure in her head went next, the ache still present but far less painful and persistent.

Another breath. Her back cricked from the base of her spine all the way up to her neck.

One symptom left to clear up. She snagged the lip of an empty tray and raised it up. A blob of unrecognizable flesh color made up her reflection in the shiny surface, but her eyes gleamed. She concentrated on those gold eyes. The color faded, flickering like a candle struggling to stay lit.

She relaxed her grip on the pan and sagged when she no longer saw the off-putting color in her makeshift mirror.

Right on time the door opened and Grady stepped in.

"Harper." He sighed and leaned back against the door. "You okay? Logan came and got me out of the office."

"Everything's under – I'm cool."

"No pun intended," he said with a small smile. "I'm going to have some words with that boy."

"You're not having words with any of them." She shook her head. "I can handle it."

"By losing your temper and causing a scene?"

"No, and also screw you."

"Hey!" He jabbed a finger at her. "Enough with the attitude. I'm trying to help."

"By being a dick?"

"How was that being a dick? I'm trying to be an uncle. A concerned uncle, who now has to go out and work damage control because I'm also your boss. Harper, you've got to stop doing this at work. People are going to start to think these fights of yours are staged. Or that I let you get away with bad behavior because we're related." He sighed and rubbed at his forehead. "We can't keep going through this."

"Screw you twice." She waved a hand toward the door. "Concerned uncle my ass. Go on then, go make sure your customers are happy."

"That's the problem! I'm more concerned with you. I don't care about those people, and I should. What happened out there?"

"He made a mom joke," she said with a growl. "And I need to stay calm right now, not argue and get worked up again."

Grady turned red, his knuckles cracked as his hands clenched into fists. "He did what?"

PURE OF HEART

"Made a joke, a stupid comment, about Mom and I lost my temper. Okay?"

"I'll kill him myself."

She shook her head again and wobbled up to her feet. "You won't and neither will I. I'm sorry I lost my temper again, alright? I couldn't help it and I'll try harder next time. He just gets under my skin and I hate him. The wolf and I agree on that at least."

He sighed. "You have to let me help. Somehow. We can't keep doing this every time he's in here. I can't ban him from the bar, or his father would have me closed down in the blink of an eye."

"If you think about it, it's amazing that hasn't happened already. I'm sorry I'm such a liability." She winced and kicked at a crate. "If you need to fire me, I understand."

"I'm not going to do that. We just need to put this fire out before it gets any bigger. He knows how to push your buttons, and we can't risk him exposing you."

"I could work in the back more? You could take over at the bar when he comes in?"

"Those sound like options. We can discuss it more later." He dug into his pocket and pried his truck keys free. "Here, take the truck home. I'll finish your shift tonight."

She raised an eyebrow. "You think sending me home won't cause more stir?"

"Less than if I let you waltz back out there like nothing happened." He snorted. "Besides, you can make sure Cooper actually goes to bed."

"Yeah, because he's going to listen to me."

"He actually believes you when you threaten him. Me he just rolls his eyes at." He shook the keys. "Look, I may be a pathetic excuse for a dad and a terrible ass of an uncle sometimes, but I'm trying. And I do love you, Harper. You and Cooper both. A lot more than my business."

He had to go and say something sappy. She rolled her eyes and looked up at the ceiling to avoid him seeing her tears. "I don't want the truck."

"You sure?"

She nodded, and once she was sure all evidence of tears had frozen, approached him. He didn't protest when she curled his fingers back over the keys. "Fresh air sounds good. I could use it and you hate walking home." He stared and she offered him a small smile. "I'll be fine."

"Alright," he said and rocked on his feet. "Um, are you good on the headache meds? I can stop on my way home and get some more."

"No, you can't. The pharmacy isn't open this late." She threw her arms around his neck and hugged him for as long as possible before her skin crawled at the closeness. "Thank you for offering. I'm okay, really. I'll see you later."

***

She snuck out the back of the bar to avoid drawing any more attention. The townies had enough drama to gossip about. No need to add more. She'd already resigned herself to the whispers that followed her around, she just wasn't in the mood to hear them again right that second.

"Lost her parents, you know," they'd say. "That's why she's so screwed up."

Harper, the troubled orphan Grady had rescued like a stray dog. Temperamental, dangerous Harper. Sometimes she found it amusing, how they acted like she was the boogeyman. Other times it was depressing.

"Gossip mongers," she muttered and looped her scarf around her neck. It smelled faintly of coconuts now. She'd have tossed it in the trash, to discourage the wolf's latest weirdness, but she did love it. Ugly yes, but it was a gift from her Aunt Naomi. Grady had been horrified when she'd gone through her knitting stage, but now the beanies and scarves were their way of remembering, cherishing another loved one they'd lost.

With her nose pressed into the soft red wool and hands jammed in her pockets, she turned down the short alley. It was clear, the sky above full of stars. She hoped that meant no more snow, at least for a little while. The break in the weather would encourage people to take down the Christmas junk.

The snowmen would melt.

She winced as she stepped onto the sidewalk and had to skirt around one of the large ones. The townies constructed them all up and down the street, like it was an adorable tradition and not just plain creeptastic. She hated having to dodge the snow people, their terrifying grins and button eyes.

"Note to self," she muttered as she leaned away from long stick arms. "Do not watch horror movies with Cooper anymore. No matter how many times he makes the chicken sounds or calls you a pussy."

In an effort to avoid the stares of both real and snow-made people she broke into a jog. Her pace didn't stay stable for long. Despite the sketchy footing, she sped up when she saw the lights of the subdivision. Her thoughts kept up, unfortunately, no matter how fast she pushed herself.

Holt, Emerson, Grady, Scott, Logan. Their voices and faces plagued her every step of the way.

Are you really so juvenile?
We can't keep doing this.
Your mom.

Her feet went out from under her as she stepped with too much confidence on a thick sheet of ice.

She laid on the cold ground, face mushed into a thick snow hedge. One eye rolled up to see the waning gibbous looming overhead. It was at its

PURE OF HEART

weakest, and yet the wolf crashed through her veins like it was the night before a full moon.

AJ, she thought but dismissed it immediately. She'd already bothered AJ enough. If she continued running to her for help she'd develop an unhealthy habit. Dependence.

She lurched back to her feet and wobbled a few steps before starting to jog once again. Her feet directed her down the wrong side of the subdivision and she caught a stronger whiff of coconuts. Not just from the scarf still wrapped around her neck.

"No you don't," she said and corrected her runaway body. "You've done enough."

Heat rushed down, from the crown of her head to the tips of her toes. She gagged at the sensation and almost tripped again. A new form of temper tantrum to contend with.

She hit the front steps of the house, and stumbled up them as she struggled to a stop. Heart pounding and breath escaping in short, visible puffs, she stood on the porch and braved a glance back. Fincher looked peaceful, Christmas lights and street lamps glittering under the small moon.

Sometimes it reminded her enough of Anchorage to quell her homesickness. In silent moments she could almost pretend she belonged here among the packs of gossip hounds and their snowmen.

A loud crash inside the house caught her attention. She turned with a sigh and a shake of her head.

Finally, a good distraction.

She thumped her boots down to clear the snow clinging and threw open the front door.

"Cooper!" She shouted, rolling her eyes as she locked the door behind her. "How many times do you have to get in trouble before you obey?"

"You complain when it's locked and you can't get in. Then you complain when it's not. I can't win. Either way I'm in trouble," Cooper yelled from the living room. "You're always mad, no matter what I do."

"I'm not mad," she said and dropped her coat and scarf on the waiting hat-rack. "More like I don't want to get in trouble on your behalf again." She grunted and shoved Cooper's backpack off the entryway bench to clear space to sit. Her boot laces were half frozen and her stiff fingers didn't want to cooperate to untie them anyway. She groaned and tried to keep from ripping them off. "Did you eat dinner?"

"No, I've become anorexic. Thanks for bringing it up."

"Cooper." She rolled her eyes again and kicked both boots off. "I'm not in the mood."

"Why are you home?"

"Let out early for good behavior." She stared at the tower of wet shoes and winced. They'd be getting a lecture about that later. "Did you save me any food?"

"Uh, no, but there's some of the leftover goop Dad made."

The idea of trying to shovel down any more of Grady's cooking made her choke. She peered around the corner and rolled her lips together to keep from laughing. Cooper stood on the couch in all of his nerdiest superhero attire. Flash shirt, Batman pajama pants, and the Superman robe to top it off. He'd never be caught dead wearing that outside the house, but when there weren't any teenage girls around his inner nerd came out.

He spared her a glance, a quick one, before his eyes moved right back to the TV. The controller in his hands was turned almost sideways as he slapped his thumb against a button with prejudice. She crossed the room and planted herself in the middle of the screen.

"So you ate all the food, forgot to lock the door." She ticked off each offense on her fingers in a bored fashion. "Made a mess, and have been playing video games since you got home?"

"I'm a teenager, it's what we do." He waved a hand at her. "You're in the way."

"I'm a grown up, it's what we do," she said but stepped to the side.

He ran a hand through his shaggy blond hair and collapsed back on the couch. "You hulked out again, didn't you?"

"I hate it when you call it that."

"Only 'cause it's true." He patted the cushion next to him and pouted.

"I don't turn green." Her eyes closed in bliss as she propped her feet up on the coffee table. Another no-no, but Grady wasn't there, yet. "I hate it because it's insulting and inaccurate."

"If you'd read the comics…" He snagged the second controller and dropped it in her lap.

"I outgrew picture books in the second grade," she said and held the controller like it was some sort of puzzle. "What are we playing?"

"Do you care?"

"Nah. Let's shoot some bad guys and save the girl – world – whatever."

Blessed silence. Sort of. Explosions rocked the modest sound system along with gunfire and yelps and other strange warlike sounds. She enjoyed it though, chasing after Cooper in some other reality and having a mission. It always took her a moment to remember how all the buttons worked but she liked to think she was a quick study.

"You know," Cooper said out the side of his mouth. He tapped at the controls for a moment with an adorable growl. "Uh, you're a pretty cool cousin. Sometimes, I guess. Sorry you had a crappy night at work."

"Awww, so sappy." She knocked her shoulder into his. "You're pretty okay sometimes too. Thanks for letting me play with you."

"You could be so good if you worked at it. Killer reflexes. It's almost not fair to the other bozos."

Killer. She froze. The word bounced around her head a few times. "I'll, uh, I'll never be as good as you are, bud."

"With me as your teacher you'd be the best. We could rule the gaming world as Master and Padawan."

She shook her head and happened to catch sight of the grandfather clock in the corner. "Oh shit!"

The game stopped as she smacked the pause button.

"Harper!" Cooper huffed and poked her in the ribs. "What gives? I was totally about to own that tank."

"Sorry, Coop, bedtime is now." She handed him the controller and dragged herself off the couch. "Actually it was a long time ago, but we'll call it now because Grady's going to be home soon. I am the worst babysitter ever."

"It's Friday," he whined. "Bedtime shouldn't exist on Friday's. Side note, can we not call it bedtime? Or babysitting? I'm not a little kid anymore."

"Says the puppy in superhero attire. Take it up with the powers that be. I'm not taking the heat for letting you stay up." She gestured at the empty glasses, plates, and chip bags strewn across the coffee table. "Come on, we've got to clean this up and go to bed. I don't care if you sleep, but you'd better pretend when he comes to check on you. I'm talking an Oscar-worthy performance."

"This sucks."

Despite his protests, they made quick work of the mess. She listened to him grumble as she shoved him ahead of her up the stairs. He dragged his feet, of course, but went.

"We can play more tomorrow, okay?"

He stopped on the top floor and turned to her with a crazy grin. "Really?"

"Sure," she said and shrugged. Staying inside as long as possible, away from coconuts and strange wolfy reactions, sounded like a great idea. "You get your chores done first and we can finish what we started."

"Awesome." He grinned and grabbed her in a smaller version of Grady's infamous bear hugs. "Goodnight, Harp."

"Yeah, goodnight, Coop." Her shoulders sagged the second his door closed. The idea of going to lay in her bed to stew over things didn't sound appealing, but waiting around for Grady wouldn't be any better. She imagined her thoughts being visible, gathering over her head like storm clouds.

Killer.

She moved through her dark bedroom, right past the rumpled bed, and threw open the window. The chill of the air bit at the skin exposed by her shirt, but it wasn't enough to dissuade her. She climbed out on the roof and sat cross-legged on the snow covered shingles.

In the distance she could hear people, cars, as activity dwindled in the heart of town. She turned her attention over the swaying treetops and took a deep breath of pine scented air. The moon called to her, and even though it lacked most of its power she couldn't resist its pull. Her body hummed under the dim glow and she tilted her head back.

There it sat, as it always did. Singing its siren song, making her blood simmer and muscles twitch. She clenched her teeth to keep from howling.

"My mistress the moon," she muttered, unable to look away. "What is this new bullshit you're throwing at me? Haven't I given you enough?"

The moon didn't respond, of course. It never did when she wanted it to, or how she wanted it to. Danu, the moon Goddess, certainly wasn't much like the folk tales. Some Great Mother she'd turned out to be. "You're more like the Crone, you know that? Always throwing a monkey wrench into things."

Her joints ached, the lunar pull drawing her upward. She wanted to be closer to the light, always closer, to bask in it. The skin on her arms erupted with goosebumps and her hair stood on end. Her vision shifted and the world around her brightened, but she only had eyes for the moon. Golden eyes reflecting the beast inside that yearned for its luminous mistress.

"I don't know what you're up to," she said, and hummed. As much as she hated it, she always felt more alive bathed in that glow. Better than the warm touch of the sun could ever be. She belonged in the night, under a blanket of stars, guided by Danu while she stalked the forest.

Or that could be the wolf messing with her head again.

The rumble of Grady's truck coming toward the house broke the spell. She twisted around, heightened eyesight picking out the battered truck approaching.

"I'm not playing your game." She glared up at the moon and slid back into her room.

CHAPTER NINE

Emerson

Emerson could see Oscar's thoughts brewing. He stared at her, or more like through her, as he fidgeted with his carry on. She smiled at him in a small, sad, sort of way. They stood just outside the car in the snow-covered parking lot – as close to the airport as she'd managed to coax him. They'd been arguing the whole way there. She considered it a victory that she'd gotten him out of the vehicle at all.

The berms of snow surrounding the lot glittered in the sunlight. A nice winter day in Montana. A good day to be flying. Part of her wished it would storm, blizzard, to postpone having to say goodbye. She'd become accustomed to saying goodbye to her daddy, she wished she didn't have to get used to the same with her brother.

"Oz, I'll be fine," she said for the fifteenth time. It hadn't worked the first fourteen either. "You have to go back to New York."

"I could stay another week." He gave up on his leather messenger bag, dropping it to his feet. "I'm staying another week."

She shook her head and fixed the collar of his sport coat. "No, you're not. One week will turn into another and then another. You are getting on that plane and going home. Back to work and the lovely Claire. Don't think I haven't noticed her blowing up your phone."

"You're my sister, you're more important. I can get the time off."

"And a new girlfriend?" She raised an eyebrow. "Those Broadway darlings are hard to come by."

He huffed and shoved his hands in his pockets. "I don't like leaving you with that bunch. Not until after the hornets have calmed back down. You really kicked the nest this time. I can feel it. There's something off about them."

"Holt and the 'mysterious' Harper? Please," she said and rolled her eyes. Harper, maybe, had something different about her, but she wouldn't admit that to him. "I survived High School, I think I can manage."

"But see that's... trouble, Emerson. Trouble with a capital T. I know you, you're not going to leave this alone. You're too curious for your own good."

"I admit I'm intrigued. But it doesn't mean I'm going to throw myself right back in the middle of things. Harper did basically call me a dimwitted whore and Holt an STD riddled playboy." She sighed and picked his bag up for him. "I'll be using the cold shoulder technique until they grow up."

"What if they never do?" he asked and slipped the strap back over his shoulder. "You do know that's a possibility? Or she really is a psycho and he's a plague carrying sex fiend."

"Then I guess I won't be making friends as quickly as I thought."

He groaned. "Emerson."

"No." She shook her head. "I can handle this. I'm going to live in that town and I'll have to learn to deal with everyone else that calls it home. Besides, it's only a small mystery." The mystery of the playboy and the monster of Fincher.

"And that right there." He pinched the bridge of his nose. "That worries me the most. You and your mysteries, I swear. Not everyone is fond of your Scooby-Doo routine. Especially strangers."

"I'll be fine." Sixteen, and he still didn't appear persuaded. "They have to learn to deal with me too. It's an adjustment period and it won't all be bad. We haven't even seen the two of them since their argument." She looked beyond him, to the tiny airport entrance. "You're going to miss your flight."

"They're probably hiding from me, that's why. Or Harper killed him and is on the run or hiding in a cave somewhere. Listen, if I get on that plane I won't be here to deter Holt from sniffing around and Harper from, I don't know, chewing your arm off?"

"I know this may come as a shock, but I don't need you to build a moat around the house. Or to pretend to be the fire breathing dragon keeping me locked away." She leaned into him, stealing warmth and a last bit of comfort. For his sake, of course. "That only encourages white knights on stallions anyway. I'm quite capable of voicing my own opinions and sending away unwanted sniffers and arm chewers."

"Just promise me something," he said, turning as she pushed at his shoulders. "I know you're — " he lowered his voice and leaned toward her ear. "Ambidextrous."

"Really, Oscar." She scoffed, but linked arms with him as they trekked toward the door at a snail's pace. "Now you bring that up?"

PURE OF HEART

"It needed to be mentioned." He blushed. "With this Harper and Holt thing, it really needed to be mentioned. She's crazy and he's an ape. Messing with them both when they already don't like each other — just promise me you won't — that you'll be safe."

"Safe?" She smiled wider and watched him squirm. "Dear sweet, uncomfortable brother of mine. Safe is my middle name."

"If that were true, it would be very ironic," he said with a snort.

She held up a hand. "I, Emerson Austen Grey, solemnly swear I will not allow my ambidexterity to cause too much trouble in the small town of Fincher."

"If only I felt reassured." He nudged her and shook his head. "You used the wrong hand to swear."

"I'm ambidextrous." She smiled her most winning smile and delighted in his scandalized expression.

"Not for swearing things. You'll call me later?"

"Oh, not you too. It'll have to be after I talk Mother down again. I'm starting to think she'll come up here and drag me back to Atherton in the middle of the night."

"But you like talking to me."

"Do I?"

"Don't tease me," he said and let go of her arm as they approached the doors to the terminal. "Alright, Dorothy, I'm going. But if you need me all you have to do is call. You know I'll come running."

"You're the perfect gentleman and an exemplary brother." She hugged him tight and laughed as tears welled. "Look at us, you'd think you were going off to war."

"I'm not, but I wonder about you. Try not to blow up any sheds or take too many hearts prisoner."

"The shed wasn't my fault," she said. He pulled back and she sniffled when he ducked to kiss her forehead. "Love you, Oz."

"I love you, and I'm going to miss you terribly. I think I'll even miss that furry gremlin you call a pet."

She let him go and backed away, not bothering to wipe at the wet streaks on her cheeks. "You're ridiculous and stalling. Go on. I'll call you after I lock up tonight. We'll video chat too. I'll need your help with things from time to time."

He walked backward toward the ticket counter. "Lock the doors and the windows, and for the love of your worried brother draw the blinds!"

"Talk to you soon." She left when he turned around, not wanting to watch him go. It had been hard enough when he'd gone to New York the first time. Somehow this felt more permanent.

Still, she wiped her eyes and raised her chin as she stepped back out into the bright sun and snow. The wind tossed her hair and tousled her skirt as she made her way to her car. She sat inside for a moment, the engine silent, and looked at herself in the rearview mirror.

"You can do this Emerson, you can. It'll be fun. You'll see." She turned the key and gripped the steering wheel. "I'll be fine."

Seventeen times.

***

What little bravado she'd managed to find disappeared in one long sigh as she pulled up to the house. Her house now, but she still thought of it as her grandparent's. She stared at the front door waiting for Papa to come outside and shuffle over to the porch swing. Nana would follow along shortly with two cups of coffee, even in the middle of the afternoon.

They didn't come outside this time. Oscar wouldn't be walking out to scold her for sitting in the cold either.

"I'm alone," she blurted, startling herself in the silence of the car.

She'd lived at home during college and always had a gaggle of girls to spend time with, boys to flirt with. Even her mother had been a companion of sorts. An unwanted one, most of the time, but a person nevertheless.

I might even miss those tennis matches, she thought. "Just don't start talking to yourself or you're in trouble."

Laughing at her own joke, she opened the car door and stuck a foot out into the snow. The laughter gave way to a gasp when the cold bit into her exposed toes. She high-stepped across the snow covered drive, staying upright by sheer will power. Her eyes widened when she realized she'd have to shovel her own driveway clear. She couldn't even park in the garage because all her boxes were still stacked inside, along with things her grandparents left behind.

Her beautiful shoes were wet and had snow packed in along the edges. She winced, looked around the empty neighborhood, and then stooped to take them off. Wet Prada's in one hand, she struggled to arrange her keys so she could unlock the front door.

She missed Oscar's teasing already and he'd only been gone a couple hours.

"*C'est la vie,*" she muttered and eased the door open.

A merry jingling sound bounced toward her. She bent down with a smile and scooped Mr. Darcy up as he wound around her ankles. Her shoes lay where she'd dropped them in the entryway and she paused in the living room. Then she grinned and continued on her way. It was her house now.

She stopped again half way up the stairs, put the cat down and hurried back to her favorite pair of peeptoes. "So I'll keep some rules," she said to the cat. "Only a few, and you can't ever breathe a word to mother."

He mewed, like he agreed to her terms, and followed her upstairs. She went to the guest room first, to see if Oscar left anything behind. He'd made the bed, cleaned off the dresser. She doubted he'd left a sock behind.

Next she checked the office. The bookcases were still stuffed to the brim. Her computer sat in place of Oscar's with a sticky note on the monitor.

I left a document with instructions on how to use the new software on your desktop. Oh, and I changed that awful wallpaper.

She smiled and touched a finger to his chicken-scratch.

Shoes still dangling from one hand, she entered the master bedroom. Her room. The quilt her grandmother had made covered the mattress. Patches of white and blue stitched together with painstaking care. She trailed a hand over the cool blanket and then sat down on the end of the bed. Oscar had suggested re-painting the room, changing the theme to something more her. The blues and whites didn't scream Emerson. They reminded her of early mornings when she'd get cold and run down the hall to climb into bed with Nana and Papa. He'd grumble about chilly toes and fingers and Nana would laugh.

The paint would stay. She sniffled and scooted back on the bed until her back hit the pillows piled in front of the headboard. Mr. Darcy jumped up beside her and made himself at home in her lap, purring away.

She spoke to his twitching ears. "No mother to force me to go shopping. No daddy to come home with surprises. No brother to tell my secrets and schemes to." She hugged him. "At least I still have you, Dee."

He bumped his head against her chin.

***

She stepped inside Early Bird Books and smiled at the dust free shelves and somewhat more orderly stacks. A few books remained on the floor. She'd had to leave them due to the incident with the now broken shelf. But it had gone from a mess of epic proportions to something more manageable. Between her and Oscar's hard work, it looked more like a bookstore and less like a hoarder's spare room.

"Well, Mr. Darcy, shall we continue where we left off?" She bent down to smile at him through his cat-carrier grate. He blinked at her and gave a faint meow. "That's what I thought."

She opened his crate and scratched him behind the ears when he lingered for a moment. "You know, if it wasn't called Early Bird Books I'd say you could be the mascot for this place, but if we called it Siamese Books people would get the wrong idea, I think."

He purred and dropped off the desk to go about his prowling. When the jingle of his collar faded, she realized how alone she was. Oscar would not be coming in to complain about the weather or lack of familiar stores. He would not be heard making a racket in the back office as he pored over the ledgers. Nor would he be there to tease her when he caught her reading instead of shelving.

As if she could resist opening a few, here and there, as she shelved new and old stories. They all but begged to be opened. There were so many tales she hadn't read or that were favorites, just sitting on shelves waiting to be picked up and appreciated. Some author had poured their heart and soul onto blank pages, and she felt she at least owed it to them to take a peek. Not to mention if someone came in and had a question she should know a thing or two about the books she carried.

"Best stay away from the classics today," she said with a shake of her head. The beautiful stained oak bookshelves to her right drew her attention and she grinned at the shiny plate on the side. It read Children's Section. "Much safer."

Like the rest of the cases, this section had become wildly out of order. She couldn't tell if her papa had tried some new arrangement for sorting, or if he'd stopped caring altogether.

She widened her eyes, and snatched a thick blue-spined book off the nearest shelf. "Harry, what are you doing all by yourself over here?" She moved down the length of the shelf scanning for the rest of the series, holding Order of the Phoenix close to her chest. One by one she pulled them each from the odd places they'd been tucked into. "Alphabetical by title," she said, finally recognizing the method of organization adopted by her grandfather. "That won't do."

She carried the entire Harry Potter series over to the front desk and heaved the stack onto it. Light reading for later.

"I'm my first costumer," she said as she scanned each book into the computer. At least she'd find out if the cash register still worked.

Books paid for, she turned her attention to the sorting cart. She paused, hands resting on the handle and frowned at the ceiling. No music, not even speakers. One more thing she needed to add. It wasn't a library, after all, and she always preferred to read with something playing in the background to further stimulate her imagination.

"Mr. Darcy, please remind me to look into commercial sound systems later," she called and shoved the cart into motion. Her fingers trailed along a wall as she walked through a back aisle. All the walls were the same purple-red color. She pondered what might be better, more attractive to the bookworms. Bright and cheerful? Or maybe something soothing and warm to draw customers into the embrace of a good book. A color like coffee with the perfect amount of cream in it?

Resigned to an afternoon of re-ordering she grabbed the first title in the A's and set it on the cart. In her mind, she planned out how she would get this done. First she'd move one letter at a time and sort by author. Then she could re-shelve them appropriately.

"Heaven help me if every section is like this, I'll be here for a year."

A loud knock on the front door scared her so badly she dropped the books in her hands. She whirled around, a hand to the five-beat-pile-up in her chest and peered around the shelf to see who had stopped by.

PURE OF HEART

Holt stood on the other side of the glass door, a bouquet in his hands and a winning, hopeful smile on his handsome face.

She whipped back around the corner and backed herself up against the shelf. "Okay, Em. You can do this. Don't accept an apology too fast, no matter how cute those dimples are. He was rude."

With a scowl she shook out her hair, took off her glasses, and then walked toward him. She made sure each step looked confident and glared at him for a moment before opening the door. "Can I help you, Holt?"

"Uh, hi?" His smile faded. "Is Oscar here?"

She considered lying to watch him squirm longer. "No."

He stared at her until she raised an eyebrow and then thrust the flowers at her. "These are for you."

They were not store bought. She could tell because the roots were still attached. They were a pretty purple-blue and shaped like long cones. An odd flower, but unique. "They're lovely. What are they?"

"Lupine," he said and stuffed his hands in his pockets when she accepted the gift. "My mom has a greenhouse with a bunch of native flowers. You know, for the tourists."

"Of course."

"Look, about the other night I — "

"You were a jerk," she supplied.

"Yeah." He scuffed his shoe against the pavement. "It's just Harper and I don't get along anymore. I told you we got into a fight recently."

"So you thought you'd take my brother and I to the bar where she works? Did you want us to witness another firsthand?"

"You were curious about her, and I thought maybe she'd be nicer if there were new people with me."

She leaned against the door and narrowed her eyes. "And the things she said?"

He scratched at the back of his neck. "I do have a bit of a reputation, I admit. But I swear that was a long time ago."

"How long?"

"High School?" He shrugged. "I'm not perfect, Emmy. I do dumb stuff sometimes and I used to chase girls a lot. I'm trying to grow up. You seem like a really nice girl and I'm sorry you had to see and hear all that shi — junk the other night. Can you forgive me?"

Not just yet, Em. Steady girl. "I'm not sure I should trust you."

"Please? Let me prove to you I'm not that guy. I promise I'll be a perfect gentleman, just like you deserve."

"And how do I know you're a man of your word? After that embarrassing display, it doesn't seem likely you'll keep your promise. We are still strangers after all."

"Let me take you to dinner," he said, pleading with his bronzy brown eyes. "At The Lodge. It's nice, the fanciest place in town. That's a start, right?"

She sniffed the flowers and pretended to mull it over.

"Please, Emmy. Give me another chance?"

"One more," she said and held up a finger before he could babble any more. "I mean it. If you can't behave like an adult, then I'm done. You understand? No amount of flowers and puppy dog expressions will change my mind after that."

"I got it." He grinned. "So dinner, tonight?"

"Yes." She nodded. "Pick me up at six."

CHAPTER TEN

Harper

It felt like she'd swallowed a rock and then washed it down with a pinecone chaser.

Harper half stomped and half dragged her way down the street, holding onto her stomach. She delayed swallowing as long as possible. It only helped a little, if she waited too long her throat would start itching and she'd end up hacking up a lung. There weren't too many people out on the sidewalks, but she wore a scowl to frighten off anyone she passed. They didn't even whisper as she stormed by, though she did catch a few wide-eyed looks.

That's right, she thought with a sneer, *I'm scary and in no mood for your bullshit*.

That morning her alarm clock had summoned her from the depths of a bloody nightmare. Her nightmare followed her into the daylight, vivid and terrifying. Flesh had torn under her hands, blood sprayed, bones snapped. She could still picture Holt's face, frozen in terror, as she ripped open his chest. He'd screamed and she'd howled in response.

She shook her head as the images played again. The wolf simmered under her skin. Her stomach clenched again and her fingers gripped her shirt.

She'd never liked Holt and may have dreamed about kicking him in the balls once or twice – this was different. The wolf seemed to have murder on her mind.

"Another new symptom of Emersonitis?" She wondered out loud and pushed her free hand against her aching skull. "Step one is admitting you have a problem. I'm admitting it, I have a serious problem. How do I get to whatever step two is?"

More disturbing than the gory night and day terrors — the more she thought about Emerson, the stronger her reaction. Her head spun in circles, trying to keep up. Emerson equaled happy, jittery energy that inevitably turned to raw, sickening anger. Because Holt. Always back to Holt. Round and round she went again. Emerson, Holt. Holt and Emerson. Holt, Emerson, the wolf and Harper. There wasn't room for all of them in her head.

"How am I supposed to fix this?" It wasn't like she could talk to Grady. He'd get that constipated look on his face and stammer for hours. No, she'd have to leave him out of it for now. Logan didn't know about the wolf, by some small miracle. He also seemed to be of the opinion if he tried hard enough, she'd see him as a romantic option. That left AJ. Again.

"She should charge by the hour." She rolled her eyes and winced.

Her nose twitched and she stumbled midstride.

"Coconuts!"

With a mouse-like squeak of alarm she hurled herself into the thick brush alongside the road. One hand clamped over her mouth to muffle a whine as she pressed herself into the dirt. The wolf howled and her spine twisted. Her nose burned along with her throat. The smell got stronger, coming her direction. Her ears pricked up at the sound of heels clipping along on the sidewalk. Of course Emerson, little miss lady, would be wearing shoes with a heel on slippery sidewalks. Trish had once said poor weather was no excuse for poor fashion. She'd love Emerson.

The clicking drew nearer still, and through the leaves and twigs Harper saw her. Or at least her legs and those loud ankle boots. She waited for the numbness, the loss of control. Maybe this time she'd loll her tongue out and leap from her hiding place like an excited retriever. Her fingers dug deep into the cold earth, scratching long lines.

Emerson passed her, not slowing.

She poked her head up and saw her clip-clopping away, nose buried in a book, open on top of a sizeable stack. Nausea struck hard and she gagged. She dropped back into the shrubbery, hoping Emerson hadn't heard or seen anything. Heat prickled over her and she choked when her stomach rolled. She muffled a groan with a palm and turned onto her back. The sun hit her right in the eyes.

Then the wolf bubbled to the surface. Her legs tensed and one arm twitched. The hand not clamped over her mouth dug into the dirt. She closed her eyes and wished it all away.

"Harper."

She opened her eyes and saw an upside down Emerson frowning down at her. "Oh. Er, present?"

"So you're hiding from me now?"

PURE OF HEART

Shit, shit, shit. "Um…" Was she trying to wag a tail she didn't have? *God.*

"I wasn't planning on stopping or speaking to you at all. But then I thought you might have tripped."

"I'm not known for being graceful," she said with a grimace.

"Are you alright?"

Her right arm snapped. "Never better," she said through gritted teeth.

Emerson tilted her head to the side. "What was that noise?"

"Twig."

Blue eyes narrowed. "Well since you're alright, I'm going to go ahead and speak my mind. Lord knows when I'll get the chance again. I don't think I'll be stepping into your uncle's bar anymore. Not after that little episode of yours."

"Uh?" Harper's jaw snapped shut and she squirmed in discomfort. The wolf cocked her head, and she whined.

"You insulted me the other night. I don't know how things work around here, but I have to tell you I'm appalled at the way you acted. How dare you cast such aspersions on my character."

"Ass what?" She screwed up her face and then eeped when Emerson glared.

"You were violent and unaccountably rude. Maybe that's how you and Holt normally do things, but I will not stand by and let you say such horrible things about me." Emerson huffed, and the books in her arms shifted. "Look, I don't know what's going on with the two of you, and frankly I don't care to. Kindly keep me out of the crossfire of your little Hatfield-McCoy feud."

Another whine. Harper cowered in the dirt, overcome with a sense of immense misery. Damn wolf.

"You intrigue me, Harper. You are an ineffable curiosity, but I will not subject myself to someone who can be that nasty to a stranger."

Ever hear of stranger danger? She wondered, looking up into a very annoyed expression. *I am the epitome of a dangerous stranger.*

"Do you have anything to say to me?" Emerson drew herself up to her laughable full height.

The wolf wanted to grovel, but it dawned on her what a perfect opportunity she'd fallen into. If she could strangle the wolf into silence, Emerson would be offended. With any shred of Irish Luck, offended enough to stay away.

She bit down so hard her jaw popped. Her stomach gurgled loudly and her hands grabbed fistfuls of dirt. She trembled and felt sweat gathering. Those pretty pale eyes narrowed to a squint. She waited, struggling more with each passing second.

Emerson slumped, her face falling with her shoulders. "Goodbye, Harper." She turned and left, heels clicking away faster than before.

A howl got caught in her lungs. She gasped and rolled onto her stomach, holding her mouth again. Her lips trembled. She blurped into her palm, breakfast poking the back of her throat.

Tears came again, stinging her eyes and blurring everything. She'd never felt so rejected in her life.

***

She made it to AJ's, slinking through town and feeling more dejected with every step. The tears had gone, but the lingering, near gut-wrenching, sadness stayed. Her toes dragged across the ground, hands held tight to her sides. She whimpered in the back of her throat.

She'd done it. Emerson would want nothing to do with her anymore. That was best for both of them, but didn't make it any easier to deal with. She slumped against the front door to the clinic, and eased it open. Trish grinned, and leaned forward against her desk, pointed chin in her open palm.

"Harper. Here for a flea bath?"

"Hi, Trish," she said and headed for the door to the back rooms. The smell of butterscotch didn't even perk her up. She followed the trail easy enough, and ignored Trish's concerned call of her name.

"Hey, AJ?"

The dogs and cats went berserk. Barking and hissing, throwing themselves around their cages. She couldn't sneak in anywhere.

"Harper!" AJ looked up from a file. Her smile slipped into a frown. "Oh no, what happened."

What did you do now?

Return of the tears. Goddamned wolf. "I got rid of Emerson."

"You what?" The file fell onto the desk. AJ crossed the room in a few quick strides. Her hands were cool against Harper's elbows as she led her to a spare chair. "Guys, hush, it's just Harper!"

"Not like that." The animals settled back down, aside from the occasional growl or yowl. She fell into the seat and covered her face. "She was unhappy about the things I said at the bar the other night. Wanted an apology. I didn't give her one, and I'm pretty sure this whole mess is over."

"What happened the other night?"

She groaned and scratched her dirty nails against her scalp. "Grady didn't tell you?"

"Believe it or not, we don't talk about you all the time."

"Holt happened. He came in — with Emerson — and he made a mom joke. You know, 'your mom'?" She let AJ pull her hands away. "I lost it, AJ. I just lost my shit."

"He should know better. I'm sorry, Sweets." AJ's frown deepened. She pulled a hand through her hair and sighed.

"I grabbed him, threatened him. Emerson saw the whole thing, and I couldn't control my mouth. She and her brother stormed off, and I damn near wolfed out right there I was so furious."

"Understandable. That's a lot to deal with. Holt pushing your buttons and Emerson there too. I'd like to give him a piece of my mind."

"He was trying to make me jealous," she said and barked a short laugh. "Jealous of Emerson, I think. He knew exactly what to say to get to me too. Now I look like a maniac to her."

"Were you? Jealous, I mean." AJ crouched down and after a long look raised her hand to touch Harper's forehead. "You've got a fever again."

"Unbelievably. My wolf thinks Emerson is hers. I heard it, in my head. Mine." A sharp breath drew her attention from the floor. She glanced up and saw AJ chewing on her lip. "What?"

"Nothing just yet. I think you've given me another clue into what's going on, though." She moved away and dug into a nearby glass cabinet. "I'm going to try to get your fever down, alright? What happened today?"

Harper watched her soak a white rag and sighed. "She chewed me out about what I'd said to her. I might have implied she was a slut." She winced as she accepted the damp cloth. The frigid water felt fantastic against her boiling forehead. "She wanted an apology, and the 'or else' seemed pretty clear. I didn't give her one so she left."

"And you think she'll stay away from you now?"

"Yes, and I feel terrible. My wolf is, I don't know. It's awful. Like the world has ended."

"Harper." AJ took the rag, flipped it over and returned it to her clammy forehead.

"It's dangerous, whatever this is. It's not right, and it's dangerous. How the hell do I know what's going on? For all I know I'm drawn to her because she's some sort of favorite prey. Spoiled rich girl. Yum, yum. She wouldn't be stringy and tough like the jerks around here." *Like Ben probably was.* She shuddered.

"We've talked about this." AJ tossed the rag away and put her damp hands over Harper's knees. "This is not hunting behavior. You're not stalking her."

"Well what is it then?" Harper pushed backwards, the wheels on her chair squealing. "What the hell is it? If you're so sure then tell me, oh great werewolf whisperer! You tell me why it feels like this."

AJ stood up, tousled her own hair again, bottom lip back in her teeth.

Harper pointed and stood. "You don't know, or you won't tell me what you suspect. It must be bad then. We've never kept secrets from each other." Anger swept through her, a new and fantastic sensation covering the lethargy and depression. With a snarl she kicked over the chair, setting off a fresh round of noise from AJ's patients. "You should have shot me, Jay. Put me out of my misery when you had the chance."

She headed for the door with her fists clenched and mouth bleeding where she'd bitten down on her cheek.

"Harper, wait."

"Stay away from me."

"Harper."

She turned, vision flashing. "It's for your own damn good. Stay away."

***

Grady left her alone all afternoon, holed up in her room with a blanket over her head, but she couldn't think of a good enough excuse to get out of family dinner. First he'd called for her, a couple of times. Then he'd sent Cooper. A few minutes later he showed up himself and ripped the blanket off her.

"Hey, you can throw a pity party after we eat. You've been in here for hours."

"Go away."

Much to her mounting frustration, he took that as an invitation to sit down. Why did he pull out the comforting parental crap when it was the last thing she wanted?

"Harper, I don't know what's going on now, and I get you don't want to talk about it. See, I'm trying this whole giving you space thing. I'm not going to ask what's wrong. But you are going to come downstairs and have dinner with us. You don't have to talk. Let your food fill your mouth, and I'll do the same." He patted her shoulder awkwardly. "Come on, I made your favorite."

Ribs. Juicy slabs of meat smothered in sauce and cooked to perfection. Her stomach growled and she salivated. Of course she'd been able to smell them cooking. She'd hoped he'd leave her a plate. Then she could sneak down later and gobble it up without having to be social. That would be giving her space.

"I'm not taking no for an answer. Get up."

She went without verbal protest. Glaring at him worked just as well. He didn't say a word either. Not to her. He talked to Cooper about school and commented on his awesome barbecue skills. She glared harder, let her lip curl, and he smiled back with his mouth full and sauce smeared in his beard.

A bone cracked between her teeth and his eyebrow twitched. It arched when she dropped the splintered halves onto her plate with a clatter. Her fingers were stained red. She thought about licking them clean, but the image of Holt's broken body came stampeding back into her head.

Her hands trembled. She looked at her plate and her stomach twisted up.

"Coop, help Harper with the dishes. I'm going to-"

Heat came over her, like someone had opened the door to the oven. Or maybe the door to Hell, the Devil had decided to come get her himself. She gagged and thumped her fists down onto the table.

Grady stood up. "Harper?"

"Did she swallow a bone?" Cooper asked and lurched away.

She threw up on herself, gagged again at the smell and heaved some more. The bones in her hands cracked. Her fingernails extended and fingers snapped in on themselves. Fur sprouted on her arms and her nails darkened, turned black and hooked. Numbness blanketed her.

"Harper!" Grady grabbed Cooper by the back of his shirt and dragged him away from the table.

Her throat constricted and her gums itched. She fell sideways off her chair as her hips shifted out of socket. On the way down her hand snagged on the tablecloth, dragging it and all the dishes onto the floor with her. Plates shattered and food scattered. Her breastbone and ribs crunched and pushed out, forming the deeper chest of the wolf.

"Cooper, call AJ!" Grady yelled. She lolled her head in his direction, vertebrae in her neck and spine popping.

He dropped to his knees next to her, just out of reach. His hands stretched toward her.

She bared her teeth at him and heard her nose fracture. "Run."

The wolf surfaced, surging forward. Darkness crowded around. She saw Grady's expression turn to fear as her canine jaw, nose, and cheeks began to take shape.

"Run," she whispered. Her legs kicked out, she pressed her hands against the floor and staggered up on bare human feet. Doubled over, she swayed down the hall toward the back door, body no longer under her control. The pressure on her feet caused a pins and needles sensation bordering on pain. Every muscle bunched, shifting beneath her skin. Twin cramps knotted her calves, then both biceps, and her fingers twisted up again, stuck in odd positions.

Unable to figure out the doorknob the runaway wolf snarled, her half formed snout wrinkling.

Grady caught her elbow and pulled. She whipped around with a furious growl and lunged. He stumbled back from a swiping paw-hand and fell on his ass.

"Mine," she said and watched his pupils dilate.

"Harper, it's okay. Come on, Harper." He stammered, hands held up in surrender.

Both paws grappled with the doorknob, nails biting into wood. One hard yank tore the door off its hinges with a sound like a thunderclap. Chunks of wood bounced off the walls and slid down the hall.

"Harper!"

She tossed the door behind her, sneering when Grady balled up to avoid getting knocked in the head.

Stop this, stop it. She tried to take the reins back, wiggle a single finger in defiance. Anything. Her efforts were rewarded with more numbness, a heaviness in her limbs and an unbelievable sleepiness.

Don't go to sleep! Oh God, don't sleep.

She made it to the middle of the yard before her knees buckled. The last bit of the sun winked at her, she felt the draw of the moon. Paws heavy on her thighs she tilted her head back, eyes rolling. Her face crunched again, shoulders wrenched forward.

Darkness swallowed her whole.

CHAPTER ELEVEN

Emerson

"Hey, Earth to Emerson. Come back, Emerson." She blinked and looked up from her plate. Holt smiled. "You're a zillion miles away. What's going on in that pretty head of yours?"

Harper, actually, but she couldn't very well say that. Not yet, anyway. Some subtlety would be required for that subject. She shook her head and dabbed at her lips with her napkin. "I was thinking this was unnecessary," she said. "You didn't have to take me to dinner, Holt. Though I do appreciate the gesture."

He waved a hand. "It's part of the apology. I ruined your first night out in Fincher. Besides, I should have brought you to the Lodge in the first place. Better service and food."

"Saying the words was enough, really." She ducked her head and peered once more at her dinner. He had insisted on ordering for her, and she hadn't quite figured out if she liked the venison or not. Or if she liked the fact he'd ordered for her. That was something Gabriel would do. It didn't help she couldn't stop visualizing Bambi with every bite.

"Maybe I wanted to take a nice girl out to dinner." He sat back in his chair, still chewing, and swiped a bit of sauce away from the corner of his mouth. "What do you think?"

"Of you?"

He pointed his fork at her, Bambi flesh speared on the end. "We'll come back to that. I mean the Lodge. What do you think?"

She hummed, sipped her water, and glanced around. Rustic was the first word that sprang to mind. A fitting atmosphere for a hunting lodge turned restaurant and inn. Polished wood gleamed in the low light, the banister on the staircase, the walls, and the floor. All of them were made of beautiful, light hardwood. Bear skin rugs covered the sparse open spaces. Antlers decorated most everything else, from lamps to walls. The nature paintings she could see were in frames also formed from antlers. She turned in her chair and tried not to stare too long at the massive elk head mounted over the ornate mantle. The two chairs on either side of the fireplace were big enough for a giant to recline in comfortably. They were also constructed of animals.

The firelight danced over the glossy black fur. If she dared to sit there, it would have been like sitting in the lap of a black bear. The armrests even had claws.

If she decided to go with honesty she would surely offend him. Her honest answer was she found the whole place a disturbing, gaudy celebration of death, and a monument to man's unquenchable thirst for blood and conquest. Pointless violence, not for food or protection, but for sport and... decoration.

"It's..." she caught sight of a wolf's head, permanently frozen in a ferocious snarl. Her stomach clenched. The poor creature. "Quite the shrine."

Holt's dimples deepened as his smile stretched. "My dad got some of the trophies himself, but a lot of them are mine."

"Are they?" She took a bigger sip than her mother would approve of.

"Not to brag, or anything, but I'm probably the best hunter this side of Montana." He leaned toward her as he spoke. "You like that wolf?"

I would have loved to see it in the wild, alive. "It's beautiful."

"I snared it two years ago."

"Snared?"

"Trapped, you know?" He gestured like he was wrapping a noose around his neck.

"O-oh." She clutched her glass. That wasn't a pretty picture in her head. She thought of White Fang, Buck from Call of the Wild, and imagined them caught in some vicious trap. Unable to break free, bloodied and terrified, how they would cry for help.

"You okay?"

She glanced up and found him frowning at her, forehead furrowed over eyes that appeared even darker in the low light.

"I'm not much of a hunter. The only exotic animals I've seen have been at the zoo or on television." *Oh, and I'm a pacifist.*

"I could take you out with me sometime."

"I don't think I'm cut out for that sort of thing," she said, and offered a thin smile. He returned it after a beat and then chuckled.

"You're probably right."

He went back to eating, and she was drawn back to the wolf.

"Holt?" She sighed, and wrenched her attention back to the table. "I'm sorry to ask. You've already apologized and been so nice, but... what is it, exactly, with you and Harper?"

His knife stopped sawing and his frown reappeared.

"I know it's really not polite to ask," she hastened to say. "Nor is it any of my business, I'm sure. I'm just so curious. The way you talk about her and that display at the bar. It's almost like you believe she really is a monster of some sort."

Silence stretched, and she tried not to fidget. He scratched the back of his head and smiled again. It wasn't the same one he'd been aiming at her all night.

"I've known her for a long time. Since Grady brought her down from Alaska after her parents died."

She about swallowed her tongue. "Her parents – I assumed she chose to live here with family."

"Harper?" He snorted. "She hates it here. Her parents died in some freak fire up in Anchorage when she was a kid. Poor Grady didn't know what he'd gotten himself into."

"What do you mean?"

"Everyone says Harper's cursed."

"Don't be ridiculous," she said with a scoff. "Cursed. Everyone is touched by tragedy in some way."

He shook his head and dropped all pretense of finishing his meal. "No, listen. It wasn't just the fire. Right after Grady took her in, his wife died. Dropped dead in the kitchen. An aneurysm or something. Then Harper's boyfriend, Ben, he was on the football team with me. He got ripped to pieces by a bear." He dropped his voice, leaned in again. "I think he was out in the woods with her, trying to get some action. He was too smart to wander out alone in the dark."

She licked her lips and sipped more water to soothe her dry mouth. "That doesn't mean she's cursed."

"She's like an omen. I mean, I tried to be there for her, but she went off the deep end after Ben. I didn't care what people were saying about her, but she about tore my head off. Told me to fu – uh, eff off."

"And now you don't get along?"

He shrugged. "I think I remind her too much of Ben. Not that it matters anymore. She's completely insane. You saw her at the bar."

"What did you say to her anyway? I couldn't hear over the noise."

"I don't know what set her off," he said and ran a finger along the opening of his beer glass. "I asked for a beer, she freaked out."

"Just like that?" She narrowed her eyes.

"It doesn't take much anymore to set her off. One time a guy at school told her she looked pretty, or something, and Harper broke his nose. Grady's on a first name basis with the local Sheriff thanks to her."

That sounded an awful lot like a lie. She sipped her water again, let him sit with his half-truth while she stared at him. "So she has a history of violent 'freak outs'?"

"Well, I mean, she tosses people out of the bar all the time."

And I'm sure it's for no reason whatsoever. Just like that boy just said she 'looked pretty' and you simply asked for a beer. "That doesn't make her an omen. She's had more than her share of misfortune. Anyone would have a hard time with that."

"You taking her side?" He squinted at her.

"I'm saying I understand her behavior better now."

"Sure, I guess. Wish she'd quit taking it out on the rest of us though."

She pushed her plate away and cleared her throat. "I'm sorry to bring it up. I ran into her again today and she's just — well she wasn't very civil."

"That's Harper. Trust me, you're better off leaving her alone. Logan follows her around like a love-sick puppy, and she's just as mean to him. They're supposed to be best friends." He drained the rest of his beer and smacked the glass back on the table. "Let's talk about something else. How about I show you the trophy room? There's a Grizzly in there I think you'll like."

More dead animals. Her stomach turned. *After this*, she thought, *I'm going to be a vegetarian. Even if the meat is cage-free, grass-fed organic.*

He stood and offered her his arm with his charming smile back in place. She hid a wince, and tucked a hand into the crook of his arm anyway. He led her out of the dining area, through several occupied tables. People stopped mid-chew to gawk. She blushed, but kept her head high. Holt's smile turned into more of a smirk, and he squeezed her fingers with his elbow.

It was all starting to feel familiar in a bad way. She pulled her hand away and used the banister on the staircase instead. He shot her a look and she smiled. "I don't need you to keep me steady, as kind of you as that is. If I couldn't walk in these shoes I wouldn't wear them."

Her smile took the bite out of her words as she'd intended. He shrugged and glanced down at her feet. "You do look nice. Did I tell you that?"

Repeatedly. "Yes, thank you."

He grabbed her hand again as they crested the top of the staircase. She stuffed down a sigh. The open hallway stretched forever, her heels clicked on the polished hardwood. She tried not to drag her feet.

"The guest rooms are all down here," he said, pointing. "My dad was going to put the trophy room downstairs by the gift shop. I told him it should be up here, so people could see it as they head for their rooms."

"Okay." She hesitated at the doorway, tugging back on his hand.

PURE OF HEART

"Um…"

"It's okay, there's no one up here right now." He grinned and pulled at her. "Besides, we have to go through here to get to the balcony. Wait 'til you see the view, Emmy. It's really something."

She closed her eyes as he towed her into the room.

"Ah, want it to be a surprise?" He asked. His arm felt heavy over her shoulders. "You can look now."

When she dared to peek, she almost stumbled backwards. A massive Grizzly stood before her on a pedestal of fake rocks. Its paws reached for her, claws spread, and its mouth gaped to show off impressive teeth.

"Isn't he awesome?"

"I'm not sure that's the word I would use," she whispered.

He chuckled and steered her around the bear. Right into something out of her nightmares.

The room was massive, and filled with trophies. Deer frozen mid-step, a mountain lion coiled to spring. Birds stuck with their wings spread in a desperate, futile attempt to fly away.

She swallowed as Holt took his time moving from one to the next. He continued to talk to her, but his words sounded muffled, distant.

In the far corner of the room she saw a wolf. Not just a head mounted like downstairs. It sneered at her, ears pricked forward and body hunched. The light of the fire in the room cast an eerie glow on dull glass eyes.

"Hey, Emerson, are you paying attention?"

He pouted at her and she shook her head. "I'm sorry. I was distracted."

"You really like wolves, huh?" He pressed her closer to the wolf and she leaned away from the teeth. "This guy is quite a catch. He put up one hell of a fight, but I won in the end. You want to touch it?"

She shook her head again, but he took her hand and set it on the grey and white fur.

"Don't be scared," he said.

Her breath lodged somewhere in her throat. She stroked down the wiry fur and then snatched her hand back to her side. "I'm not scared."

Horrified was more like it. Or disgusted.

He didn't notice. His mind appeared to be on other things.

She knew that look, but before she had a chance to clear the air and stop him he had already decided to act. He dipped his head, aiming for her mouth.

"Holt." *Wait, wait, wait.*

Her phone rang and he jumped away like she'd hit him.

Saved by the bell, or in this case the timely singing of her current favorite song.

She smiled at him, trying not to show her relief, and pulled her phone from her purse. "I'm sorry. That's probably Oscar."

"You can't call him back later?" He took a step back.

"He'll just call again. He's a bit of a Worried William."

Holt frowned. "A what?"

She ignored him. "I must have missed our call time. Excuse me."

Back out in the hall, she blew out a long exhale and leaned back against the wall. The phone stopped singing and then started all over from the top. She ran a hand through her hair and tapped the screen. "Oscar I swear you have some sort of freaky sixth sense. Maybe there's something to that twin thing after all."

"Miss Grey?"

Not Oscar.

"Yes?"

"This is Sanctuary Security Systems. We detected an alert with a sensor in your home. Would you like us to call the authorities?"

"What?" She stood up from the wall, phone clutched harder to her ear. "Someone broke in?" *My shoes!* "Yes, call the Sheriff, I'll be right there!"

"Do you want me to stay on the line with you?"

"No. Thank you though." She hung up and chewed on her bottom lip. At least she had a solid excuse to get out of the Lodge. "Holt?"

Two men had entered the trophy room since she'd left. They must have come in from the balcony. Holt laughed and pointed at an elk head. She fidgeted as she stepped toward him.

"Holt?"

"Oh, hey, this is Emerson. She just moved here. Emerson these guys are up for the ski season. Brandon and Mark, right?"

Both of them stared at her, making no attempt to hide their leers. She held on to her composure by a thread. "Hello. It's nice to meet you, may I borrow Holt?"

"Tell them about the bear," another voice boomed.

She spun around. Yet another gentleman entered the room. This one had on a sport coat and tie. He grinned at them as he approached and slapped Holt on the back. "My boy is the best hunter you're ever going to meet. There's not an animal out there he can't bring home for this room. Bears, cougars, wolves. You name it, he's bagged it."

"Uh, Dad this is Brandon, Mark, and Emerson." Holt winced.

"Emerson!" He stuck out his meaty hand. "I'm Adam Markham. Welcome to my Lodge." He shook hands with Brandon and Mark, but his attention quickly returned to her. "Holt has talked about you non-stop. His mother banned your name from our dinner table so we could eat without hearing it every five seconds."

"Oh, I... " She blushed. "That's very sweet. I'm sorry to take him aw — "

"Holt, why don't you give these fine gentlemen a tour of the gunroom?

PURE OF HEART

I'm sure they'd be very impressed." Mr. Markham slung an arm over Holt's shoulders and gestured to the far door. "You know, Holt's been thinking about leading some hunting parties? Now that's an adventure."

Holt shot her a desperate glance and shrugged. They all filed into the next room, leaving her standing among dead animals with tears welling in her eyes.

Left alone, again.

She sucked in a shaky breath. "Well, I guess I'll be walking home."

***

The sun had set while they'd been inside. Dense fog floated over the ground and clung to the trees on either side of the gravel road. Quaint Victorian-style street lamps offered dim light isolated to the places where they stood.

She tried not to run from one light source to the next. Not that she could, with her choice of evening footwear. While cute and a complement to her outfit, they weren't designed for hiking.

Pine trees loomed over her, casting long, dark shadows like spidery fingers reaching for her. She shivered. Her short skirt left her legs exposed to the bite of the cold air.

She kept checking over her shoulder, expecting Holt to come charging down the lane in his truck. That's what would happen in a romance. Except maybe it would be raining, or at least snowing. Something a little more dramatic.

The current setting was more appropriate for a horror novel.

A sharp snap rang out and she stopped, head turning the direction she thought it came from. The wind picked up, tossing her hair over her face and causing the tops of the trees to dance. They made a rustling noise as branches and leaves brushed together. Snow fell into the light and shone like glitter. If she hadn't been so cold she might have found it beautiful.

Another snap.

"Just a tree, Em. Steady girl." She pulled her coat tighter and walked faster, aiming for the next lamp post.

Again. Snap. Followed by a deep huffing noise.

"It's not a bear," she said, eyes closed tight. "It's not. A bear would be too smart to come within three paces of that place."

She stiffened as a heavy feeling came over her. The fine hairs along her arms stood on end. Every muscle in her neck locked up. She thought she heard it creak as she forced herself to look.

Among the shadows of the trees two gold eyes, gleaming, stared at her.

"Oh God," she whispered. "What would Hermione do? Wand. I don't have one. Next option."

Her mind raced, multiple options coming forward for her to discard. She trembled with each slow step, like a helpless bunny in the sights of a hungry hawk. Running away and screaming at the top of her lungs wouldn't work. Predators chased prey. If she ran she'd define herself as prey.

"I'm not afraid. Not afraid." She repeated it, but the urge to flee grew stronger. "Stay steady. Show no fear."

All the while, whatever it was watched her, hidden in the trees just out of sight. She widened her eyes in an attempt to track its movements. That didn't help her peripheral vision at all. Her pace quickened with her heart-rate, not to a run, but a mall walk. Finally, something her mother taught her had proven somewhat useful.

A wolf leapt from the bushes ahead of her. She screamed, heels digging into shifting gravel with the suddenness of her stop. It didn't move and she didn't dare breathe.

The head alone was double the size of the two she'd seen in the Lodge. Black fur rippled. It took a step toward her and paused again, gold eyes locked on her face.

"Nice wolfy," she said with a small squeak. "God, please don't let it eat me."

Pointed ears swiveled back and forth as she spoke. It stepped again, and she backed away, purse held in front of her like a shield. She hadn't brought her mace, and didn't have so much as a whistle.

It padded closer, paws pressing into the snow with no sound. She turned to keep her bag between them as it looped around to flank her. It sniffed the air, sneezed and then sprang forward. She screamed and swatted, it caught the leather bag in its teeth and pulled. The contents spilled across the snow. Bright pink accessories, her cell phone, keys, everything.

Her knees knocked together and her stomach plummeted. Tears burned her frozen face. It sniffed and nosed at her things and then headed toward her again. She backed up, her now empty hands extended in front of her. Her feet sank into an ice covered puddle. One shoe stayed behind, stuck in the muck. She whimpered, limping backwards. Pine needles and small rocks dug into the bottom of her exposed foot.

The animal pressed closer, and she stumbled in her haste to stay away. Her eyes widened and more tears obscured her vision. It was herding her up an incline, into the forest.

"Listen, *s'il vous plaît*, I'm not like the others." Those hellish eyes, glowing like coals in a dying fire, blinked at her. "I didn't even like the venison, I swear. That was Holt, he ordered and – oh God, can you smell it on me?"

Her back hit a tree. She squealed and twisted her face away. "Please, I can't die like this."

She sobbed and squeezed her eyes shut, waiting for the pain.

It whined.

PURE OF HEART

A wet nose poked at one hand.

A rough tongue licked tentatively.

She cracked an eye open. It cocked its head at her and whined again.

Its tail wagged.

"W-what?"

Another nudge to her hand, and this time it pressed its long muzzle into her palm, let her hand slide up its broad head. The soft bristles tickled her skin.

"You want me to... pet you?"

It plopped down, right at her feet and pressed its head into her chest. Both ears pricked forward and it whuffed softly. Its tail swished twice against the snowy ground.

She knew some people kept wolves as pets. This one wasn't wearing a collar.

"You are not somebody's pet," she said. Her teeth chattered. "You're a wild animal, and I should not touch you. Then again a wild animal would be feasting on my flesh right about now."

It nuzzled her hand again, let out another strange huff.

"You are a very large wolf."

It hunched over, making itself smaller.

"And very smart, clearly." A tentative smile pulled up one corner of her mouth. "You're a strange creature, aren't you?"

Its tail thumped and it sat back up. She looked into its eyes and warmth surrounded her. Like an imaginary blanket around her cold shoulders. "You won't hurt me, will you?"

It snorted, and to her disbelief shook its head.

She reached out with a fist, slowly. Her fingers uncurled as she neared the top of its head. She set her palm down on the fuzzy fur between its ears and shivered.

Its ears flattened, and it shuffled closer, leaning against her.

"I'm petting a wolf. No need to panic, it's perfectly normal." She swiped the lingering tears off her cheeks. "Oscar is never going to believe this story. I'm not sure I do."

It sighed and closed its eyes.

"Good boy?" she guessed.

It snorted.

"Girl. I'm sorry. Good girl. Nice wolf."

"Emerson!"

She flinched, and her new friend jumped away with a snarl. It moved in front of her, ears back against its head. A low growl rumbled.

"Emerson! Where are you?"

The thick ridge of fur along its spine stood on end. It stiffened its legs and rolled back its upper lip.

"No!" She reached down and tugged on the long bushy tail. The wolf made a strange garbled noise and twisted around. "Don't hurt him, please."

"Emerson!"

It shook all over, tossing melted snow on her, and stalked away. Headed deeper into the forest, not toward Holt.

She sighed and let the tree prop her up. Holding on to it for balance, she peeked around to make sure the wolf was gone. It paused, halfway up the hill behind them and looked back. Since she'd already lost her mind, she gestured for it to leave, thinking it would know what she meant.

"Emerson, damn it, answer me!"

"I'm here!" She called and shooed the wolf again.

Holt came crashing through the woods and the wolf melted back into the night.

"Oh my God, Emmy." He tripped on a tree, caught his balance and ran to her. "You scared the – are you okay? You're not hurt are you? I found your stuff and I thought…"

She eyed the rifle in his hands. "I – um – I thought I saw something. A bear, maybe, and I panicked."

He sagged with a heavy sigh and scrubbed a hand over his messy curls. "Okay. I'm just so glad you're alright. C'mere. It's okay now."

"I'm sorry for leaving without – My house! Someone broke into my house! Can you take me home? Now?" She snatched her shoe from him and slipped it back on with a grimace. It was full of muddy, gritty gunk.

"Someone broke in?"

She let him wrap his arm around her and guide them back to the road. "Yes, the security people called me. You were busy so I thought I'd walk home."

"I'm so sorry. If you'd said so I would've left right then. My dad's just trying to get more tourists up here. For the business."

"I need to remember my mace," she said, looking at the gun slung in his free arm.

"Here's your purse," he said, snagging it off the road and holding it out to her.

"Thank you."

"Look, Emmy." He opened the truck door and helped her in. "If you think you see something like a bear again, the woods aren't really the best place to run."

"I know that now."

He set his rifle in the back seat. "I'll get you some bear repellent, okay?"

"Okay," she said with a nod. Her wolf wouldn't have been afraid of bear repellent, but she couldn't tell him the truth. He'd want to go after it. A wolf that size would be a main attraction in that trophy room.

"Your hands are like ice." He stretched across her and turned on the

PURE OF HEART

heat, full blast. She tried not to squirm when he kissed the side of her head. "Let's get you home."

"Thank you for rescuing me," she said, looking out toward the woods.

She thought she heard howling.

CHAPTER TWELVE

Harper

A bulky figure swathed in shadows stepped out of the house. She recognized the wide shoulders and muscled frame of a large man. He paused on the porch, glanced back at the broken front door. His shoulders rounded forward, she saw his voice in wisps of steam as he whispered. In the suffocating silence that had followed the last howl of a scream from inside her home, a match scratched, loud and clear. Flame leapt to life between his hands. He cradled the light like an injured bird.

A whimper escaped her mud caked lips. She slammed a hand over her mouth, keening into her palm as he turned her direction with predatory swiftness. He raised his head and she sank deep into her mud hole.

The match fell, flickering valiantly, and landed on the porch. It lit up, wood catching with ease, and a trail of consuming heat led into the house. The burning porch whined plaintively as he rocked from his heels to his toes and back. She got a better look at him in the dancing firelight. The black of his leather jacket, the dark stains on his pants, but his face remained a mystery thanks to his baseball hat, wide brim pulled low over his forehead.

He reached into his jacket again and she saw flowers. Deep purple flowers with odd drooping, bulbous petals. He treated them with the same tender care as the match, placing them almost lovingly to the side of the steps.

Flowers at a grave.

Flowers…

"Flowers!" Harper surged upwards. Her wrists caught, arms stretched out to her sides. She fell back onto something soft and warm.

"Harper, easy. It's alright, calm down."

"Wha — ?" Her wrists were tied to the bed. She flexed her feet and found her ankles also strapped down. The bed-frame creaked when she jerked at the restraints.

"Hold on. I'm sorry, I thought you'd be asleep longer. That metabolism of yours is hard to predict."

"Jay?" She frowned at the croak of her voice. "AJ, why're you here? What happened?"

The ropes slackened and fell away from one wrist. She clapped that hand over her eyes. Her room swirled in nauseating circles, greens and browns blending together into an unfortunate pukish color. "Full moon hangover? The full moon isn't for a few days."

"Just hold on, we can talk in a second, I'll explain what I can." Cold fingers dug into the knots binding her ankles.

"I turned without the moon? That's not possible."

"Right, and werewolves don't exist."

"Where's Grady? Is he – and Cooper?" She growled and spread her fingers to see AJ standing at the foot of the bed.

She held up her hands, ropes dangling from her fingers. "Everyone's fine physically. Mentally, I'd say we're all due for a visit with a shrink."

Her wrists and ankles burned, she sat up to inspect the damage even though it would heal. The fleece blanket covering her fell to her lap. "Why the hell am I naked? Again!"

A weak smile perked up AJ's solemn expression. "It's not like I haven't seen it before. You know what happens to your clothes when you transform in them."

"You could have dressed me!" She snatched the blanket back up to cover her chest. "What the fucking hell?"

"I know you're freaked out –"

"Really, what gave it away?"

AJ pursed her lips, hands still in the air with the ropes. "Harper, hush. I get it, but you have to stay calm. We don't know for sure what triggered this episode and I don't want to sedate you again. Now shut up and let's deal with one thing at a time before we add more complications. Like a tiger-sized wolf rampaging in broad daylight."

Wrong time to growl, but she couldn't keep it caged behind her teeth. "Fine."

AJ stared at the ropes in her hands and then dropped them to the floor. "I don't know what I was planning on doing with those." She came around the bed and handed over a glass of water. "How many of these migraine pills are you taking now?"

"As many as it takes," she grumbled, eyeing the orange pill bottle. AJ tapped out two and held them out.

"Slam those, then we can talk. If you think you can keep a lid on that temper of yours?"

Harper ignored the verbal jab and gulped the water, gagging at the sensation of the pills going down.

"What question do you want answered first?"

Temper, temper, control your damn temper. "What happened?"

AJ sat down in the chair by the bed. She ran a hand through her hair and rubbed at her cheek. "What do you remember last?"

"Eating dinner." Harper scratched at the side of her twitching nose. "I'm tingly and twitchy. Why am I tingly and twitchy?"

"Probably something to do with your out-of-sync transformation."

AJ sounded exhausted, voice lower and thicker than normal. Harper took a closer look and saw dark circles under her eyes. A crumpled blanket lay draped over the back of the chair.

"You were here all night."

"Cooper called. You collapsed in the kitchen last night. By the time I got here you'd fully transformed and taken off. When we finally caught up with you… well, we took some precautions." AJ inclined her head to where the ropes had fallen. "Of course I stayed."

The kitchen, dinner, ribs, being mad at Grady, she clutched the blanket tighter to her chest. "You're sure everyone's okay?"

"Yes. Grady's got a couple of scrapes, but he's fine. Cooper…" She winced. "Cooper had a rough night. You didn't hurt him, but I think he was in shock. It reminded him of Na — "

"I get it. Don't." She shook her head, guilt clawing at her insides. "I turned. In the kitchen. Without the full moon and just took off like usual?"

"Not like usual."

"What do you mean? Besides the great werewolf coup of last night, what's different?"

"You didn't go to your usual spot. We tracked you out to the lodge and then back around to the Grey's place."

The Grey's, she knew that name. She licked at her chapped lips and cleared her throat. "The Grey's? The older couple one street over? Didn't Mr. Grey pass away a couple months ago?"

"He did." AJ hesitated, mouth catching on nothing. Her eyelids drooped. "It's now occupied by their granddaughter."

Anyone else. Sweet Jesus on toast, let it be anyone else.

"Emerson Grey."

Damn it. Goosebumps erupted all over her body. She shivered and leaned back into the embrace of her pillows. "All things lead back here, don't they."

"It could be a coincidence?"

She snorted. "Yeah, sure."

They slipped into uncomfortable silence. The old clock clicked on the wall, the blanket rasped against her bare skin, AJ's breathing intermixed with her own. She could hear both their hearts thumping away.

"Sweets –"

"Did you talk to her?" She looked out the window.

"No. No need. You were in the woods behind her house. And it's damn lucky too. Blalock was there. Apparently someone broke in. Nobody noticed you. Thank God."

"You're kidding, nobody saw me? Or you and Grady dragging me back home?"

"Haven't heard a peep out of anybody. You know I'm the first person they call when we have animal sightings in town."

"Animal sightings." She knocked the side of her fist against her forehead. "Jesus H. God. What is happening?"

"You don't remember anything? Even a tiny detail?"

She quirked an eyebrow at the familiar 'mad scientist' expression being aimed at her. "No, Dr. Frankenstein, you know I never do."

Air rushed into her lungs. She blinked rapidly as her brain made her a liar. Flashes of color, snippets of sounds, smells, blended together in unrecognizable mush. Her headache attacked with renewed fervor. It struck so hard her vision went hazy around the edges. Foggy tunnel vision, complete with floating flecks of white light. Not enough to obscure the clearer image of eyes, glacier blue. Her nose stung with the reeking scent of fear and salty tears. "Emerson. I saw Emerson last night."

"What? At her house?"

"No, I don't –" she shook her head and swallowed nothing. Her mouth had gone dry. "I think it was somewhere else? I can't – it's not clear."

More chunks of information. Snow and trees, a lamppost. She bristled at the familiar scent memory of leather and moss. His rough voice cut through the white noise in her ears. "Holt was there too."

She turned her head and AJ had gone pale. Well, paler than normal. Her freckles stood out against ashen skin and her eyes turned into black holes. "Do you remember… anything else?"

"No," she said with a huff. "You're the one always saying I'm not a monster, and now you think I hurt him? If I wanted to hurt him I would have already. This is probably just some whacked-out wolf dream."

"Do you dream about them a lot? Emerson and Holt?"

"Absolutely, we have threesomes in my dreams every night." She glared until color returned to AJ in the form of a deep blush. "No, but this was a dream. Not the transformation part, obviously, but the rest. Probably because you shot me full of drugs again."

"But you're remembering it."

"Not clearly. Snippets of random shit. A dream, nothing more."

PURE OF HEART

"I don't think so," AJ said carefully. She looked up from her examining her hands. "I think you know it, too."

"That's an awful lot of thinking this early in the morning."

"Sweets…"

"It's a fucking nightmare, okay? A jumble of feelings and urges. Could be a memory or a drug induced hallucination. How the hell would I know the difference? I'm leaning toward the drugs. That makes way more sense."

"Telazol wouldn't cause hallucinations. It never has before. This is something else, something new, and it has to do with Emerson."

"Oh does it?" She sneered and gripped the blanket until her knuckles hurt.

"Yes. Which is why you're being defensive and cranky. It scares you. Ever since she came into town you've been different. We can't ignore that fact. You were guarding her house last night, Harper."

"How about we stop ignoring the fact you clearly have a theory about all of this? Why don't you just spit it out and quit making me guess?"

"I'm guessing too."

"Guess out loud. Since it concerns me, and we're all so fucking concerned anyway."

"It's not like there's some scientific journal I can reference!" AJ stood and flung her hands in the air. "All I have is a theory based on your behavior. I'm not an expert, okay? I could be way off base and I don't want to – God, Harper, I don't want to make this any harder."

"Please," she said with a roll of her eyes. "What could you possibly have to say that could make my life any harder?"

"Grady knows more than I do, and he's just as confused. Your grandparents didn't include him on wolf matters because he's not a wolf. Now, because I'm a vet, it's somehow my responsibility to figure out a mythical creature."

She paced, wringing her hands. Harper watched her with a frown.

"AJ."

"Veterinarian, not a Xenobiologist or monster hunter. I don't even like monster movies. I hate horror movies." She pinched the bridge of her nose and waved her other hand through the air. "I've dug through every website and book. I watched every stupid movie. Ever since I found out about you my spare time has been spent researching the ridiculous."

"AJ."

"I didn't believe in werewolves, you, until I walked in one morning and the wolf I'd tranquilized had morphed into a naked human."

"AJ." She raised her voice to cut through the frantic mumbling. "My patience is wearing thin over here."

"Most of what I read is complete crap. Or, at least, I think it's crap until you turn around and do something —"

"AJ!"

Her pacing stopped. AJ released her nose and stared, panting and disheveled.

"You're ranting," she said. "That adorable thing you do when you're upset? Stop. Just say it. I don't need to see your notes or check your work. Just spit it out. How much worse could it really be than the things that have already happened?"

"I think you went after Emerson last night. You were upset about how it went the last time you saw her and you went after her." Her cheeks puffed out with a held breath. It all whooshed out and she slumped back into her seat. Head in her hands. "I think you knew something wasn't right with her and you went to check it out."

"Oh, that makes a lot of sense. I thought you were going to say something awful," she scoffed. "Hey, this stranger I just met is suddenly, creepily important to me. I'm going to wolf out and check on her because I blew her off. That'd be the polite thing to do."

"I told you, it's just a guess."

Her head hit the headboard with a dull thunk. She groaned. "Why would I do that?"

"Because you've imprinted on her."

"That would be worse than things that already happened, good joke." She barked a laugh and shook her head. "Imprinted. Right."

"I'm not joking. I'm dead serious. Harper, I think you imprinted. On Emerson."

"What?" The joke lost its humor. She shook her head again and wiggled a fingertip in her ear. "What?"

"Look, I've done my reading. The internet and books can't seem to agree about it. I mean, it's all myth anyway, or I thought it was all myth, but…"

"But what? You think I imprinted like a baby duck because the internet sort of says so? The internet can't even agree that Elvis is dead." She glared when AJ had the nerve to blush. "I think I'm offended. Yeah, I'm definitely offended."

"Not like a duckling. Like a werewolf."

The guilty expression did not help with the flutter of nerves. "Explain."

"Um, you see, it's a fact that real wolves…"

"Real wolves what? Eat elk?" She narrowed her eyes, anxiety jumping another notch. "Stalk blonde girls?"

"Real wolves they… they mate for life."

A pro wrestler might as well have come barreling into the room and collided with her. Her ears rang and her stomach dropped through the bed. "No, no, no. No. Nope. Definitely not tha – this is not a – No." She would have bolted from the bed, nudity be damned, if a single hand to the knee hadn't anchored her in place. AJ's fingers flexed, cold and strong. "I take it back, I'll be a duck."

"From what I gathered from my various sources, this is a good thing, okay? At least, if I'm right, we know for sure you're not going to kill her."

"How could this be a good thing?" She pulled away, swatting at AJ's hand. It gripped tighter instead of releasing. "It doesn't make any damn sense. The internet lies. Elvis is dead."

"Generally I'd agree with you, but I looked at every single site, and a lot of the things they talked about are things you've exhibited or talked to me about. The paralysis, loss of control, fixation, and feeling like you recognize her. Your behavior yesterday. Harper, it's all right there in bullet points."

"She's a girl."

AJ cleared her throat. "Yes, she is."

"That makes zero sense. Zero, zilch, nil, none!" She managed to get free from the hand holding her still and lurched from the bed. Wrapped in her blanket like a burrito she headed for the door. A shower would fix it. She just needed to take a nice hot shower. That would wake her from the nightmare she'd fallen into. "I'm still dreaming. It's the damn Telazol."

"Harper, sit. We have to talk about this."

"The hell we do. Go away, dream AJ. Far away." Fingers pinched her none-too-gently on the behind. "Ow!"

Before she had time to retaliate or make a tactical retreat she found herself seated on the bed again. AJ stooped down and picked the ropes back up. "Don't make me tie you down."

"Try it," she said with a snarl and started to get up again.

"Fine. Run. You can have this conversation with Grady instead."

Her traitorous legs went right out from under her. "You talked to Grady about this?" she whispered in horror. She'd meant to whisper it anyway; it came out half a shriek despite her intentions. At least she now had a better measure of what true mortification felt like. The tips of her ears burned. "Oh God."

"This isn't any easier on me, alright?"

"I hate you." She whimpered and hid her face with her hands. "We are not having the werewolf sex talk. Not you and me, and not Grady and me either. Fuck you both."

"I wouldn't call it a sex talk, *per se*." AJ squirmed and rubbed at the back of her neck, not making eye contact. "I'm just going to keep going, okay? At least until one of us passes out or combusts. When it's over we'll go downstairs and find something incredibly strong to drink. The whiskey Grady hides in the clock should work."

Silence. She glanced at the window, calculating her chances of making the jump straight through. Out the window, to the woods, up a mountain where nobody could find her ever again. The cold air could keep her face from melting off. "You think I imprinted on Emerson. In some sort of weird werewolf... mating ritual."

"The things that have happened since she came into the picture can be explained that way, yes. Though I wouldn't use that exact, uh, terminology."

"No, of course not." She scoffed and bared her teeth. "How would you phrase it exactly? Lycanthropy Courtship Rituals?"

AJ sighed. "Harper. The internet isn't a reliable source, granted. Especially for creatures that supposedly don't exist. Maybe I'm wrong. I could be. But I believe that's what happened. You imprinted on her. She's your — "

"If you say mate, I will throw up and then I will stuff you in a trunk with my puke and mail you to the North Pole."

"Your one? Your person? Better half? Any of those better?"

"Not in the slightest." She stared at the side of AJ's face. The rhythm of her heart tripped. "She's a she."

"That's accurate."

"Why would I – the wolf, I mean. Why would it imprint on a girl? A human too. That's stupid, we can't make little werewolves." She gagged on nothing. "I don't even like..."

"I don't know, Sweets." AJ cleared her throat. "What I do know is you are the wolf. The wolf is you. This distinction you're making isn't real. There's no separation."

"You don't know that either," she said and clenched her teeth until her jaw popped. "You're not in my head."

"You react with wolf instincts. You've said so yourself. When you get upset you 'lose control' of it. Like losing your temper. It's you, part of your personality you've been suppressing. Because you're afraid."

"Of fucking course I'm afraid! I ripped my boyfriend up, I change into a wolf with, and now without, the full moon. That's a monster!"

She grabbed the water from the nightstand and tossed it at the door. It shattered, spraying water and glass.

AJ stood up, nice and slow, lips pursed. "I'm sorry. I know this is hard to accept, or hear."

"You don't know a damn thing, AJ. I know what I am."

"Be angry. Fine. And you're right, I'm not you." She paused with her hand on the doorknob, feet spread to avoid standing in the puddle on the floor. "But please, think about what I said."

"Thought about it, thanks."

"Okay," AJ said with a nod. "If you need me, call."

She slipped out of the room. Harper rolled over onto her stomach, loosed a howl into her pillow, and pounded on the mattress.

**

The full moon approached. Each night her yearning pulled harder, stronger than ever. Like her insides were trying to become outsides, and gravity had increased tenfold.

Her temperature spiked, her joints creaked. She couldn't keep much food down.

Ducks and howling wolves frequented her turbulent dreams. Co-starring with a terrified, bloodied Holt and smiling Emerson. The shadow man with his flowers and Ben guest-starred.

It seemed easier to avoid sleeping. Among other things.

Like thinking about imprints.

"Absence makes the heart grow fonder," she quoted to herself and made a face in the mirror. Her cheeks were sunken, her eyes bloodshot gold, and her hair hung limp around her face, bangs plastered over one eye. "Should be absence makes the heart sick."

Ben frowned at her in the mirror, shaking his head.

"You can shut up and go away. I don't need the audience."

"Hey, Harp?" Grady said, wincing as he pushed open the bathroom door.

She glared at him and reached for her toothbrush.

"Um, right, okay. I know we aren't talking about this but –"

"No buts." She jabbed the toothbrush at him. "No. Not unless it's you butting out, that is."

"You look like a zombie," he said.

"Ah, bluntness. What a sweet, sweet sound."

"I called AJ, she's coming over to examine you." He stilled her hand. "Harper, we're worried."

"You're always worried," she said, mouth full of toothpaste. She spat into the sink and turned the water on to rinse away the red-tinged foam. A quick check with her tongue revealed three wolf teeth. "Now that you've joined Team AJ with the bullshit imprint theory I suppose I can understand your worry. But I'm handling it just fine. See, here I am, not wolfing out or chasing after blondes."

"You look like death."

"Well zombies are dead, Grady. That's kind of the point."

"Harper."

"This isn't easy!" She smacked her toothbrush down, snapping it in half. Great, now the gingivitis would win. The cabinet trembled when she ripped it open to remove her pill bottle.

"It's making you sick," he whispered. "You're howling in your sleep. Sleep walking. You can't keep going like this."

"Which is why I'm knocking myself out and tying myself down at night. I've got it handled." She shook her head and shouldered past him. "If the howling is keeping you up invest in some ear plugs. Figure it out."

"Is this really your plan?" He followed her down the hall. "You can't avoid it forever. Not like this."

"Why? Because according to you and AJ I'm a werewolf with a crush? How absurd is that sentence?"

"We have to figure something out. You can't bottle it up forever."

"You know what? Right now my plan is to make it through this full moon. After that, I'm open to suggestions. Maybe a lobotomy would do the trick. This will all blow over eventually."

"You don't know that."

"Yeah? Then I'm in good company, aren't I? Seeing as nobody seems to know anything. I'm going to try this and if it doesn't work I'll try something else." She stopped on the threshold of her room. There were long tears in her mattress, all hand shaped, with mattress innards poking out. One more thing added to her growing list of stuff to fix. "If you don't mind, I'm going to take a nap before AJ gets here. I need to rest up before another arguing match. Tell Cooper to stay out. He's been sneaking into my room. Not a great idea."

"He's scared for you."

"Do you see that mattress?" She waved a hand at the evidence. "Want him to have matching scars? Keep him out."

"It doesn't bother me, you know."

"That I've turned into Freddie Krueger?" She stopped clearing off the bed, hands hovering over her blanket. "What?"

He sighed. "That – that she's a she. You haven't said a word to me, but I've heard you screaming at AJ. I wanted to tell you… it's okay. I don't care and I don't want you thinking it would disappoint me, or something. I'm not going to kick you out or disown you or anything."

"Everything's not about you," she muttered. "But congrats. I'll get you a rainbow sticker and World's Best Uncle mug."

"That's not what I meant. I just didn't want you to be worried about that. I love you and it doesn't matter that you've imprinted on Emerson."

"If I imprinted on her. Which I didn't."

He bowed his head, scratched at his forehead. "If you imprinted on her. What scares me is it could be causing this much damage to you."

"I don't want this," she said and collapsed on the bed. She couldn't sit like a calm, sane person with her knees wobbling. Couldn't stop the tears either, even though she'd been getting tons of practice. She tried to hide them by folding her hands over her eyes. "Why can't I be normal?"

"Who the hell said you aren't?" He sat next to her, put an arm around her shoulders. "There's nothing wrong with you. At all. I promise to flatten anybody's nose who says otherwise."

"I'm a werewolf."

He chuckled and then coughed. "Sorry. Yeah, that you are. But you know what? I grew up with a werewolf for a sister. From what I remember about her, you're perfectly normal."

"Did Mom… Did she imprint on Dad?" She grimaced at her knees, unable to look at his face.

"I don't know. She didn't exactly bash my door down to tell me her secrets. We definitely didn't talk about imprinting, or boys." He sighed and squeezed her into his side. "I thought your mom went all twitterpated when she met John. They were one of those couples. The sappy, gooey ones that make you want to throw stuff at them."

"Why didn't they tell me this could happen? They didn't even tell me I was a werewolf." She sniffled and laid her head on his shoulder. "They could have left me a note. Something. A sticky note that said 'congratulations on being a werewolf, watch out for that imprint.' Anything."

"You were eight," he said, hoarsely. "You were eight and they thought they were going to be here, Harper. We all did."

Tears dripped down her cheeks and onto his ugly flannel shirt. "As if being a werewolf isn't bad enough." She choked out a soggy laugh. "I have no idea how any of this shit works."

He kissed her forehead. "We'll figure it out, Harp. Together."

CHAPTER THIRTEEN

She sat on the roof to get fresh air. Her hands and feet trembled and twitched, fingers and toes curled and stretched in a constant, frustrating pattern. The cold air and smell of the trees soothed her burning skin and inflamed sinuses. It also made her want to sprint into the woods. Her ears perked at the sound of footsteps. She tensed, waiting for the bedroom door to open.

"Grady, for the last time, I'm not hungry," she muttered. Thirsty, yes. Her liquid consumption had tripled. Water, juice, tequila, it didn't matter. She'd drink a gallon of it to fix her awful cottonmouth. Food tasted horrid and she didn't want to spend her day with her head hanging over the toilet.

"Harper?"

Goosebumps prickled her skin; her hair stood on end. Her wheezing breath stopped and her heart stumbled. She turned around slowly, her heavy-lidded eyes wide open for the first time in days. "Emerson?"

Sure as shit, a smiling Emerson stood in her room with a plate of cookies in her hands. "Hi," she said. Her white dress fluttered in the breeze from the open window.

Blessed moisture flooded her mouth; she tried to stand or move inside, but her legs had stiffened and numbed. Tingles lit up her nerves and her belly flip-flopped. She licked her lips and twisted her mother's ring around and around her finger. "Uh, what are — what are you doing here?" she asked, voice cracking.

"Harper? I'm here to check on you, remember?"

"You what?" She shook her head, tipped backwards as the room tilted, and squeezed her eyes shut. Grady and AJ wouldn't dare be so bold. She hadn't called Emerson either. She wasn't stupid. Not to mention she didn't have the number. Imprint or no imprint, being anywhere near Emerson wasn't a good idea. Not before AJ's theory, and definitely not after the bomb had been dropped. "Go away, please."

Her chest hurt. She wanted to go back inside and lay down in the nest of blankets and heating pads she'd assembled. Warm and soft, surrounded in her own scent, far away from coconuts or butterscotch or anything else. It had been compromised now, the smell of coconuts would linger when Emerson left. If she could find the strength to get her to leave, because she had to, before something happened. It already had, seeing her again had stirred up everything she didn't want to deal with. Her palms were sweating, even her eyelids were hot. Emerson had to leave before she did something awful, like reach for her.

She inhaled through her mouth, to avoid the scent that made her crazy. A taste of it invaded her senses anyway and she frowned. Instead of coconut she tasted butterscotch.

Butterscotch meant...

"Sweets."

"AJ," she said, shivering, and wiped at her clammy forehead. Eyes still closed. "Is Emerson in the room with you?"

"No, it's just me."

"Do you have cookies?"

"Yes."

"Fuck." All the tension in her shoulders slid out, and she slumped. She caught the pendant hanging around her neck and grasped it in her fist, the edges of her Sita Knot bit into her palm.

"You're hallucinating Emerson?"

The butterscotch smell grew stronger. She heard hesitant footsteps. "Guess so."

AJ's perpetually chilled fingers wrapped around her fist. "How long?"

"Not long." She opened blurry eyes and tried for a smile. Even her face muscles were too tired to respond.

AJ frowned down at her, then stooped and crawled through the window. She sat cross legged on the snowy roof. "It's escalating."

Her mind was too gummed up to generate an appropriate response, or even an inappropriate one. She leaned into AJ's sturdy shoulder. A warm arm came around, holding her in a loose side hug. "I'm sorry, 'bout earlier. The yelling, chair kicking, and the glass throwing."

"It's okay. I know this sucks. I'd be more worried if you hadn't had a meltdown."

"I shouldn't have taken it out on you though. You're just trying to help. Like always."

AJ rubbed her shoulder. "I take it as a compliment."

"Really? You take me throwing a tantrum at you as a compliment?"

"I take it to mean you trust me enough to show me how scared you are.

PURE OF HEART

We're close, aren't we? Close enough to occasionally have shouting matches, and then apologize later."

"You're the closest thing I've got to a mom."

Chapped lips brushed her hair. "I believe being angry at family is pretty normal. I certainly got into it with my mom when I was younger."

"You? I don't believe it."

"Ha!" She laughed. "Harper, if we'd met when I was your age the world wouldn't have survived our screaming matches. My poor mom called me her devil child on more than one occasion."

"And your dad?"

"Mostly he would hide in the garage. He'd come out when the yelling died down to send me to my room and ground me. He avoided the actual fighting part at all costs. We pretended to fight one time just so we could peek into the garage to see what he actually did in there."

"What was he doing?"

"Sitting in the car, listening to the radio."

Her laugh came out part rasp, part cough. "That sounds like something Grady would do."

"Probably part of the reason I like him so much. His low tolerance for drama is appealing, and fun to watch when he can't escape it."

Their heads knocked together. Harper sighed and let go of her necklace. "So imprinting?"

AJ swallowed and nodded. "That's the theory."

"If I don't want... that," she said and coughed again. Or any part of love at first sniff. Not with Emerson or anybody else. "If I don't want that and the wolf is me, do you have any brainy ideas on how I control it? Me? Control myself, I mean?"

"I might. But first, let's get you inside and see if we can bring this fever down, huh? You're going to cook your brain, and then how would you come up with those Harperisms?"

***

AJ's brainy idea turned out to be meditation.

"Feel things," she said, sitting on her knees on a yoga mat. "Feel them, make peace with them, and let them go."

"If I wasn't desperate, I would so be making fun of you for this," Harper replied with a sigh. She shifted on her own yoga mat, wincing at the discomfort in her knees. "I hate this."

"You hate almost everything."

Sweat dripped from her hairline and soaked her neck. Her hair clung to her itchy skin. She flexed her fingers and sucked in a deep breath.

"That's it. Now hold it for ten seconds, then let it out slowly through your nose. When you exhale think of breathing out the feelings, or things you don't want to think about."

She sputtered on her exhalation of bad and opened her eyes. "Oh my God, Yoda. How am I supposed to focus with you being all mystic and weird?"

AJ sighed and cocked her head. "This is only as difficult and weird as you make it. You wanted my help. This is the best thing I could think of." She leaned back and tilted her face up toward the ceiling in the basement. The quietest place they'd come up with for this exercise. Also the place Harper most associated with her other half.

The cage was open, close enough she could have touched the bars with no effort. She looked at the mattress and blanket inside, and then around the large room. A box of chains sat near AJ. Grady's first tactic for restraining the wolf when she'd begged him for help. The chains she'd snapped like rubber bands stretched too far the night Ben had died.

She shivered, heard her neck and shoulders pop, then closed her eyes.

"Think about what you want to let go of."

Stale basement air filled her lungs. She pictured Emerson, and gritted her teeth at the warm sensation that came with the thought. Her lips clamped together in a thin, tingly line.

"Hold the breath, and sit in the feelings that come with it."

Her heart raced, eye's throbbing in time with the accelerated beat. In her lap her fingers twitched, nails scratching at her sweat pants. Hair rose up on her neck and arms. She licked at her lips and raised her chin.

"Now let it go."

Warm air streamed out her nose, much faster than she'd intended. She could feel AJ's frown. "Sorry."

"No, it's okay. It takes practice."

"I don't feel any different," she said. When she opened her eyes again, she had to blink to adjust to the sudden onslaught of heightened vision. "Um, did I do it wrong? This isn't going in the right direction. I thought we were leashing the wolf, not letting it run wild."

AJ shrugged and pulled the tie out of her hair. She held it out with a smile. "Here, you look uncomfortable."

Harper put her hair back and dodged AJ's all-knowing gaze. "Did you bring a tranquilizer with you? I don't want to wolf out and take out the wall trying to escape."

"This is going to take time, Sweets, and patience. It's not going to be a one and done. You'll have to learn to control it. Activating that side of yourself is good, actually, it'll help you work on this."

"But what if I..."

"I'm prepared, don't worry. Let's just try again, keep at it."

She huffed and slapped her hands back down on her thighs. Both quads ached, the well-formed muscles hard as rocks and bunched, ready to propel her into action. "We should have done this forever ago. Before it became a do or die situation."

"In our defense, I didn't know about you until a few months ago. I doubt Grady knows anything about meditation or would have suggested it. Try once more."

With a growl she closed her eyes again and thought *Emerson*.

Her stomach clenched, and her heart went nuts. She exhaled with a groan and leaned forward until her head hit the mat.

***

While AJ attempted to teach her the art of meditation to control her wolfier impulses, Harper decided to do some work on another aspect of her newest issue. The part that confused her.

There were no guidebooks titled "So You Think You Might Be Gay" or "How to Tell if You're a Lesbian." She checked, searched library catalogues and bookstores. Nothing. The internet didn't even have any suggestions, though it did offer several quizzes to test her gayness level. She opted out.

Downstairs on the couch, she glared at her laptop. Grady and Cooper had long-since gone to bed, leaving her in the dark and to her own devices. Since she couldn't sleep, research seemed the best use of her extra time. AJ loved this stuff, but the longer Harper stared at the glowing monitor the more annoyed she got.

She cleared out her search field and typed in a new query. Werewolf imprinting.

The search engine thought for a moment and then threw up link after helpful link. That is if she needed help being crazier. All of the top hits had something to do with a book series she thought sounded familiar. Or maybe it was a movie.

Her eyes widened at one link in particular. How to tell if a werewolf has imprinted on your baby. She wrinkled her nose. "Alright, we've reached a new level of yuck. What is wrong with people?"

She slammed the laptop closed, snuffing out the only light source. "So much for that brilliant idea."

The grandfather clock ticked along, her ears twitched with each tick and tock. Upstairs she heard Grady snoring like a chainsaw wielding bear trapped in a swimming pool. She pouted in the dark. At least he could sleep. If she dared try for an hour nap she'd wake the whole house with her howling, yowling, and growling.

"Why her?" She rubbed at her gritty eyes and spoke into her palms. "Makes no sense at all. Ben made sense. At least biologically. But no, I ate him instead. How is this real? I am not gay."

Prove it. She sneered at herself for even thinking such a thing. "I already did, moron. Ben did not have lady parts."

The few things she'd bothered to click on during her hours of internet search had suggested sexuality was fluid; it could change. She could have been attracted to Ben, and then found herself attracted to Emerson. A person by person attraction, not a set gender.

That all sounded like a load of bull with a heaping side order of shit.

Prove it.

"Fine." She huffed and snagged the remote off the coffee table. "Let's do an experiment. AJ would approve."

The TV did its best to blind her when it came to life. She scrambled to punch down the volume as a sportscaster's voice boomed in the silence. "Fuck, Grady. Get a hearing aid."

Ears ringing, she messed with the settings and found the right station for Cooper's game station box thing. It took her a moment to figure out how to work it, but eventually their streaming TV service came online.

She stared, chewing on her bottom lip. "No going back after this."

Coward. You're afraid they're right.

"Am not."

She set her shoulders and put in the name of a show one of the many websites had suggested.

It started out harmless enough. Some shaggy-haired blonde chick taking pictures of another chick. Blonde photographer lady had an interesting accent, not an Irish accent like her grandparents, but thicker, Scottish.

They were both pretty, she admitted, but she didn't feel attracted to them. Her heart hadn't tried to break her ribs. She didn't feel the tingles or struggle to breathe like when she thought about Emerson. The model kept eyeballing the photographer, and their conversation took on a different tone. Awkward.

Her chin hit her chest when Shaggy pounced on Model. "Uh…"

They were kissing. Not in a sweet kind of romantic way either. More like the kind of way that said she should avert her eyes if she didn't want to see things.

"Do not want!" She threw a blanket off the couch, groaning when the remote didn't appear magically.

Shaggy stepped it up a notch. She ripped open Model's shirt for some aggressive groping. The heavy breathing and whimpering coming out of the speakers made her blush. If Grady or Cooper heard it upstairs they'd think all sorts of things. Shaggy undid Model's pants and shoved her hand down them. Harper's hand closed around the remote where it had lodged itself between the couch cushions.

"Nope! No. I am not old enough for this show."

She switched the channel away, back to the regular cable stations, and slid down in her seat. Her ears burned and her heart pounded. "Oh my God. Worst idea ever."

Some new sports themed something or other droned on in the background while she got her breathing back under control. She coughed, cleared her throat, and rubbed at her damp forehead. "Lesson learned."

She changed the channel, and two women locked in a passionate kiss appeared.

"Lesbians!" She turned off the TV and tossed the remote into the recliner, well out of reach. "Okay, curiosity murdered and buried under the house. I'm done, I swear."

"Harper?"

"I didn't see anything!" She fell off the couch, landing between it and the coffee table. One arm stayed on the cushions, bent backwards in an uncomfortable angle.

Cooper helped her untangle herself and sit up. He slumped down next to her and stole her blanket. "What didn't you see?"

"Nothing. I saw nothing," she said with a wince. A blush tickled her neck and cheeks. She huffed and crossed her arms. "What are you doing awake anyway? Did you... hear something?"

"Nah, had a crappy dream." He picked at lint on the blanket. "How come you aren't in your room?"

"I figured insomnia is better than rope burns and keeping the whole house awake."

"Oh."

"Yeah." She looked over at him and frowned. He had dark circles under both eyes and his head kept bobbing. "You want to talk about it?"

"About what?"

"The dreams."

He shrugged and leaned his head back against the couch, like it weighed a thousand pounds and he couldn't keep it up any more. "I keep dreaming you die in the kitchen. Or sometimes I think you're dead, but then the wolf explodes out of you. Like that alien thing from that guy's chest?" He put a hand to his chest and then made an explosion sound and screech. "Then you run off into the woods, and we can't find you."

She pawed at her greasy, sweaty hair and sighed. "I'm sorry, Coop. I'm sorry you had to see that, and you're dreaming about it."

"It's not your fault."

Her stomach twisted at his tone. He'd always been so sure of her, even after what happened with Ben. "I'm still sorry."

He shrugged again. "Are you feeling better?"

Not in the slightest. She glanced at the TV and curled up her lip. That hadn't helped at all. "Yeah, I feel better. AJ's hippie kumbaya meditation stuff seems to be working."

"You're not going to, um, go anywhere are you?" He ducked his head, frowning at the edge of the blanket twisted between his hands.

She frowned and set her hands on his. "Where would I go?"

"I don't know," he said, blinking heavily up at her. "I just have this feeling you're going to leave."

His mother had died in the kitchen, inches from where she had collapsed. Tears gathered as she watched him fidget, staring toward the TV. Naomi had been making them lunches for school, and then she'd crumpled. The sound of Cooper's screaming had kept her awake for months. It gave her the chills, remembering his terrified wails.

She squeezed his hand and smiled weakly at him. "I'm not going anywhere, Cooper. I promise, okay? I'm not going to leave you."

"Promise, promise?" His chin wobbled but he smiled back at her.

"Promise, promise," she said and held out her other hand, pinky out. "I'll even pinky swear."

He rolled his eyes and snorted. "Nobody does that anymore. How old are you? A hundred and five?"

"Smart ass." She ruffled his hair.

"Hey, Harp?" He shoved her hand away and sighed. "Dad won't tell me what's going on with – you know, why you're so sick. You never get sick."

"This is a different kind of sick," she said. *Love sick. Ugh.* "It's a wolf thing, we think. Nobody's really for sure."

"Like the wolf flu or something?"

"Or something."

He crossed his arms and squinted at her. "Harper."

"Cooper."

"Come on, everybody else knows, why can't I know too? I can help!"

"I don't think you want to know," she said. "I didn't want to know. If I could go back in time and erase that whole conversation with AJ, I would."

"You shouldn't mess with time travel," he said with a slow shake of his head, lips pursed. "You can mess up all sorts of stuff. Changing the past can seriously damage the future."

"You build a time machine and not tell me?"

"Nope. Just watch a lot of sci-fi."

She groaned and hid her face with her hands. If she didn't tell him, he'd pester all of them until someone cracked under the whining and attitude throwing pressure. But if she told him, she'd have to deal with him knowing. She peeked between her fingers to see his jaw set and arms still crossed.

Lesser of two evils it was.

"You remember the blonde girl in the red dress?"

"The one that made you freak out and punch me in the eye twice, and kick dad in the balls? Yeah. Kind of hard to forget."

"Right." She bit her lip and rubbed the back of her neck. "AJ thinks I imprinted on her, that's why I've been acting so crazy."

His eyes widened and jaw dropped. "You're gay?"

She snorted. "How is it I have no idea what imprinting meant or means, but I say it once and you conclude I'm gay for Emerson?"

"What else would it mean?" he asked, shaking his head. "Wow. I mean, think about it. You imprinted on someone. What else would it mean?"

She did not mention her baby duck theory, instead she glared at him. "I don't know, genius. It may not even mean what we think it means. But that's why I'm sick, I'm trying to undo it."

"So is it like love at first sight or something? It's not like she's been around here. Do you even know her at all?"

"More like love at first sniff," she joked. Her throat tightened up. "No, I don't know her. I don't know how to explain it. I just know I'd rather not have imprinted on her. I'm not gay. That's why all the meditation crap is going on. I'm trying to control the wolf."

"Some romantic you are," he said.

"I don't want to romance her, that's the whole point."

"So don't."

"I won't." She huffed and poked him. "This is why nobody told you. Jerk."

He laughed and pushed her away. "No. Dude, look, you're thinking about this the totally wrong way."

"Oh am I? Please, clear it up for me Mr. Know-it-all."

"Girls," he said and blew his bangs out of his eyes. "You're always so freakin' dramatic. Who said you have to romance her? Did you think maybe you could be just friends with her? Maybe that'll do the trick. Or is there some rule that said you have to be girlfriend and, uh, girlfriend with her because you probably imprinted?"

She couldn't help it, she gawked at him. Her shoulders dropped forward and she groaned into her hands. "I don't know if I should strangle you or hug you."

"You'll try both later anyway, you know it and I know it." He patted her on the back. "How about for now you let me have the glorious moment of being right."

"I hate you."

CHAPTER FOURTEEN

Emerson

"Oscar, no, for the hundredth time, you don't need to come back." Emerson sighed and rubbed at her forehead. "Nothing was stolen. The house is fine, I'm fine, everything is under control."

Over the phone, she heard drawers opening and slamming. "Like hell it is."

"Oscar."

"Your house was broken into! What if you'd been home? I can't even think about it. I already bought a ticket, alright?"

She stopped pacing and narrowed her eyes. "You what?"

"I bought a ticket. I'm flying out tomorrow morning. I should have flown out when you first called."

"I am not an infant."

"You're my baby sister."

"By an hour, Oz." She groaned. "Look, I understand and I appreciate you wanting to charge to my rescue. It's just not necessary any more. We're not five-year-olds facing down playground bullies."

"No, we're adults, and the trouble you're getting into now is a thousand times scarier."

"Return the ticket," she said, raising her chin. "I can't have you running to my rescue every time something happens. I have to be able to be on my own. I need you to trust me. When I say things are under control I need you to believe me."

"But –"

"I will tell you when or if I need you to fly back here. Trust me, please."

"Did you at least get the door fixed?"

"Not yet." She shook her head and winced when she caught sight of the back door, boards nailed in place to cover the gaping hole in the bottom. The frame had shattered all the way around it. Someone large had rammed her door with the force of a cannon ball. "As soon as I get off the phone with you I'm going to get that taken care of."

He sighed and she could picture him pulling at his hair. "It was nice of Holt to get you a room at the lodge."

"Are you admitting the monkey might not be so bad?"

"No. I'm saying the monkey did a nice thing. He's still a lower primate. I don't suppose he has the mental capacity to fix the door?"

"I didn't ask," she said and sat down on the arm of the couch. Oscar quieted and she rolled her eyes. "You can say whatever it is you're thinking."

"I was going to remark about trouble in paradise, but the idea of him being in paradise made me queasy."

"He is a touch overzealous." She drew her hair over one shoulder and groaned up at the ceiling. "Our recent outing has made it clear to me we're probably not compatible beyond a friendship."

"Because he's a monkey?"

Her lips twitched up at the corners. "Because he reminds me too much of Gabriel, and not in any good ways."

"How terrible."

"Don't gloat, it's not gentlemanly. Anyway, that's why I didn't ask for his assistance with the door. I don't want to get his hopes up more than I already have."

"You mean besides letting him in your home after just meeting him? Or going on a date with him after that little show at the bar? Or letting him procure you a room at his father's lavish lodge?"

"You know you're not helping." She raised an eyebrow. Mr. Darcy leapt up onto the couch beside her, purring away. She scratched his furry chin and smiled at his antics. "I'll let him know where I draw the line."

"You couldn't just send him a text?"

She thought about Holt's attempt to kiss her, and shuddered. "That would be rude, and I think we've passed the point where a text would be enough. No, this will have to be a face to face conversation and I'll have to wait for the right time."

Oscar huffed. "I don't want to know."

"Probably not."

"What about the mysterious Harper? Any news on that front?"

"Uh, no, I haven't seen her for awhile," she said and cleared her throat. "She's still a mystery at this point. One I'm not sure I'll ever solve."

"Trouble."

PURE OF HEART

"Not really." Heat stained her cheeks and flooded her neck. She hadn't mentioned their last encounter to him. The idea of him belittling Harper, giving her a nickname like Holt's, made her angry. Not with the Harper situation, but with Oscar. Certainly now that she knew more about her past, she didn't want to think about anyone giving Harper a hard time. Her hand curled into a fist on Mr. Darcy's back, she set her jaw, and glared at the wall. "She's not trouble. She's different, and hard to get to know, that's all. A challenge, Oz, a worthy challenge."

And she seems like she needs a friend, she thought with a frown.

"More worthy than Holt?"

Her heart said yes. "Time will tell."

"I know you think they're interesting, but remember there are other people in town you can make friends with. These two don't seem housebroken, or properly socialized. You have a habit of bringing home strays. Does it have to be these two?"

"Maybe I'm attracted to damaged souls," she said, stiffly. "Just because they're damaged doesn't mean they need to be put down, or I can't adopt them."

"You and your stupid big heart." He sighed again. "Alright, alright. You're sure you're okay? Nothing's missing?"

"No, they didn't take anything," she said, glancing around the living room. Her brand-new flat screen was still on the wall. All her expensive artwork and knickknacks were still in their respective places. None of her shoes had gone missing. "I guess they saw all the books and thought I didn't have anything they wanted."

"Clearly they didn't know your wardrobe is worth hundreds of thousands of dollars," he said with a strangled laugh. "You know that's not exactly a good sign? If they didn't take anything, it's more likely they were there for you. For ransom or to cut off a lock of your hair for their collection and murder you."

"You've been watching too much television. No more cop shows for you."

"It's not all paranoia. Promise me you'll be cautious for the next couple of weeks."

She nodded. "I will. I'm going to buy an extra lock for the doors, too."

"You're not scared?"

"Not enough to require a visit from you," she said, gently. "I've given some thought to getting a dog. Something that might be more of a deterrent to breaking into my home again, like a Rottweiler."

"I'm sure Hellspawn would appreciate that. You know you can't put a Rottweiler in one of those carrier purses, right? Also, I would not recommend painting its nails or naming if Fluffy."

"I would not name it Fluffy." She scoffed. "It was a thought, that's all.

Besides the possible kidnappers, I thought the bears might reconsider visiting me if I had Cujo in my backyard."

"Cujo was a Saint Bernard."

"I'm aware. They shed more, and lack the temperament to ward off intruders."

"So Rottweiler was your next choice?"

"Well, I can't very well go out into the woods to find my wolf," she said without thinking. Her eyes widened at her slip. She pulled the phone away and shook her head. Even with the extra space she heard him suck in a noisy breath.

"Your wolf? What wolf! What? Emerson…"

She hadn't lied by not telling him about her wolf. She'd simply not mentioned it. "A wolf, I meant a wolf."

"I'm not buying it. I know you better than anyone. You put emphasis on my, as in ownership. As in you need to get to talking right now, and it better be a charming story about a petting zoo. There was a wolf in your backyard?"

A loud knock on the front door saved her from having to respond. She yelped and fumbled the phone. "Oscar, someone's at the door. Might be the Sheriff for a follow up. Do not fly out here."

"Emerson!"

"I'll call you back later. Love you! Bye."

She disconnected the call and dropped the phone onto the couch, eyes fastened on the door. A second, lighter, knock came. As if the person knew she'd been waiting for confirmation of a visitor. With the curtains drawn she couldn't check out the front window to see who had stopped by.

"It's the Sheriff," she told herself and stood. "Or Holt. Robbers and kidnappers do not knock politely."

Mr. Darcy padded toward the door, but froze two feet away. His tail puffed up and he sank to the floor with a vicious growling yowl.

"Dee?"

He hissed and took off, shooting past her and up the stairs making more unhappy sounds.

She clutched the sleeves of her oversized cardigan and approached the door on stiff legs, bare feet silent on the hardwood. Her hand hovered over the doorknob. She leaned up on her toes, and pressed an eye to the peephole.

The keen green eyes of Harper Cahill stared right back.

She fell back onto her heels and whirled around to press her back to the door. Her heart banged against her ribs and butterflies did loop-di-loops in her stomach. She rubbed at the side of her neck and across her collarbones, shook her head and licked at her lips. Harper had appeared on her doorstep, uninvited, and she didn't have a plan of any sort to deal with it.

"I'm not even dressed for this," she whispered in dismay and looked down. Her shirt had a studded heart on it, and her yoga pants were not meant to be seen by anyone, ever. She grabbed both sides of her favorite cardigan and pulled them over like a robe. "No, no, no."

"Emerson?"

Harper's voice, more of a growl than anything else. Emerson shivered at the sound and turned back around. "Okay, I can do this. *Pas de panique*. It's just Harper. The woman who bled all over a bar, was rude to you, and is somewhat terrifying." She paused, then said louder, "Just a second!"

Just Harper. She rolled her eyes and finger-combed her hair. "What is wrong with me?"

With a deep breath, she set her shoulders and grasped the doorknob firmly. Or as firmly as she could, with the tremors racing up and down her forearms. She managed to open the door, not yank it hard enough to betray her nervousness. "Hello, Harper."

"Uh, hi?" Harper swallowed and shoved her hands into her back pockets. "I was… in the neighborhood?"

"We live in the same neighborhood."

"Yup."

She pressed her lips together and scratched at the side of her neck. "Okay? Did you need something?"

Harper's smile wavered. She averted her eyes downward, and rocked back and forth. "I was thinking," she said and hummed a low note. "I was thinking that – that I should apologize. For the other day."

"Oh." She wrinkled her nose and smoothed out imaginary wrinkles in her pants. "Well, that's – I suppose I appreciate the thought."

"I'm not… good at this," she shrugged.

"Apologizing?"

She hummed again and nodded. "Not because I don't have practice. God knows I do, especially lately. I should be an expert." She sighed and scuffed a boot against the welcome mat. "I feel really shitty about what I said and how I acted. You were right, you didn't deserve that. I don't even know you. Could you forgive me for being a monstrous jerk?"

"You're not a monster," she said and then clamped her lips together. So much for staying in control. Her mouth had gained a mind of its own, uttering things she'd rather stayed in her head. "Please, don't say things like that."

Harper's dark eyebrows drew together, she tilted her head, and peered up through her lashes. Which should have been funny, considering their height difference, the top of Emmerson's head just reached Harper's broad shoulders.

Emerson pulled in a slow breath, fighting the sudden tightness in her chest. "I don't like hearing anyone say things like that about… themselves.

All I wanted was an apology anyway, and you've done that, even if it's a bit late."

"I had to dig my head out of my ass first," she replied and loosed a raspy laugh. "It was firmly lodged, so it took awhile. I'm sorry."

"What if we start over?" she blurted, eyes widening as her mouth formed words without her permission again. "I mean –"

"No, yeah, that sounds like a – I would like that. From the beginning, like I didn't bulldoze you the first time."

The crooked grin she wielded made Emerson's head spin. Her stomach plummeted to her toes. Then returned to its proper place so quickly she had to grab the door to steady herself. Bulldozer indeed, more like a steamroller. "Okay, so." She cleared her throat and held out the hand not gripping the door for dear life. "Hello, I'm Emerson Grey. It's nice to meet you."

"Harper Cahill. Welcome to Fincher."

Coarse calluses dragged across her hand. Emerson gasped. Along with the sensation of hardened skin against her palm, tingles crackled up her arm. Just like they had the last time she'd touched Harper.

"Sorry," Harper said, pulling her hand back. "I know my hands are rough."

"Oh no, it's not," she said and shook her head. "It's not that, they're really warm. It surprised me, that's all. You're not wearing gloves. I expected cold."

"I'm hot blooded." Another crooked grin.

"Apparently." She grinned back and leaned against the door. Her grin faltered when she noticed a few other things about her new acquaintance. The angular features she remembered were more pronounced since their last encounter. High cheekbones jutted, dark circles occupied the underside of both glassy eyes. She glanced lower and caught a peek of collarbone straining against pale skin. Harper didn't have a coat on either, just a loose and baggy V-neck with a faded, checkered shirt over the top. She looked smaller. "I know we're starting over, but you look different."

"Been sick."

"Oh. Oh!" She shook her head and opened the door wider. A wave of heat from inside the house swept passed her. Harper shivered. "And you came over here without a coat or gloves? In this weather? Would you like to come in? Warm up before you walk home?"

"You let people you just met into your house? That doesn't seem safe." Gold flashed in those distracting irises.

Or she thought it did. She shook her head again. When she checked the color was gone. "A bad habit I haven't broken yet."

"You might want to work on that. I'm fine, thanks for asking though. I feel a lot better."

PURE OF HEART

I don't want you to go, she thought and blushed. Not a normal thought to have, or something she could understand. After all, Harper was the last person she should want to get to know so desperately, despite her tragic back-story. Oscar's words returned.

You always bring home strays, Emerson. These two don't seem housebroken or properly socialized.

"I don't want to go, either," Harper blurted and turned bright pink. "I mean, uh, sorry."

"I said that out loud?" She swallowed a groan and cursed her mouth's continued betrayal. "Well, that's awkward. I mean, I'm sorry, I just…" *Desperately want to be your friend, for some reason.* "My brother says I'm nosey, I call it curiosity. I'd like to get to know you, that's all. You really should come in, you're shivering. I know it's not far to your house, but I could make you some tea before you go? That would be the polite thing to do. You did walk over here to apologize, the least I could do is invite you in."

The crooked grin returned in full force. "Are you nervous?"

She found herself smiling back as some of the tension rolled out of her shoulders. "What gave me away?"

"The speed talking. AJ does that when she gets nervous."

AJ. She filed that name away for later, and gestured for Harper to come inside. "I guess you know my 'tell' now."

"It's kind of obvious." Harper stepped inside and shivered more viciously than when she'd been outside. She rubbed at her arms, head turning as she glanced around. "You like books, huh?"

"My grandparents owned the bookstore in town, and they left it to me. Love of literature runs in the family," she said and slipped past Harper, trying not to touch her. It was even harder not to look over her shoulder constantly as she led the way to the kitchen. "Sometimes I think I could open the house to the public as a small library."

"You could. Is there a bookcase every five feet?"

She giggled and shook her head. "Not quite. But there are several."

"So you do a lot of light reading then?" Harper paused at the kitchen table and picked up the book left open. "In Praise of Love." She cocked an eyebrow and grinned.

Emerson blushed anew and retrieved her book, careful not to bend any pages as she set it back down. "Yes, that's a favorite."

"It's in English. Those books you had the other day were in French."

"I studied literature and French at Stanford," she explained, trying not to run to the stove for her teapot. "I always prefer to read in French, it's beautiful. That book is written by a French philosopher. It's really very good."

"Yeah?" Harper sat down at the table, but didn't touch the book again. "It looks like it would be pretty sappy."

"I suppose it is." She cleared her throat and moved her foot stool over so she could reach the cabinet holding her mugs. "But it's moving in the best of ways. Inspiring."

"Inspiring?"

"We could say that love is a tenacious adventure. The adventurous side is necessary, but equally so is the need for tenacity. To give up at the first hurdle, the first quarrel, is only to distort love." She quoted from memory, shaking hands flat against the counter. "Real love is one that triumphs lastingly, sometimes painfully, over the hurdles erected by time, space and the world." She could feel Harper staring, but ignored the goosebumps and tingle in her spine as she filled the teapot. "You can't tell me that's not inspiring."

The sound of water sloshing in the teapot was the only sound for several beats.

"You can quote it from memory?" Harper's voice was deeper, the gravel in it more pronounced. "Why read it again if you know it by heart?"

She shrugged and moved the pot to the stove. "Because I enjoy it. There are many books I haven't had the time to read yet, but I saw it on the shelf and had to pick it up again. I've got time on my hands now, so I didn't feel the need to rush into something new right away."

"Oh?"

"My social calendar is wide open," she said and wrinkled her nose. "At home I had things to do. Parties to attend, outings with my mother, classes, that sort of thing."

"There's not a whole lot to do around Fincher anyway."

"Certainly not when you're the new girl."

"You won't be new forever," Harper said. "Pretty soon your calendar will fill up, and you won't have as much time for reading."

She sighed and picked at the side of one of the mugs. "That sounds both awful and wonderful. I love to read, but I would also love to make some friends around town. I'd hate to develop another bad habit."

"What habit would that be?"

"Talking to my cat," she said with a smirk.

"You have a cat?"

"I do, Mr. Darcy. I'm not sure where he scurried off to. Normally he's friendlier with visitors." She glanced over and saw Harper holding onto the lip of the table. "You don't like cats?"

"We don't… get along. I'm more of a dog person."

"Oh!" She grinned. "I've been thinking about getting a dog."

"Let me guess, a Pomeranian?"

The teapot whistled, and Harper jerked like she'd been kicked. Emerson frowned and snatched it off the stove. "No, I was thinking more like a Rottweiler."

PURE OF HEART

As soon as the whistling ceased, Harper visibly relaxed again. She almost sagged against the table. "A Rottweiler? What's a girl like you want with a dog like that?"

"A girl like me would like to feel a bit more secure in my home," she said, trying not to bristle at the implication. "I don't know if you've heard – my mother said small town gossip travels swiftly – my house was broken into."

Harper shifted in her seat and pursed her lips. "I might have heard something about it. Are you alright? They didn't take anything?"

"I'm fine, I wasn't even home, and they didn't take anything."

"I meant – you don't feel scared or anything? Sounds like it would have been scary."

"I stayed at the lodge for a few nights to get over it," she said and finished steeping the tea. "Do you want some cream or sugar?"

"Uh, no."

Both added to her own cup, Emerson smiled gamely and carried the steaming mugs to the table. "I think a Rottweiler would make someone think twice about trying something like that again. First, I need to get my door fixed."

"Your door?" Harper clutched the mug with both hands, her upper lip curling at the corner.

"Yes, they smashed through it." She frowned again and tilted her head. "Though I don't understand why they did it the way they did. The bottom half looks like a wrecking ball went through it. Why not the whole thing?"

Harper swallowed hard. "Don't know. But I could take a look at it, if you want. I've got some experience with home repair. I can even install the new door for you."

"Is this part of your apology?" Emerson asked over the lip of her mug. "That seems to be the Fincher protocol."

A shrug was her only answer.

CHAPTER FIFTEEN

Harper

People were staring. A lot. She could feel the eyes on her and smirked to herself. Beyond the staring, she could hear them whispering from the end of the aisle.

"What's Harper doing here? Break something again?"

"Her and that temper."

"Who's that with her?"

"I don't know, someone new. Pretty little thing."

"You're kind of like a local celebrity, or something," Emerson commented.

Harper looked up from the door she'd been examining. She leaned to the side and saw Mrs. Asher and Mrs. Landy eyeballing Emerson. "You get used to it. Some days I even find it amusing. Watch this." She waved at the gossip paparazzi, and the women quickly left, chattering low to each other. Scandalized for sure. "See?"

"Is it because of your reputation?"

Great, the gossip network had been busy. She sighed. "Depends. What have you heard?"

Emerson raised a hand to tick off each one. "Vampire, serial killer, cannibal, curse, omen, crazy person, bouncer."

Harper cringed and leaned back on her heels. "I wouldn't agree with all of those."

"Which ones would you agree with?"

"I'll let you decide what I am and what I'm not, okay? That seems fair." Being so close to Emerson, talking to her, helped, but also made things difficult. She had to be careful with her reactions, what she said. Her brain-to-mouth filter was on the fritz again. "Did you hear anything else?"

"That you flattened a boy's nose in high school because he said you were pretty. And you're adept at throwing people out of the bar."

"I have no recollection of the events to which you're referring," she said in as snotty a tone as she could manage. AJ had taught her that line. She used it more often than she cared to admit.

"Very good," Emerson said with a laugh. "Did a cop teach you that phrase or was it an overworked lawyer?"

"Neither. It was a veterinarian." She grinned and rattled the door she'd been poking at. "This door should do the trick."

"You are very strange, Harper." She shook her head.

"Says the mysterious newcomer."

"I'm mysterious?" Emerson scoffed and followed her toward the front of the store. "How am I the mysterious one?"

"You said it yourself, remember? You're new, and none of us know much about you. Besides the fact that you've moved here, like books, and speak French."

"How terrible, how do we fix this?"

"Pretty simple. You tell me about you, I tell you about me." She turned around with a grin, walking backwards with her hands in her pockets. Safer that way, kept her from touching. "You first."

"There's not that much to tell, honestly. I can't really be all that mysterious. I told you I went to Stanford. I own the bookstore. What more is there?" she asked, smiling back. "I used to visit my grandparents here in the summer when I was younger. I'm surprised we never met."

"I didn't move down here until I was eight, so I could have missed you. Even if you were around, unless you were hanging out in the woods we wouldn't have seen each other. I kept to myself," Harper said, careful to keep her tone neutral. She could almost feel the curiosity pouring off of Emerson and wondered how she could avoid the topic. They were headed for murky waters and she'd rather not go there. She banged on the bell sitting on the counter.

"I still get a sense of déjà vu, like we've met before and I don't remember."

"I would remember you," she said, in almost a whisper. Then shook her head and glared behind the counter. "Where the hell is Rob?"

"Maybe we met in a past life." She cocked her head. "You moved down here from Alaska, right?"

Harper tensed. "You've been talking to Holt about me."

"I'm sorry, yes."

"I can't say I'm surprised," she said and smacked the bell again, imaging it was Holt's face. "Yeah, I'm from Alaska."

"Like Polar bears and Penguins, Alaska?"

She sighed and turned around to lean back on the counter. "Anchorage. There are no penguins in Alaska, and there definitely aren't any polar bears that far south."

Emerson bit the corner of her bottom lip. "You probably don't like to talk about it."

"Not really, but I'll enlighten you since you're so curious and probably have all the wrong information from Holt the dolt." Harper scratched at her cheek and blew her bangs out of her eye. "Grady came up and got me after my parents died. That I don't – I'd really like to not talk about that. So I live here now, with Grady and my cousin, Cooper. That's the story of Harper. The end."

The end indeed. She set her jaw and clenched it rhythmically as she stared through the dirty linoleum floor.

Emerson put her hands in the pockets of the dress she'd changed into. Because heaven forbid she be seen in public in normal people attire. She licked her lips and took a hesitant step forward. "Harper, I'm sorry. I'm being nosey."

"Let me guess what else Holt told you," she said, still looking at the floor. "He said I'm an omen, or a curse, because when I moved here my aunt died, followed by my boyfriend." Her jaw flexed, a muscle jumped in her cheek and her eyes went super focused for a second. "By the way, that shitstain at school I punched out? He said my ass was to die for, and Ben proved it."

It had felt good to break his nose, and see the group of boys surrounding her go pale at all the blood. The suspension and long lecture from Grady had sucked, but Holt and his buddies left her alone after that. Worth it.

"Harper." A cold hand gripped hers and squeezed. The tingles came buzzing back to life, and her stomach rolled over. "I'm sorry."

"Don't ask Holt any more about me, okay? If you want to know something you can come straight to the source." She pulled her hand away, missing the contact immediately but unwilling to risk more. "Let's talk about you instead. There aren't a lot of happy, good things to talk about involving me."

"Harper Cahill," Rob said as he sauntered up. He wiped his hands on a rag, but still smudged his bearded face with grease when he rubbed his nose. "Break another door? Or the fence again?"

"Damn bears," Harper said, voice huskier than ever. She smiled at Emerson and slowly twisted to aim that smirk at Rob. At last, a friendly face that didn't make her insane. "Not me this time. Miss Grey here had a door broken, and I told her I could replace it for her."

Rob leaned around and grinned at Emerson. "Miss Grey, huh? Not related to Nate and Annie?"

"I'm their granddaughter," she said and held out her hand. Which, of course, he shook and smeared with grease. Emerson didn't even frown, though she held her hand far away from her body when it was released.

Harper tried not to snicker.

"They were nice folks, I'm very sorry for your loss."

"Thank you."

He inclined his head at Harper. "This one breaks things on a regular basis, so should be more than able to fix your door for you."

"And here I was thinking she's just good for witty repartee and scaring off old ladies."

She rolled her eyes. "You don't know the half of it. Rob, can you bring the door down to the Grey's house? I want to get it installed before it snows again."

"Sure. I could use a break. Show me which one you want and I'll load it right up."

***

True to his word, Rob followed them back to Emerson's with the new door in the back of the store truck.

Harper stood in the back hallway, scratching her head as she took in the damaged door. It was familiar in the worst way. Grady's door had looked similar several times, generally right after a full moon. Her wolf had done this. Broken into the house the night that... She jumped when Emerson touched her elbow and a zap traveled up to her ear. "Sorry."

Emerson pointed at the door. "Tell me that's not bizarre."

"It's... weird, yeah." She gulped and shook her head. "You have a tool box somewhere in this library, or do I have to rip the rest off with my bare hands?"

"As exciting as that would be, Oscar made me get a tool box and I even have a new wrench!" She grinned and whirled around, leaving Harper standing there to study her own handiwork. At least now she could fix what she'd done.

She turned when she heard a soft grunt and fought back a wide grin when she saw tiny Emerson lugging a massive toolbox. Both of her hands were wrapped around the solitary handle which rocked and rattled with each lurching step.

"Don't smirk at me like that," Emerson scolded, stopping a foot away wearing an adorable pout.

"Sorry, I'm sorry." Harper grabbed for the box, and hefted it with one hand, only to set it on the floor. "I was thinking about you trying to fix things. Do you have a hardhat too?"

"I'll have you know the internet and I are more than capable of completing small home repairs." She planted both hands on her hips and leveled a glare worthy of a teacup Chihuahua.

PURE OF HEART

"And what is a small home repair? Hanging a picture?"

"I fixed the shower all by myself and put together a desk and two bookshelves," she said with a satisfied smile. "I'm sure with help from the internet I could attach the new door. At least it wouldn't make smart comments."

Still chuckling, Harper opened the tool box and peered at the contents. "Where's the fun in that?"

"My mother can't even run the dishwasher." She huffed. "I refuse to be like that. I like to be able to do things myself."

"How do you go through life not knowing how to use a dishwasher?"

A bright blush lit up porcelain cheeks, and blue eyes darted away to the nearby painting. "We have staff to take care of that. My mother can't cook, and I don't think she's ever held a mop. She's completely helpless."

Images of mansions and butlers danced through Harper's head. She paused her rummaging and sat back on her heels. "You're rich."

Emerson crossed her arms and cleared her throat. "My parents are. Daddy's a cinematographer, and he has an inheritance."

"Cinematographer? Like movies?"

"Television."

"Anything I'd know?" She smiled, but Emerson bit her lip and looked down.

"Probably not."

Harper frowned and scratched the side of her cheek. "And now I'm the one bringing up uncomfortable things apparently."

"What safe topics are left?"

"How about the weather?" She shrugged and selected a screwdriver from the tools laid out before her. "What do you think of the snow?"

"It's cold?"

"Nice."

"Thank you."

"Okay, so, how about I walk you through what I'm about to do? That way, if you ever need to replace another door you can do it yourself, Miss Independent?"

Emerson nodded and reached for the screwdriver. Their hands brushed and she sucked in a sharp breath. "With one change," she said. "I do the work while you walk me through each step."

"Deal."

The door didn't take long to install, even with Harper having to patiently explain every part. Emerson let her do all the heavy lifting, after an unsuccessful attempt at lifting the door herself.

"There, good as new, and you did it."

"Most of it," she said. "You're pretty handy."

"I'm used to fixing things."

"I don't suppose you'd be good at fixing dryers as well?" She raised an eyebrow and opened the new door. "That is my dryer right now," she said, pointing outside. "My sheets froze."

"Drywall, yes. Dryer, no," Harper said, peeking around to see a clothesline stretching across the yard. She packed all of the tools away and then scratched at her cheek.

"Do I want to know why you're proficient with drywall repair?"

"Nope, but how about I take a look at the dryer anyway?"

"Are you looking for an excuse to poke around?"

"Maybe. Is there a reason you're answering my questions with questions?"

"Keeps us away from dangerous topics, doesn't it?"

She laughed and rolled her eyes. "Okay, *touché*. Show me the dryer, let's see what I can do."

"Holt already messed with it, but he couldn't do anything."

Harper rubbed her fingers over her lips to keep Emerson from seeing how it curled up. She couldn't suppress the growl that followed. Ignoring Emerson's quizzical look she rolled up her sleeves and headed for the laundry room off the kitchen.

The dryer was in pieces inside. Harper picked up a hose of some sort and wrinkled her nose. When she turned around Emerson was leaning against the doorway, one pale eyebrow arched.

"I think you need a new dryer."

"Why thank you, I don't know what I would have done without your expert advice."

Harper smirked and wagged a finger. "No, no. I do the sarcasm thing, so you have to find your own thing."

"Can we share custody?" Emerson asked.

"We'll discuss it." Harper set the part on the dryer. "Here lies your dryer. It was a good dryer, always made clothes warm and fluffy. It will be missed."

Emerson snorted, and then her eyes widened. Harper wondered if it was the first time she'd ever done such an un-ladylike thing.

"How about this," Harper said and gestured at the laundry basket sitting on the washer. "You come over to my house and use our dryer until your new one arrives?"

"I have the clothesline."

Harper put a hand to her chest. "You would rather hang your fancy clothes outside where unspeakable things could happen to them than allow me to help?"

"I hope you know you're ridiculous," Emerson replied, and rolled those pretty blue eyes. She sighed and tapped a finger against her chin. "Hmm, go to a strangers house and dry my unmentionables or air dry them?"

PURE OF HEART

"I promise to be on my best behavior and never mention the color of your underwear. But I draw the line at folding them."

Emerson laughed and threw a wadded up sock at Harper. "Now the answer is definitely no."

***

Harper felt a strange energy invade her limbs as she pushed open the door to the house. Unlocked, again. She took Emerson's laundry basket away from her, and headed straight for the back of the house. Not that she was embarrassed by the state of things, but she knew the pictures around would arouse Emerson's curiosity. They'd managed to find inane things to talk about and tease one another about on their walk over. She didn't want to go back to that awkward phase from earlier.

"So here it is," she said and did her best Vanna White impression in showing off the dryer. "I trust you know how to work one of these? Or have you been using a clothesline for too long?"

Emerson elbowed her. "Do you ever stop?"

"Never," Harper said. "Everything's self-explanatory and it shouldn't shrink anything. If it does it's not my fault."

The sound of a veritable stampede assaulted Harper's ears. She hid a smile and looked toward the door, waiting. It didn't take long. Cooper came bounding into the room, dressed only in boxers with some cartoon on them. He pulled up short when he saw Harper wasn't alone.

"And this is my cousin, Cooper," Harper introduced.

Cooper stared goggle-eyed at Emerson and clapped his hands over himself. "Harper!"

He disappeared in an instant. She could hear him running up the stairs, and grinned wider when his door slammed so hard the house seemed to shake.

"That's normal, don't worry about it," she said.

Emerson giggled. "I hope he's not embarrassed."

"Cooper? Like all teenaged boys, he'll be furious for all of five seconds. I expect him to return in his Sunday best oozing charm like he thinks he's James Bond." Harper cocked her head and grinned wider when she picked up the sound of dresser drawers opening and closing. "He usually walks around in his underwear, so maybe this will teach him to be more careful."

"You are cruel," Emerson said, still grinning. "Poor kid. I can't imagine growing up with you around."

"Are you kidding? He's lucky. If it weren't for me he'd wear superhero clothes to school every day."

"That's adorable."

"I don't think the High School girls would agree."

Emerson shrugged. "High School girls are mean just to be mean."

"We know that, but he's still figuring it out," Harper said with a sigh.

"Anyway. Soap's up on the shelf." She pointed up and realized how strange it must be for her to see four opened boxes. Grady had been experimenting with different scents, and each one had made Harper queasy. She looked back at Emerson's puzzled face.

"Um, we like variety? I recommend that one. It's the least obnoxious smelling."

"Harper? Want to explain what that — " Grady stopped, much like Cooper had, just inside the door. His eyes went wide and ping-ponged back and forth between Emerson and Harper. "Hello?"

"Grady, I think you've met Emerson," Harper said, glaring hard in an attempt to communicate with her eyes alone.

"Right, yeah, Emerson. Hello... again. Harper can I talk to you for a minute?"

No. "Sure."

Grady grabbed her elbow, shot a tight smile at Emerson, and then dragged Harper out of the small room. Harper didn't resist as he pulled her down the hall and into the kitchen. The second they were alone, however, she pried her arm from his grasp. "Nice caveman routine, I'm sure that didn't look strange."

"What is she doing here? Have you lost your mind?"

"Her dryer's broken?" Harper offered. The hair on the back of her neck stood on end. If she'd been a wolf she would have been bristling. Warning number one. "Grady — "

"You had me throw you in the basement the other night to stay away from her, and now you've brought her home?" Grady scrubbed his hands over his beard and huffed. "What's going on?"

"I feel sick." She held up a hand before he could interrupt her. "Not bad sick. Queasy, jumpy. Everything's on high alert. She does something to me and I can't figure it out. But I know it's worse if I ignore it."

"That doesn't mean you bring her home."

"The full moon is coming," Harper said. "I feel like I drank a hundred cups of coffee. That's normal. What I don't want is for things to get worse because I'm – I don't know, aggravating it. If buddying up to Emerson keeps things under control, then I'm going to do it."

"But what about the..." Grady narrowed his eyes at the wide open doorway and then leaned in close to whisper. "What about the control problem? You were like a..."

"Wild animal?" Harper supplied, trying not to snarl at the bad taste it left in her mouth.

"When she was here last," he finished with a nod. "What am I supposed to do with you if it happens again?"

"I don't know."

"Helpful."

PURE OF HEART

"I don't think it will now that I'm doing what it wants, things are better." Harper closed her eyes and listened. "I don't feel any urges now."

"That's not exactly comforting either," Grady mumbled. "I don't like this, at all."

Harper snorted. "Join the club. I'm just as blind, and I'm the one having out of body experiences."

He didn't seem to have another retort, and Harper didn't know what else to say.

She shrugged and held her hands out. "Looks like it's going to be the blind leading the blind."

"Hey, Harper?"

Grady about flew up to the ceiling, and Harper, who'd heard Emerson coming, smiled at his shocked expression. "Yup?"

"Holt sent me a text asking if I could meet him for dinner. I don't want to impose, but could I leave my laundry here? I promise I'll come back for it."

With her back to Emerson, Harper stared at Grady, felt her vision flicker and shut her eyes. Her chest burned like she'd swallowed something scalding. "Trying to get me to do your laundry for you?"

"You'd like that too much," Emerson said.

Harper couldn't turn around, she couldn't move. Every muscle had locked up and pain radiated from every joint. Her voice came out rough from between her gritted teeth. "Caught me. It's fine. Leave it here and finish it tomorrow."

"You sure?"

When she opened her mouth to assure her it was okay, nothing came out but a strangled growl.

"We're positive," Grady said. Harper opened her eyes and Grady gave her the worst look he could, pity written all over his features.

CHAPTER SIXTEEN

Emerson

Emerson decided to let Harper and Grady continue their argument without her as an audience. The awkward tension she'd felt earlier with Harper had returned tenfold. She didn't want to wallow in it or force Harper and Grady to either.

On her way back to the laundry room she happened to look up from the floor in time to see Cooper. He leaned against the banister and grinned at her. She stifled the urge to laugh. Harper had hit the nail on the head. Cooper had retreated upstairs and donned what she suspected was the one suit he owned. No doubt a hand-me-down from his father, judging from how it swamped his lanky frame. He'd even slicked his hair and she almost sneezed when the smell of too much cologne hit her nose. Holt over-did it too, which made her wonder if all men in Fincher thought the appropriate amount of cologne was the entire bottle.

"Hello again. Cooper, right?" She asked, hiding a smile behind a hand. "You look very handsome."

He puffed his chest out and tugged at his lapels. "You can call me Coop."

"I'm Emerson," she said and held out her hand, expecting a polite handshake.

He grabbed it and kissed her knuckles. "Charmed."

Oh my God he's adorable, she thought and bit her lip. *Must run in the family.* "A real gentleman. Don't see many of those these days."

His face turned bright red. "Uh, well, I try? Are you new in town?"

"I am, yes. Your cousin was nice enough to let me use your laundry room. My dryer suffered an unfortunate death." She leaned in closer to whisper in a conspiratorial tone. "I think it was heat stroke."

"Cool!" He said, with a grin. "I mean, not cool that your dryer broke but – so you and Harper are friends?"

"I think we may be."

"Awesome. Do you need any help with the folding or... anything?"

She put both hands on her hips while she pretended to ponder his query. "I think I've got it for now. But I may have an idea. How old are you?"

"Sixteen."

"Do you have a job?"

He shook his head, disrupting his neatly combed hair.

Emerson hummed and looked him up and down. She fought another laugh back when she saw he'd even put on a pair of shiny shoes. Her humor faded when she realized he probably didn't wear the suit often. It was all black, even the shirt and tie. Like a suit one would wear to a funeral.

She cleared her throat and smiled again. "Listen, I own the bookstore in town. I need to do some number crunching – but how would you like to work for me?"

His blue eyes went wide. "Dude, really?"

"Really. I could use some help around there, and I think a gentleman, like you, is just what I need."

The James Bondsian facade disappeared with a fist pump. "Awesome!"

She held up her hands. "Let's not get ahead of ourselves. I've still got to check and make sure I can afford to hire you. But I'll come by and let you know when I figure it out."

He turned bashful again in an instant. "Can I talk to my dad about it?"

"Of course," she said, and straightened his tie. "I'll go over the books tomorrow morning. Should have an answer for you by the time I close."

"This is way better than working at the vet clinic with Harper and AJ."

"I thought Harper worked at the bar with Grady?"

"She does, but she volunteers to do stuff at the clinic." He wrinkled his nose. "She's crazy. No way would I clean up animal crap for free."

And the mystery deepened. She smiled and patted his shoulder. "Probably should go talk to your dad. He's in the kitchen with Harper."

"Thanks, Emerson!"

"You're welcome," she said and watched him take off. Shaking her head at the amount of energy she may have just cursed the bookstore with, she continued back toward the laundry room.

She couldn't find a good place in the small space for the hamper. It seemed rude to leave it on top of their washer. There were three other doors in the hall, besides the one that led out to the backyard. The first she opened was a bathroom. She paused at the second.

Hitching the hamper on a hip, she reached with her free hand and

PURE OF HEART

touched the frame. While the door appeared to be brand new, the frame was broken. Not even a quarter of it remained intact, like something had blown through the previous door. Just like the door at her house Harper had replaced. Had someone tried to break in there too? She grabbed the doorknob and eased it open.

Through the crack, she saw nothing but black and the outline of stairs leading down.

She yelped when a hand smacked against the wood, forcing the door back in place. The hamper hit the floor as she spun around to see Harper. She put a hand to her the base of her throat, her pulse hammering against her fingertips.

"Harper!" She shook her head, but stopped when she thought she saw something flicker. Harper's eyes, for a split second, looked like they'd flashed gold. Again. Too many times now for it to be a coincidence.

"That's the basement. You don't want to go down there."

"I was going to put my hamper — " she tugged a hand through her hair and huffed. "You scared the life out of me."

"I'll take it upstairs. Sorry I scared you. The basement's a disaster. Full of junk and… spiders. The stairs are rickety too. I wouldn't want you to get hurt."

"What happened to the door?"

She stiffened and glanced at the damaged frame. "I tripped coming up the stairs and broke it. We just replaced it. I haven't had time to redo the frame yet."

"Oh." She bent to pick up her scattered clothes and jumped again when Harper knelt as well. "Harper?"

"You don't want to be late for your dinner. I've got this."

"Are you sure you're not looking for an excuse to paw through my underthings?"

Harper's irises went from green to gold. She almost commented, but Harper looked away, back at the floor, and her shoulders slumped.

"Nope. You better go. Don't keep Holt waiting."

***

Emerson replayed the encounter with Harper over and over in her head as she got ready. By the time Holt picked her up, she'd shaken the entire incident off. Harper had been arguing with Grady, no doubt over her. Her behavior could be explained as a reaction to whatever conversation they'd had.

The change of color in her eyes, which continued to nag at her more than the rest, she wrote off as the light. Harper's eyes were a very pale lime green. No doubt a myriad of things would play off that color. A reaction to outside light was the simplest and most logical explanation.

She chewed on her bottom lip as Holt led her down the street toward

Sullivan's. Not the ideal place for her to have the boundaries conversation. Harper would be there, and she could ignite the two of them without meaning to. "Holt, I don't know. Maybe we could go somewhere else?"

"You nervous about seeing Harper? Don't worry, I won't let her be mean."

She stopped and tugged at the crook of his arm. "Holt, please don't. She and I are doing better now. We're friends."

He looked up at the street lamp and puffed his cheeks out. "Sorry. I just don't — Harper plays games and she's moody. I promise to be on my best behavior. Can't make any promises for her though."

"Thank you," she smiled. "I think Harper deserves a real friend. She's probably been really lonely."

He grumbled something under his breath and shook his head. "We've tried. I've tried for years. Logan's been her friend for the longest, and she gives him the cold shoulder."

"There's more to it than that. I'm telling you." She eyed the shamrock sign hanging above the noisy bar and set her shoulders. "I'll prove it."

With a grin he wrapped his arm around her shoulders. "Hey, if it makes you happy to try, I won't even say I told you so if you're wrong."

"Comforting." She rolled her eyes and poked his side. It gained her some space, his arm dropped from around her, giving her some breathing room. "What do I get if I'm right?"

"The satisfaction of being right? How about the look of shock on my face?"

I am right. She shook her head. "Good prize."

He wiggled his eyebrows up and down, and reached out to hold the door open for her. "I thought so."

Sullivan's wasn't full like before, but just as noisy. She smiled a greeting at all the strange faces. Logan was bussing a nearby table and she offered him a wave. He stared at her for a long moment and then gave a half-hearted return.

"I don't think Logan likes me much," she remarked.

Holt sighed. "Everybody who meets you likes you. Ignore him, he's weird."

"You think everyone is weird."

He shrugged and steered her toward the bar. She started to protest, knowing what he was up to, but then caught sight of Harper. Those sharp features paled and her eyes flicked back and forth – as though she was looking for an escape.

She grabbed for Holt's elbow and dragged him the rest of the way to the counter. "Harper! How good to see you."

"Oh, hey… you." She pulled a strange face that morphed into the worst fake smile Emerson had ever seen. "And Holt too. Must be my lucky day."

"Harper," Holt said, leaning his elbows against the bar. He wrapped his arm around her shoulders again, but he was focused on Harper. She didn't much care for his grin either.

"You –" Harper sighed and threw a rag down. "What can I get you?"

"Emmy?" Holt asked.

Her eyes flashed that gold color again. Emerson thought she heard a growl, but dismissed it as a chair scraping across the floor.

"I'm not really feeling the Guinness tonight. Why don't you surprise me?" She watched Harper, noted the way she was breathing. Shallow, quick, almost like she was trying not to hyperventilate. She didn't look all that good. There was a waxy sheen to her face and her shirt hung off her shoulders. Maybe it had been something else. "You okay?"

"Fine." Her voice squeaked and she cleared her throat. "Peachy, even. I'll make you something." She turned to Holt and the gold flared again. "Holt?"

"The usual."

Harper turned around and Emerson frowned. "Holt?"

"Hmm?"

"Did you see Harper's eyes just now?" She leaned over to whisper at him, watching Harper the whole time. It could have been her imagination but she thought she saw Harper twitch. She definitely clenched the liquor bottle in her hand. "They changed colors."

He shrugged and jerked his chair closer. "She's got freaky eyes. They've always been like that. She explained it to us once in High School, something about the light and reflections."

"Oh." She pulled back and smiled when Harper returned with their drinks. "Harper, thank you again for fixing the door for me, and for letting me leave my laundry at your house." She reached over and smacked Holt's back a couple of times when he choked on his beer.

"No problem." Harper looked like she'd swallowed something nasty. She backed away from the counter and gestured toward the back. "It's my break, so I'm going to just go do… that. Yell at Logan if you need anything else."

She all but ran through the swinging doors into the kitchen area. Emerson turned to Holt, he held his hands out.

"That's your friend."

"What is going on? She wasn't like this earlier." The mention of Holt changed Harper's behavior. Seeing him in person doubled her transformation.

"Jumpy, irritable, running from the room at every given opportunity?" He ticked off each one on a finger. She ran through her own mental evidence checklist. "Only thing that encounter was missing was the sarcasm. I think that was for you though, not for me."

She picked up her glass and took a sniff of the concoction. The amber colored beverage swirled enticingly, but she wrinkled her nose at the heavy scent of alcohol. "What is this?"

"Harper's version of a Long Island Ice Tea, I think."

She took a sip of it and blinked in surprise. "It's sweet!"

He laughed and took a hearty pull of his dark beer. "Yeah. She's a pain in the ass, but she's a pretty good bartender."

Taking a less cautious drink Emerson smiled and set the glass down. "She remembered I like tea."

"Of course you do. Weird French books and tea. I don't know how you can drink that stuff."

"Coffee is just as bitter," she said. "And it gives you horrible breath."

"Tea stains your insides and your teeth."

"It does not stain your insides!"

"You hope." He grinned at her and swiveled on his stool. "See, this wasn't so bad, was it?"

She shook her head and pushed some hair behind her ear. "No, I suppose not." Her eyes were continually drawn back toward the doors leading to the back. Where Harper had disappeared. "Holt, I think I'm going to –"

"You're kidding."

"No, I feel like I should follow her."

"Emmy…"

"I'll be right back, I promise." She touched his arm and slid off her stool. Trying to appear nonchalant, she eased past the few tables and patrons in her way and headed straight for the doors to the kitchen. The thrill of doing something she knew she shouldn't made it even more exciting. Her heart hammered in her chest, and she wondered if someone would stop her. Would she have to make up an excuse?

She stopped in front of the doors and glanced around. Nobody was paying her any attention. Raising her chin and setting her shoulders she marched into the back, pretending she belonged.

Her heels clicked against the tile as she crossed the long room. The smell of food and dish soap was almost overpowering. She smiled over at the cooks who shot her a cursory glance. "Harper?"

"Check the freezer," the burlier of the two answered. She wrinkled her nose, confused when he bumped his elbow against the thinner man at his side. They whispered to one another, and both made no effort to hide their long-lasting glances at her.

"The freezer?"

PURE OF HEART

"That's where the Ice Queen likes to hide," the thin one said. He pointed her in the right direction with his chin.

She tried her best to look undaunted as she eased past the greasy, sweaty men. She also tried not to think about morgues and dead bodies as she sized up the large metal door. The handle was cold to her touch when she grabbed it. With her audience watching her she couldn't falter. Clearing her throat, she yanked.

Nothing happened.

She yanked again, and again. Then pulled on the handle and leaned all of her weight backwards. *"C'est des conneries*! Is she holding the door closed?"

Snickers came from behind her. She glared at the cooks over her shoulder. "Gentleman, that is hardly helpful."

"Pull up, then back," the burly one said with another snicker.

"Of course," she said, summoning up the haughty air her mother had perfected. *Snooty, she could be snooty.* "Everyone knows that."

She hastened into the metal room, the sound of their laughter chasing her. The door didn't slam behind her like she'd hoped, but settled into place with a hiss and a dull whump. She leaned back against the cold door and looked up at the ceiling. Fog billowed out from the vents. She wondered why it wasn't snowing in the small room.

"Emerson?"

Harper stood up from her perch on a crate in the back. Steam came off her body, but she didn't appear affected by the cold beyond that.

Emerson gaped at her. "How are you not freezing?"

"What are you doing in here?" Her eyes darted back and forth, much like they had when Emerson first stepped into the bar.

"This is a strange place to take a break," she said, arms wrapped tight around her midsection. "You're not even wearing a coat."

"I am wearing pants though." Harper pointed at Emerson's bare legs. "Do you even own a pair of jeans? This isn't California, you know. Or summer."

"Really? I hadn't noticed." She rolled her eyes. "I like skirts."

"I thought we agreed sarcasm was my thing?"

"I thought we agreed to joint custody?"

Harper rubbed her nose and snorted.

Emerson growled and hopped in place. Her legs felt like they were turning into blocks of ice. "I also thought we agreed to be friends?"

"We did. We are. Friends, we're friends."

"Then why are you running away the second I come in here? Is it really just Holt?" Emerson asked. "We were fine this afternoon, all the way up until I mentioned Holt, and then when I showed up with him you took off.

I understand you two don't like each other, but I was really hoping we could all be grownups."

"I should've known this wouldn't be easy."

"What was that?"

Harper ran her fingers over her upper lip. She shook her head and sighed. "Look, I'm sorry. I've had a lot going on and I didn't — "

Cagey might as well be her middle name. She threw her hands in the air. "Harper, I'm getting whiplash! What is it?"

"I'm weird, okay?" She scuffed the toe of her shoes on the floor. "I'm really weird and I'm not used to having people interested in being my friend."

"Logan's your friend."

"Logan's different," Harper whispered. Her shoulders hunched and when she looked up... there went her eyes again. So gold they almost burned with it.

She swallowed and thought of another pair of eyes. Which was completely ridiculous. Her mother's voice spoke up in the back of her mind. *Get your head out of the clouds, Emerson.*

Right. She'd follow up on that later. With a better source of information. For the moment... She tilted her head and studied Harper, who seemed to be finding her shoelaces very interesting.

"Oh," she said. "What you mean is I'm different because I'm not a man?"

Harper blushed bright red. "I – yeah, that's definitely part of it. I don't get along with girls usually. Except AJ."

"Who's AJ?"

"The vet."

"The vet who taught you that phrase you used earlier?"

"Yes."

"It's not a bad thing," she said and sucked in a lungful of frigid air. One way to fix it. Start over. "Can we try this again?"

Harper arched an eyebrow, but a smile twitched up the corners of her pale lips. "This super awkward conversation? Why not, I've already tasted humiliation."

"Must you be so difficult?" she huffed, but softened it with a small smile of her own. "I mean the friends thing. I really want us to be friends." *Not that I understand why, but it has to happen.*

It could have been her imagination, but she could have sworn Harper swayed on her feet. The cold must have been getting to her.

"You mean it?"

She shrugged and held out her hand. "Two dramatic, possibly messed up women, trying to be friends. This could be fun."

Harper's calluses scraped against the softness of her palm. Her grip was strong, almost too strong for such a delicate looking hand. "What could possibly go wrong?"

***

Harper decided to stay in the freezer for the rest of her break. Since they were starting over, and she was worried about being weird, Emerson hadn't said anything about it. What she did do was file it away for later, more evidence to think over.

She hadn't been in there long and the cold had her shivering. Harper looked calm, almost comfortable sitting amongst the frozen food. Without a coat. With steam coming off her body in noticeable wisps.

She had a plan. Not a great one, but a plan. She had too many questions, and her curiosity would not be denied. She stepped back into the bar and saw Holt, surrounded by a bunch of men. He didn't notice her, which would work out great for part one of Operation Sasquatch.

Logan was at the back of the room, clearing another table. He paused every now and then to glare toward the bar.

The reason she needed Holt distracted.

She eased through the crowd, smiling at anyone who spared her a glance. All the while trying to figure out how to approach him. Harper had agreed to a do over. She could try that.

"Hey," she said, stopping just beside Logan. He jerked like she'd dropped a glass.

"Oh, hey."

"It's Logan, right?"

He nodded, eyeing her with a wariness she found amusing. Like she could ever be any sort of threat. "Yeah. Can I – did you need something?"

"I was hoping maybe we could talk? We didn't really start off great with the whole scarf thing."

"Uh, no I guess not." He stopped mopping up the table and glanced back toward the bar. His shoulders hunched up and his hand balled up the rag. "I probably shouldn't though. Talk to you, I mean. I'm kind of working, and Holt'll be all over me for talking to his girl."

"I'm not his girl," she said and slipped into the booth. He leaned away from her. "Just for a minute, I promise."

"You're kind of weird."

Now isn't that ironic. "Am I?"

He sighed, shrugged and sank down across from her. She grinned when he started wiping at the table again. "So I don't look like I'm totally slacking," he explained with a blush. "What did you want to talk about?"

"I feel bad about the other day."

"I was kind of a jerk."

She shook her head. "No you weren't, you were just looking out for your friend."

"I could have been nicer about it."

"I probably could have too."

He ran a hand through his messy, floppy hair. "So we're both sorry. Cool."

"Cool," she repeated, the word tasted foreign. "I'm sorry about Holt too. He has this thing when other people are around. I don't quite get it. He's really nice when it's just the two of us."

"He's an ape." He started scrubbing with a little more vigor at a stain. "Sorry."

She laughed and reached over to pat his hand. "It's okay. I get it. My brother calls him the monkey."

"Your brother is a smart guy. Holt picked on me and Harper a lot when we were younger." He raised his chin in the direction of the bar. She turned and saw Harper standing close to the various liquor bottles, her lip curled in obvious disdain. Then she saw gold again, and bit her bottom lip.

"What is it with him and Harper anyway?"

"That's probably something you should talk to them about." He frowned, almost pouting, and scratched a nail against the stain. "I don't really get it either. I'm sure it has something do with Harper's boyfriend, Ben, and all the bullying."

"Speaking of Harper," she said and cleared her throat. *Nonchalant, act nonchalant.* "I've been around her a bit –"

His head snapped up so fast she winced, imagining how hard it had to have been on his neck. "Really?"

"I like her, she's funny. Kind of quirky. We're... friends."

"You've been here less than two months, and you made friends with Harper?"

She made a face at him. "Am I that bad?"

"No." He shook his head, hair falling back over his forehead. "It's just it took me over a year to get her to say more than two words to me."

"How old were you?" She imagined teenage Harper would have been a bomb waiting to go off.

"Eight."

The same age as Harper when she'd become orphaned and been transplanted to a new town.

"Oh well, that's because she didn't want your cooties," she said and winked.

The blush returned, scorching all the way to his hairline. He coughed and swiped at his hair again. "Yeah. Some things don't change."

How intriguing. She leaned toward him. "So you know her really well, I was curious – that thing with her eyes?"

"How come they look freaky gold sometimes?"

"Yes, exactly!" She frowned, realizing she'd whisper-yelled that. In a bar.

PURE OF HEART

Logan leaned in as well. She repeated herself at normal volume and he nodded.

"I didn't notice it at first," he said. "But sometimes it's super obvious. It's the light. She's got spooky yellow green eyes anyway. Light hits them at the right angle and it makes the yellow stand out. She said it's her clothes sometimes too." He picked at the collar of his grey t-shirt. "Like black makes them really green. Blue makes them more yellow." He made a face. "At least that's how she explained it. Not that I keep track of stuff like that."

"No, of course not." She tried to sneak another peek at the bar, and found two people watching her. Harper and Holt had located her. "I think they're on to me."

"Have fun navigating that minefield." He threw the rag into the bin of dirty glasses and scooted out off the bench. "It was nice talking to you."

"You too." She watched him go and then raised her hand to wiggle her fingers at the bar. Harper quickly went back to mixing drinks. Holt grinned and waved for her to come back. He went as far as to raise his voice over all the noise.

"Emerson, come meet the guys!"

"Minefield indeed," she muttered to herself and shook her head. "What am I getting myself into?"

CHAPTER SEVENTEEN

Brunch. When Harper had called and asked to hang out, her first thought had been brunch. A nice cup of tea, maybe a scone. Pleasant conversation.

Brunch didn't usually take place at the local vet clinic.

Two steps behind Harper, Emerson stopped, frowning at the big dog-shaped sign. "Harper?"

"Yeah?"

She pointed at the sign and arched an eyebrow. "Is this a cute, but confusing, mascot for a quaint diner?"

Harper grinned and shrugged. "Does this look like a diner to you?"

"Is this payback for asking you to help me with my house?" She narrowed her eyes. "Because I don't think it's necessary. I'd be happy to compensate you with more pizza."

"You like pineapple on your pizza," Harper said and made a face. Emerson fought a smile. Watching her pick pineapple off her slice with an offended look had been a highlight of her evening. "It's bring a friend to work day."

"You're a terrible liar," she said and crossed her arms. "Why didn't you tell me where we were going? Am I even wearing the right clothes for this?"

"You can borrow some sneakers, I keep a spare pair here."

"At the vet's office?" She narrowed her eyes. "Why?"

"Come on, Emers. It'll be fun, I promise. Cute puppies and kitties for you to snuggle with."

The puppy dog look Harper made wasn't fair. Neither was the new unique nickname she'd been gifted with. Not Em, not the horrible Emmy, Emers, delivered in Harper's trademark growl. She groaned and ducked her head. "Fine. But can we please go to lunch after? Like normal friends?"

"You're like a magic eight ball that gives questions instead of annoyingly vague answers." She laughed and started toward the front door again, a slight spring in her step. "We'll hit the deli after. I won't even make fun of the way you eat."

"Like a normal person?" She glared at the back of Harper's head as she followed her. "Some of us like to taste our food."

Harper held open the door for her, grinning again. "You eat like a mouse."

"You eat like a starved coyote."

The grin slipped, just a little, but came back quickly. "Do I?"

She'd noticed a lot of that. A seemingly innocuous comment had the power to make Harper twitch. If they were animal comparisons, that is. Her smile would falter. She'd pause in the middle of something.

What's going on in that head? She wanted to ask, but instead put on her best innocent expression. "Watching you eat is like watching a special on wild animals."

There it went again, almost too small to be noticed. But she knew how to look for it now. The slight tick in the corner of Harper's left eye.

Harper shook it off and huffed. Back to her regularly scheduled programming. She waved her hand at the open doorway. "I'll be getting you back for that."

"I'll look forward to it."

Walking into a veterinarian's office, she expected to see furry patients and worried owners lining the walls. Like a hospital ER for quadrupeds. Instead, she faltered once inside. Because there weren't rows of chairs filled with owners and a variety of pets. The floor was hardwood, not linoleum. Natural light spilled in through the windows. A single receptionist, not wearing scrubs, sat behind an impressive circular desk. She glanced up from her computer screen and smiled.

"Can I help you?"

She started to reply, but the door closed behind her with too loud a bang and she turned around to glare at Harper.

But Harper stared at the receptionist with such a predatory expression she forgot to scold her.

"Oh hey, Trish." She crossed her arms and bared her teeth in a very scary, fake smile. "Kill any cats lately?"

She blinked rapidly at the quip. That seemed an odd way to greet anyone. Let alone someone you worked with on a regular basis. She shot a glance back at the receptionist and frowned when she saw a similar expression.

What was wrong with these two? Harper couldn't possibly have another frienemy in such a small town.

"Well you're still alive, so no," Trish said. She leaned her chin into her palm and rolled her eyes. "But feel free to stand in front of my car sometime and we'll see what happens."

Harper put a hand to her chest. "Now you've gone and hurt my feelings. I'll bill you for the therapy needed to get over that."

"Assuming you have feelings to hurt."

"You're calling me an emotionless robot?" Harper cooed and waved her hand at her face. "How sweet. Apology accepted."

Trish nodded her head at Emerson, but didn't look at her. Probably afraid to take her eyes off of Harper. Considering the way she was being sized up, Emerson didn't blame her. "Who's this? Did you finally find someone who can stand you for more than five minutes?"

Was it a game? Harper didn't appear angry. In fact, if Emerson knew her right, that expression was amusement. They were playing? Her eyes ping-ponged back and forth between them.

Children. She was in a town full of adults who acted like kids.

"Well, I'm blind and mostly deaf," she said with a shake of her head. Might as well throw herself into the ring. "It's a gift and a curse."

"Ooh, and she's quick on her feet, too." Trish straightened with a laugh. "I like her. I'm Trish, as you probably heard."

These people were so weird. Her mother would faint being anywhere near such behavior. "Emerson."

"You should get a leash for your cat, Emerson."

It felt nice to be included, even if it was the strangest ritual she'd ever been involved in. "I was thinking a studded collar, hot pink with a heart shaped id tag."

Trish looked delighted. Sort of. "Don't forget to chip her too."

"Jesus H. God." Harper groaned and grabbed Emerson by the elbow. "Come on, Emers. Is AJ in the back?"

"She's expecting you. Try not to break anything else. Oh, and feel free to come back out this way so I can laugh at the claw marks."

"Are you two always like that?" she asked as Harper steered her toward a door in the back.

"I don't know how it started exactly, but yeah." She shook her head and pulled Emerson through a small exam room. "We weren't kidding at first. I don't think. Back in school we had shouting matches at lunch and recess. Now it's sort of a game."

"How evolved of you. You know you're weird, don't you?" she asked with a fond smile. Weird could be good. Different was fun.

***

The second Harper stepped into the back, all hell broke loose. Cats hunched up and hissed from the corner of their crates. Dogs whined, barked and growled. Some of the braver canines went right up against the bars, teeth snapping and paws digging. Others followed the cats' lead, curling into a ball in the corner.

Emerson raised an eyebrow and looked to Harper. "You're as popular with the pets as you are with the receptionist."

"Very funny," she grumbled and stalked further into the room, hands on her hips. "Hey, knock it off!"

The barking ceased, though it echoed off the walls longer. However, the cats didn't stop. Which didn't surprise her. Mr. Darcy didn't listen to her either. What did surprise her was the growl she heard.

She cocked her head and stared at Harper's back. The growling continued. Deep and murderous. Yes, that was all Harper. Last she checked human beings weren't supposed to make sounds like that.

"Harper?"

Harper stiffened and took several deep breaths. Her shoulders rose and fell several times. "Sorry. They'll be good now. Won't you guys?"

"Do they do that to anyone who comes in?"

Another door opened and a woman in a white lab coat came out. Chart in her hands, she didn't look up at first. None of the animals made a peep. "Harper, right on time. You'll love today, Snowball's back in."

Harper cleared her throat. "Yay. Um, I brought an extra hand."

The vet still didn't look up from her chart. She ran a hand through her ink-colored hair and flipped a page over. "You talked Coop into coming to help? Is he outside flirting with Trish?"

"Not Cooper."

Emerson raised an eyebrow. The vet frowned and looked up. Her dark espresso eyes widened and her mouth opened. A reaction Emerson had imagined a few times, but not under such circumstances.

Something passed between the pair. A lot of that happened around Harper. *Have they somehow learned to communicate using their eyes alone?* That wasn't possible. She'd tried multiple times to have a conversation using only her eyes. It didn't work. Ever. Not even in the mirror with herself.

But Harper had a lot of eye conversations. She didn't think it could be telepathy. Something though. An elaborate secret, she had a feeling.

"AJ this is Emerson. Emerson, AJ." Harper crossed her arms, crooked smile in place.

"It's nice to meet you," AJ said. She shot Harper another look, and then held out a hand. "Harper's said a lot about you."

Interesting. "Has she?"

"Only good things." AJ smiled, glanced at Harper, and then cleared her throat. "Shall we get to it then?"

PURE OF HEART

"I thought maybe Emerson could observe at first, draw her own conclusions on if she wants to get more hands on."

AJ coughed and nodded. "Absolutely."

All business then. Emerson smiled, trying to appear game. AJ had vomit on her lab coat. Yellow, chunky vomit. That so did not bode well. She didn't seem bothered by it, which made her want to ask if she knew.

Harper beat her to it, in her own Harper way.

"Jay, did you know you've got dog puke on you? I mean, if you're trying a new perfume I have to tell you... it's a little pungent."

"Nice," Emerson said, nudging her. "I'm proud of you."

"I can die happy now." Harper made a face.

AJ held out her lab coat. "Oh. Crispin, that little terrier over there, he got into a poisonous plant. Poor guy."

The terrier in question, a brown and black splotched mop-like creature, shivered in its crate. He stared out at them, focused on Harper.

They were all focused on Harper. Still.

Every move she made, they watched with rapt attention.

The plot thickened.

AJ dropped the chart on the exam table. "Right. Harper, I'm going to get Snowball out. Think you can help me draw some blood?"

Harper narrowed her eyes. "Draw some blood?"

More secret, silent talk passed between them. Emerson wanted to scream. What were they saying?

Snowball didn't seem too thrilled with the idea either. She flattened her fluffy white body close the bottom of her crate and yowled when AJ opened it. Yowled at Harper.

AJ didn't react at all. She picked the cat up, cradled her close and set her on the table. "Okay. So, Harp remember what we talked about."

"Harper," Emerson whispered. Harper's lip twitched and another thick growl came out between her clenched teeth. "Harper." *Not a cat person. Right.* "Do you want me to help? I'm accustomed to angry felines."

"No, I got this."

AJ arched a dark eyebrow, and nodded toward the hissing cat. "Come on, Sweets."

"Nice kitty," Harper said. "I'm your friend."

Emerson bit her lip as Harper approached the table. She knew unhappy cat when she saw it. Blood was going to be drawn. Not all of it from Snowball.

"Relax," Harper said, her voice lower and scratchy. Like it had been when they'd first met. "I promise I'm not going to hurt you. We're buddies, okay?"

A hand reached out, and lightning fast Snowball responded in kind, claws extended. Harper didn't yelp or jump away. She growled and Emerson heard a snap, like a twig breaking.

"Harper!" She jumped forward and snatched Harper's hand away from the cat.

"Wait!" AJ said with a wince.

Snowball jumped off the table with a squall and made a beeline for the nearest hiding spot. Harper wrested her hand free from Emerson's grasp and dove after the cat.

"Harper!"

"Harper, I'll get her. Don't corner her!"

But she didn't listen. The cat had flattened itself under a cabinet, and Harper's head, shoulders, and left arm went underneath after it. A rumbling growl boomed in the room, chased by a high-pitched snarl from Snowball. Harper's legs flexed as she tried to shove herself farther under.

"Harper, you leave that cat alone!" AJ bellowed and swatted Harper on the behind with a folder.

The scuffling and squeaking of Harper's wet shoes on the linoleum ceased. She backed out and aimed a sheepish grin up at them. "Sorry, got carried away. She got me good."

AJ pulled her up off the floor. "She did."

Emerson grabbed her bleeding and torn hand, wincing as she got a close look at the damage. Five track marks marred Harper's skin from her knuckles to her wrist. Blood welled in each one and smeared over the back of her hand.

"It's okay," Harper grumbled. She tried to pull her hand back and Emerson noticed a shudder go through her.

"It happens all the time," AJ said, kneeling and peering under the cabinet for Snowball. The cat growled. "We're working on it. Harper loves animals, they're just slightly frightened of her."

Slightly, sure. She pursed her lips and ran her thumb over the claw marks on the back of Harper's pale hand. "That's sweet of you, Harper. But maybe you should stick to dogs."

"Yeah, maybe."

Her breath caught in her throat when Harper turned her head. Under the fluorescent light Harper's eyes glowed a deep golden color. Again. That close up she could see, really see. It couldn't be a trick of the light. Those eyes, that color, she'd seen it before.

AJ coughed and Harper jerked like she'd been struck. "Let's try this again."

***

Emerson tried to let it go. She told herself her over-active imagination

PURE OF HEART

had conjured up some new fantasy. The mystery of the glowing gold eyes nagged at her, always in the corner of her mind, and her biggest piece of evidence in support of Operation Sasquatch.

It shouldn't have been such a big deal. She'd grown accustomed to writing things off as silly ideas brought on from reading too much. The problem with Harper and this latest intriguing oddness — it reminded Emerson of another set of eyes. Ones that belonged in the head of a large black wolf she shouldn't be seeing in Harper's face.

She could blame it on her imagination all she wanted, but the idea didn't seem to be going anywhere any time soon.

The logical explanation had been presented not only by Holt and Logan, but she'd thought of the same thing. A simple trick of the light. Harper's eyes were a distracting shade of green, pale enough they looked yellowish anyway. The right reflection off of them could play that up.

Simple. Logical.

Except she didn't believe it for a second.

Harper's eyes didn't just look gold, they gleamed with it. Like when the beam of a flashlight bounced off a cat's eyes in the dark.

That left the fantastical explanation, the one she didn't dare ever say out loud for fear of acknowledging her encroaching insanity.

Harper couldn't be a werewolf. Some things were too far-fetched. If true, that would mean other things existed too. She wasn't ready to say vampires, unicorns, or trolls were real.

But what would be the harm in indulging her imagination a little longer? It did give her something to do, and maybe she'd write a book of her own about it someday.

She paused in the midst of shelving and turned to Cooper. They'd been working in silence for the better part of a half hour. The occasional request for a book, or a question about a title had provided the few breaks. He seemed content to stand beside her and use his longer arms to place the books on shelves she couldn't reach without a stool or ladder.

"Coop?" She cleared her throat and smiled over at him. "May I ask a question?"

"You mean besides that one?" He grinned right back as he stretched up to deposit another book on the topmost shelf. "Sure."

"It's about Harper. Her parents," she said. Harper had asked her not to talk to Holt about it anymore. She hadn't said anything about Cooper.

He stilled and then pulled the book he'd been holding against his chest. "Um, maybe you should ask her?"

"You're right, I should, and I would." She sighed and shook her head. "It's just she's a vault and really good at deflecting." *Or outright denying me answers.* "I was wondering if maybe there's some sort of connection to…

Maybe it's not me, is what I'm trying to figure out."

"It's not you," he said. "She likes you."

"I'd like to know what happened, I'm afraid to ask her and upset her more than I probably already do with all of my other questions."

"It's not something we talk about. Everybody already knows, and I — she wouldn't want me talking about it, you know?"

"I promise I won't tell her you said anything. I've heard the rumors, and I don't know what's true or not. I don't want to assume something, or ask her when it's so painful."

He fidgeted with the book in his hands, opening and closing the front cover. "I don't know what to say. I never met them. We have pictures. They look nice. Dad talks about Aunt Cassidy sometimes, tells me stories about when he was a kid."

"Holt said there was an accident?"

"Yeah." He sighed and looked over at her. "A fire. Harper was eight."

She tried not to allow her brain to conjure the images for her, but they appeared nonetheless and she shuddered. A small child with dark hair and giant green eyes, crying and covered in dirt, curled up in a closet as smoke billowed in. "That's awful."

"Harper has dreams about it," he whispered, looking around like Harper might pop out from behind a shelf. "She doesn't like to talk about those either."

"Of course not," Emerson said and blinked back the rush of tears that threatened. Poor Harper. "That would explain why she doesn't like to get close to anyone."

"Yeah." He nodded. "I kind of got like that when my mom died."

She winced and inched over closer to him. "I heard about that, too. Holt said some people think Harper caused it."

He swallowed, his Adam's apple bobbing. "She had an aneurysm. Harper didn't put it in her head."

He shuffled his feet and stared over her shoulder. She could see a wet film over his eyes and put a hand on his arm. "I'm sorry, Coop. I didn't want to upset you either. Forget I said anything."

"It's okay. You're new and don't know all the… stuff." He shrugged and offered a weak smile. "And Harper would definitely clam up if you asked her. She's private."

I don't blame her. She wanted to ask about the boyfriend too, but didn't want to push him any further. "I get curious." She shrugged and went back to the book cart. "My mother hates it."

"You don't talk much about you. What are your parents like?"

"My dadd- uh, my father, he wasn't around much. And my mother's kind of a nut. If you know what I mean." She shrugged again. The awkward tension would go away soon. If she could just muddle through it a little longer, it would. "She is very worried out about me moving up here."

"Are you an only child or something?"

"No." Stroking the spine of an HG Wells book she glanced up at him over the frame of her glasses. "I have a twin brother. She's just protective and wants me to be – well, what she wants me to be. Unfortunately I inherited my father's stubbornness."

His lopsided grin reminded her of Harper. "That's cool. I mean, that you have a twin and came up here, even if your mom didn't want you to. I'm glad you're here."

She smiled back. "Me too."

He ducked his head and grabbed another book. "Harper's – Harper's happy too. I know she's weird and moody, or whatever. But I'm glad you're friends. She's alone a lot, and she's been... better since you came to town."

The giggle couldn't be stopped. He just looked so adorable. When he blushed it made it worse. She wanted to hug him. "You're very sweet, Coop."

"Yeah," he said and cleared his throat. "Don't tell, okay?"

"What happens between these shelves stays here," she said and crossed her heart.

Now if she could just get some answers out of Harper.

CHAPTER EIGHTEEN

Harper

Harper crept into the bookstore, all her senses on high alert. A wolfish grin stole across her face. She didn't know why stealth mode was necessary, just that her body had dipped into an easy crouch on its own as she approached Early Bird Books. It seemed harmless enough. Ike did a similar sort of slow sneak attack when they played.

She glanced around at various stacks as she padded deeper into the store. Cooper had gone home already and had plenty to say about his new job and boss. Enough that she couldn't sit there any longer and listen to it. The mere mention of Emerson sparked her need to see her. She had to get her fix.

The sound of books scraping together, pages fluttering, and the rustle of fabric guided her through the store. She grinned and cocked her head, ears straining. Emerson's scent grew stronger.

She passed several open boxes and half-full shelves. Last time they'd spoken Emerson had gone on and on about working on the bookstore. All the things she wanted to do to change it up, put her own stamp on it, while somehow still leaving a touch of her grandparent's original vision. A charming local bookstore with a modern twist.

Whatever that meant.

It wasn't the type of thing she'd pay attention to normally, but something that didn't involve the bar, Holt, or her werewolfism was a nice change. She'd be more than happy to listen to Emerson ramble about genres, labels, and creating new inventory because it was different. It also made Emerson smile and wave her hands around as she spoke, all excited about books. Anything that made her that happy Harper was willing to listen to, just to see her smile.

Jesus H. God, I'm turning into a sap. She slowed, on the balls of her feet, prowling closer toward the humming Emerson. The melody didn't quite ring a bell, probably some insipid pop song. One of those that would get stuck in her head and make her wish for an ice pick to jab into her ears and make it stop.

She stood on the other side of the row, hemmed in by books. A wolf in a forest of shelved adventures. Through a gap in the texts she saw Emerson, in yet another dress despite the freezing temperatures outside. This time it was yellow, sunny and adorable, much like her personality. She had her nose wedged between the pages of the book in her hands, and smiled as she read.

She wore glasses, the thick black framed kind that had become trendy for some reason.

Since when did Emerson wear glasses? And why did she have to be so damn cute all the time? A small growl reverberated in her chest, but not in warning. The wolf pressed against her skin, but didn't feel dangerous.

It felt playful, excited, like someone had offered her a bacon-wrapped steak. If she'd been in her wolf body, she knew her tail would be wagging, tongue lolling out of her mouth. More like a happy-go-lucky Golden Retriever than a massive werewolf.

There goes my street cred, she thought with an eye roll. *Get a grip. You're embarrassing us.*

Emerson giggled and set the book aside. She ran her fingers over the title and then sighed.

The moment had arrived for a sneak attack. Harper grinned as she slipped around the shelf. Every muscle tensed in anticipation, and her heart did back flips in her chest. She inched closer and closer. The smell of coconuts with that hint of vanilla swamped her senses. She swallowed a whine and paused before she lost her cool and jumped on Emerson. Her mouth went dry, a grin stretched her lips far enough her cheeks ached. She stopped again, just behind Emerson's shoulder, and considered her next move. Tackling was out of the question.

She reached up and tapped Emerson's cardigan covered shoulder. "Emers."

Emerson jumped like she'd been poked with a cattle prod and let loose a squeal.

Harper jumped back, in case Emerson had armed herself with a thick tome. She didn't need another bruise on her stomach, even if it would disappear in a few minutes. "Don't throw the book at me, I come in peace!"

"Harper!" Emerson pressed the large book in her hands against her heart with a small laugh. "I didn't hear you come in."

"I'm sneaky," she said, jerking her thumb toward the door. "You need to put a door chime in. Or hang some bells on it. Never know what kind of things might be lurking around."

"I doubt a bear would be interested in a bookstore. What I should do is put a bell on you." She chewed her bottom lip for a moment, then turned to face the front door. "The door chime though, that's a good idea. I'll add it to my list of things to do. Which at this rate should be completed sometime next year."

Her shoulders slumped and Harper touched her elbow. "You'll get it finished before then, and it's going to be awesome. Might even convert some locals from TV to books."

"I hope so. It would break my heart if I had to sell the store. I'm surprised it's still open, to be honest. But I know I can turn it back around." She stroked the polished shelf and sighed. "This was their dream."

Harper licked her lips and swallowed another whine. "If you – I could, uh, install the chime for you."

The smile came back to Emerson's face. "You really are handy, aren't you? You don't have to, though. I appreciate the offer, but I can figure it out."

"I want to help," she said. Hell, if Emerson wanted the moon for better lighting, she'd do her damndest to rip it out of the sky. "I know you and the internet can get it done, but I'd like to do it for you. You've done so much already on your own. It all looks great, by the way, beautiful and classy." *Just like you.*

A blush stained Emerson's cheeks, and Harper knew she almost had her.

She flashed her best puppy dog eyes. "Let me help, Emers. Please? That's what friends are for."

Emerson liked that word. Harper could tell by the change in her posture, the book pulled tighter to her chest, and how her smile turned shy. "Alright. Because we're friends."

"Yup." She nodded, heart thudding heavy against her ribs. "Friends."

"Well, since you're feeling so friendly and helpful this evening... Could you maybe stay for a minute and help me with some of these?" She asked, waving the book at all the others on the shelving cart.

"Absolutely." She snatched one off the cart and wrinkled her nose at the title. "Othello?"

"Shakespeare, Harper, don't tell me you've never heard of him." Emerson clucked her tongue and rescued the book, stacking it with the other one already in her hands. Like Harper might try and eat it.

"I know who he is. I just didn't know people read that stuff outside of High School English classes."

"*Mon Dieu,*" she said, and put the books back on the cart with the utmost care. "O, beware, my lord, of jealousy! It is the green-eyed monster which doth mock the meat it feeds on."

"Did you just quote Shakespeare from memory?" Harper blinked and shook her head. "Doth what? Is that even English?"

"I can see I have my work cut out with you."

"Smarty pants. Say it in French."

Emerson smirked. "O, méfiez-vous, mon seigneur, de la jalousie! Il est le monstre aux yeux verts qui doth maquette de la viande, il se nourrit de."

"Look at that, I understood the same amount in a foreign language. Blah, blah, accent, blah." She grinned and earned herself a huff.

"Right. Should I explain alphabetical order, then?"

"Oooh, there're claws on the kitten," she said and arched an eyebrow. "Be nice to your friends, buddy."

"You started it, I was merely responding in a way I thought you might understand."

"Be still my beating heart."

"That's not Shakespeare," Emerson said with a smug smirk. She handed over a book. "William Mountfort, *Zelmane*, 1705. 'Ha! Hold my brain; be still my beating heart.'"

"Holy shit, forget running a bookstore, we need to get you on some sort of nerd game show. Easy money."

"Strangely, I think you and Shakespeare would have gotten along. He would have loved your wit."

"Yeah, I can see it now. Me and Will drinking beer, playing pool and talking trash." Her easy grin widened when Emerson pouted at being unable to reach the top shelf, even in her ridiculous shoes. "Hey, maybe while I'm out picking up your customer alarm system I should also get you a step stool? It's kind of hazardous to have you climbing shelves to reach things. Probably embarrassing too, if the owner of the store can't reach half the books."

A sharp elbow connected with her ribcage.

"Hey!"

"Keep it up with the short jokes and see where that lands you."

"I thought Munchkins were supposed to be sweet," she mumbled, rubbing the tender area. "What are you going to do, not welcome me to Munchkin Land? You're in the Lullaby League, right? Or was it the Lollipop Guild?"

"Ugh, Harper. There are no words for you." Emerson rolled her eyes and laughed. "You know the Wizard of Oz is also a book, yes? A series, in fact."

"Is there anything you don't know?" She froze, noticing how close they'd become. The paralysis didn't return, but her brain went numb. Her mouth hung open partway, the scent of coconut so strong she could taste it in every shallow breath. She swallowed and licked her lips, wondering what

PURE OF HEART

Emerson was thinking. She also seemed to be stunned stupid, like they'd both run into a bug-zapper.

"A ladder would probably work better," Emerson said, clearing her throat, breaking their staring contest. "Instead of the stool."

"Remind me later, we should watch The Mummy with Rachel Weisz before I get you a ladder," she replied, fighting down a ferocious blush.

"That sounds adventurous." Emerson nodded and snatched another book from the cart. "I guess for now you're going to have to do."

"I'll do? I'll do for what?"

"A ladder. Or rather a taller person to put these up for me until I get a ladder."

"Hold on a second, I'll just do? Are you saying you'd prefer a ladder over me?"

"Ladders don't tease."

"Yeah, but they're lousy conversationalists in general."

"Just... put this one up there, please?"

She stood up on her toes and slid the book into place. "Can I ask you something?"

"May I."

"May you what?"

"No." Emerson laughed and brushed her hand down Harper's arm, leaving tingles in its wake. "No, I meant it's 'may I ask you something,' not can you. I know you're capable of asking. You meant to ask for permission."

"Oh my God," she said and groaned. "May I ask you something, your highness?"

"Yes, you may. You may also call me Emerson, I don't think we need to be so formal here."

The most adorable, mischievous look crossed her face, and Harper forgot to breathe. *How do I do that thing... where I... air?*

"Are you alright?"

"Peachy," she said with a wheezy breath. *Oh yeah, that's how you air.* "Um, so, I was wondering about your family."

Emerson's spine locked straight, her smile shook at the corner. "Oh?"

And that's why I wanted to ask. The wolf stirred from its content doze. She narrowed her eyes and watched closely for any other sign of distress. One whiff of any sort of abuse and she'd be on a plane to California to whoop some ass. "You don't talk about you much. Or about your family."

"That's funny," she said while managing to make it sound like the least funny thing in the world. "Cooper said the same thing earlier."

"It's a Sullivan thing, we're a perceptive bunch of lunatics." *Also protective and loyal, like any good dog.* "Is it... bad?"

"No." Emerson fumbled a book, caught it and sighed. "No, not at all, if anything my brother and I were spoiled, privileged. I think most people expect us to be awful brats."

"Is he older?"

"Barely," she said. "We're twins."

"Uh-huh." That explained the nearly identical note in their scents. "So how come you never talk about your family?"

"Harper, it's not like we've spent hours talking about... everything."

"We're talking now."

She sighed again. "We are. What do you want to know?"

All of it. "How come you got so uncomfortable when I asked about your dad?"

"I don't know." She frowned and tapped her fingers against the spines of a few books. "It's not something we usually talk about. At home everyone is always bragging about who does what and whose family is worth more. Oscar and I find it rude, and so we don't... it's just not something we talk about."

Some of the pressure eased out of her shoulders. She'd been expecting some dirty secret that would make her want to go on a bloody rampage for justice. "So you and your dad have a good relationship?"

"He's gone a lot, for filming," she said with a one shouldered shrug. "But yes, we have a very good relationship, I would say."

"And your mom? What does she do?"

Another pause, longer this time. "The official line is my mother is a photographer."

"And the unofficial one?" *In other words, the actual truth.* She raised an eyebrow.

"She takes care of the house in California, or stays with Daddy in Vancouver. Oscar and I were her job, but now that we've both moved out I'm not sure what she'll do." Emerson shook her head and pushed her glasses back up her nose. "She was a photographer, that's how she met Daddy. But she stopped after they got married and we came along."

There was something else, something underneath. She shuffled closer, acting like she wanted to get another book. "Huh. Think she'll go back to photography now?"

"I hope so." Emerson frowned and thumbed through a few pages. "Honestly, I'm not sure she wanted to be a mother, or if it was something she felt like she had to do. She never seemed very happy. Maybe taking pictures again would fix that."

She pictured a bored mother, running her kids around like employees instead of children, and swallowed the hot lump that formed in her throat. "That doesn't sound like it was all that fun for you."

"Oh, no, like I said we never... we had a wonderful childhood. Glamorous, even. And we're twins, so we always had each other." She winced and snapped the book shut. "Our parents were distant, but they love us."

After that the conversation died, Emerson fidgeted for a moment and then went right back to shelving books, forehead pinched and lips pursed. Harper stole side glances whenever she could, a frown of her own dragging down both her mouth and her mood.

There was something else, she knew it. Maybe not as unpleasant as her vivid imagination conjured, but not a bed of roses either. It sounded more like neglect than anything else. An absent father and a drill sergeant mother.

Her fists clenched around the edges of some fancy hardcover. "Hey."

Blue eyes darted up to her face, larger than ever behind the lenses of those geeky glasses.

"I'm sorry, I didn't mean to make you uncomfortable. I don't like talking about my family either. I should know better than to be so nosey."

"It's alright. No harm done." She bit the corner of her lip and looked down at her shoes. "I should…"

Nothing, the sentence went unfinished. Harper blew her bangs out of her eye and dipped her head to reestablish eye contact. "Hmm?"

Emerson sighed and handed her another book after a long couple of seconds of breathing and avoidance. "Could you put this on the top shelf for me? Please?"

Disappointed, but determined not to upset her any further, she took the book and smiled. "Sure thing."

She raised up on her toes again, placed the book, and dropped back down. Only then she suddenly realized one of them had closed the respectable gap between them. Emerson was much, much closer than she remembered. Startled, she stumbled, tripping over her own feet as she hurried to regain her personal bubble boundary. Emerson reached out, caught her by the waist to steady her, and destroyed Harper's plan.

Her knees wobbled, chest constricted, and mouth flooded. She gasped for a breath, and it was laced with Emerson, who was now pressed against her side, looking up at her with a concerned expression. Her head spun and she had to close her eyes for a moment and order herself not to pass out.

But the smell. That sweet, beautiful smell. It was so intoxicating she didn't realize she'd moved again until it was too late. She wasn't moving away from Emerson to restore her equilibrium, she was moving closer. Not something new friends should do, or even old friends.

The wolf asserted itself with little effort, taking advantage of her stupor. She flailed a hand, shocked it still moved, and latched onto the shelf. It did little to ground her and didn't stop her body from continuing forward.

She'd been possessed. The hand not desperately clinging to the bookshelf slid around Emerson's trim waist and tugged. A hug. A hug she could deal with, not that bad, not crossing too many boundaries. But still, that smell, and if her head got any lighter it would float away.

Emerson's breath hitched, and that didn't really help.

Her nose slid against silky strands of blonde hair and she lost the will to fight anymore. She'd found Heaven. So warm, soft. A hand landed on her hip, fingers squeezed gently.

Her nose slid along the warm skin of Emerson's cheek, and if she'd thought Emerson's hair was Heaven, she'd been wrong. She could smell how alive Emerson was, felt the heat of her blush. She heard her small squeak over the pounding of her heartbeat when she pressed her face against the side of Emerson's neck.

As much as she'd wanted to fight the imprint, she couldn't deny it felt right. Like she was meant to be here, this was home. The wolf was calm, almost lazy, not fighting her anymore, just as long as she stayed where she was. As long as she kept nuzzling.

Nuzzling. Nose deep in Emerson's neck, almost purring.

She jerked back, tripped over a box of books and crashed into the wall. Behind Emerson, leaning casually against the bookshelf, Ben raised an eyebrow at her.

"I'm sorry," she said, voice cracking. "Emerson, I'm sorry."

Emerson seemed to be in a trance of some sort, swaying in the aisle.

She kept breathing through her mouth, hoping to avoid a repeat performance. Her eyes stung, and her face hurt from the blush that burned her cheeks, throat, and chest. Even her ears had turned red.

She'd ruined everything.

"Wait, Harper, hold on a — It was just a hug, it's fine, I don't — " Emerson snagged her hand and reeled her back. Harper dug her heels in, shaking her head. Then Emerson stopped tugging and her breath hiccupped. "Harper, your hand."

Her hand? Her hand! The scratches from the cat. She'd let Emerson put Band-Aids on them, to hide the fast healing, but she had peeled them off as soon as she got home without thinking. They weren't necessary and she hadn't thought about anyone noticing.

"Your hand," Emerson said again, shaking her head and running her fingers over the back. Right where the scratches had been. "There aren't even any scabs!"

"I have to go," she all but shouted, scrambling backwards. She needed a clear mind, had to get away.

"Harper, wait!"

Her traitorous feet obeyed. She clutched at the shelf beside her with one hand, the other pressed against her nose.

"Please," Emerson said, near whispered. "Harper, it's – we can – can we talk about it?"

PURE OF HEART

They had nothing to talk about. A monster lived in Harper and it wanted to nuzzle Emerson's neck. What could go wrong with that topic?

Or the fact Harper knew it was more than that.

"Harper."

"Nothing to talk about." Harper turned just enough and Emerson flinched away. "I – I sprayed it with one of those skin-tone Band-Aid things. That's all. I really have to go now."

She deflated for a second, then drew herself up, shoulders pulling back, chin lifting. "I'll wait for you to be ready then."

Harper ran from the bookstore like a puppy frightened by the vacuum. It was mortifying, but the first lungful of cold air helped soothe the sting. Her legs were aching to run, so she turned toward home and took off.

CHAPTER NINETEEN

Emerson

It wasn't the light. Emerson shook with the weight of the revelation. She couldn't deny it. Not anymore. It wasn't the light. Harper's eyes burned gold with the same intensity as the wolf's. The wolf that haunted her dreams, the same one she kept looking for in every shadow.

"It's not possible," she said, holding on to a shelf. "It's not, it's not."

But it was, somehow it was. When Harper had pulled back, right before she'd jumped away, she'd seen it. They'd been far too close for her not to notice.

The evidence piled up in her mind as she staggered through the shelves. Rough palms, gold eyes, the animalistic behavior. How she twitched, and changed the subject or acted uncomfortable when Emerson compared her to wild beasts. The way the other animals responded to her presence. Her cagey behavior. The wolf.

What had just happened? She'd been nuzzling, sniffing. Like a dog. Her brain still ran sluggishly, in need of a reboot after that close encounter with Harper. It had started out as a hug, she'd thought. A warm surprise, one she hadn't minded in the slightest. Being that close to Harper, held like that by one strong arm and pressed up against a long lean torso had blown her mind. She'd never understood that expression, because it seemed dramatic, even for her tastes. Now she understood and could appreciate it. Every thought had stopped, all she could do was feel, and it was glorious. Her body had hummed with a new and thrilling current at the full contact. Harper held on to her like she was the most precious thing in the world, and then the nuzzling started. She'd been snuggled with before, but it always seemed like a precursor to sex. This was different and amazing. She didn't want it to stop, and then Harper had jerked away, like she'd been burned. The loss was indescribable. A hole had opened in her chest.

It wasn't normal. None of it. She had no rational explanation for any of it.

"I have lost my mind. It's happened. I belong in a psych ward." She grabbed onto her desk, like she needed it to stay standing. Maybe she did, her whole body shook. She pulled her keyboard close, closed her eyes and tapped a single word into the catalogue search.

Werewolf.

"God help me, I've become Bella Swan."

***

Faoladh. The name repeated in her head. Over and over and over. Clear and sharp. It had burned itself into her retinas the moment she first read it on her laptop. She'd said it out loud, several times, as though she needed to further cement it.

The Irish version of the werewolf legend. Not a ferocious man-eating beast, cursed to turn into a monster under the light of the full moon. According to legend the Faoladh was a hero. Someone who protected lost children and travelers, guarded villages and towns, family, with the tenacity and loyalty of a pack of German Shepherds.

It was Harper. Emerson knew it in her bones. Her friend was a Faoladh. The black wolf she'd seen outside the lodge was Harper, and she needed to prove it to keep her sanity.

She shook her head and set her hands on her hips, surveyed her attire for the evening laid out on her bed. Black leggings, black long sleeved shirt and jacket. A black beanie to tuck her hair into. The cheapest outfit she'd ever picked up, and the first time she'd ever been in a super store. It would be her first time breaking into someone's house too.

Her doorbell rang. With a frown, she glanced at the clock and checked her bedroom window. The sun had yet to set. Harper had begged off on movie night, so it couldn't be her.

"Oscar, if you ignored me and flew up here anyway, I swear there will be yelling." She shook her head and went down the stairs. Mr. Darcy darted between her legs, going up the stairs instead of down. "Okay, not Oscar."

She twisted the hem of her sweater as she approached the door. The one other possibility made her stomach flip over, and not in a pleasant way. She still wasn't ready for that conversation yet.

Up on her tiptoes, she spied through the peephole and sighed. Holt stood there, as she suspected. With flowers in his hand.

"Holt, I want to be friends with you. You're a nice guy, but I'm not in a place here where I'm ready to date anyone," she said under her breath. Cringing, she rubbed at her neck. He would not take it well, and she didn't want to hurt his feelings. Or tell him on her doorstep. "Trouble. This is

PURE OF HEART

trouble. *Merde*, Oscar was right."

She didn't think he'd meant possible werewolves when he said it, but he had nailed the potential trouble with Holt and Harper. Except more than her usual trouble was on the way, involving a werewolf and a hunter.

"How is this my life?" An idea of how to get him to leave sooner rather than later came to mind. One that wouldn't require her giving him the 'just friends' speech. She slumped out of her perfect posture, mussed her hair, and tried to look as small as possible.

Holt grinned at her when she opened the door and held out his bouquet. "Surprise!"

"Holt," she said and faked a small cough. "How... lovely. Thank you for the flowers."

His grin faded. "Are you sick?"

"I have caught a bit of a cold," she lied and hid a wince behind another pathetic cough.

"Well that sucks. Want me to make you some soup or something?"

I want you to go away so I can execute my mission. She offered him a weak smile. "No, thank you. That's very sweet. I'm alright, I had some soup earlier and have lots of tea."

"We could watch a movie or something? I don't want you to be all alone and sick, that's the worst." He shuffled his feet and blasted her with a pout.

"As kind an offer as that is, I'm going to go to bed." At his interested look she hastened to add, "Alone. I'm sorry, thank you for coming by. I promise we'll talk later."

"When you're feeling better?"

"Yes, when I'm feeling better."

"Okay. Um, I'll see you later then. Text me if you get bored or want some company." He waved, then shoved his hands into his pockets and tromped off her porch. She watched him go, made sure he left, and then slammed the door.

"*Fantastique*, could this night get any more messed up?"

Oh yes, of course it could. She was going to find the neighborhood werewolf's den.

***

She looked up and shivered. Above her the moon hung fat in a field of stars. It offered plenty of light for her to sneak around. The quote-unquote experts all agreed. A werewolf would turn under the light of the full moon. It also served as a reminder of her insanity now that she had a head full of werewolf facts. Things about a mythical creature that were too fantastical to be true. She wouldn't normally think of website authors as experts of any kind either.

Grady's battered truck sat in the driveway. She'd been hiding in the bushes long enough to see him stomp into the house. Cooper had left soon after, his backpack slung over his shoulder.

And Harper was in there, somewhere.

Since their incident at the bookstore, she'd disappeared. Poof. Most likely from embarrassment. But it wasn't that particular night she wanted answers for. An explanation was due for all of it, the whole picture.

She pulled her beanie further down on her head, over the tips of her ears. The cheap fabric kept riding up and it itched. Nothing she'd ever owned had itched, yet another reason to burn it when she finished using it.

Mindful of her footing and wary of creaky boards, she slipped up the porch steps. She tried the knob quietly, and discovered the front door was unlocked. She chewed on her bottom lip after pushing it open a crack. Moonlight spilled across the entryway and cast shadows down the long hallway.

She jumped and almost screamed when something crashed and clattered. The ice-maker kicking on.

"Get a grip. What would Sherlock do?" She rolled her eyes at her thought, and opened the door wide enough to slip inside. "Probably not go into a dark house looking for a werewolf."

Upstairs she heard the quiet drone of a TV. Grady, hopefully asleep in his room or office with some sort of sports game on. After a momentary pause, she decided not to lock the door behind her. It would make things easier if she needed to make a quick escape. From angry human Harper or angry... not-human Harper. Or Grady, who would probably not be thrilled to find her in his home. Either way, she had an out. Not her greatest plan, but it would have to do.

She set her shoulders back and crept down the hall on her tiptoes. She hadn't forgotten Harper's reaction to the basement. Even if there wasn't a werewolf down there, she'd been hiding something. Harper wouldn't have reacted like that because of spiders, or even boxes full of embarrassing baby pictures, if any had survived the fire. Hopefully they weren't hiding a messy basement and nothing more. That would be disappointing.

The door loomed in front of her. While she understood it was a door, looking at it in the dark, polished white surface glinting at her, it made her feel small. She'd adjusted to being short, but this was different. She felt vulnerable and tiny before something that could be shielding an amazing secret.

She never did like feeling that way. It helped her find enough courage to grip the doorknob. Still, she counted to three before she twisted and pushed. Dank air blew into her face. She swallowed hard and looked down the stairwell. The natural light didn't go far past the first landing. From this point, if she went in, she went in the dark.

It was enough of a blow to her fake bravado that she almost talked herself out of the whole thing. "Stupide, Emerson. *C'est tellement stupide.*"

PURE OF HEART

A clattering noise bounced off the walls down below, follow by a pained sound. A human sound. She had a feeling it wasn't a thief.

"Harper?"

No response.

She sucked in a deep breath, wincing at the damp taste. "Harper, if you're down there, would you just tell me? Please? I'm sorry for coming in uninvited, but I thought you might be sick." She tried for a laugh but it came out strange. Like the nervous tittering she imagined characters in books having. "Um, I thought I'd keep you company?"

She cocked her head, straining her ears for even the faintest sound.

Another whimper, so weak she almost didn't hear it.

It hadn't occurred to her that something else might be going on. She'd jumped for the least plausible explanation, after all.

What if she's hurt?

"Harper? Are you okay? I'm coming down."

"Don't!"

Goosebumps broke out all over her body, and she froze on the stairs. She knew Harper's voice, and it was her down there all right. But the gravel in it, the thick, guttural tone was different. She always had a rumble of a voice, but this sounded sickly. "Are you hurt?"

"No. I'm... cleaning the basement. Go away."

"You're cleaning the basement in the dark?" She continued down the creaking steps with caution. Her fingers trailed along the walls, to help her keep from cartwheeling to her death. "You don't sound okay."

"Emerson, please. Please go away."

The more she spoke, the more feeble she sounded. Maybe she'd tripped herself, and was too embarrassed to say so. "Where's the light switch?"

Harper groaned.

She stumbled when she hit the bottom of the stairs. "Where are you?"

"You have to leave."

Turning in the direction of the voice, she shuffled toward it. Her toes bumped against boxes. Things she couldn't identify toppled over, and she felt more than ridiculous walking around with her hands out in front of her. "No. I'm not leaving until you tell me what's going on." She crashed into something that wobbled and fell. Judging from the metal clanging against the floor, she guessed a box of silverware. "*Merde.*"

"I can't, I can't tell you."

"Oh yes you can." She fumbled around some more, like a drunk mummy, until she remembered... Cell phone. Exasperated, she dug the device out of her pocket and turned on the flashlight. The beam wasn't wide and it didn't go far.

It went far enough.

A cage took up one corner in the basement. The box she'd knocked over? Not silverware. Chains. Her eyes widened as she swept the light around. The thin beam wavered as her hand shook. "Oh my God."

She turned back to the cage, the hair on her arms and neck standing on end. Her lips and chin trembled, she blinked and wiped her clammy hands one at a time on her leggings, switching the phone from one to the other. This was it. "Harper?"

The light bounced off of Harper's eyes, she shrank away from it with a rasping growl. She'd been thinner with dark circles under her eyes the last time they'd seen each other. Now she looked worse, drenched in sweat, even paler than usual.

And she was sitting on a concrete floor in a cage in her uncle's basement.

"Emerson, please get out of here."

All thoughts of werewolves flew right out of her head. "*Fils de pute!*" She rushed toward the cage, not caring that she knocked over more things in her way. "Harper, where's the light switch? I need more – I have to – why are you in a cage?"

Harper recoiled when their hands made contact. She backed away against the wall on top of a flimsy mattress, out of reach. The blanket she had draped over herself slipped, revealing a bare and bruised shoulder.

"Did Grady do this? Is this because of his wife? Does he blame you for – forget it. I'm calling the sheriff." She shook her head. "I'm so stupid. I came up with this idea you were a werewolf, and that was why you – Stupid, stupid, Emerson. Hold on, okay? I'll get you out of there."

The smile that crossed Harper's face was more of a wince. It quickly fell away as she tucked her knees to her chest and groaned. "Don't call anyone. You can't. Just leave me. It's not safe and I don't want you to see this."

"If you think I'm leaving you in a basement in a cage, you have lost your mind." She knelt down and grasped a bar with her free hand. "Where's the key? I'm getting you out of there and someplace safe. And I am calling the police. He can't do this to you."

"Go!" Harper roared.

Gold eyes glowed in the shallow light, and teeth that didn't belong in a human mouth glistened.

She'd had it right the first time. The implausible, impossible explanation. "You – you're a –"

"Monster. I'm the monster here, not Grady." Harper squeezed her eyes shut and fisted her hair on either side of her head. "I can't stop it anymore. Get out!"

But Emerson couldn't move, her body locked up as Harper doubled over. She was living in her own horror movie and she couldn't look away. Her eyes refused to close.

One of Harper's hands struck out, slapping against the concrete.

PURE OF HEART

She heard grinding sounds, cracks and pops.

Bones, she heard Harper's bones breaking.

The hand on the floor contorted. Knuckles snapped and fingers twisted in on themselves. Then they shrank back into the palm as fingernails turned black and elongated into claws. Black fur sprouted in a wave, moving up her arm.

Harper stared at her with wide, gold eyes. She grimaced and groaned again, showing off that mouthful of pointed teeth. Her nose, jaw, lips pushed outwards with a horrible creaking noise. A wolf snout took shape. More bones crunched and reformed. Her ears crawled up to the top of her head and grew upwards, became pointy. All of her hair sucked back into her scalp.

Emerson still couldn't move, or even scream. Not even when the transformation slowed, and for several seconds Harper sat with a wolf's head on her human shoulders.

Then Harper fell over, front paws slashing at the air and scratching against the floor. Ribs cracked one by one, her shoulders dislocated. Sloshing, slurping sounds added to the bones snapping and crunching. The fur swept down, covering every inch of skin still exposed. Her knees reversed direction with two snaps. Pads burst out on the bottom of Harper's feet, turned dark and rough.

The wolf, Harper, thrashed and panted for several unbearable seconds. Her tail grew, her limbs shrank, and the gurgles petered out. Then she was still, lying on her side with her eyes closed.

"Harper?" Emerson whispered. She shook her head, closed her eyes and opened them again. Harper was still there, still a wolf. The wolf from the month before.

Harper shuddered, her claws gripped at the floor. She rolled and then staggered to her feet. Her head tilted back and she howled, long, loud, and low.

Then she turned and stared, ears flicking back and forth.

That was Harper. Harper was in there, behind those gold eyes. Under all that fur and muscle and heavy bone. She'd seen it.

A werewolf. Harper was a werewolf.

She might as well have stuck her fingers in a light socket. Shocked and panicked, she stumbled and tried to back away. Her feet stirred up the chains she'd dumped earlier. The scream that had been threatening the entire time Harper had changed broke free as she tripped, caught in the mangled mass of heavy chain. She fell back, unable to see anything, and heard her head connect with the floor.

CHAPTER TWENTY

Someone screamed.
Emerson jerked, flailed, and struck something. She realized the scream had come from her. Instead of stopping, she screamed again, louder, and with her eyes clenched shut threw her hand out again. She made contact and felt cloth.

"Emerson!"

A man's voice. Not Holt, too deep for Holt. She opened one eye and Grady glared back at her. "Mr. Sullivan?"

"What in the hell are you doing in my house?" he bellowed.

She cringed away from him, and put a hand to the back of her head. A nice lump had formed, hot to the touch. "I – I –"

"You – you what?" His eyes bulged. "You broke into my house!"

Memory flooded back. With it came guilt, because she *had* broken into his house. Horror came too, because she knew what was probably still in the basement. Then anger, swift and fiery, stormed in to wipe out the other emotions.

"I did because I was worried about Harper, and I was right to be!" She sat up too fast and the room spun. "You have her in a cage!"

The red flush in his face drained, leaving him pale and wide-eyed. He leaned down and grabbed her shoulders. "You listen to me –"

"No. I don't have to," she said and shoved him away. "Why is she in a cage? Looking like death, alone, in the dark. That's your niece!"

"You think I don't know that?" He whipped the pageboy cap off his head and tossed it at the wall. "Do you have any idea what you've done?"

"Do you?" She stood up and shaky legs and headed back toward the hall. The shock had worn off. She couldn't leave Harper down there like that. "No wonder she's always hiding from people. You've made her think she's some kind of monster."

"She's a werewolf!" Grady caught her wrist and tugged her back. "She's dangerous."

"No she's not, I've seen her. Let go of me." She twisted in his grasp and leaned backwards.

"You don't know anything about it," he yanked harder, pulling her into the living room. She fought him, but he held on, shook her, and pushed her, none to gently, onto the couch.

"Don't talk to me like –"

"Shut up," he said, pointing a finger. "Stop. You sneak into my house, you stick your nose into things that aren't your business, and you want to lecture me?" He sighed through his nose, like an enraged bull, and ran a hand through his hair. "How am I supposed to clean up this mess?"

"Faoladh," she whispered and glared at him through teary eyes.

He froze and then dropped his hand. "What did you say?"

"Faoladh," she repeated with more strength. "You're Irish. Harper's Irish. The Faoladh, the Irish werewolf, is not a monster, but a protector."

"Fway-luh," he said and then barked a sarcastic laugh. "We pronounce it fway-luh. Where did you hear that?"

She huffed and wiped at her eyes. "Harper – Harper's been acting weird, I had a suspicion. I read up on werewolves. Which is a very silly thing to say out loud."

A muffled howl drifted down the hall. They both turned.

"Good soundproofing," she said with a sniffle. He handed her a tissue box and then flopped next to her.

"It was Harper's idea," he said. "So was the cage."

"Why?"

He swallowed and leaned forward, elbows on his knees. "There's more going on here than I should explain. But you know the big part now and – I can't see any other way." He turned to her and smiled. Sort of. "Everything happens for a reason, I guess."

"For what it's worth, I'm sorry for breaking into your house." She pulled her beanie off and blew a strand of hair out of her sticky face. "I'm not sorry for checking on Harper, but I'm sorry about this."

"I'm sorry for yelling at you. This is really dangerous, Miss Grey. For all of us."

"Emerson," she said. "I think we're past formalities."

He nodded and then pointed up at a picture above the fireplace. "My parents were a mixed couple. My old man was a wolf, my mother wasn't. They had my sister, Cassidy, and she inherited the wolf gene. Then me, and I didn't. Cassidy met John Cahill, another wolf of Irish blood. They had Harper." He scrubbed at his forehead and glanced at her. "They died before Harper started the change. She doesn't know how to control it."

She thought of the last time she'd seen Harper as the wolf. Docile, almost playful, she hadn't seemed dangerous at all.

"She's had… problems. In the past," he said, as though reading her mind. "She begged me to lock her up. Which doesn't always work. She's strong and smart. AJ found out by accident, so now if Harper breaks out, we go get her and bring her back."

Problems. She sucked in a big breath and stared at the side of his bowed head. "Your wife? Did Harper…"

"No, no. Naomi had an aneurysm. Harper didn't have anything to do with her death."

She didn't mention Cooper had said the same thing. He probably wouldn't appreciate that she'd brought the subject up to his teenage son. Yet she knew something else was there. She had a feeling problems didn't translate to Harper-wolf digging through the trash. "I want to see her."

"She wouldn't want you down there," he said, not unkindly. "But if you want to wait here, I can get some coffee going."

"You stay up all night when she's, uh, like this?"

He nodded. "Not just because she could break out. I don't want her to – I feel like I'm leaving her alone. Even if I'm not in the room with her, I can't just abandon her like that."

"How does she break out?" she asked, hoping to steer the conversation into less treacherous waters. To her relief he smiled and it was a bit more genuine. He tugged at his beard and tilted his head toward the kitchen.

"Let me get the coffee started, I'll tell you all about it. Maybe you can help me figure out a better place for her to stay."

***

The howling never died down. All through the long night Harper kept it up. Never a constant. She'd howl and then pause, on occasion for over an hour. Emerson flinched every time she heard it. Though she'd never heard a wolf howl before in her life, she thought it sounded sadder than it should.

She and Grady stayed up, sitting side by side on the couch in their vigil. The coffee was burnt and really not her thing, but she drank it anyway. It seemed to make Grady happy. He relaxed after that first cup, and she found despite his grumble he wasn't all that bad. At least he could hold a conversation.

"The sun's about to come up," he said during a lull.

Blinking the need for sleep away, she glanced at her watch and then peered out the nearest window. "Is it?"

The old Grandfather clock in the corner of the room started to chime. In the basement Harper howled yet again. This time she didn't hold it as long and it sounded more distant.

"Give it thirty minutes. I'll go get her, but you may want to wait a bit before you try talking to her," he said. "She'll be sleepy, so I don't know if she'll say much. If she even wakes up."

She stiffened and shot him a look. "What do you mean if?"

"Not like that. I mean she sleeps pretty hard the day after. It takes a lot out of her."

"Oh." She sagged back against the couch and rubbed the bridge of her nose. "Of course. I'm sorry, I shouldn't have assumed. Been awhile since I pulled an all-nighter." He squinted and she shrugged. "College. Midterms are awful."

"You want another cup?"

The idea of any more coffee made her stomach turn. "No, thank you, I think I've met my caffeine quota for the month."

He shook his head and smiled. "I see why the two of you get along so well. You mind if I turn on the news?"

"So the weatherman can tell us it's going to snow more?"

"Exactly."

She shrugged. "Sure. It's always good to be informed of things you already know."

The TV, a modern flat screen out of place with the rest of the rustic interior, didn't provide much of a distraction. She kept listening for sounds from Harper to rise over the drone of the news anchors, but nothing did. The house had gone almost eerily still. Even Grady seemed afraid to make too much noise. He kept the volume on the TV low.

He had the routine down. She'd almost fallen asleep when he stood up and stretched, full on, as though preparing for a grueling session at the gym. She arched an eyebrow and cracked a grin when he blushed.

"I know she doesn't look it, but that girl is heavy as a log."

"Wait, you're going to carry her out of there?"

"To be honest, we usually leave her in there to avoid getting knocked around," he said, scratching the back of his head. "But I don't think she'd be thrilled if I let you back down there."

"And how mad is she going to be in general?" She grimaced at the thought. Harper had not been pleased at all the night before. Somehow she doubted that would go away easily.

"With the full moon hangover? You might want to prepare yourself."

She couldn't help it, she giggled. Giggled. She'd officially been awake too long. "You call it a full moon hangover?"

"You'll see," he said before stretching one more time. "Alright. I'll come get you when I get her more or less settled. Maybe she'll be nicer if she's in her room."

Her curiosity had already gotten her in more than a little trouble, but she followed him anyway. Not all the way to the basement. She waited in the living room with her head peeking around the corner.

His shoes clomped down the stairs and she winced with each footfall. That would not help any sort of hangover. She chewed on her lip and waited as silence fell once again. The clock ticked behind her, letting her know every second that passed.

The stairs creaked, and she wanted to hold her breath. Grady eased out of the basement, Harper wrapped in the blanket and limp in his arms.

She blushed when he smiled at her, like he'd known she'd be there. "She's okay. Really out of it, but okay." He did an odd sort of jumping wiggle thing to adjust his sleeping burden. Harper's head settled in place against his shoulder. Emerson thought she saw a sliver of gold under heavy eyelids.

Not adorable. She's not adorable, Emerson. You're angry, very angry about all of this. Not to mention confused, frightened, in shock, and going insane. Besides, she'd had fur and pointy teeth not more than an hour ago.

Grady stopped at the base of the stairs and sighed. "If anyone asks, I'm very strong and manly and didn't make a single sound carrying her up these damn things."

"I promise I will never tell anyone your werewolf niece is so heavy you threw your back out carrying her upstairs."

"My God, there're two of them," he said and grunted as he took the first step.

***

On the other side of the door she heard Harper, slurring her words as she talked with Grady. Nonsensical babble, for the most part, interspersed with rough giggles.

"You're tucking me in like I'm a kid. Am I a kid?"

"You're high as a cloud, that's what."

Another giggle. Shivers slithered down her spine at the sound.

"I'm in a cloud! Do I get a bedtime story too? Does it end in happily ever after? I like those ones."

"You really stepped in it this time, Harp."

"I'm not stepping, I'm laying. Or lying. No, that's not right. What am I doing?"

Grady sighed, loud enough for her to hear, and stepped out of the bedroom shaking his head. "She is pretty out of it. You should come back later."

"Leave? Now?" Emerson crossed her arms and fixed him with a glare. "After what I saw last night? I don't think so. I can't leave without some answers. If you're not going to give them to me, Harper will. I think I've earned that."

"Earned?" He scoffed and matched her glare with one of his own. "Little girl, you've earned her wrath is what you've earned. She's going to be pissed. I'm not comfortable letting you in there with her like this. She's not in any state of mind to answer anything."

"I'm not going anywhere," she said and raised her chin. "The questions aren't going either. She's going to be mad, and I would be willing to bet my favorite pair of Prada's she'll run for the mountain if I wait. Then I'll be right back here, pestering you."

"Sleep is like a time machine!" Harper interrupted from the bedroom with a snicker. "I'm a genius!"

He raised an eyebrow and jerked his thumb at the open door. "You think that's going to answer your questions?"

"Look, I'm not going to run into town and announce that Harper's a werewolf. Nobody would believe me anyway. I want to talk to her before she's furious. This is the only chance I've got."

"It's not. She'll –" he wiped at his mouth and looked to the ceiling. "It's not your only chance."

"I'm not going to hurt her. I swear," she said, touching his elbow. "I couldn't. I'm in this now, and I can help. You said you have to go to work. I can stay here with her, make sure she's alright. I'm an ally now. She needs someone here doesn't she, while she's still… what did you call it?"

"Full moon high," he said with a groan. "This is such a bad idea. She'll remember everything. How does that factor into this plan of yours? She's not going to be happy with either of us."

"We're all adults." Though she used the term loosely for Harper. "She tends to be unhappy anyway, from what I've gathered. Certainly she wasn't thrilled last night. At least this way I'll be better prepared, less frustrated, when she stomps over to yell at me."

He snorted. "There is no way to be prepared for a Harper meltdown."

"I'll manage. Don't you need to go open the bar? Paperwork to do?"

"I'm being dismissed from my own house," he mumbled, but nodded and eased past her. "I'll be out in ten minutes. Try to keep her from jumping out the window or running into the street."

Her eyes widened. "That's happened before?"

"No, but she's Harper."

She watched him cross the hall and go into another bedroom. The door closed with a soft snick, and she straightened up, set her shoulders. "Into the wolf's den."

Harper, bundled up in a mass of blankets, greeted her with a lazy grin. "Hi."

Not the reaction she'd been expecting. She smoothed the front of her sweatshirt and tried to organize her thoughts. "Hello, Harper."

"You're pretty."

"Thank you." She inched closer to the bed and sat down in the chair beside it. Gold eyes shimmered over at her with disconcerting focus.

"Are you okay?"

"I should be asking you that," she said and cleared her throat. Head tilted to the side, she leaned in. "Do you remember last night?"

Harped nodded like her head had gained a few thousand pounds. "You saw the wolf. Me."

"I did, yes. But that wasn't the first time, was it?"

"Nope. I got out, went to see you."

"Why? Why me?"

" 'Cause of the coconuts," she whispered and winked sloppily.

"Coconuts?"

"Yup."

"Well that clears that right up," she grumbled.

"I heard that!" She pointed at her ears. "Wolf ears."

"What about the coconuts, Harper? What does that mean?"

"Lime in the coconut?" She started humming, feet waving back and forth under the blankets.

"This cute thing is not fair."

"I'm cute?" She closed her eyes and hummed some more. "Best day ever. Except I'm sleepy, and my head hurts. But it's all good. I'm cute."

"*Mon dieu*, Harper." She rolled her eyes and fought the smile twitching up her lips. An absurd buzzing filled her head, along with the return of the flutters in her stomach. "I don't understand this."

"Did you know I'm super strong? And fast! Like an X-Men, man, woman? Thing."

"You're not a thing," she said, frowning. "How does it work?"

"X-Men are mutants."

"No, not the – the wolf, I meant. How does that work? It's not just during the full moon. Is it always there? When you're human?"

"Sometimes we want different things." She reached out and tangled two fingers in Emerson's hair. "Sometimes she breaks free. When I'm mad or sad or afraid. Makes my eyes look scary."

Her scalp tingled. Heat suffused her face, traveled down her neck and chest. "This is getting ridiculous. Um, does it hurt? The transformation?"

"Nope. Waking up does. I'm all alone and it makes me sad."

Tears burned her eyes remembering the wolf's, Harper's, sad cries through the night. Her chin quivered. She grabbed Harper's hand and pulled it away from her hair, but didn't release the spasming fingers. "Do you stay alone on purpose?"

Harper's eyelids fell to half-mast. "It's not safe."

"Why?"

"I'm a monster. Killed Ben. I'm dangerous."

"You're not dangerous, you're like a kitten."

"People leave me. You should too. It's not safe."

"Harper." She squeezed her fingers. "I'm not going. I'm not leaving."

"I killed Ben. It could get you." Harper pulled her hand away and rubbed at her eyes. "And you don't know about the…" She licked at her lips. "P? Something P. Poison Oak. No. Poison Oak sucks."

"The what?"

"Huh?"

"What don't I know about, Harper?" She pressed closer, watching green flicker against the gold. It sounded important, it felt important that she know the answer. "Harper?"

"I'm Harper," she said with a dazzling smile. "Nice to meet you."

Back down the rabbit hole. She passed a hand over her tired eyes and smiled back. "What am I going to do with you?"

"You're pretty."

"Thank you."

"Welcome."

She took Harper's hand back and squeezed. Goosebumps raised up along her arms. "Hey. You were saying I didn't know something. It sounded important."

"Can't remember," she said and nuzzled her pillow. "AJ said it. I'm sleepy, Emers." Her eyes closed and seconds later a wheeze of a snore graced Emerson's ears.

She sighed and tucked the limp hand in hers under the blankets. "That's that, I suppose. I'll see you soon."

CHAPTER TWENTY-ONE

Harper

The note read simply: sometimes they stay.

Her first instinct had been to wad it up. Smudge out Emerson's girlish cursive and the intent behind those three words.

She re-read it five times, until she could hear it as though Emerson had said it aloud. Then she shoved it into her bedside table drawer before she could change her mind.

That didn't mean she wasn't angry. Oh no. Furious came closer. Just shy of homicidal better. As if she hadn't been embarrassed enough when she woke up and remembered their mortifying conversation, now she had a note to remind her what she'd said, a perfect memento of her own awkwardness.

The anger felt safer. She had a good reason for it after all. It came from the human too, not the wolf. The wolf didn't seem to be bothered in the slightest that they'd been taken advantage of, or that it had been discovered.

She almost ripped the front door off Emerson's bookstore. Bells jingled and clacked against the glass, announcing her presence. She glared at the three sleigh bells for ruining her moment.

Seated behind the front desk, glasses crooked on her nose, Emerson didn't even glance up at her. "Harper."

A growl reverberated in her chest. She stomped over to the desk and smacked her hands down on the counter. "What the hell were you thinking? Are you actually insane?"

Emerson sighed and took her glasses off. Hair pulled back in a messy pony tail, and with dark circles under her eyes, she looked as ragged as Harper felt. "Nice to see you up and about. I see the pleasant high of this morning has worn off."

"Don't do that." She jabbed a finger at Emerson's face and growled again. "Don't act like nothing happened, and don't you dare pretend like you know anything about this."

"I know plenty," Emerson said, standing slowly from her chair. She crossed her arms over her chest and glared right back. "Yelling at me isn't going to make me forget either. If that's your plan, you need a new one. Scaring me into silence isn't going to work."

"I could have killed you."

"But you didn't. I'm not afraid of you, Harper."

"Well you should be!" She slapped her hand down again and leaned in. Her vision sharpened, and she expected at least a flinch. Emerson stared right back at her, then shook her head.

"You're not a monster in a horror movie."

"No, I'm your every-day, run of the mill, homicidal neighborhood monster," she said through her teeth. "How can you possibly not see the danger you put yourself in?"

"Which time?" Emerson raised an eyebrow and slipped around the desk. She stopped at the corner, not too close but not out of reach. "Was I in danger when you showed up on my date with four legs and a tail? How about when you were in a cage? Oh." She covered her mouth and widened her eyes. "Was it when you were so drunk on the full moon that you reminded me of a few college students I knew?"

"This isn't a joke." She stiffened as Emerson inched closer. "Dead, Emerson. Gone forever, erased from the planet, dead. Closed casket funeral because your body looks like it was fed to a wood chipper, dead."

"I'm still not afraid."

"Then you're an idiot," she said with a hiss of breath. "I've killed before."

Emerson stopped her sly shuffle. She swallowed and put her hand on the desk. Right next to Harper's, their fingers almost touching. "What happened with Ben?"

"I killed him isn't clear enough for you?" She sneered to cover up the tremble in her lips. "He wasn't afraid either. Now he's dead. His father drinks himself into a stupor every night, and I'm the one pouring his drinks. His mother hasn't left the house since the funeral. She sends me flowers to take to the headstone. I caused that. Me. Harper, the monster of Fincher."

"Stop saying that." Emerson set her jaw. Stubborn as always, but her eyes were wet and her face had gone pale. "Stop it."

"You want to know what happened?" She stepped in, closing the gap between them. "I told him the truth. He said the same things you are. That I'm not a monster, just a misunderstood creature that isn't supposed to exist." The memory struck harder than a punch to the gut. Ben's sure smile, the smell of his cologne when he hugged her to reassure them both. "He said it would be okay. We'd be okay. So we waited for Grady to go to work and Cooper to go to his friend's house. We were using chains then, not the cage."

Ben had waited upstairs. Ever the gentleman, he didn't want to embarrass her by watching the transformation. The last time she'd seen him, he'd kissed her on the forehead and jokingly said "break a leg."

"The rest of it is in fragments," she said aloud, forcing the words into existence. "Sometimes I hear him screaming in my dreams. 'Harper, stop, Harper it's me,' and then just screaming. He went into that basement thinking it was safe. The monster inside me taught us all a lesson. It – I – chased him out of the house, into the woods. I ripped him open and dragged his body deeper. They only found him because — because — because..." Her throat closed up, and her mouth went dry. Ben put his hands in his pockets, looking at her sorrowfully. She gagged and tried to swallow the horrible lump clogging her scratchy throat.

Emerson was shaking. She had one hand wrapped around her stomach, the other clenched hard over Harper's. "Harper, you don't have to — I'm sorry I — "

She expected Emerson to back away, run away in hysterics, throw something. Instead, she almost fell over her own feet when Emerson grabbed her. A hug, she was being embraced, not screamed at. Emerson's arms circled her neck and held on tight, forcing her to stoop.

The wolf pressed against her, and her fingers twitched. She grit her teeth against it, there would be no nuzzling this time. No matter how tempting Emerson's silky hair was proving to be.

"You know now." The wolf pushed harder, causing her head to bob. She'd hoped the busier than normal full moon would make it more docile and easier to handle. So much for that. Not wanting to encourage another hostile takeover, she carefully returned the hug. "I don't want you to end up as another ghost that follows me around."

Emerson nodded and started to pull away. Her arms slid down, but her hands stayed in contact, gripping Harper's shoulders. She frowned and sniffled. "You're hot."

"Um." She raised an eyebrow and tried to back away. Her arms tightened around Emerson's waist instead. The wolf had shaken off its lethargy and did not want to let go. "That's random. Thanks?"

"No, not – I didn't mean." Emerson blushed deep red. "I mean you're flushed. Are you okay?"

Who the hell said flushed anymore unless they were referring to a toilet? One of her knuckles popped. A shudder danced its way up her spine, leaving tingles in its wake. Her cue to leave. "Well that conversation was kind of intense," she said and focused on getting her feet to move backwards. They stayed fixed in place.

Her excuse hadn't appeased Emerson. She let go of one shoulder and reached up as if to check for a fever.

She had a fever alright. If Emerson didn't stop touching her it wouldn't be getting any better either. With the wolf distracted by keeping her feet glued to the floor, she managed to move a hand to intercept Emerson's. She caught her wrist before her fingers could make contact. Her plan backfired. She'd grabbed too hard, startling Emerson, who stumbled forward and pressed right up against her again.

"Don't," she said hoarsely. Too late. Her whole body trembled, a battle for control waging inside. The wolf was delighted at the feel of Emerson mashed back against her.

"Harper, your eyes."

So close, too close. Emerson's breath was against her lips, and she could see her pulse hammering away in her fair neck. The whole world narrowed, time seemed to crawl as she watched the slight jump of Emerson's heart beneath the vulnerable skin on her jugular. Thump thump, thump thump. God, she could hear it. She wrenched her attention away, up, locking onto to those pale blue eyes. Mistake, big mistake. She could drown there, pulled under some sort of spell. They were such a vivid, clear blue.

Emerson's lips parted and she started to say something. Over the muted buzzing in her ears, she heard it. "Harper."

That did it. She heard a howl, caged inside her mind. Her control snapped. She lunged forward, lips colliding with Emerson's. Fireworks didn't go off. Stars were born behind her eyelids, suns went supernova. Her muscles turned to mush, and the buzz in her head turned to furious white-noise.

Emerson squeaked and the sound cut through the haze, the fog Harper had gotten lost in. Fabric bunched under her hands, she could feel the heat of skin just underneath. Somewhere in the far back of her mind a niggle of worry popped up. Like maybe she should be paying attention to something else.

Paying attention to anything at all went right out the window along with rational thought. Emerson cupped her face, holding her in place and kissed her back. She responded, sinking into the kiss. Gently, almost reverently at first, her hands cupped her neck, thumbs stroking her jaw. She'd never been kissed like that before. Ever. Ben had always been rough, kissed her hard, like if he didn't she might leave, or he was that desperate to be good. They hadn't known what they were doing, really, not at first. Even after they'd had some more practice, he still kissed her roughly, eager to round the next base. Or rushing, because it never took long before she had to take a moment to get a leash on her rampaging other half.

The wolf had raged in her head every time. So badly she'd had to stop to put all of her energy in containing it, much to his disappointment.

Not this time. This time it had taken over and it demanded more. She pulled back to swallow air and dove back in, dying for another taste of those soft, soft lips. Everything about Emerson was different. Supple curves, silky skin, the scent of coconut, and she was so gentle. *Feminine,* some part of her drunk brain supplied.

A stronger urge started as a burn in her gut, then crawled upwards. She wanted to be gentle too, hold onto the fragile beauty clinging to her shoulders. Protect. But a louder voice screamed "mine" and wanted to possess. She nipped, as lightly as possible, and groaned when Emerson grabbed her hair and pulled.

She growled and spun them around when Emerson's teeth latched onto her bottom lip. A stack of books fell to the floor with a flutter of pages and several loud thunks. She didn't care. Emerson gasped when her back hit the lip of the desk. She took the opportunity to attach her mouth to Emerson's throat. The rapid fluttering of Emerson's heart beat against her lips. It called to her, bewitched her, made her knees wobble.

"Harper."

A grenade might as well have gone off between her ears. Not even the fingers tugging at her hair could keep reality from crashing back in. She could hear the part of her that had been screaming the whole time, yelling for her to stop and look at what she was doing.

She'd just done what she'd promised not to, and put Emerson in danger again.

"I'm sorry, I'm so sorry I don't know what —" she backed away, shaking her head to try and clear it.

Emerson stayed put. She was still breathing heavily, lips shiny and dark red. Harper could see a mark already forming on her neck. It took every ounce of shredded self-control she had left to keep from adding a matching hickey on the opposite side.

"Harper," Emerson said and cleared her throat. Not yet angry. "Wha— Wait — I'm…"

Distance. She needed space, lots of it. Somewhere far away from the sight and smell. She fumbled toward the door, lurching and swaying as the wolf fought her decision. "I can't — I can't do this. I just — this isn't and I'm not —"

"Harper, wait!"

She threw herself out the door, into the empty street. The bones in her forearm broke, one and then the other. She wrapped both arms around her stomach, held tight to the loose elbow, and kept hobbling as fast as she could. Two more painful steps toward home and the bones in her feet shattered. She limped on, biting into her sore bottom lip to keep from screaming. The headache and vertigo hit so hard she doubled over. She sucked in breath after breath and then threw up.

"You'll have to do better than that." She groaned and straightened up the best she could. Wiping at her mouth with the back of her hand she started walking again, wincing with each step. She started humming Bad Moon Rising. Loudly and proudly.

That would have to do until she could get home and find her tranquilizers.

***

The front door was locked, and she didn't have her keys. Figured.

Hunched over and with a more pronounced limp Harper headed for the closest window. Even if they remembered to lock the door, nobody remembered the windows. She threw it up, pushed aside the curtains, and dumped herself through the opening.

On the way home more things had broken. Her ribs, in particular, protested the abrupt landing on the floor. She groaned and used her still functioning hand to try and pull herself the rest of the way inside. Her feet hung out the window, she needed to get them inside before Mr. Reimann saw.

"Harper?"

Also bad for broken ribs? Jerking in surprise. She groaned, opened her eyes and groaned again. Grady stood in the living room archway with his hands on his hips, AJ right beside him. "Hi. Did someone order a werewolf?"

"What happened?" AJ rushed over and grabbed her under the armpits. Pain ripped down both sides of her body. She yelped and AJ dropped her like a hot pan. "Harper, what's wrong?"

"You want a list?" She rolled with a grunt and gagged. "Broken ribs, fractured feet, and I'm pretty sure my right arm is completely shattered. Oh, and I think I pulled muscles in my neck, back, and a hamstring."

"What?" AJ whipped around and pointed nowhere. "Grady, first aid kit. How did this happen?"

"I got hit by a bus?" *And the license plate was E-M-E-R-S-O-N.*

"Harper, come on," AJ said and raised the edge of Harper's shirt. She sucked in a noisy breath and ran her cold fingers along Harper's side. "You're bruising. Why are you bruising?"

"The wolf is mad at me." She slapped AJ's hand away. "That tickles." Her close up view of AJ revealed makeup and jeans without a splotch on them. "You look nice. I interrupted a date, didn't I? I'm just on a screw up roll tonight."

"We were just having some coffee and talking. About you actually," AJ said, blushing. "What do you mean you're on a screw up roll?"

"I really don't want to talk about it. Could you please jab me with a tranq like you promised?"

"That bad?"

"Nuclear."

Grady came back into the room carrying a tackle box.

She and AJ shared a look.

"You put the first aid stuff in a tackle box?" AJ arched an eyebrow.

"Harper never needs it," Grady said with a petulant expression. He held on to the box tighter. "Cooper uses Band-Aids. I'm the only one that would ever need this stuff. I figured if I'm going to need it, I'm probably going to be fishing."

"Don't even bother with that," she said. "Should have said something earlier, but I was too amused that AJ gets to order you around. Knock me out. The rest will take care of itself."

"You don't want me to set your arm?"

She winced and glanced down. The bones were pressing against her skin. Not yet poking through. "No, thanks. Once the hissy fit is over it should heal on its own."

"All right then." AJ stood back up and moved out of the way. Grady stared at her, cradling his tackle box. Harper tilted her head and screwed up her face at upside down AJ.

"What're you doing?" she asked when the silence stretched.

"Waiting for Grady to pick you up."

"Say what now?" Grady asked.

"Yeah, I agree. What? Also, no way."

"Well, I'm not going to leave her sprawled out and drugged on the floor."

The idea of being carried, in her current state, upstairs made her stomach hurt all over again. "Pass. I'm really comfy right here."

"Nonsense." AJ shook her head and turned to Grady. "She should be upstairs in her bed, right? Tell her."

Grady grimaced. "Come on, Harp. It's not that far."

"You are so whipped." She chewed on her torn lip and decided she couldn't win with the two of them teaming up. Several things that should never move ground together as she picked herself up, ribs and foot bones and her broken arm. She sat for a moment, panting, and tried not to throw up. "Get it over with before something else breaks."

Between the two of them, they leveraged her to her feet. Grady, with an expression of dread, bent and scooped her up. He staggered and the choppy movement shot pricks of agony through her torso. "You okay, Harp?"

"Do I look okay?" She wheezed and blinked black spots out of her eyes. "Hurry up, before I puke on your fanciest shirt."

AJ darted ahead of them toward the staircase. "Harper, where are the tranquilizers I gave you?"

"Bathroom."

Grady grunted and swayed on the first step. "I take it your talk with Emerson went well?"

"How could you tell?" She whimpered. One problem at a time would be better. Getting upstairs and drugged into oblivion would take care of the immediate one. Then she could worry about the 'Emerson issue.' Each shaky step struck another lance of pain through her. It didn't hurt half as bad as remembering the look on Emerson's face when she'd bolted out of the bookstore. "Can we not talk about it?"

CHAPTER TWENTY-TWO

"Harper, are you sure about this?" Grady asked for the millionth time. Harper rolled her eyes at him.

"I'm in the stock room. I have vapor rub up my nose. Oh, and I'm about to jab myself with a tranquilizer. Yeah, I'm totally good, thanks for asking." She curled her lip at the needle in her hand. AJ made it look way too easy. "Logan's okay with handling my shift?"

"Yeah, I told him I needed you in the back this week. He did that face," he said and scrunched his face up in a fair imitation of Logan's puzzled expression. "So I told him Holt had been bugging you, and you wanted a break."

"That's great. He'll be back here at his first opportunity to try and help. Good job." She huffed, but didn't take her eyes off the needle. *Why did it have to be a needle, anyway? Couldn't they put the telazol in pill form, or maybe just the liquid?* She could take it like a nasty shot with a lime chaser.

He held his hands up. "This was your idea, General. You don't like how I distracted your friend, next time you handle it."

"Whose side are you on anyway?" She glared at him and moved the needle toward her arm. He winced and shook his head.

"Yours. Always yours, Harp. You sure you want to stick yourself? I could –"

"You could pass out just watching me?" She snorted. Her hand shook as she approached the soft crook of her elbow. The wolf didn't like her plan any more than Grady. "Everybody's a critic," she mumbled and stuck the needle home. Right on the little **x** AJ had drawn.

True to her accusation, she glanced up to see Grady looking pale and swaying a bit on his feet. "Why are you still here? I thought that was a pretty clear cue for you to leave."

"Morbid curiosity?" He swallowed so hard she heard him gulp. "You think that dosage will work?"

"Only one way to find out," she said and pushed the plunger down. The idea was to subdue the wolf without leaving her in a stupor. If it worked, she'd be somewhat free of her wolfish impulses. If not... "Too bad AJ said this would not be a sustainable action plan. I could get used to having an easier time with my furry half." She pulled the needle out and shook her hand a couple of times. "Freakin' smarts."

"Here, I'll get rid of the evidence. Can't have people thinking you're a heroin addict." He held out his hand and she suppressed a grin at his obvious discomfort.

"Nobody will know. No bruising or track marks."

He pinched the body of the syringe with two fingers and held it away from himself.

She couldn't resist. "It's not radioactive, Uncle."

"Shut it."

"Come back and check on me in about ten minutes. Then we'll know if this is going to work. I mean, I'm sure your girlfriend got the dosage right, but I'd rather not have a repeat performance of last night."

"I think I prefer it when you're too drugged to speak." He gave her the 'evil eye' and shook a finger her direction. "She's not my girlfriend."

"I wasn't drugged enough to miss her kissing you," she said with a sigh. The telazol acted fast. Warmth suffused her muscles, leaving her calm and the wolf relaxed. She squinted up at him and chuckled at the blush high on his cheeks and reddening his ears.

"On the cheek. It was on the cheek."

"So defensive. That just makes it more adorable." She lazily waved a hand. "What do you want me working on?"

"You can do the inventory, if math isn't too hard for your druggy brain."

"I think I can count," she said and stood. "Can I start in the freezer? This storage room gives me the creeps."

"Really?" He arched an eyebrow.

She nodded. "Yes, really. Have you looked around? There's a single, bare light bulb in a brick-walled room full of boxes and shelves. Creepy. Also? It smells funny."

"How can it smell funny? You've got half a tub of vapo-rub stuffed up your nostrils."

"Trust me, it smells like death in here."

He sighed and wrapped the needle in a rag, very carefully. "You can start in the freezer. Try and actually get something done. You wanted to come to work, can't have you lazing about. Still think you should have stayed home."

"I'd rather not draw attention to myself by being out sick anymore.

PURE OF HEART

People already treat me like a walking disaster movie. You know the ones with the one word titles? Twister! Asteroid! Volcano! Sharknado! Harper!"

"Did you really just compare yourself to a movie called Sharknado?"

She brushed past him and shrugged. "If the shoe fits. It's easier this way. Then they won't think I've brought some sort of plague down on Fincher. Even if I have." She stopped next to the back door and whispered to him. "Imagine that, I'm my own one word title movie. Werewolf."

"Harper," he said with a frown.

"Relax, I'm downplaying the epic failure of my life. Blame it on the meds." The shock and sadness on his face made her want to yell at him. But at the moment, she was aiming for sarcastic indifference. She shook a finger in his face. "Don't."

"Look." He shot a glance toward the cooks, just a few steps away. "I don't know what happened with Emerson, but I'm not a fan of this new attitude."

"What part of 'don't' didn't translate?" She smacked her head a couple of times. "Let's try again. Grady, no, don't go there. Did that get through okay?"

His expression hardened, and she would have braced herself if she hadn't been too busy trying not to laugh. They were in a kitchen, at work, and he was holding a rag with a syringe hidden in it. A syringe she'd used to inject herself with an animal tranquilizer because she was a werewolf. And he was going to scold her for being moody.

"How is this funny?"

She swiped at her mouth with the back of a hand and grinned at him. "Because this is so sad, like pathetic, and frankly, ridiculous. I'm going to get to work now. See you in ten minutes."

***

She liked the freezer. Through the thick door, she could barely hear the thump and whine of the music. She couldn't hear conversations or laughter or people whispering about her. Even with her stellar wolf hearing.

With a sigh, she shook her head and turned back to her work. Counting frozen hamburger and steaks normally required her full attention. The last time she'd lost focus and ended up making herself sick on several rib-eye popsicles.

Now she barely felt the wolf with the Telazol running through her system. It was problematic, in that she felt half sedated too. But freeing. She didn't have to worry about eating raw meat on top of everything else.

She smiled a little as she scribbled on her clipboard. No wolf to deal with. If only it always worked that way. Without the drugs and stinky vapor rub.

"Harper!"

She shrieked, dropped her clipboard with a loud clatter and spun around. The downside of being in the freezer. Yes, not being able to hear the noise of the bar was mostly a bonus, but it also meant she couldn't hear people approaching.

Emerson stood just inside the door, looking about as furious as Harper had feared she would be.

"Emerson!" She clapped her hand over her nose, but it was too late to keep the faint scent of coconuts from reaching her even through the heavy odor of menthol.

"Really? You're surprised?" Emerson planted her hands on her hips, but thankfully didn't step in any farther.

"Well I – uh..."

"Eloquent as always."

Harper licked at her lips and tried to relax. She didn't want to look like a cornered animal. Another con for the freezer, she had nowhere to run. "I wasn't expecting you, that's all."

"How could you not be expecting me after that little episode the other night?"

Quick brain, think of something. "Because I was hoping you'd hit your head since then and forgotten?" A weak, strained laugh punctuated the statement. It died soon after it began when Emerson glared at her. "Do we have to talk about this?"

"Are you serious? You kissed me!" Emerson threw her hands in the air and stomped closer. She drew to a stop when Harper's back hit the wall. "First you yell at me, then you tell me why you're yelling, and then you kissed me. Oh, and then there's the small matter that you're a werewolf. What is going on?"

"I meant, you know, does it have to be right this second?" Harper tried to angle her head away, nose still covered by her palm. It didn't help, not with Emerson so close. Her vapor rub defense had been overrun. To her horror she felt the wolf stirring, struggling against her and the haze of Telazol. Not good.

"Why, is this a bad time?" Emerson poked a finger into Harper's shoulder. "I'm not letting you run again. Not without an explanation. Things have gotten too... I have questions."

"I can't," Harper said with a weak shake of her head. "It's not something you want to know. Trust me."

"Trust you?" Blue eyes narrowed and Emerson jabbed her again. "Trust you? You've got to be kidding me. Harper, I need GPS to navigate trying to talk to you, forget getting a straight answer. How am I supposed to trust you when you haven't been honest with me since we met?"

"Yeah, 'cause that would have gone over great! You're named after an author? Cool, I'm a werewolf, nice to meet you."

Her wolf bubbled up, no doubt pulled forward by her burst of anger. It wasn't at full strength, but it was there. She whimpered, half from the wolf and half from her. *Why don't my plans ever work?*

The sound agitated Emerson further. She grabbed Harper's wrist and tugged. "Why are you covering your nose? What is going on?"

With no response ready, Harper could only stare at her and take tiny breaths through her mouth.

"Is it a wolf thing? Is that why you kissed me and then ran away with your tail between your legs?"

Yes, but also no. Harper swallowed and looked up at the ceiling. With her back literally against a wall, she felt closed in. Her breath hitched as Emerson inched closer. "Sort of?"

"Is it bad?"

"Yes." Harper nodded and then paused. She hadn't finished her pro-con list for the imprint. "Wait, no. I mean – kind of?" Ben nodded and pointed at his neck.

"You can't just kiss me and then do this."

Harper smothered the whine trying to escape her lips by pressing them together as hard as possible. She made the mistake of glancing down, hoping to catch Emerson's eyes and telepathically communicate her distress. Instead she found herself captivated by Emerson's full lips. Somewhere in the back of her head, she thought she heard the echo of a howl.

Emerson huffed. "You are so frustrating. First you're all passive aggressive because you're a werewolf, then I find out and you yell at me, which I probably deserved. Followed by, surprise, a kiss I still haven't recovered from. Are we starting the pattern over again? I don't know what you want, and now, on top of it, I don't know what I want either. It's not fair for you to keep doing this. It's not a game!"

She was standing too close. Too close. The wolf flexed and Harper trembled. Afraid to breathe, she tried to hold air in her aching lungs. She couldn't speak, not sure what would come out if she opened her mouth.

"What did you do to me? Is this some sort of werewolf thing? Did you even want to kiss me?"

Harper's whole body went hot in an instant. She choked, then took in a breath laced with coconut so strong she could taste it.

Then she remembered she had tasted it. Coconut and Emerson, and it had been so good angels might as well have been singing the Hallelujah chorus.

Her stomach clenched. She snapped forward, grabbed the back of Emerson's head and crushed their mouths together.

This time Emerson didn't squeal, like perhaps she'd expected it. Harper shoved the wolf aside and tried to focus on the feel. She needed to know as much as Emerson did.

Could it be more than just the wolf?

With the wolf out of the way, by some miracle not demanding to be in charge, she calmed the kiss. No biting this time, gentle and easy, all human instead of part animal. She reached out and cupped Emerson's jaw, held her carefully.

She expected Emerson to struggle, since she was pissed about their first kiss. Emerson surprised her again. She responded with the same gentleness, tucking herself in close and stretching up on her toes.

Harper's head spun. Gooseflesh covered her arms, and a strange tingle swept over her from head to toe. Was the imprint working its magic? Or was it the kiss itself? The wolf stayed out of the equation, subdued somehow. She felt nothing but satisfaction.

She pulled away, took a shallow breath, and then ducked her head to kiss Emerson again.

It wasn't just the wolf. Maybe AJ had been right. They weren't separate beings fighting for control of one body. She was the wolf. The wolf was her.

That didn't make it safe.

Ben's screaming surfaced in her head. Flashes of blood and flesh and pure hatred from the wolf's memory came soon after.

Not safe.

She pushed Emerson away, feeling like she'd ripped her own arm off in the process, and lunged for the door. History repeating itself. She wouldn't let it repeat anything else.

"Harper!"

It's not safe. I'm not safe. Panicked, she pulled too hard on the door and heard something crack. Not a bone, the wolf was too weak, but the door hung crooked on its hinges.

She ran past the cooks who shouted after her. Past Grady, who came into the back just in time to be shoved away. She hit the back door, crushed the doorknob in her hand in her haste to get out.

Outside the frigid air stung her lungs. The tears she hadn't realized she'd been shedding froze on her cheeks.

She ran. Not because her life depended on it.

Because Emerson's did.

***

Ike greeted her as she stuck her head through his doggie door. He whined, cocked his head to the side, and offered a short tail wag. Philippe had gotten over his shyness, but lacked Ike's tact. He went straight for face licking.

"Not now," Harper told them and wiggled the rest of the way through the door. She swiped at the dog drool and lingering tears on her half frozen face. Both dogs backed off and she got to her feet.

PURE OF HEART

The lights were all off in the house, but she had excellent night vision. She had no problem moving through the living room without bumping into anything. The dogs padded along behind her as she headed straight for the hallway, following the scent of butterscotch.

AJ didn't even twitch when Harper opened the bedroom door. Under a bundle of blankets, all Harper could see of her was the splash of dark hair against a white pillow.

She knelt down at the bedside and narrowed her eyes. AJ slept on, oblivious, even when Harper pulled the blankets off of her.

"Jay?"

AJ's nose wrinkled. She grunted and turned her face into her pillow.

"AJ." Harper sighed and leaned in. "AJ!"

With a shout AJ sat up, then rolled off the other side of the bed. Her amusement over such things appeared to be broken. She couldn't even smile.

AJ's head popped up over the far edge, hair in utter disarray and mouth wide open. She snapped her teeth together, glared and slid her hands back onto the mattress. "Harper, have you lost your damn mind?"

"Sorry," Harper said and bowed her head. "I need your help."

Her tenuous control slipped again. She didn't bother struggling to keep it. The wolf had gone back under, leaving her bereft of its strength and composure. Not that it had been cool, calm and collected since leaving Emerson. She missed it. And that realization on top of all the others crowding her brain... She covered her face with her hands and cried.

"Sweets?"

"I can't do this!" She yelled and leaned into the mattress with a sob. "I can't. It's not safe and I'll – I'll kill her. Just like Ben. It's trying to get out and I want to let it. I'm so tired of fighting it all the time. I'm the wolf!"

"Harper," AJ said.

Harper sniffled and looked up and AJ was kneeling on the bed, both hands outstretched. "I can't anymore."

"Come here."

The dogs jumped up onto the bed and Harper followed. She crawled onto the rumpled blankets and curled up against AJ. Another memory snuck up on her. Of seeking shelter from bad dreams with her parents, curling up between them and feeling protected.

Except this time she was the monster. She hiccupped and held onto AJ. "Can I stay in the barn?"

"Is it that bad?"

"I kissed her."

"Oh." AJ sighed, but her hand didn't falter. She kept running her fingers over and through Harper's hair. She started rocking from side to side. "Harper, it's — it'll be okay, Sweets. Of course you can stay here as long as you need to."

Harper nodded and stuck her sticky face into AJ's throat. "Thank you."

"You don't have to thank me," AJ said and pulled the blankets back over both of them. "This will all work out, you'll see. It's going to be alright."

"You don't know that."

AJ resumed her rocking and wrapped both arms tight around Harper. She squeezed and Harper shuddered. Not out of fear, but at the chill that had replaced the burning heat the wolf had been putting out.

"I do know that. I know you, and I've got a good feeling about all of this. You're both going to be fine."

"Promise?"

"Promise promise."

CHAPTER TWENTY-THREE

The singing stopped working. She'd exhausted every song she could remember, hummed every melody she could think of to the horses in AJ's barn. It stopped working to suppress the wolf, to keep it out of her head. Ben hung around more often, staying right next to her, bleeding and silently stoic.

Only the Telazol helped, and Harper's arguments for higher dosages fell flat.

"One, I don't want you addicted," AJ said, holding up a finger. She glared and Harper shrank back from her. "Two, I'm not knocking you out every day like some twisted version of Sleeping Beauty. I'm sorry, Sweets, but no."

"Jay, please." Harper looked up from under her bangs. "It's always in my head now. The howling... I can't block it anymore."

AJ pursed her lips and knelt down in front of the hay bale chair Harper had erected. "If you want to break the imprint with Emerson, you have to do it on your own. The drugs aren't going to do it for you. If it's not what you want, the wolf needs to submit."

Harper dug her fingers into the hay. "It's not going to roll over on this. You don't know what it's like. I feel like I'm schizophrenic, and it's the stronger personality."

"You're not crazy. Or schizophrenic. You're having a minor crisis of self right now, and that's okay. I'm pretty sure most people go through this over the course of their lives. They just don't get to blame it on a wolf."

"Did you just compare imprinting to a midlife crisis?"

AJ shrugged. "Best I could think of."

"I think I'd rather the wolf wanted a convertible," Harper said. She dropped her aching head into her hands with a whimper. Her fingers scrubbed at the roots of her hair in a useless attempt to ease her pain.

"How about you come inside? Take a nap."

She shook her head and winced. Her every attempt at sleep had been inundated with nightmares. Nightmares and often ephemeral, obscure flashes of Emerson, trees and forest creatures.

"Harper," AJ said with a heavy sigh. "It's been three days. You need to sleep."

"I can't." Her voice cracked, and she swallowed back the now ever-present lump of tears. She blamed the wolf for the sudden influx of torrid emotions. It was easier that way. "I'm already starting to have day terrors. I don't want to encourage it."

"You're having day terrors because you're not sleeping. You're exhausted."

"I'm afraid," she whispered. "Not just of the dreams. What if it takes over while I'm asleep?"

"At this point?" AJ huffed. "Lack of sleep combined with your lack of eating, I think you're too weak to do much of anything. Even that wolfy strength of yours can't compensate."

She hesitated to give in. Saying no sounded safer, but as she opened her mouth, her stomach grumbled and she whined instead of speaking.

AJ nodded an I-told-you-so. "Come on, Sweets. I'll make you a grilled cheese and you can take a nap. Grady will kill me if I don't do a better job looking after you." She stood with a low groan and held out her hand.

Harper stared at the hand and looked up at AJ again. "You'll wake me up?"

"Come on, Harp. You know I will."

***

She managed half the sandwich before her stomach decided it had enough. Harper tried to get her face into an apologetic expression when she handed the plate back to AJ. "I can't eat anymore."

AJ frowned, but took it. "Is my cooking that bad?"

"It's better than Grady's," she said with a small smile.

"That's not saying much. I've been to your house for dinner." AJ grinned back and took a bite off the untouched half. "Oh well. You ate so I can't complain. Now about that nap."

Harper wrinkled her nose at the crumbs flaking off the sandwich and the loud sound of AJ chewing. Her senses had been on high alert for days. "Do I have to?"

"You need to, and you know it."

That didn't make it any easier. She fidgeted with the blanket spread over her lap. "Can I stay out here with the fire? I –" she paused and mumbled the rest. "Like the smell."

"Sure. You want an actual pillow?"

"No, I don't need one." She shook her head and stretched out on the couch under AJ's watchful eyes. "You'll be here?"

"I'm going to go look over some paperwork with Trish," AJ said and waved the sandwich at the door to the vet clinic. "But I'll only be a room away."

She couldn't demand that AJ sit and watch her sleep, not on top of everything else. The second her cheek pressed into the soft couch cushion her eyelids fluttered. "Okay."

"I think I'll include this in the book that will never be published." AJ smiled, wiped her hands on her faded jeans and adjusted Harper's blanket. "The care and feeding of a werewolf — that will be the chapter title."

Harper managed a raspy chuckle and closed her gritty feeling eyes. "You're insane."

"Most likely. I prefer to be called mad though. Insane scientist doesn't have the classic ring to it."

She cracked open one eye and smiled. "Dr. Frankenstein."

"That's Fronk-en-steen," AJ corrected. "Do you want Ike here with you?"

"Yes, please."

AJ called for the dog and had him lay down beside the couch. Harper dangled one hand over the side to touch his fur.

"There, everybody's cozy. Come get me when you wake up, we'll see if I can get some more food in you."

"Stay until I fall asleep?" Harper asked and tucked her nose under the hem of the fleece blanket. "In case the wolf…"

She heard AJ sit down and felt fingers pushing through her hair. "Of course."

***

Trees, dark and shadowy, loomed over and surrounded her. Their branches snagged at her hair, scratched her face. Rain, cold and heavy, soaked her to the bone. She ran on, bare feet splashing in muddy puddles. Ahead of her, just out of reach, she saw the blurry form of another person. She tried to shout, to call out, ask them to wait.

They turned and a flash of lightning revealed Ben. He tripped and disappeared for a moment, swallowed by the darkness of the forest. She saw his shape, his outline, stumble back up and take off again.

"Ben!" She ran faster, tearing through the brush. "Not that way!"

She leapt over logs and bounced off trees, unfocused on anything besides getting to him. He ran from her like a startled deer, almost effortlessly staying ahead of her. While she continued to get hung up on brush, slipped on rocks, crashed into trees, he kept running. Numb and clumsy her feet went out from under her again. She slammed into a creek with a yelp.

The creek… She planted her hands in the grit and rocks on the bottom and shook the water from her face. It was her creek. She knew where she was. If Ben kept the same path she could take a short cut.

Thunder rumbled as she dragged herself back to her feet. She raised her face to the sky and perked her ears. It sounded like Ben had stopped. She could faintly hear him panting and swearing. With the rain she couldn't smell him very well, but her ears still worked. She could still save him. Her vision flickered, in and out of sharp focus. It settled in wolf mode, so acute she could see individual rain drops streaming down.

She took a deep breath and darted off his trail, headed for a nearby outcrop. The rock bit into her hands, surface slick from constant rain but still sharp enough to hurt. She dug her fingers in, despite the sting and heaved herself up. Now, on higher ground, she could see him, doubled over in a clearing not too far. "Ben!"

He startled, looked around and took off running again. She gave chase, knocking small stones free as she went. They trickled down the gentle incline alerting him to her location. She watched, heart hammering in her throat, a feeling of impending doom heavy on her chest. A fresh surge of adrenaline kicked in and she ran harder, desperate to reach him first.

Another strobe of light revealed that she'd closed the gap between them. He ran alongside, close enough for her to see the fear in his eyes. She didn't think, just jumped, arms outstretched and tackled him. They hit the ground and rolled, both shouting in surprise and pain. She gripped hard at his sodden shirt, her nails ripping through the fabric. He screamed and turned over under her, hands stretching up in a defensive posture.

"Harper! Harper, it's me!"

He tried to scramble out from under her. She pushed down on his shoulders. "What are you doing?"

"Harper, don't! You know me! It's Ben!"

She leaned toward him, shoved him deeper into the muck. Of course he was Ben, who else would he be? "I don't understand. What's happening? Why did you run?"

His hands closed around her throat. She could see the muscles in his arms straining as he tried to press her away from his face. He tightened his grip, grit his teeth and threw her to the side.

She landed in a puddle, he crawled away from her got to his feet and started running again. Panic closed its icy fist around her heart. She gulped in a wet breath and shook her head. "Ben!"

Movement caught her attention. She looked down at her hands. They weren't hands, but paws as big as dinner plates. The movement she'd seen had been her reflection in the puddle. A wolf's face glared back at her, golden eyes gleaming like fire.

"No. No, not Ben." She fell back from the puddle and turned her head in the direction he'd gone. It wasn't hard to pick up the sounds of him crashing through the woods, desperate to get away. "You're going the wrong way!"

Up again and her hands were hands again. She dug her toes into the mushy ground and threw herself after him. If she could get to him first he'd be okay. Shouting his name whenever she could, she leapt back into the forest. She could hear him panting, the thick sounds of his shoes against wood.

She tackled him a second time and used her weight to hold him against the ground. He struggled, tried to hit her with his elbows, kicked his legs. "Stop! Stop it, I'm trying to save you!"

He groaned and squirmed, laced his hands together behind his neck. "Harper!"

Light blossomed along with heat. An explosion nearby rocked her, sending a jolt through her stomach like the bass at a rock concert. She jerked back and looked up to see a house. Her house, the one in Alaska, not Grady's, close enough to them for her to feel the heat from the blaze. Windows shattered as the flames devoured everything within. "Mama?"

She heard a scream. Half human, half wolf.

"Harper."

She whipped around, toward the sound of her name, said in a small childish voice. A little girl with blonde hair and massive blue eyes tiptoed toward her from the cover of the woods. An adorable shy smile put dimples into chubby cheeks.

"Harper!" Ben yelled.

Too much going on, too much. She closed her eyes, shook her head, opened them again and the little girl had disappeared, or transformed. Emerson stood a couple steps away. She eased forward, somehow untouched by the rain that still fell heavily.

"Harper."

"Harper!" Ben's fist smashed into the side of her face. She jerked, shocked to feel pain blooming through her cheek. "Harper, don't!"

Hatred, ugly and vengeful, swept over her. She stared at him, his hair plastered to his forehead, clothes ripped and blood welling from the deep scratches on his chest. He shook his head, brown eyes wide.

"Don't. Harper, please. Please, it's Ben."

"It's not you," she said around the wolf teeth crowding her mouth. "It was never supposed to be you."

He screamed as she lunged for his throat, pale and exposed. His hands struck at her shoulders, tried to shove her away and beat at her. She caught his neck in her teeth and squeezed. It popped in her mouth, crumpled under the pressure of her jaws. She growled, infuriated, clamped down and then pulled back with all her might.

She heard a tearing noise, and then blood filled her mouth. Hot, and rich with the taste of iron.

"Harper?" Emerson said. She knelt down and touched Harper's ear. "Harper, wake up."

She swallowed the mouthful of blood and turned her face into the gentle touch. "Emerson?"

"Wake up." Emerson smiled and started to back away. Back into the forest.

"Emerson!"

***

"Harper! Harper, it's okay."

Her eyes snapped open, and she found herself on her back on the couch. The blanket she'd been snuggled under was wrapped around her feet. Ike was lapping at her face and whining. Overhead AJ and Trish peered down at her.

"That must've been some nightmare," Trish said, without her usual sarcastic tone. She patted Harper's feet and smiled. "You okay now, Champ?"

AJ turned to Trish with a frown. "I've got it from here."

"Thanks for the rescue, Trish. I won't tell anyone you were being sweet," Harper said. Or more like croaked. Her throat had seized up around the first word.

"Well you know, you hear screaming and your inner badass comes out."

"Let's sit you up," AJ said as soon as Trish had gone. She helped Harper up and then kept pulling until she could embrace her. "Are you alright?"

Harper shook her head and dug her face into AJ's neck. "No."

"You want to talk about it?"

"No," she repeated and shuddered. Her mouth felt gummy and dry all at once. "Water?"

"Yeah, hold on."

She licked her lips and reached for Ike, needing some sort of contact to keep her grounded. The dog didn't protest, tail wagging as Harper drew him into her lap. He was too big to be a lap dog, but she didn't care. She stuck her nose in his downy white ruff and let him lick her ear to his heart's content. His fur stuck to her face and she realized she'd been crying in her sleep. Again. She used her shoulder to clear as many of the leftover tears as she could.

AJ reappeared holding a large cup. Harper heard ice cubes clicking against the sides and each other. She gulped down the cold water until a brain freeze forced her to stop.

"Better?"

She shook her head and closed her eyes. "How long?"

"Little under an hour."

An hour. It felt like a lifetime. "Oh."

"Sweets..."

"AJ, no. I don't want to talk about it. Not now, not ever." She glared over the rim of the cup. "I told you it would happen."

AJ nodded slowly, checked over her shoulder and then leaned in. "You weren't just screaming. You shouted his name and then hers."

Harper blushed, cracked a piece of ice between her teeth, and then resumed her glaring. "Trish's name?"

"Harper."

"Leave it alone, Jay." She gestured toward the door with her chin. "Did Trish hear?"

"At that volume, the whole town heard."

"Fantastic," she said with a groan. "That's not weird at all."

***

Harper retreated back to the barn. Back to her hideout of hay, horses and shame. Sleep tugged hard at her, but not as hard as the wolf. Every time her eyes drooped, even the slightest, or she let herself rest for a second, it was there.

Little things kept popping out of place as the wolf tried to assert itself. It screamed for her attention the only way it could. By breaking her bones. Along with constant super vision, her fingers and toes kept cricking out of place. The muscle spasms were the most obnoxious. Various cramps popped up in her calves, her arms, even one vicious one in her hamstring. She'd bitten the wooden handle of a pitchfork trying not to scream her way through that one. Left a nice imprint of non-human teeth in the wood.

At the moment a single wolf canine was jabbing her bottom lip. She touched it with the tip of her tongue and winced. AJ had been goofing around when she'd jotted "Fang" down on her records. It didn't seem so funny at the moment, even if it had never been more fitting.

The howling too, returned. She heard it as though it was coming from a long tunnel. Distant but there, and ringing from inside her own head.

"Distract yourself," she said and turned her attention to the neat bales of hay nearby. "Right."

Freckles stood in his stall, watching every move she made. She stuck her tongue out at him and went about her business. "Don't judge me."

At first she thought she'd build a hay fort, like an igloo or something. That seemed too pathetic and doglike, so she knocked it down and started over.

"You know, Freckles, it's not that I don't like Emerson," she said. With a grunt, she hoisted a bale on top of her growing tower. "I do. She's funny and sweet."

Freckles snorted.

She glared at him. "Watch it, buddy. Say the wrong thing and I'll go get the barbecue sauce."

He tossed his head and she smirked. "That's what I thought."

Another bale went up. She started building steps. "It's just... it's Ben."

Tears bit at her eyes. She slumped down on the next bale she'd been about to pick up and turned to the horse. He snuffled at her and whickered.

She wrapped her arms around herself and shook her head. "He was the first person outside of family I told about this —" she knocked on her head. "This thing living in me. He was so calm about it. Then again, he didn't believe me until I picked up the front end of his truck. Then he had a minor freak out."

She smiled wistfully, remembering how Ben had sat down, hard, when she'd reached down and hefted the truck. "It didn't matter though. I still killed him. After all that talk about how I was just scared."

Freckles stretched his long neck out and took a tentative sniff at the top of her head. She stretched out her hand for his muzzle and he pulled back with a huff. But after a moment he leaned out again and touched his whiskers to her fingers. "I have a right to be scared."

He looked at her with bright eyes, both ears pricked forward, and pawed at the ground with one hoof. She smiled and he nickered softly, then made a small whuffing noise.

Her smile fell as she followed her thoughts down. "And then Emerson and this imprint. Everybody's worried, Emerson's too curious for her own good, and then here I am. What am I supposed to do?" She bit too hard into her lip and squeaked. The single wolf tooth drew blood.

Freckles backed away, his ears swiveling back and forth as he looked toward the barn doors. She sighed and stood to continue her building, licking at her bleeding lip. Her stairs were almost done. Might as well finish something she started for once. "I mean, I'm pretty sure I'd kill her. I don't know. The wolf seems to like her... a lot. But I don't know if it's just the wolf or if it's me. AJ and Grady say we're the same creature, but then there's Ben. I loved him, the wolf didn't. What if it's just the wolf? I can't just let it lead. Not after what it's — I've done. Imprint or not, I just can't trust it."

Her stairs complete, she stood back and admired her handy work. A hay bale throne fit for Queen of the barn. She climbed up it and perched on top. With all her recent free time she might be able to put together a nice hay crown to go with it. She tugged at one earlobe as the howling rose again. The wolf wasn't a fan of her antics, apparently. Or maybe it was pissed she was talking to a horse. "Freckles, don't repeat this to anyone, okay? I'm trusting you with very personal information. I think last time, in the freezer, that was me. I kissed Emerson, not the wolf." She wrinkled her nose. "That sounds awful out loud. Does kissing a werewolf count as bestiality? I just meant... it was there and it definitely pushed, but I was in control. I, Harper, kissed her."

PURE OF HEART

The laugh that burst out of her mouth was awkward and loud. Freckles jerked his head in her direction.

"I kissed a girl and I liked it?"

He snorted.

"Not a Katy Perry fan? Me either." She lay back with a groan and rubbed circles against her throbbing temples. "It doesn't matter. The imprint, the wolf. I can't risk it. I won't risk her. I'm not letting this thing tell me what to do. Emerson will be safe as long as I stay away from her."

The problem would be making that work. Fincher wasn't huge, certainly not big enough for her to hide. They would inevitably cross paths. Which left one option; she would have to drive her away. She'd done it before, she could again. Shove her away... right into Holt's arms.

Her stomach clenched at the thought. She heard the echo of a snarl, and realized that one had been out loud, not in her head. "We have to," she said and blinked to clear the sheen of tears out of her eyes. *Damn wolf.* "We have to let her go."

Let her go and watch from afar. No longer even a friend. Watch Emerson and Holt's whirlwind romance. They'd fall in love, get married, and have a horde of hairy children that all had Emerson's eyes.

Maybe someday she could even repair the friendship. When it was safe and Emerson was forever out of her grasp. She could be Aunt Harper and choke down the wolf every time she smelled coconuts.

It could work.

Even if it hurt every second of every day for the rest of her miserable, cursed life.

The howling stopped and emptiness took up residence in her whole body. She whined and curled up, knees to her chest.

An ache speared her and spread through her limbs. Her teeth chattered.

A howl, stronger than any other she'd felt, surged up from the pit of her stomach. She let it go. An animal sound that rattled her bones and shook more tears free escaped from her human mouth and disappeared in the rafters. The wolf howled for something it couldn't have, and Harper joined it, mourning for something she wanted, but could never have either.

CHAPTER TWENTY-FOUR

Emerson

The pale blue dog sign outside of AJ's had lost its charm. Emerson sat in her car and glared at it through her tears. Her brain had turned to mush, up was down, time didn't matter. Ever since Harper had dropped off the face of the Earth she hadn't been able to sleep, not without dreaming of the wolf. She had gone crazy, it had happened for real. Not only had she discovered a real life werewolf living in Montana, working as a bartender, she'd gone ahead and kissed her.

She touched her forehead with a shaking hand. Touched her lips, remembering the rush of kissing Harper, the full body explosion that had occurred when Harper had surprised her with a response best described as wolfish.

Time was no longer her friend. She'd thought having some time apart would help un-muddle things. It only made them worse. Three days of nothing but time had not cured whatever ailed her.

She suspected Harper was both cure and disease.

"How did this happen?" she asked the rearview mirror as she flexed her hands around the steering wheel.

Talking to herself wouldn't bring her any answers. She wanted to talk to someone, anyone. But the people who already knew about Harper weren't an option. If she talked to Grady, Harper would be more pissed, or whatever she was. AJ was out. She definitely couldn't talk to Cooper. That left her alone. Though she did think AJ would be a more sympathetic ear than any of the others.

She reached into her purse and grabbed her phone, dialed Oscar, and slumped back against the seat.

He picked up after the second ring. "You know it's kind of late?"

"Oz?" She choked on tears and wrapped an arm around her stomach.

"Em, what's wrong?"

"I made a mess," she said, sinking lower in her seat. *I became friends with a werewolf. Then she kissed me and freaked out. Then she kissed me again and freaked out again. Now she's gone and I feel so alone.* "You were right."

"Harper or Holt? Do you want me to come up there? I will. I swear I will come out there and run them over with the Prius."

She imagined him trying to sneak up on Harper in the car. Her dull laugh bounced off the windows. The dissonant tone made her wince. "It's Harper. It's... complicated."

"Of course it is. Did she hurt you, Emerson?"

"No." She shook her head. "No, she didn't do anything wrong. I think I messed up."

"What happened?"

"She kissed me."

Silence.

"Oz?"

"I'm sorry, I'm just trying to figure out – was this a surprise to you?"

She chewed on her bottom lip. Her stomach roiled. "Yes. I don't think she intended to, it just sort of happened."

"Like an accident?" He sighed. "How do you accidently kiss someone?"

"It wasn't an accident, it was a surprise for both of us, but I wouldn't say it was an accident. It feels like we've been headed this direction, but it wasn't the right moment."

"You and your moments. So she kissed you and ran for the hills. Did she look scared?"

"Shocked is more like it, but..."

"But?"

"But then when I saw her again, she kissed me... again." She left out the part about how she'd cornered Harper in the freezer right before. Or that they'd been arguing about werewolf things.

"Oh. Okay, now I'm confused."

You and me both. "We were having a discussion. She kissed me. She ran. Then she kissed me and ran again. I haven't seen her in three days and I don't know what to do."

"Em, maybe she needed some time to sort things out. Do you even know if she is, uh, monolingual? Or ambidextrous, at least?"

"The topic didn't exactly come up."

"Sounds like you might have blown her mind a bit, and she wanted some space to figure it out. Kind of like how you locked yourself in your room for a week after you kissed Madeline? Remember? You freaked out."

This is different, she wanted to say, but couldn't explain it. "I guess so. I'm just – I want to talk to her. I have so much to say, and questions and..."

"And you really like her, don't you?"

"I think I do." *But I can't know for sure, because she's a werewolf.* She groaned and rubbed at her temple. "I really do."

"This is just like those books you love. You know that, right?"

"I love to read about it," she said, cringing. "Living it is not as fun. I've been lied to."

"Fiction does that."

"I know where she is. She's surprisingly horrible at hiding. A plus to living in a small town, if I'm looking for someone there aren't a lot of places for them to go."

"Ah, my sister the stalker."

"I want to go talk to her, work this out."

He sighed again and she heard him flop onto his couch. "In my opinion, you should leave her alone. Let her get a handle on what she wants first. But I know you, and I know you're not the world's most patient person. What are you going to do, and how can I help?"

"Can you tell me you love me and support me even when I'm being a psycho?"

"I love you and I will support you in your psychosis. I'll even make sure they don't try to feed you pudding at the psych ward."

She laughed. "You're the best brother ever. I'm sorry for calling so late. I needed to talk to someone and I don't have anyone else. It's not like I can call Holt."

"You can always call me. That will never change, even if we are worlds apart."

She slouched down in her seat and glared out the window at the trees beyond. "I'm beyond annoyed with this situation."

He snorted. "You're loving every second."

"I am not. It's incredibly frustrating when you don't know what you want, and you don't know what someone else wants either."

"Seems to me someone wants to kiss you. You could start there."

"With kissing?"

"No. Unless you want to try it backwards and see what happens." He laughed again and she rolled her eyes. "Ask about the spontaneous kissing first. See where it goes from there."

"Alright," she said. "I can do that."

***

She marched up to AJ's house, shoulders squared and mouth set in a thin line. Oscar called it her 'no mess' face. Her more practical choice in footwear for the evening meant she could move in the stale snow without getting stuck, or risking frostbite. They weren't the cutest pair of boots she'd ever owned, but they carried her toward her goal a lot faster than peeptoes would.

Angry, she told herself as she stomped snow onto the welcome mat before AJ's front door. *You are very angry, and you will not take no for an answer. No more secrets or deflections or being turned away. Not this time.*

AJ opened the door, both her eyebrows at her hairline instead of the trademark single eyebrow arch. "Emerson?"

"Hello, Doctor Bell. Where's Harper?"

"Harper? She's not here."

"Oh yes she is." She narrowed her eyes and crossed her arms. "I really appreciate you being a good friend to her. I do. However, she and I have a lot to discuss, and she's been missing for three days."

"That's not a good idea," AJ said, wincing and ruffling her hair. "She's not in a good space, and I don't want to make things worse."

In other words, I don't want you to make it worse. She let her proud stance fall away, licked at her lips, and took a deep breath. "Please, Doctor. It's not just Harper who's in a bad space. I need to talk to her. Too much happened and I need answers."

"Call me AJ," she said and opened the door wider. A Border Collie stuck its head around it, tongue hanging out the side of its mouth. It cocked its head and whined up at her. "Why don't you come inside for a minute, you look like you could use some coffee."

"No, thank you." She shook her head and felt her smile wobble at the edges. The tears returned. "I need to see her. I'm losing my mind, and I need to talk to her, now. I promise I'll get out of your hair after that. Is she in there?"

AJ tilted her head and leaned forward. Dark eyes flitted over every inch of Emerson's face. Finally, she inhaled sharply and backed up a step. "She's in the barn. I'll be out in an hour to check on her, and you. Understand?"

"Yes," she said and nodded. "Thank you."

"Be careful."

"She won't hurt me."

"That's not what I'm worried about."

***

"Why wasn't I crate trained at a young age?"

Emerson paused outside the half-open barn door at the tone in Harper's voice. Her heart lurched in her chest, crawled up to her throat where she could feel her pulse thump away. A fresh shot of adrenaline rejuvenated her, warmth spread through her ribcage. Her thoughts scattered and her frustration seeped away, leaving behind only determination.

She set her jaw, tightened her hands into fists and slipped into the barn. "Harper!"

Harper, who had been sitting on a ridiculous throne-like chair made of hay, squealed and tipped over backwards. She popped back up around the side within a second, hay sticking out of her hair and a wild look in her gold eyes. "Emerson!"

"Were you really expecting someone else?" She marched toward her cowardly werewolf with her shoulders back, chin held high. The tension that had lingered in her chest for the last three days eased. She felt calm and in control. Time to get the wolf some courage. "We need to talk."

"Do we?" She said, voice cracking, and clutched at her necklace, still behind her hay barrier. "I'm good. I think. Nice seeing you. Get out."

"Make me. Is it the wolf, Harper?"

"Is what the wolf? Me? Yes, I'm the wolf, and Harper, and maybe having a psychotic break."

She stifled a laugh. "I had a similar thought about psychotic breaks, which is why we really need to figure this out."

"Now?"

"Now," she said and crossed her arms. "I need to know why."

"Why what?"

Her eyes narrowed, she pursed her lips. "You're not stupid, and neither am I. So stop acting like it. While we're at it, why don't you stop acting like a child and come out here."

"This is not a good idea. This is the worst idea ever, and I've had some bad ones lately." Harper eased out into the open, but kept her back plastered to the hay. "I don't know what to say. I'm trying to protect you."

"Protect me from what, exactly? I thought the big secret was the wolf. But – you've done something to me." She huffed and pinned her in place with a glare. "What did you do?"

"I didn't do anything to you, it happened to me."

"What happened?"

"You did."

Emerson tossed her hands in the air and then stuck her fists to her hips. "Oh, yes, that makes sense. Somehow this is all my fault? Since I met you I haven't been able to stop thinking about you. You kissed me, and I probably shouldn't have, but I kissed you back, if you care to remember. I can't help myself. It's like you've stripped away all my self-restraint."

"You didn't want to kiss me?" She made a choked noise and lowered her head, shoulders hunched, lips pressed tight together.

"I did, that's what I'm saying. I wanted it so badly and it's odd, even for me, to want to kiss someone I just found out is a werewolf." She rolled her eyes and glanced over at the horse side-eyeing them. "What are you looking at, Nosey?" He moved away with a snort, and she turned back to a rapidly reddening Harper. "And then – then you kissed me and left me with my head spinning to go hide in a barn with Mr. Ed?"

"I –"

She stamped her foot. "Was that the wolf, Harper? Did you want to kiss me? Or would you have shoved your tongue in anyone's mouth if they'd been there instead?" Her stomach burned and she clenched her teeth at the thought.

"I didn't – No, that's not – Of course not! Fuck!" She heaved a breath and the gold flared brighter. "I don't know how to explain this to you, and I don't even want to. It doesn't even fucking matter. Emerson, you have to stay away from me, do you understand? I could kill you. I can't control it, and it's worse when I'm around you. I'm terrified for you. When will you understand I'm a monster?"

"Stop!" Emerson stomped forward, closing the distance between them to a couple feet. Within slapping range. She ground her teeth and Harper curled her lip. "Stop it. You're not a monster. I can't stand to hear you say it anymore. It's not true. I'm so done watching you hide yourself away to wallow in depression and loneliness because you've labeled yourself as something atrocious. You're a good person."

"How would you know? You barely know me, and you're already accusing me of doing something to you." Her left eye twitched. "What's your definition of monster? Fangs and claws? Check. A body count? Check. People die around me – I can't – I won't let you be my next victim."

"Was it the wolf?" she whispered.

"Are you listening to me?"

She stepped closer still, stared up into Harper's glare. "Answer the question."

"I could kill you. Please," she said, and grabbed Emerson's shoulders. "Please. I could kill you."

"I'm not Ben." She grabbed for Harper's wrists, keeping her from pulling away. "I'm not him. I'm Emerson. And you're not the same person you were, not the monster you think you are. Answer the question."

"I can't." Fat tears slipped down her face, catching on her lips and a couple dripped off her chin. "Please. You have to go. Get as far away from me as you can. You don't want this."

"Don't you dare tell me what I want or don't want." She shook her head and blinked free some tears of her own. A strangled laugh came from her scratchy throat. They were crying like a couple of drama queens on a soap opera. "It's my choice to stay, and I told you I would. I'm not running."

"You will."

"No."

"I wanted to. The wolf pushed, but I wanted to kiss you. It's you. The wolf – I – I imprinted on you."

She wrinkled her nose. "You what?"

"Imprinted, we think." Harper laughed and shoved her hair out of her face. "I don't know how to explain this."

"Try."

"Wolves and probably werewolves, they – they mate for life." She groaned and squeezed her eyes shut. "Jesus H. God. I said it out loud and it's even worse when I'm the idiot saying it. I'm so sorry."

"I don't —" Her mouth opened, but nothing came out. She cleared her throat and tried again. "Are you saying I'm... You think I'm your mate? How does – hm – what?"

"The monster inside me imprinted on you," she said through gritted teeth.

The sound of a smack resonated through the barn. Emerson drew her hand back, gaping at the red mark she'd left on Harper's cheek. "I – oh – I'm sorry, I told you not to say that again."

"You...Ow!" Harper rubbed her cheek and glared with one eye.

"So that's it then? That's why you kissed me, and why my head has been a disaster since running into you? Is it some sort of werewolf magic forcing us together?" Her hands shook at her sides. Every bit of her wanted to reach out and smooth the sting she'd caused. It felt like she'd kicked a puppy.

"I don't know. Grady didn't know about it. AJ found some information online."

"Oh good, online resources are always so trustworthy," she said with a scoff. "I suppose that would explain some things though. We don't get a choice in the matter? What if you don't want me forever? Or I don't want to be your... mate."

"I don't know." Harper sat down on an overturned bale and pressed her palms against her eyes. "I don't know, okay? I've just been trying to stay away from you, so you could have a choice. To keep you safe from the wolf, me, the imprint, all of it."

"I'm safe. I'm aggravated, and confused, but I'm safe. Actually, I can't think of anything safer than being under the protection of a werewolf." She laughed again, but cut herself off and cleared her throat. "What's it doing to you? The imprint."

"It howls for you. It's obsessed, and I couldn't keep fighting it. And then I gave in and started spending time with you. Cooper thought maybe it would be happy with us just being friends." She snorted. "And now the line is so blurred. I kissed you the second time to test and see if..."

"To see if it was you."

"Yes."

"And?"

"And it doesn't matter, Emerson. It doesn't matter if I have feelings for you. It's dangerous, and you don't feel the same."

"You don't know if it's dangerous, I doubt it would be. An imprint wouldn't be worth much if you were a threat to your mate." She cringed. "We need a different name for that. Wait. Feelings?"

"I have – I like you. A lot."

That's good, isn't it? She held her breath and chewed on the corner of her mouth. Harper refused to make eye contact, preferring to glower over at the horse who had begun to eavesdrop again. "Harper."

"It doesn't change anything. Not when we don't know anything about this imprint. It could just be that, screwing with us."

"Who said I don't have feelings for you?"

Harper shook her head. "It's the imprint. Somehow it's messing with you too. No sane person would... you know."

"Does that matter?"

"How about the fact that I'm not a man, did you add that into your calculations for how fucked this all is?" she said.

Emerson took a seat next to her, grabbed for Harper's hand, and stared at the barn door. "Is that the part that's really bothering you?"

"Nope. Just another thing that doesn't make sense. I'm not – I've never been interested in women before. Though to be honest, I've never been much interested in anyone, except for Ben."

"This could all be some werewolf thing neither of us is ever going to understand," she said. Sitting that close to Harper had stirred up all kinds of flutters and jolts throughout her body. Not exactly helpful in this situation. She turned and observed Harper's pulse, thumping away with enough strength for her to see it under the pale skin of her neck. "But I should probably disclose that I'm ambidextrous."

Harper snorted. "You can use both hands? That does seem important for you to tell me right this second. Thanks for clearing that up."

"No, Harper. It's a more... well, Oscar and I feel it's a more polite way to say that I am bisexual."

"That's not polite, it's sneaky."

"Fine, it's sneaky." She shook her head and slid her hand up to Harper's wrist, smoothing her thumb over the thrum of a thundering pulse. Her breath caught in her throat as her heart raced to catch up with the allegro tempo. "Point is, that's one less hurdle from where I'm sitting. Maybe that's the reason it's me, because I'm already... but that doesn't explain –"

"Doesn't matter, it really doesn't. We can't give in to this."

"What if I want to? Not give in, per se, but I can't deny I feel things when I'm with you. Thrilling new things. Could it hurt to explore them? Explore the imprint? It doesn't feel like a bad thing."

"That's the choice you want to make? How do you know if it's even yours?" Gold eyes locked onto her, held her in place. They lowered to her mouth, lingered for a second, then raised back up. "This is your decision. I won't let it force you into anything."

"This is my choice."

"It's a stupid one."

"Do you want to get slapped again?" She smiled. They were closer. The hair rose on the back of her neck, her hands trembled around Harper's. She swallowed and held those shining eyes with her own. "This is going to sound cliché, and you can make fun of me later. I give you permission. But when I'm around you, it's magic. Werewolf imprint or magic or whatever, I don't care. I want to chase that feeling because it makes me feel like I can fly, like anything could be possible. And since you're still you, that anything will probably be annoying, frustrating, and insane."

"You sure you want that? Me? It's not going to be easy."

Her smile grew, she shifted nearer. "I never thought it would be. I want to try. But what do you want? All of you, not just the wolfish side."

Harper swallowed hard and grinned weakly. "You."

"I'm going to kiss you now," she said, already leaning in, but she paused and frowned. "Don't run."

"Okay."

She tried to be gentle, to keep from overwhelming them both again. The brush of their lips erased that option. Her ears started to ring at the slight caress, and her lips tingled. Harper shivered and caught Emerson's chin in a rough palm, drawing her back for a firmer contact. It took every bit of willpower she had to pull away instead of press for more. "There," she said with a gasp, nose grazing Harper's. "Was that so hard?" She tugged at a lock of dark hair and grinned. "You're so thick headed."

"The better to head-butt people."

"Do you have a comeback for everything?"

"Not yet. I'm working on it. Sometimes I cheat and check my notebook. The Holy Bible of Sarcasm."

She groaned and kissed her again. "You're lucky I think you're charming."

"That's not luck, Emers. That's good genetics."

"You think you're so badass, don't you?"

"Nope. Not at all. But I'm in a pretty good mood. My shitty week just turned awesome." She grinned her lopsided grin and pressed a lingering kiss to her forehead. "I can't believe this is real. Well, the slap part was pretty real. My face still hurts."

"I'm sorry, again, for slapping you. I should probably stick to my words when expressing myself."

"I don't know, the kissing thing works. I think it's supposed to help things that hurt too." She pointed to her cheek.

Unable to resist her pout, she quickly righted her wrong and kissed the pink skin. "Already incorrigible. I see I've got my work cut out for me."

"I swear I'm potty trained."

"Now I know it's the wolf imprint," she said and raised her chin for another kiss. Which turned into two, then three. By the fifth she lost count, brain blanked by the incredible sensations.

Harper growled and dug both hands into her hair, cupping her ears and holding her in place. Emerson clung to the front of her shirt to keep from floating away.

Freezing water sluiced over both of them. She shrieked and fell off the hay bale. Harper tumbled backwards with a strangled yelp.

She shoved her wet hair out of her face and blew off a piece of hay stuck to her chin. AJ stood over her with a smirk, bucket balanced on her hip.

"I'm so happy for both of you, but take this literal roll in the hay elsewhere. You're spooking my horses."

"Jay!"

CHAPTER TWENTY-FIVE

The smile on her face could not be contained. She couldn't put it away, nor did she want to. Harper took her hand and led her out of the barn. Warmth radiated through her body from the gentle contact. The calluses on Harper's hand tickled her palm and her heartbeat took off, drumming a crazy beat at the lopsided smile directed down at her.

AJ glared at them, hands on her hips, but she smiled too. "I'm watching you two."

"Yes Ma'am." Harper grinned and tugged at Emerson's hand.

Outside, night had taken over, the moon riding high in a clear sky. The snowy landscape took on the lunar glow, making everything brighter than it had any right to be.

She looked up at Harper in the light and caught bright gold eyes. Her cheeks were flushed. Something about seeing her out under the moon made her thoughts scatter, unable to lock onto any one thing.

She felt jittery, like she'd had one too many cups of Grady's tar-like coffee. Harper, wolf, woman, she'd never looked so much like both at one time. The moon brought it all up to the surface, and instead of being afraid she was invigorated, fascinated. Various expressions played across Harper's features, too fast for her to pinpoint one before it changed.

"So, um..." Harper tugged at her hair, bit her lip, and kicked up some snow. "Hi?"

She smiled and squeezed the warm hand and bottled up her breath to get control of her heart. "Hello."

"I don't know what to do now."

"I'm not entirely sure myself," she said. "We should probably go to bed."

Harper dropped her hand and backed up a step, jaw hanging open, whole face pink. "Whoa, that's, uh, maybe we could back it up a step or five?"

Blood rushed to her cheeks. "No, I didn't..." she stammered. "I meant go home. We should go home, to our separate homes. Not that I don't enjoy your – not that I don't want to – I didn't mean that we should... not that. Not right now, I mean. Because eventually, if you want, that would be –"

"Emerson!" Harper laughed, ducked her head, and rubbed at her flushed cheeks. "I got it. Please stop before you prove spontaneous human combustion is a real thing. At least in werewolves. Spontaneous werewolf combustion."

"I'm — I..." She tangled her fingers and puffed up her cheeks. "There's no getting out of this hole I've dug, is there?"

"Nope. But don't worry, I have plenty of practice digging holes and climbing out of 'em. You'll live." She grinned and put her hands into her pockets. "Goodnight, then, I guess."

She turned around and headed toward the woods instead of the street. Emerson frowned and followed. "Where are you going?"

"Walking home."

"Through the woods?"

"Yeah, why not?"

She reached out and snagged two fingers in the folds of Harper's worn and faded plaid shirt. The fabric was soft, old, and it swamped Harper's thin frame. For the first time she wondered who the previous owner had been. Ben? Grady? Harper's father? "Why not through the town? It's dark and what about the... bears?"

"Bears? They're hibernating. I'm not really concerned about cranky bears. They can smell the wolf on me, and I think we've agreed it's best if we avoid each other."

"You made a pact with the local bears?" She pictured them gathered in a clearing, deep in the woods. A small herd of giant grizzlies and one massive wolf the color of sin with fiery eyes. "Does the barking and growling translate?"

"You're funny," Harper said and cocked her head. "But it wasn't a round table conversation, like you're thinking. I had a run in with a black bear a few years ago. Scared me half to death, but it got punched in the head, took a big whiff, and decided not to play with me anymore."

Emerson chewed her lower lip, pinched the fabric between her fingers and tugged. Harper didn't budge and she ended up moving instead, pressed right up against a strong arm. Heat rolled off of her, a nice comfort overriding the chill of the night. A bear had attacked her. A bear. And it had lost.

"What is it? I'm going to be fine, I promise."

"It's not that I – I want to go with you." She shook her head and wrapped her arms around Harper's.

"What about your car?"

She sighed, her poor car. "I think it'll be okay overnight. I'll come get it tomorrow. Dr. Bell seemed rather adamant we take ourselves elsewhere immediately."

Harper snorted and headed for the woods again, Emerson tagging along holding her shirt sleeve. "What gave you that impression? Was it the pointing out of the barn, the smug smirk, or the freezing bucket of water?"

"Yes?"

"Was that a question or an answer?" She paused and looked down her arm. "Can I –" Her fingers twitched. "Is it still okay if I hold your hand?"

With a wide grin she let go of the shirt and twined her fingers between Harper's. A bolt of that same unnamed something tingled through her fingers and up her arm. "May I."

"Emers." Harper growled and rolled her eyes.

"I'm sorry, it's a habit," she said, still grinning.

"Who's English are you correcting so often it's become a habit? Oscar doesn't strike me as the type who needs help with that." Clear green eyes narrowed and then widened. "Oh, it's everyone. Here I was feeling special."

"I know it comes off as annoying and snotty." She ducked her head and tucked some hair behind an ear. Happy to be walking with Harper and back to the way they were before. No secrets or yelling. She didn't have to snoop anymore. Operation Sasquatch had been completed, successfully.

Harper shrugged. "It's kind of adorable in an irritating way. Come on, before AJ returns with a hose."

"She wouldn't."

"She's done it before, to break up a tussle between me and Ike."

"Who's Ike?"

"Stopped yourself, didn't you?" She smirked and helped her over a log. Warm hands steady on her waist. "Ike's her dog."

"You were fighting with her dog?"

"We were playing. Got a little loud."

She giggled, imagining Harper on all fours with the Border Collie, growling and wrestling over a rope toy. One end in Harper's teeth, the other held tight in Ike's.

They walked in silence for awhile, pausing on occasion for Harper to help her over one obstacle or another. She enjoyed the silence, content to spend the time observing. The way the corner of Harper's mouth twitched just before she smiled. How she moved through the woods with such ease and grace, like she was a part of them, belonged here. More than anything she liked feeling so safe, cared for, in the way Harper helped her along. She held on so carefully, lifted her like she weighed nothing, and always, always smirked when she set her back down. Then she would stop again, her expression slack and eyes glossy.

"What's your middle name?" She asked, out of curiosity more than an urge to kill the silence.

"Random," Harper quipped and turned around to lift her over another log. She set her down and held on until Emerson nodded that she had her footing. "No, that's not it. It's Quinn."

"Sorry, I'm just trying to get to know you. I feel like we're going backwards somehow. I feel like I should know more about the woman who imprinted on me." She blushed anew at the thought. The whole thing could be just that. An imprint, werewolf magic, working on both of them. But Harper licked her lips, hummed a low note and she stopped caring about that. This magical, mysterious creature was hers if she wanted, and she did.

"You sure that doesn't bother you?" Harper pushed her bangs out of her eyes and sighed. "I wouldn't blame you, you know. It's weird, I'm a werewolf, and I think it's weirder than Tim Burton's vision of Hell. How's that for messed up?"

"I'm not that bad, am I?"

"No, not at all. It's strange though, can we agree on that?"

She nodded, then shook her head, unsure of the correct response. "It's... unusual. Especially for it to feel this way so quickly. Like I've known you forever, even though I hardly know a thing about you."

"Are you sure – because I can – we could be friends, I think."

"Harper, we couldn't. I would spend the rest of my life chasing this feeling." She laughed, stopped, and swallowed hard. "Which is somewhat problematic when one thinks in terms of free will. However, I also believe in fate, love at first sight, and you love who you love. Sometimes it's not a choice."

"It's always a choice. You're choosing to act on this or to ignore it."

"It doesn't feel like that to me." She looked at the hand holding hers, large and rough, but gentle at the same time. She saw the ripple of defined muscles up her arm, and shoulder, though they were slim and feminine. A sharp jaw line, green eyes that glittered with mischief. All that dark hair, tousled and falling over her shoulders in soft, messy waves. She was a riddle, wrapped in a conundrum. Beauty and the beast all in one alluring package. "How could I not choose you?"

"Love at first sight, huh?" Harper chuckled roughly and scratched the back of her head. "You saying you love me, Emers?"

"No," she said and licked at her lips. "I'm saying I feel like I could, and I'm not the type of girl to run from that."

"You must've had a lot of fixer-upper boyfriends." Harper's smirk fell. She sighed and shook her head. "Sorry. My manners are pretty atrocious."

"It's alright, you're not wrong. Oscar calls them strays." She winced, knowing she'd have to call him back soon. The second she got home, before he panicked, if he hadn't already. "But what it's like with you – it was never like that with any of my previous suitors."

"Suitors. We're going to have to work on this highbrow talk. I feel like I need one of those foreign language guide-book things."

"Don't sell yourself short." She rubbed her thumb against the tendons on the back of Harper's hand. "Part of what intrigues me about you is how smart you are."

"I'm smart?"

"You seem to have a certain intelligence about you. Certainly you use those witty barbs of yours quite deftly."

"Thank you?"

"You're welcome." She peeked up at Harper's little smirk. "It also doesn't hurt that you're easy on the eyes."

"Jesus H. God," Harper said with a groan. That smirk stretched into a pleased smile. "So... Middle names. Hm. Emerson Anne Grey?"

"No, though I wouldn't have complained. I love Anne of Green Gables."

"Never heard of it."

"I'll have to fix that. Perhaps the movie would be a better place to start."

"And there goes your opinion of my intelligence. I can read, you know."

"I'm sure you can. Which comic book is your favorite?"

"X-Men." Harper's face stayed blank, serious, for the span of seconds. Emerson rearranged her own expression into one of shock and outrage. It earned her the response she'd wanted. Harper broke first and laughed. "Kidding! If it's not Anne, then, uh, what are the popular ones. Grace?"

Of course as soon as the name passed her lips, Emerson tripped on a submerged rock. She would have landed face down in the snow if Harper hadn't reacted faster than any human could. "That would have been ironic, but no," Emerson said with a laugh, holding on to the arm around her stomach.

Harper scoffed and pulled her upright. "I agree. You're more delicate anyway. More like a... Rose?"

"Think less traditional."

"Right, your parents are probably book nerds too."

"Hey!" She swatted at her, laughing as Harper swayed out of reach.

"Call it like I see it." She grinned and came right back, taking her hand like they'd been doing that for years instead of minutes. "I can't think of any author names."

"Shall I end your needless suffering? All that thinking must hurt."

"How many IQ points did that cost me? Smart-ass."

She sighed and reached out to touch some snow clinging to the side of a tree. "My father picked our names, thankfully. My mother wanted to name us whatever was trendiest at the time. Liam and Emma were her top picks, I believe."

"Liam's not bad, good Irish name."

"I wouldn't have minded Emma horribly either. It makes me think of Emma Woodhouse." At Harper's blank look she stifled a laugh. "Emma, by Jane Austen? I thought you said you could read."

"Doesn't mean I make a habit of it."

"We're going to have to see about encouraging that." She started making a list in the back of her head of all the titles she loved. Classics and new fiction. "I think you'd be a Harry Potter fan. There's even a werewolf."

"Goody. Sign me up. As long as the werewolf is the hero and not the blood dripping villain." Harper sighed and squinted up at the moon. "Middle name?"

"I just said it."

"Emerson Harry? Nope, that's no good. Emerson Emma? No. Jane?"

"So close."

"Emerson... Austin? Your middle name is Austin? Like the capital of Texas?"

"Austen with an e, like Jane Austen."

"Of course." She chuckled. "Emerson Austen with an E Grey."

"Harper Quinn Cahill," she said, pleased to know something else, something normal about this abnormal person.

"Well, now at least I'll know what to yell when you're in trouble."

"You foresee me being a lot of trouble?"

"Oh you're trouble. Doesn't take a genius to figure that out." Harper's smirk deepened. "Dating strange werewolves, that's definitely trouble."

"Are we dating now?"

"What else would we call what we're doing?"

"I don't know, but as long as it doesn't involve the word mate, I am on-board." She frowned, not wanting to spend time on that particular word just yet. There'd be plenty of chances to mull it over, and all its connotations. "We haven't even had a proper date."

"I took you to the vet clinic."

"That does not count," she said with a tsk. Harper had never done this, she knew that. She also knew it had been awhile since anyone had taken Harper out. *Ease her into it*, she thought, *be gentle, don't go too fast*. "Since you're new to this, allow me to rectify the situation. Harper, would you like to come over to my house tomorrow night for dinner?"

"I don't know, I've got a flea bath scheduled, and I think there are some neighborhood cats that need to be harassed. Not to mention I've gotten lazy about marking my territory. Lots of wolfy things to do."

"You're not funny."

"I'm funny and I know it." Harper wiggled in a ridiculous dance move, grin wide and charming. "I'm bringing funny back?"

"*Mon Dieu.* Harper."

"No fair with the French stuff. Mess with me, bright eyes, and I'll break out my Irish to level the playing field."

"You speak Irish ?" She pulled Harper to a stop, eyes widening. Another new layer to the already complex woman.

"Had to learn a little, my grandparents spoke it." Harper shrugged.

"That's fantastic! You'll have to teach me some."

"On a first date? How scandalous."

Their pace slowed to a stroll. Harper steered her around a thick tree and the town lights stood out, winking at them from the snowy valley. Almost home, almost to the end of their peaceful idyll. She didn't know what tomorrow would be like, but she had a feeling moments like this wouldn't always be available. "You're saying yes to dinner tomorrow?"

"Yeah, I am."

"I'll cook." Unlike her mother, she could, thanks to several expensive private lessons. Her mother's idea, strangely enough. Despite avoiding the kitchen herself, she swore up and down Emerson would never find and keep a man without knowing her way around a stove. She doubted Harper would be interested in any of her French cuisine, but a simple steak dinner might be better anyway. "Are you allergic to anything?"

"Vegetables?" Again she delivered it with the perfect deadpan expression. One that had Emerson staring at her, waiting for the punchline. Surely she was joking. "You caught on to that trick way too fast. Yeah, I'm kidding. I am a carnivore for the most part, but I can handle veggies. Just don't expect me to eat tofu."

A pity, but nothing she couldn't work around, at least for now. "So noted. Tomorrow at six?"

"I'll be there." Snow crunched and slid down the short hill they stood on top of. Harper scratched her cheek. "Is there a dress code?"

"What if I said yes?" She asked, wondering if Harper would show up in a dress and heels if she said so. A long look at Harper's lean side profile had her brain working to conjure up an image worthy of that glorious shape. Something tight, black, exposing what had to be magnificent legs and toned arms.

"I'd be breaking rules already."

"Hmm, I'll have to roll up a newspaper in preparation."

"Who even reads the newspaper anymore? You have the internet, I know you do. Don't go trying to smack me with that either."

She laughed and sighed, looking down at the back of her home. All that thick snow burying the patio furniture, obscuring everything in her yard. Long icicles dangled off the roof like clear teeth. She shivered and snuggled under Harper's arm, right up against her side. "This is beautiful."

"It is." Harper's lips brushed against her temple, barely there and gone the next second. "Do you want me to walk you to the door?"

"Please?"

"You don't have to say please."

"I'm saying it anyway." She grinned and remained tucked in safe and sound against Harper as they inched down the hill. Her feet went out from under her a couple of times, but a steady hand kept her from sledding the rest of the way minus the actual sled.

"You know you should probably invest in some snow boots and jeans. As cute as those dresses are, you're going to lose a leg to frostbite."

"You think my dresses are cute?" She leaned up and dropped a sweet kiss to Harper's cheek. "Thank you."

Harper groaned. "So much trouble. Jeans, woman, jeans and boots. I'm sure there's some over-priced designer ones you can pick up with glitter and fake diamonds on them. No four inch heels though, alright? That kind of ruins the point."

"Fake diamonds?" She gasped in fake outrage, unable to manage the same deadpan look Harper had perfected.

"Good one."

They came up on the back door, the new and pristine one Harper had replaced the broken one with. She touched the wood, frowning as a thought hit her. "Harper?"

"Mhm?"

"Did you –" she pointed at the door and put her hands on her hips. Harper immediately looked guilty, a sheepish smile crossing her face, and her toes kicking the mat. "You did."

"I sort of lost my shit." She winced and rubbed at the back of her neck. "That night. But I fixed it."

"Do I have more of this to look forward to?"

"I'll try not to?"

She sighed and shook her head. "And you think I'm trouble."

"You are, I just happen to bring a bit of my own too," Harper said and tilted her head back toward the woods. "I should probably get going. Even though I don't want to."

"I'll see you tomorrow." She looped her arms around Harper's neck and stood up on her toes. Another sigh seeped out at the return of the tingles, this time running up her spine. Harper growled and kissed her cheek.

"Tomorrow."

CHAPTER TWENTY-SIX

Harper

She chugged a carton of orange juice to combat hellacious dry mouth. Her back twitched, and her hands shook as she tossed the empty container into the trash can across the room. "Swish," she said and shook out her hands.

"Do I even want to know?" Cooper asked, leaning against the doorway. He arched an eyebrow when she laughed in response.

"Nope. Not at all, probably not, I don't think so." Harper grinned and tripped over her shoes as she danced toward the coat closet. Emerson sent her a text earlier telling her to wear a coat, even if she didn't need it.

She giggled, snagged her trusty Sherpa lined sweatshirt and zipped it up over her shirt.

"Harp, you're giggling, and that's terrifying."

"Happy, Coop, I'm happy," she said with a sigh. *Insane and somewhat delirious, but happy.* She scraped a hand through her hair and cleared her throat. "So, you're in charge of the house while I'm gone. Don't eat all the food, and please go to bed at a decent hour."

He cocked his head. "Did you make friends with Emerson? Is that what this is?"

"Huh? Friends? Oh, yeah, we're friends." *Friends who held hands as they traipsed through the woods all the way back to the house from AJ's. Friends who kissed each other goodbye and hopefully hello. Girlfriends.* She giggled again. "I'm going over there for dinner and to answer some more werewolf questions."

"It doesn't freak you out that she knows?"

She shook her head so fast it made her dizzy. "It did and now it doesn't."

He scurried around her and closed the front door before she could make her escape. His eyes widened. "Dude, you told her about the imprint, didn't you?"

"Get out of the way, Cooper," she said with a growl and yanked at the door, knocking him into her.

"You did!" He grinned. "Did you kiss her? Are you girlfriends now?"

"None of your business!"

He whistled a low note and waggled his eyebrows. "Uh-huh. Going over for dinner? Like a date?"

"I swear, if you don't get out of my way I'm going to duct tape you to the wall and turn you into a makeshift coat rack." Her eyes flicked in and out of beast-mode. "I mean it. Move."

"Tell me first," he said and crossed his arms, still grinning.

"Oh for – yeah, okay? She's my…" Her mouth went slack in what had to be the dopiest expression in the world. She couldn't help it. "She's my girlfriend."

"I was right, Dad owes me." He stepped out of the way and bowed low, one arm across his stomach the other stretched toward the door. "Don't let me keep you."

She narrowed her eyes at him, and opened the door. One foot had crossed the threshold when he started chanting.

"Harper's got a girlfriend, Harper's got a girlfriend."

She slammed the door in his face and grinned.

"Rude!" he shouted.

"Be good!" With a shake of her head she headed down the stairs humming the horrid tune: "Harper's got a girlfriend."

***

"I've got an addiction," she said by way of greeting.

Emerson grinned at her and opened her front door. "Do you?"

"Yeah." She nodded and kicked the door shut behind her before advancing with a growl. Blue eyes glinted up at her as Emerson backed away, always one step out of reach. "I was hoping you'd be my dealer."

"You've accepted this faster than I thought," she said and turned to press her back against the wall. She licked her lips. "You sure you're okay with all of this?"

Her fingers ached to touch; she curled them back into her palms, forearms trembling with the strain. "I – it's weird. I still don't understand, but I can't stop now. This should feel alien, but it doesn't." The sensation of the wolf had changed, morphed into something exciting. She didn't fight it anymore, or want to hide it. Not with Emerson. "It's an addiction, and you're the drug in my blood now, I swear, and I don't want to stop. I can't. Are you having second thoughts?"

"No, not at all. I was concerned about you. I suppose I should still be when you use words like addiction and combine it with your wolfish side.

But as long as we're in agreement, and you aren't uncomfortable," Emerson said. Pink flooded her cheeks, spilled down her neck. She drew a shuddering breath and tilted her head up. "I thought about it all night. You, I thought about you all night. I don't care if it's werewolf magic."

She sighed and slid her palms up the wall, framing Emerson's head. "I know you have questions."

"So many questions," she said thickly. Her eyelashes fluttered and Harper's pulse surged in her throat.

"I should probably answer those before you think of more." She leaned in and slid the tip of her nose along a cheekbone. Mirroring what she'd done in the library. Another growl warmed her chest. "Do you have a list?"

"I do." Emerson squeaked and slipped her cold hands into Harper's sweatshirt pockets. "Numbered and organized."

"Of course you do. I bet it's even typed out and — "

"Harper, shut up and kiss me."

"Yes, ma'am." She captured parted pink lips and tried not to fall over. Unbelievable power engulfed her, threatened to drown her. Her eyes rolled back behind quivering eyelids. Hair stood on end, goosebumps broke out over her skin, and heat swamped her. The urge to clamp her teeth down grew so strong she had to pull away and gasp for air. Air that tasted of coconut and vanilla. She stared at Emerson's neck and clenched her teeth. "You're like the moon," she said, to distract herself, and shook her head. It wasn't a dissimilar feeling. Moonlight infused her with energy, strength, and her body reacted to it much the same. "A little moon."

"Is that bad?"

"No, I don't think so. New." Her smile wobbled at the corners. *Bite, mark, mine*, her brain screamed. She shoved it down and shook her head again. "Very new." She wrapped a strand of blonde hair around two fingers. "Little Moon."

Emerson shuddered and grabbed Harper's wrist, gently untangling her hair. "Normally I am not a fan of pet names. That one you may keep."

"Yeah?"

"Yes," she said and smiled. "Now, as much as I'd love to stay right here and let you have your fix, I did make dinner and the steak is probably getting cold."

Her ears perked up at the mention of food. She backed away and took a sniff. The coconut stained everything but underneath her super focus on that particular scent she caught a whiff of meat. Mouth-watering, delicious, melt on your tongue meat. She grabbed Emerson's hand and towed her toward the kitchen. "You made me steak?"

"You are a carnivore, are you not?"

"Funny." She stopped at the table and took a moment to appreciate the hard work Emerson had put in. It was set beautifully. Not the table so much as what waited for her on it. There were no candles or lavish centerpieces, and she couldn't care less. Not with what she assumed to be her dinner waiting for her. Heaps of mashed potatoes and a steak the size of her head sat on a white plate. She could smell the blood in the beef and see the juice gathering under it. "Am I drooling?"

Emerson chuckled and gave her a slight push forward. "Not yet. Your eyes have gone gold though."

"Does it bother you?"

"No. It'll take some getting used to, but it doesn't bother me." She inclined her head toward the food. "Go ahead. Do you want some wine?"

She shook her head and tried to remember her manners as she sat down. Her gums itched at the strong smell. Emerson had cooked it perfectly without having to be told. "No, thanks."

"Not a fan?"

"Can't get drunk, so don't see the point. And I have sensitive taste buds, alcohol is an overwhelming flavor."

"Good to know. Will the smell bother you if I have some?"

"Emers, all I smell is steak right now. A parade of skunks could march through here and I wouldn't notice," she said and pressed her hands together to keep from grabbing the steak. "Go for it."

Emerson sat down beside her and unfurled a cloth napkin over her lap. All prim and proper, with perfect posture and everything. Meanwhile, she was struggling to not eat with her hands.

You're not actually an animal, she scolded herself.

"If you concentrate any harder you're going to pass out," Emerson said with a laugh. "I've seen your table manners before. While I wouldn't recommend showing anyone else that side of you, it's just us here. Please eat."

She held her fork and knife, caveman style, and grinned. "Remember how you said I sometimes eat like a starved coyote? You should have made me a smoothie version. "

"Yes, I remember, but I don't think we can sip steak. I'll try not to comment on your eating habits." Emerson cut a piece of her smaller portion with surgical precision and raised an eyebrow. So delicate and feminine, Harper had to wonder how she could infuse girlishness into every little thing.

How the hell is she like that? she thought. *Why am I not like that? I'm a girl too.* "Alright, I gave you fair warning. You might want to avert your eyes."

Emerson chewed her dainty bite, dabbed at her lips with a second napkin, and shook her head. "Now that I know why you eat like that, I think I'll be alright. Thank you for the warning."

"Yup."

When she went right back to sawing off more tiny chunks, Harper took a deep breath and dove in.

She managed not to get anything on the pristine tablecloth.

***

"I think I'm steak drunk," she commented as Emerson helped her into the living room. She sank down onto the plush red sofa with a groan and managed a sleepy, sheepish grin. "Thanks for feeding me and not swatting me with a newspaper for my table manners."

"Thank you for appreciating my cooking so thoroughly," Emerson said, easing down next to her. "I don't think you needed to lick the plate, but it was quite the ego boost."

Harper raised her arm in silent invitation and almost purred when Emerson curled in next to her and sighed. "You have questions."

"I do. Are you ready to answer them?"

"Get this list," she said and hardened her expression into something more serious. "Bring it on."

"I was kidding about the list."

"Is it sad that I'm somewhat disappointed?" She pouted.

"Does it hurt?"

"Being disappointed? I was joking," she said.

Emerson poked her in the ribs and huffed. "Harper. This is going to be a very long night if you don't attempt to be somewhat serious. Does the transformation hurt?"

"No, but it's not very comfortable. Mostly it feels like pressure. Everything goes numb before any of the serious contorting happens."

"Numb like when you get Novocain at the dentist?"

"I don't know, I've never been to the dentist." She giggled at the scandalized expression on her face. "I've never needed to go."

"How would you know?"

She shrugged. "AJ checked them and then went off on a tangent about how unfair genetics could be. I still brush though."

"I take it you've never been to a doctor either? Aside from Doctor Bell."

"I heal on my own. AJ does more studying than doctoring."

Emerson squirmed over and resettled against the opposite arm of the sofa. "Sorry, I need to see your face. How old were you when you – when the first transformation happened?"

"Eleven." She scratched at her neck and winced at the memory. "It was not a fun age anyway. Grady taught me how to shave my legs, and I thought he was going to throw up when he talked to me about periods and sex." She swung her legs up and crossed them. "You should have seen him sitting on the side of the tub with his pants rolled up and razor in hand."

"Did he tell you about the wolf?"

"He tried, but I thought he was full of shit or trying to come up with some less awkward way to discuss puberty."

"It must have been terrifying the first time."

"It was. I felt this wild thing, out of control and trying to take over. It possesses me. Or did," she said with a frown. "That's – I begged Grady to lock me up. Ended up breaking the basement door for the first time. Woke up in the woods. I don't know who was more scared, me or him."

"Your…" Emerson ran a hand through her hair and then propped the side of her head up. She bit her lip. "Your mother, Grady said she was a wolf too. I would think he'd know more about you."

"My grandpa took Mama to a cabin for her first full moon. Grady never saw any of it."

"But it's not just during the full moon?"

She shrugged. "I guess not. I can't help it during the full moon. That other night, I'm not sure what triggered it. Maybe the imprint."

"It's not contagious, is it? The werewolf part. Clearly the imprint is working on both of us."

"No. At least, I don't think so. I'm pretty sure the whole infection through bite and claw is a Hollywood thing."

"What if…" she licked her lips and looked down at her hands. "What if you get hurt? When you're a wolf. Are you injured when you change back?"

"One time I woke up in the cage with a gash in my shoulder, probably from the fence. But it healed."

"What about silver?"

She coughed and rubbed the back of her neck. "I, um…" Her voice softened to a whisper and her chest tightened. She fidgeted and dropped her head. "After Ben. I tried to – with silver – I thought it would work. Stabbed myself with a silver knife I ordered online."

"Harper."

"It hurt, a lot," she said, cringing deeper into the couch. "Took forever to heal too. Even after Grady found me and pulled it out. Only thing that's ever left a scar."

"Where?" Emerson asked, shakily.

"Over my heart." She touched her fingertips there and felt the bump through her shirt. "I thought it would work. Held it against the wall and ran into it as hard as I could. It paralyzed me for awhile, but didn't kill me."

Time had dragged second by agonizing second as she laid there, blood spilling out and soaking everything. Her hair, her clothes, the floor. She couldn't move at all, not to pull the knife out or even open her mouth and scream. Her heart had slowed, so sluggish she thought it might have worked. It almost did. "I couldn't live with what I'd done."

Cold fingers tipped her chin back up. Blue eyes swam into focus. Emerson leaned in and kissed her forehead, the tip of her nose, her cheek. Without asking first she tugged the collar of Harper's shirt down, the thin fabric giving with ease. Breath quaking, she touched the scar, then slid her palm over Harper's pounding heartbeat. "Promise me you won't ever try something like that again. Right now. You promise."

"I promise," she said. "Promise promise."

"You didn't mean to, it was an accident. A horrible accident." Half in Harper's lap already, she folded herself in the rest of the way. "You're not a monster."

Harper hugged her closer and balanced her chin on top of her head. "You alright?"

"No." She sniffled. "Whatever this connection is – the imprint. It feels like I swallowed boiling water thinking about you doing that. My hormones have gone haywire. We need to do some research."

Fix this, you jerk, she kicked herself internally and pulled back far enough to see Emerson's hand resting inside her shirt. "You know you're touching my boob? Maybe that's what's got your hormones all crazy."

She smiled when Emerson puffed a laugh against her collarbone. "I am not. You'd know if I was."

"Pretty sure I know already."

Emerson's hand pulled away and dropped to her hip instead. "What are we going to do about this?"

"Research sounds good, but when I tried to look it up online all I got was weird shit. Maybe there are some books about it?" She hummed and nuzzled against silky blonde hair. "We should definitely see if there are any other side-effects besides crying and boob grabbing."

"Harper." The hand on her hip pinched. "I'll start looking tomorrow. There might be something particular to the Faoladh. Maybe I'll go see AJ too. I don't know what she can do, but at least she can do a cursory check, see if anything's abnormal."

"She'll love that," she said with a snort. "I can hear it now. I'm not a people doctor. Do you have four legs and a tail? No."

"Is that a discussion you've had often?"

"Grady went over to see if she could check him for the flu or something. I could hear her yelling from the back. He only tried it because he sucks at flirting."

"That's cute." Emerson backed away and swiped a hand across her cheeks. "We should help him."

Harper wrinkled her nose. "Let's not. He's a big boy, he can figure it out himself. Plus, he gets cranky when we tease him about it. All better now?"

"Yes."

"Any more questions?"

She sighed. "Lots. But I think I'm good for the night. What about you? Questions?"

"How did you..." She squirmed and then shivered as the movement stirred little flurries in her chest. Would being around Emerson always have such side-effects? "Um, how did you realize you liked girls?"

"I always have, looking back I can see that now." She shrugged and played with the hem of Harper's shirt. "I suppose the eye-opening moment was when I kissed my friend Madeline the first time. It was impulsive, and it scared me. I locked myself in my room and worked through it. When I came out I was a new person."

"Just like that?"

"I wouldn't say that. I still struggled for awhile. Fortunately, Oscar was there and very supportive. That helped immensely. I also did a lot of reading."

"Of course you did," she said and chuckled. "I tried that, by the way. But I couldn't find any books. I thought now that I've turned gay I might want to figure it out. Didn't really work."

"You didn't turn gay. Have you ever heard of the Kinsey scale?"

"A thing that tells you if you're gay if you stand on it?"

"What? No!" She laughed and swatted at Harper's hip. "It's a scale to describe your inclination toward hetero or homosexuality."

"So, yes, it will tell me if I'm gay."

"It's more like... how gay. It doesn't tell you what you don't already know. Would you be interested in taking a test to see where you are on the scale? It might help."

"Oh, yeah, sure, why not. It has to be better than my attempts to test myself."

Emerson stood and raised an eyebrow. "Do I want to know?"

"Nope."

"Okay, let me go get my laptop." She grinned and scurried out of the room, reappearing moments later with a pink monstrosity.

"Jesus H. God. If anyone sees me with that thing it will totally ruin my street cred."

Emerson sat beside her and clicked away at the keyboard, squinting at the screen and down at the keys. "I left my glasses at the bookstore. Here, it's this one I believe."

The computer slid over across her legs. Harper sighed and read the first question. "Age." She tapped two keys. "Why the hell does that matter? Is my age gayer than another age?"

"Just answer the questions."

"Fine. What gender do I identify as?" She clicked and moved on. "Number of..." she mumbled the rest of the question, already blushing. "Sexual partners."

She stared at the screen and then glanced over at Emerson, who was politely looking away. "Well, this is embarrassing."

"Would you like me to cover my ears?"

"No." She sighed and then grinned as an idea came to her. Watching

Emerson's face she tapped a key, paused, then added two more clicks.

Emerson blinked and cleared her throat.

Harper giggled and backspaced three times. Made sure Emerson did not see the zero she filled in.

"Harper!"

"Sorry, I couldn't help it. I'll be serious now, promise." She finished the remaining questions in silence. No need to embarrass herself any further.

"Right, so, results. A one. Predominantly heterosexual, only incidentally homosexual?" She said as she finished, and passed the laptop back to its owner. "Thank God, it's all so clear now."

"It's not very comprehensive, I know."

"What did you get?"

"A three. Equally homosexual and heterosexual."

"So you're gayer than me? Ha. Nobody would ever guess."

"Why would you say that?"

"Because you're you, and I'm me. You're like a perfect little lady Princess and I'm… not." She pointed over at her and then back at her own chest. "Beauty. Beast."

"I don't think that really has as much to do with it as you think." Emerson put the laptop aside after closing it and scooted back over. She smiled and kissed Harper's cheek before cuddling back against her side. "More like beauty and beauty. Did you know you do look different now?"

"I do?"

"Softer," she said, one finger tracing Harper's bottom lip. "Your face, your eyes. It's beautiful."

"I think they call it happy."

"I make you happy?"

"You know you do. I still don't know how this is going to work, and it's scary, but I'm happy. Happier than I've been in a very long time."

"We'll figure it out." She leaned up and kissed her. "You make me happy too."

CHAPTER TWENTY-SEVEN

They decided to watch a movie to get their odd "first date" back on track. Except neither of them remembered to push play once the DVD had been inserted. Somewhere between walking back to the couch and asking if she wanted popcorn, Emerson had gotten distracted. Which had distracted Harper.

The song on the DVD menu played on loop in the background while Harper got some more practice at kissing Emerson. Glorious, wonderful, practice.

She'd expected a woman's kiss to be softer, but Emerson was also affectionate and kind of silly about it. She giggled in between short breaths of air, and gave little kisses in between kisses, played with her hair. It wasn't hot, or sexy, like their explosive interlude in the bookstore. It was sweet, and fun, turning from kisses to hugs and giggles and back to kissing again. She didn't feel like they were trying to get to a destination, it didn't progress any further, so it was perfect. They'd already arrived.

"Mers."

"Hm?" Emerson hummed into her lips.

They would have to stop eventually, and Harper wanted to pause things before they spent all night making out on the couch like a couple of teenagers. Problem was, if they stopped it would mean there would have to be a last kiss. One really awesome final kiss to summarize the experience. Every time she tried for that she ended up starting all over again, until she regained her sense long enough to realize she couldn't even remember her own name.

"Hang on, hold," she said, gathering enough willpower to tilt her mouth back out of reach. "Sorry, I need to –"

"It's okay. I know," Emerson said. "We're getting out of hand."

"That's the problem with an addiction." She took a breath and tried not to look at Emerson's lips. "I really – I want this, a lot. The real deal and…"

"I do too." Emerson sat up on her elbows. "And?"

"I don't want to… rush. I want to be careful and not screw it up. I have no idea how this is going to work, but I want it to be right. Can we – slow? While I wrap my head around this?" She smiled and shook her head. "This is like our first date and you already tagged second."

"I did not touch your boob!" An adorable pout took up residence on Emerson's face.

"Point is," she said. "It's hard enough to restrain myself. I don't want to push it. Not so fast. It's still new and we're still trying to figure out the imprint stuff. So I'm going to go home and howl at the moon and I'll see you tomorrow. Alright, Little Moon?"

"When did you become the adult?" Emerson wondered.

"When I got you to say boob." She slipped off the couch and that warm body. "Walk me out? I've got separation anxiety already."

"Do you need a leash?"

"Funny," she said and raised an eyebrow. "I thought we decided sarcasm was my thing."

"There was mention of joint custody."

Harper stepped out into the night and swayed for a few moments, eyes closed, drinking in the last bit of warmth and the smell of coconuts. She heard shuffling and turned to see Emerson stuffing her feet into pink slippers. "What are you doing?"

"Coming outside with you."

"Don't," she said and pressed her back into the house.

"Are you ashamed to be seen with me?" She looked heartbroken at the idea.

"No, not at all. More like I'm trying to keep you from becoming gossip material. More than usual, anyhow. I might also have a rational fear of angry mobs with pitchforks, torches, and silver bullets."

Emerson laughed. "Harper, no one can see us, it's too dark without the porch light."

"The moon is plenty bright and your hair is like a beacon." She shook her head. "Aliens can probably see it from space. Have you ever been abducted? I think you're at risk."

"Aliens aren't real."

"Really?" She smirked. "Two months ago you thought werewolves weren't real."

"Lucky for me, I was wrong."

"There you go, saying dumb things," she said and stooped for a long goodbye kiss. "I'll come help you at the bookstore tomorrow."

"I'm going over early, so text me when you're on your way. We can go get breakfast."

"Goodnight, Little Moon." She grinned and backed away from the door.

PURE OF HEART

Her heart lunged forward, hammering against her ribs.

Emerson drifted forward and then leaned back with a shake of her head. "Goodnight, *Loup*."

"Lou? Did you just call me Lou? Is that French for something? What's it mean?"

"Look it up."

The door closed with a dull whump that echoed in her ears. She whined and turned around before she gave in and went back inside. "You'll see her tomorrow, calm yourself."

Her lips continued to tingle and she had the dopiest grin on her face, but she didn't care. What she did care about was getting home, trying to sleep, so she could wake up and see Emerson again. She'd have to ask Grady to mess with her schedule some so she could spend her days at the bookstore. Or take her on a date.

"I need a plan," she said to herself, turning around to grin at the house. "A great plan."

She was almost past Emerson's long driveway when the smell hit. Leather and moss. Her nostrils flared and a warning growl vibrated her teeth. Holt.

"You know, you've always been a lot of things, Harper," he said, stepping out of the shadows. "Bitchy, annoying, arrogant. I always thought you might be a dyke too. But I never pegged you for a girlfriend thief."

"Holt." She clenched her fists and curled her lip. "Stalk much?"

"Is this your way of getting revenge?" He stomped closer and jabbed a finger at her face. "I didn't want you anymore, so you went after my girl?"

"She's not your girl." With a huff, she whirled around and shoved her hands into her pockets. His footsteps followed, crunching hardened snow. "Go away, dickhead. You're ruining my good mood."

"I saw you kiss her!"

"Hooray for you." She grit her teeth and walked faster. It hadn't occurred to her to ask Emerson if she'd dealt with Holt. Great. She eyed the nearby fences and considered climbing over them to escape. The neighbors wouldn't like it, and he'd probably follow her anyway. With her luck he'd fall and break something other than his neck, then turn around and sue her for it. "Did I not say it clear enough? Get lost."

"No!" He grabbed her elbow and whipped her around. "What is your problem? And how the hell did you talk Emerson into this scheme of yours?"

"Scheme?" She snorted. "What scheme?"

"To make me jealous."

"Everything is not about you." She shoved him, and resumed her seemingly endless walk. She didn't mind time slowing down when she was kissing Emerson, but now it was annoying. Time needed to speed up, fast forward to her being home, or all the way to morning.

Wait. She stopped and slowly turned again, the wolf snarling in the back of her mind. Holt had obviously been sitting outside, there was nothing stopping him from going back. Or from showing up and raining on her parade later. "How's this for a scheme? I catch you snooping around Emerson's house again and I'll make sure they never find your body."

There. She shook her head, spun on her heel and increased her pace.

"I'm not giving up on her, Harper. I don't care if you threaten me."

A snowball hit her in the shoulder. Her eyes sparked into focus. She stopped again, took a deep breath and let it out through her nose. *Don't do it*, she thought. *He's not worth it. You're happy, remember? Don't let him ruin it.* "It's over, Holt. She picked me. Move on."

"Like hell!"

Another snowball struck the back of her head, this one more ice than snow. Her eyes burned, not from the sting, but from the all-consuming rage it stirred. He hadn't stooped as low as throwing snow at her since they were children. Her breath wheezed passed her lips, noisy and thin. Lip curled, teeth bared, she whipped around and stalked toward him. Her knuckles cracked when she clenched her fists, nails digging into her palms.

He planted his feet and had the balls to look smug. She wiped it off his face when she grabbed the lapels of his stupid pea-coat and yanked him down to her eye level. A flicker of fear caught her attention. Perfect.

"Look you inbred, leg-humping, trout-faced fuckwit." She snarled and gave him a shake, no doubt rattling what marbles he had left in his head. "I'll slow down and say it in Earthling for you. Go. Suck. An ass biscuit. I'm not interested. Emerson's not interested. Leave us alone, or I'll fuck you up so bad you'll be able to register as a dick amputee. Get me?"

She let him go and marched once more for home. More snow splattered between her shoulders.

"You know Ben said there might be something wrong with you."

Her feet dug into the snow and refused to budge.

"Yeah, he said he thought you might be a pussy puncher and didn't know it yet. Something about refusing to put out and acting like a bi-polar, crazy-ass ice bitch." He laughed. "We told him you just needed to get laid and it'd thaw you right out. Didn't turn out so good for him, did it? Guess it was bad advice. He's dead and you're worse than before!"

Breathe, breathe, she chanted in her head. Cold air rushed in through her open mouth, made her lungs ache, but it didn't douse the fire burning in her stomach. *It's not true, it can't be.* "I'm going to rip the lying, piss licking tongue out of your head."

He wadded up another snowball and widened his stance. "You don't deserve her!"

You're not a monster, Harper. She stopped again, half-way to him, eyes widening.

You're not a monster. Emerson had smiled as she said it, fingers combing through her hair and scratching at her scalp in the best way.

You're not.

She smiled at Holt and then laughed. Laughed until it hurt more than anything else. Until she had to grab her stomach and bend over to relieve the cramp.

He stared at her, face scrunched up. She swiped at frozen tears and shook her head. "You know what? You're absolutely right, asswipe. I don't deserve her. But neither do you. Have a nice night, okay?"

"That's it?" He called after her and she heard him running to catch up. "I'm not done."

"Oh, you're done," she said and kept walking, hands in her pockets and a smile on her face. "I'm not listening and I don't care. Say whatever you want. It doesn't matter."

He followed her all the way home, yelling and throwing more snow. Her smile grew wider at his childish antics. She knew she'd won. Emerson would tell him herself later and he would whine for awhile, but in the end she won. He could rally the whole town to his cause and it still wouldn't matter. She had Emerson and he never would. There would be no herd of hairy children; she wouldn't have to be the fun aunt. She snorted, and made a note to tell Emerson about her horrifying vision of the possible future. It would be fun to see her reaction.

"Harper!" He bellowed as she crested the steps of the porch.

"Yeah, Holt?"

"You can't just walk away from me!"

"What do you call this?" She opened the front door, waved at him over her shoulder and slammed it closed. "I hate him," she said to the stack of shoes. "And no, that's not an exaggeration."

"Harper?"

Cooper popped around the corner, frying pan in one hand, grilled cheese in the other. "What are you doing back so soon?"

"So soon?" She smirked and shook a finger at him. Too giddy to get after him about staying up so late. "Your awareness of time is lacking. Isn't that a problem for a Time Lord?"

He rolled his eyes. "Whatever. Who's outside yelling at the house?"

"Holt."

His eyebrows disappeared into his mussed bangs. "Why?"

"Sore loser," she said with a shrug. "I'm going to bed. You might want to wear headphones, he'll probably stay out there until frostbite sets in."

"Joy. Should I call Dad?"

"Not worth it. Grady'd be mad you were still awake anyway. You should probably head to bed soon." She patted him on the head and whistled on her way up the stairs.

"Are you whistling Harper's got a Girlfriend?"

"Goodnight, Cooper."

She shouldered her way into her room and threw her jacket across the foot of the bed. A rock hit her window and she rolled her eyes.

"Harper!"

"Tenacious little sheep fucker, aren't you?" She pulled back the curtain on her window and saw Holt in the back yard. The lights came on at their next door neighbors. "Great, he'll get the Sheriff called in all by himself."

Her window sill groaned in protest when she wrenched the window open. "Holt, you moron. Do you want to get arrested? You weren't dating her and you didn't sleep with her, so I'm not understanding your problem."

"You slept with her?" His face turned purple.

"None of your business."

"Come down here, fucking slut!"

"Since you asked so nicely, no." Another rock zinged by her ear. She ducked and glared down at him. "Have you lost your pea sized brain? Why don't you go look for it over a cliff?"

"Fuck you!"

"Fuck yourself! It's your only option anyway." A dog started barking and more lights came on. She sighed and pinched the bridge of her nose. "Go away!"

"Make me!"

"Either go away or I'll call the Sheriff myself."

"You stole my girlfriend!"

"I can't steal something that was never yours," she shouted. "How old are you?"

He started searching the ground for another rock and she rubbed at her forehead. When he stopped, she glared and tensed, waiting for another volley. Instead of reaching down for whatever piece of garbage, he knelt and pawed at the stale snow.

A strong jolt zapped her spine and she straightened up with a gasp.

It hadn't snowed in days.

Not since the last time she'd been out in the yard.

The night her wolf had taken over and she'd transformed out there.

"The prints," she whispered and gripped the window sill with both hands, splintering it. "Holt!"

The prints, the prints, the damn prints. They would clearly show human to wolf. She swallowed a wave of bile and smacked the window sill. "Holt!"

He stood up so fast he lost his balance and fell back to his knees. Even from that distance she could see his bunched forehead, wide eyes, and slack jaw.

"You!" He yelled. "It's you!"

PURE OF HEART

Oh no. Her heart plummeted to her toes. "What?"

He didn't respond and scurried out of her yard, right over the busted fence.

"Shit!" She spun around and ran straight into the footboard of the bed. "Damn it!"

Fury and panic warred for control. She gripped the bed and flipped it out of the way. "No!"

Her nails shot out and down, curved and hardened. Cricks and pops chased each other down her back. Her biceps bulged, straining the fabric of her long-sleeve shirt until the seams ripped.

Kill him.

Kill him. Protect her.

Holt screamed in her head and flashes of blood and gore played out across her eyes. She slammed into her bedroom door, gums itching and canines leaping forward, ready to tear into him.

Cooper stood on the other side, gaping like a fish. He still had the frying pan in one hand. "Harper?"

"Get out of the way! He knows!" She tried to muscle past him, but he moved over to block her path.

"Whoa, Harper. You can't go outside like that."

"Cooper get out of the way or I'll make you," she said with a growl.

She pushed him and he staggered back into the open landing, but stepped right in her way again, blocking the stairs. There wasn't time to play anymore. She grabbed the banister and threw herself over. Both ankles rolled over when she landed. She hobbled over to the wall and groaned when seconds later the bones re-set themselves with two awful crunches. Upstairs she heard a door slam.

"Harper, no!"

He ran down the stairs and leapt, hitting her back and sending them both to the floor. She bucked him off and staggered to her feet, aiming for the door.

Something glinted at her from his hand. Not the frying pan. She ignored it and grabbed the doorknob. It crumpled in her hand like a soda can.

"I'm sorry!"

A hard impact on the back of her head sent her reeling face first to the floor again. Her ears rang with a hollow metallic sound. She tasted blood at the back of her mouth.

"Stay down," Cooper ordered.

Emerson. He would go after Emerson. She planted her palms, more like paws, and drove herself upwards.

Clang!

She dropped, brain fuzzy and vision blurred around the edges. The ringing in her ears became more painful and something dripped out of them. "No," she whimpered. "No."

"Harper, I'm sorry."

A sharp prick lit up the nerve endings in her thigh. She slumped to the floor and curled up, caught sight of a needle sticking out of the side of her leg. Cooper stood over her, frying pan held aloft. He had his phone against his ear.

"Dad? Code Red. Code Red. Come home now!" He tossed it away and grabbed the handle of his improvised weapon with both hands. "Harper, I'm sorry, easy, okay? Just – everything's going to be okay."

The familiar sluggishness of Telazol swamped her weakening limbs and further muddled her thoughts. Her tongue went heavy in her mouth.

"Emerson," she said, right before the lights went out.

CHAPTER TWENTY-EIGHT

Emerson

Emerson smiled as she unlocked the front door to the bookstore. The jingle-bells she'd hung rang and clicked against the glass. One lay on the floor. She stooped and picked it up. "We'll have to fix you, won't we?"

Mr. Darcy ran toward her meowing loudly. She knelt down and scratched him behind the ears. "Good morning, Dee. Sorry you had to stay here last night. I didn't want you and Harper to bother each other."

He mewled and bounced his head against her palm. Sharp blue eyes blinked up at her.

"I know, I'm a bad Mommy. We'll work on making you two friends, okay? How about some food?"

At the word he raced off toward the office where she'd stashed his dishes. Her smile broadened as she dropped her purse on the counter and dug out a baggie of kibble and can of wet food. She took a second to check her phone, hoping for a message from Harper. Nothing yet, but she couldn't resist sending a message of her own.

At the store. See you soon! :-*

The sound of books falling to the floor in the office told her Mr. Darcy was impatient.

"Coming!" She put her phone back in her purse and tucked the bag out of sight. "I'm coming, sorry!"

Bells jingled and clacked against the door again. When she turned around, she saw Holt. He didn't smile or offer her flowers, he had his hands in his pockets and his head tipped down. A chill danced down her spine and slipped around to take up residence in her belly.

"Holt?"

He looked up and she wished he hadn't. A muscle jumped in his jaw, dimples nowhere in sight. His thick eyebrows drew together and his eyes had lost the adorable childish spark.

She backed up a step. "Holt? Are you alright?"

"No," he said with a new and terrifying deep tone. Like he hadn't slept and stayed up all night smoking cigars. "No, I'm not alright, Emmy."

Why, why didn't I talk to him earlier? She wondered and toyed with her fingers. He stepped toward her and she backed up another step. She glanced over her shoulder, toward the back door. "Oh – I – hm, how can I – what's wrong?"

"Harper." He paused, face pinched, and shook his head. "Harper is what's wrong."

She swallowed, wishing desperately Harper would show up. *Come on, please*, she tried to think it hard enough so her attempt at telepathy would work. But the door remained closed and Holt was still there, glaring at her. He moved closer and her legs locked up. She gripped the counter with one hand and held her stomach with the other. "I don't understand."

"I saw it at your house last night. I came by to check on you," he said. "I saw it kiss you."

"You were at my house in the middle of the night?" she asked, voice shrill. He smacked a hand down on the counter and she flinched, blinking back tears. "That's not okay, you know that don't you?"

"None of it's okay, not you kissing that thing, and definitely not Harper." He leaned in and dropped his voice to a whisper. "I know what it is. I saw the tracks in her yard."

"You followed her home?" She glared at him and tightened her hands into fists.

"I was trying to protect you and I was right. It's a fucking werewolf. I found proof in the vet's office. That bitch has been covering up for Harper. For that whole damn family. Grady's been keeping a monster in his house, near his kid, and now it's got its claws in you."

"She doesn't have – that's not what happened!" She drew herself up to her full height. "Holt, I know you're angry and upset right now. But please, you have to listen to me. She's not a monster, she's good. She's a Faoladh."

"It's a werewolf, that's a monster," he said with a snort. "Listen to yourself, defending it. It probably killed Ben, not some bear. Now it's done something to you and I'm not going to let it. It'll be okay, Emmy, I'm going to save you."

His hand closed around her upper arm and tugged her up against him. She leaned away and pushed against his chest. "Holt, no, I don't need saving! I chose Harper, I chose her, and I'm sorry I didn't tell you. I want her, not you."

She winced at his hiss of breath, so close she felt the heat of it graze her cheek.

"You don't want it. It's some sick werewolf shit. You're under its spell or something, but I'm going to fix it. I promise you, I'll free you of this or die trying."

He would die. She shivered at the thought. If Harper saw him like this, or he tried anything else she doubted anyone could stop the wolf. "I'm not under a spell! Listen to me, you have to let me go and forget about Harper. Please, don't –"

"Don't what? Save you and the town?" He curled his lip and shook her. "Listen to yourself. This isn't you, Emmy."

"We aren't in some fairytale where you're the hero who rides in, slays the monster, and gets the girl. I'm not that girl!"

An odd glint appeared in his eye, and her stomach turned over. "There's an idea."

"Don't you-"

He cut her off, smashing his mouth against hers and swallowing her squeal of protest. She lashed out with all her strength, smacking her open hand against the side of his head. He staggered away and she wiped at her mouth as she eased toward the back of the counter and her purse. Which held her mace.

"Son of a bitch!" He punched a bookcase, and she jerked, rushing for her bag. His hand slammed down on hers before she could retrieve it. She screamed and tried to run, but he held her down, his weight coming down against her back. "I'll forgive you for that. I know it's not you. We're going to go for a little ride, okay? I hate it, but I know it'll bring that freak out. Everything is going to be fine once it's dead."

Dead, dead, Harper, dead. "No!" She twisted against him to no avail. His hand was strong and his weight was too much. The tears that had been threatening broke free, running down her face in a steady stream. "No!"

"I'm sorry, I'm sorry," he said and reached behind himself. A line of rope came across her hands. He forced her palms together and tied them, then tied a thick knot to his own hand, leashing them together. "It's for you. I'm doing this for you."

"Don't," she said through her tears.

"I've got it all worked out. Did research and everything." He yanked her upright and dragged her through the store toward the back. They passed the office, and Mr. Darcy peeked his head out long enough to hiss. "I couldn't find silver bullets, and didn't have time to make any. But I've got something better. The vet, she's got all this stuff I found when I broke in. I made some changes. It'll be quick. Quicker than Harper deserves."

She shook her head and leaned her weight back on her heels to slow him down. Her plan backfired when he grabbed her and clamped a hand over her mouth. He lifted her and carried her out the back into the alley.

His truck waited for them, driver-side door open and ready.

He shoved her inside, and after a moment of hesitation stretched across her to seatbelt her in. She considered biting him, his ear so close, but he must have sensed her thought and pulled away. "Don't. Don't make this any harder. Don't scream and don't fight me. I don't want to hurt you anymore."

"Then don't," she said and held up her bound hands. "Let me go. It's not too late."

His jaw clenched. "I don't like this, but it has to be done. I have to protect you and the whole town. All those tourists who went missing in the woods over the years were probably Harper. Hunting, feeding, like human beings are elk or deer." He pounded on the steering wheel. "No more. I won't let it take another human life and I'm not letting it take you either."

She licked her lips and watched the town go by, giving way to trees. "If she's such a beast, how do you think Grady survived? Or Cooper, or AJ, or Logan. You, you're still alive."

"It knows better than to mess with me," he said. "I'm a hunter, the best, I've taken down grizzlies. If anyone could hunt it and kill it, it's me."

But she can't die, she thought, a flare of hope lighting her heart. *She can't die, she heals.*

He pointed at the rifle sitting on the dashboard. "I know what you're thinking, werewolf is different from bear. Or regular wolf, but I've got it worked out, don't worry. See, I got the tranquilizer rifle from the vet office. And my mom, she has all these exotic flowers. Even poisonous ones."

"Why are you telling me all of this," she said through her teeth. *How did he get so damn smart all of the sudden?*

"I want you to know, even when you're still under its power. I know you're still in there somewhere, and maybe this will help you break its hold, if you know I've got a plan."

"I'm not under a spell!" She raised her hands and hit his shoulder. Over and over. He grabbed her wrists and bashed them into the dash. "I'm not under a spell, you – you *morceau de merde.* Asshole! Let me go!"

"Knock it off!" He smacked her, driving her head into the window. Lightning flashed in her vision, she whimpered and slumped in her seat, hands against her burning cheek. "I've got wolfsbane. Do you hear me? I've got wolfsbane loaded in a dart and it'll kill it. Please, Emmy, listen. I'm sorry, but it'll work and then you'll be free!"

"She's not an it, she's Harper! Harper Quinn Cahill and you're going to murder her. Do you understand that? She's a person and you're going to kill her."

"It's not a person, it's a werewolf and it's fucked up your head and killed people. I'm not murdering anything, I'm putting down an animal. An animal that's tasted human flesh. It's a fucking man-eater. If this was Africa,

PURE OF HEART

it would be the man-eating lion and I'm the guy that has to get rid of it."

There'd be no arguing with him. She whimpered and licked the blood on her lip. "Where are you taking me?"

"Somewhere safe, where I can set everything up." He spun the steering wheel and the truck jostled violently off the pavement onto a rough, snow-covered road. "I brought you a blanket so you won't get too cold."

"How kind," she spat and eyed the lock on the door. In a book, a heroine might throw herself out of the moving vehicle and make a grand escape. With her hands tied to Holt's wrist it wouldn't work. She'd either drag him out with her and get hit again for her trouble, or worse he'd drag her alongside until he stopped or muscled her back inside. Harper would find her, she was certain but... she stared at the rifle. *Wolfsbane. Wolfsbane could kill her.* It was poisonous to humans as well, deadly, and from what she'd read, ten times as toxic to a werewolf.

Holt turned on the radio and even started singing along to some country song she didn't recognize. His heavy hands trembled, he fidgeted, tapped on the steering wheel, and ran a hand through his hair. Psyching himself up.

She shivered and turned her attention to the knots on her hands. While she had some range of motion, she wouldn't be able to untie them, unless she used her teeth.

"What's your plan for after," she asked, to break the washout of the upbeat music and his sonorous singing. *Talk to him,* she thought, *calm him, he'll make a mistake.*

"I don't know. If it turns back human I'll have to get rid of the body, I guess. Like in the movies, they always turn back into a person. But I don't know, it's so fucked up. If it's still a monster maybe I'll hang the head, or take it to the cops."

Harper's head, human, green eyes replaced by fake lenses that gleamed in the firelight, hung beside the wolf in the trophy room. She swallowed as bile burned the back of her mouth. Her heart sped up further, and her nausea increased. She put her hands against her chest and pressed down, attempting to still it, or slow it before it broke her ribs.

The truck braked, and Holt scrubbed at his hair again before untying the rope from his wrist. He reattached it to the steering wheel and then stretched for the rifle. "Sit tight, I've got to get some stuff ready."

There were in a clearing, hemmed in by trees and dead bushes. The sun lit up the snow, making it glisten almost invitingly. Holt walked past the truck with a dark green duffle. He dropped another length of rope by the biggest tree and then reached into the bag to toss something large and metal beside it. A chain rattled against itself; she twitched at the sound and craned her neck wanting to see what it was.

He looked up, caught her staring, and smiled. "Bear traps. See? Got it all figured out."

She recoiled against the seat, flashing back to the images of Buck and White Fang caught in such devices. It mutated, until she saw Harper, her black wolf, snarling and snapping, shackled to the Earth in its teeth. The vomit she'd been choking down rose higher, she put her hands to her mouth and coughed. "Holt!"

Two more bear traps hit the ground.

"Holt, let me out!" She kicked at the glove box, tried to undo her seatbelt. "Let me out!"

"What?"

Too late. She leaned over and threw up. Not much came out, since she hadn't eaten since the night before, but enough to stain his seat. She wiped at her tears and looked at the puddle and wondered if it was karma.

"Christ!" Holt groaned and untied the rope from the steering wheel. "Well, that's just great, now the truck's going to smell like puke." She didn't apologize. He grumbled and threw the end of the rope at her. "Just stay there."

He slammed the door closed and marched around the front. She took a deep breath through her mouth. This was her last chance. As soon as the passenger door opened, she whirled around and launched herself at him, half falling from the tall truck. He grunted at the impact and staggered back. She hit him as hard as she could and took off running. By no small stroke of luck, and due to more teasing from Harper, she'd gone for denim and flats for the day. Without a skirt and heels to impede her, she flew down the gravel path, crying and yelling for help at the top of her lungs.

Arms wrapped around her waist like steel bands, lifted her easily off her feet, and spun her. She screamed again, in both rage and fear.

"Emerson! Stop it, stop it!"

"No!" She jerked her head back, hoping to hit his nose but came up with nothing but air. "No!"

"Nobody is going to hear you out here," he said against her ear. "Nobody but me and the animals."

"Harper!" She thrashed and kicked at his knees. "Harper!"

"It's not time for that yet." He grunted again, and spun them around. She kicked at him, swearing viciously in a combination of French and English. He gripped under her knees and swung her upwards in a typical hero carry. "It can't hear you."

"Let me go, let me go, let me go," she sobbed.

The truck came back into sight and she squirmed, crying louder. It felt like the end, her death in a snowy, pretty clearing. All the fight drained from her limbs. He kissed her forehead and she turned away with a whimper.

He set her down at the base of the tree. She stared at the pile of bear traps while he looped the rope around her, securing her to the trunk. He pulled her bonds tight, tight enough they hurt. The pain shocked her system enough to return some clarity. She shook her head and glared at him as he came back around with a bandana in his hands.

"It's clean," he said, looking apologetic.

"Fuck you."

"Now I know it's not you running the show. My Emerson would never swear." He tied the bandana around her head to gag her, tangling her hair in the knot at the back. "It won't be long, I don't think. It can't stay away."

She shuddered as his fingers ran down her cheek and then across her upper lip. His eyes softened at the corners, and he smiled.

"It'll be over soon."

He moved away, grabbed a trap and set it. Around in a half circle he went, kneeling in the snow, setting one after the other and covering them in snow. With his line ready, he went up to a tree and pulled a knife. He cut down a sizable limb and stabbed the thicker end down into one.

She flinched when it snapped into action, biting the limb in half. Holt grinned and nodded, then bent over and re-set the trap, covering it with a fresh pile of snow.

"Perfect," he said, hands on his hips. He surveyed his handiwork, and then made his way back to the tree. She twisted against it, screaming at him through the gag. He ignored her and scooped up a gun, not the one that had been sitting on the dashboard.

"Shotgun," he told her. "The wolfsbane will knock it down, give me an advantage. I figured a couple slugs would finish the job. Ruin the head for mounting, but you do what you got to do."

He racked the weapon and put it over his shoulder.

She whimpered and let her head fall back against the rough bark.

CHAPTER TWENTY-NINE

Harper

Her room, her sanctuary, had become a prison. They'd been drugging her throughout the night. The edges of her mind felt fuzzy, and the wolf was dazed. It wasn't enough to dull the memory of the night before. The Telazol didn't stop the rage from burning up her insides. She'd never felt fury like it before. Her whole body trembled, the sheets underneath her saturated with sweat. The salty scent, mixed with the odor of their fear made her stomach turn and gurgle.

She tasted blood. Her own from a cut on her lip, and the nicks on her sensitive, itchy gums. The wolf teeth in her human jaw clicked together, snapping at air. She growled and yanked on the ropes once again holding her to her own bed frame.

"Let me out of here right this second!"

"Harper we can't, not until you calm down," AJ said with a wince. She bent down with a damp rag.

"Stop doctoring me. He knows, and he's going to go right back after Emerson." She tugged again, snarling at the pale, worried faces of her family. They crowded around her. Grady with a fresh tranquilizer in his hand, Cooper still clutching the frying pan, AJ with her rag.

"I don't want to dose you again, I don't know what that much tranquilizer will do to your system. Calm down, and let's figure this out." AJ turned to Grady. "Maybe we should call Sheriff Blalock?"

"And tell him what?" Cooper asked with a snort. "My cousin, the werewolf – oh, you don't know about the werewolf? Well, she says that the local douchehole might have kidnapped her girlfriend. Does that count as an emergency?"

"Not might have," she said through her teeth, every tendon in her neck tightening. "He did. I know it. I can feel her!"

"What do you mean you can feel her?" Grady's eyebrows shot up.

"Is there a disturbance in the werewolf Force?" Cooper added.

"This is not the time for explanations. Let me go!" Her heart sped up again, beating faster than any heart should. It half choked her and the extra rush of blood had her twitching. She turned her head and saw her biceps straining, the veins in her hand bloated and dark. "Let me go. If he hurts her because you stooges kept me from getting to her in time…"

"Maybe you should dose her again," Grady said.

"I have no idea what that will do. She's had too much the past few days. I'm surprised she's not sick already."

Cooper waved the pan around. "We could –"

"Don't even think about hitting me with that again."

"What if I go get Emerson?" Grady smiled at her, placating. She swallowed vomit and blood. Tears obscured her vision and a wave of despair swamped her.

"She's not – she's in danger. I feel it. These aren't my tears."

"If that's true and Holt has her," AJ said. "You go near him like this and what do you think you'll do?"

Rip out his throat. Tear into his chest and yank out his black heart. Mummify him alive and add him to his own trophy collection. She snarled as the blood soaked images danced through her head. "I'll make sure he doesn't hurt her again."

"That's what I thought you'd say." She shook her head and shrugged at Grady. "I could administer a smaller dose, against my own advice, and we could move her downstairs?"

"She can get out of that cage."

"You have a better idea? We need to get her calmed down before she has a heart attack, or changes. And one of us really needs to deal with this Holt situation."

"Uh, guys?" Cooper interrupted them and pointed to the bed.

The posts of her headboard groaned. She bared her teeth at them, ropes pulled taught against her wrists. "I can break out of that cage. You want to know what else I can break out of?"

She pulled, harder than she'd ever dared. Both posts cracked and splintered with one more ferocious tug. The bed broke, the front falling to the floor. She rolled off the side and stood, used her teeth to cut through the world's ugliest bracelets.

"I've always been so careful not to use my full strength," she said and tossed the ropes at Grady's head. "I could have broken out of those any time. Chains can't hold me and you thought rope would?"

"Harper, wait." Grady approached with the needle.

Cooper backed up against a wall, frying pan in front of him like a shield. AJ grabbed him and yanked him toward the door.

"Wait. You're not thinking clearly. The wolf –"

"The wolf is me!" She kicked the bed, sending it screeching across the floor into the opposite wall. Right where Cooper had been. "I am the wolf. Right now I have to go save Emerson. With or without your help."

The window felt cold against her back. She grabbed a shoe off the floor and hurled it at Grady.

"Harper!"

She stalked toward him. AJ jumped forward and wrapped her arms around his chest, pulled him back as well.

Perfect. Now she had room. "I'll try not to kill him," she said.

Fists clenched, teeth grinding together, bare toes digging into the floor, she whirled around and ran full tilt at the window.

"Harper!"

The glass shattered, cutting her skin and ripping her shirt. Frigid air dried out her eyes, slapped her in the face. She fell, head first, into the fence and blasted right through it. Boards snapped and twisted under her weight. Shards of wood joined the glass sticking out of her face, hands, and arms. She screamed and howled at the same time, laying in a heap of bloody snow and busted fence.

"Goddamnit!" Grady shouted from her bedroom.

Sorry about the fence, Uncle, she thought woozily. Her vision flickered in and out of sharp focus then settled with everything in hi-def. The dirt in the snow, the individual particles that made up the icy mush, the bright red of her own blood – she could see everything. She put her palms down to lurch to her feet and screamed again. The bones in her right forearm had pierced the skin. White bone glistened, blood gushed from the split, steaming and filling the air with the smell of iron.

She rolled over, biting right through her bottom lip to contain the noise. The bones shifted, exposing nerve endings and shooting agony through her body. A tooth broke in her mouth. She hissed and clamped her good hand down on the bones, shoving them back into her mangled arm.

Ben approached, hands shoved in his pocket, flaps of torn skin moving with each step. He knelt down beside her and reached out to touch her, but his fingers curled back into his palms.

"Ben, I'm sorry. I'm so sorry. It was me, I did it. I killed you. Please, forgive me."

He smiled at her, bent down and kissed her forehead. He didn't disappear, like she expected, he stood and walked away without looking back. Right through the neighbor's fence.

She spit out the tip of a canine and staggered to her feet. Her left knee realigned, fixing her limp, and the sudden jerk caused her to veer off course and trip into the snow again.

The busted bones cracked and heat shot down to her numb fingertips.

She flexed her right hand over and over until the sensation fled. With a grunt, she crawled to her feet again, felt the rough calluses against the bite of the snow.

"Harper!" AJ yelled from the front porch.

Don't stop me. Don't even try. She ran toward the nearest fence, hooked her clawed fingers into the wood and rolled over the top.

"I'm coming, Little Moon. Hang on, Emerson," she said in short puffs. Spine tingling, body overheated, and muscles heavy she took off for the next fence. "I'm coming."

***

She hit the back door she'd just installed for Emerson without slowing. Her shoulder took the brunt of the impact. The door cracked down the middle, one half bouncing against the wall on the hinges. The other half clattered to the floor.

"Emerson!" She stepped into the house, senses straining for any sign she'd been wrong. Everything smelled of Emerson and there were faint echoes of her own scent, mingling with even smaller undertones. Including the steak they'd had the night before. She pricked her ears and cocked her head, but heard nothing besides the hum of electronics. No footsteps running down the stairs, no yelling for the breaking and entering. Not even the cat's stupid jingle collar. "She's not here."

Stability seeped out of her knees, she wobbled into the wall, gasping for air. Her chest tightened, and she put a hand over her heart to keep it caged behind her ribs.

She couldn't stay. Grady and AJ would be along shortly, armed with tranquilizer darts and "rationale."

"Bookstore," she said and ran back out of the house, making a mental note to fix the damage again when things were safe.

She hopped fence after fence. Her feet hit first, she tucked and rolled through the snow and then dashed for the next. Several faces peered out of windows. She ignored them and ran harder. The Sheriff would be notified eventually, and that would be one more person looking for her.

First I'll find Emerson, she thought, launching over the last fence in the neighborhood. *Then I'll turn myself in.*

She tore down the hill, bare feet digging into rocks, snow, and other debris. It hurt in a distant way. She welcomed the reminder of reality. Each prick of pain settled her frantic thoughts and turbulent emotions.

Right as she turned the corner onto the main drag the front door of Sullivan's opened. She plowed straight into Logan as he stepped outside. They hit the salt-strewn, icy, wet sidewalk and slid. Curious onlookers halted on either side of the road, pointing and gawking.

"Harper, what the hell? Where's the fire?" Logan grabbed her biceps and started to sit them both up. "Is this blood? You're bleeding! Oh my

God, where are your shoes? What happened?"

She pushed down on his chest and wrenched her arms away. No time for an explanation or an apology.

"Harper!"

He almost caught her foot. She felt his fingers graze her ankle. She jerked away and broke into a dead sprint down the sidewalk.

Making a scene, you're making a scene. She shook her head and ran faster, breath puffing out, lungs ready to explode. *I won't be around long enough for them to catch me,* she thought and shoved open the door to Early Bird Books.

The smell hit her, so strong it knocked what little air she had gulped down out of her body. She groaned and gripped the metal bar dividing the door hard enough to warp it, leaving an impression of her hand.

Fear hung thick, stinging her already inflamed sinuses. Fear and coconuts mixed with leather, moss, and tears.

Her hackles rose, a current zipping down her back. She growled and leapt over the desk. The hair on the back of her neck stood up. She grabbed Emerson's floppy leather bag, the contents already strewn out across the desk. A can of mace, lipstick, perfume, all the things Emerson thought necessary to have with her at all times.

A cellphone.

She grabbed the phone with her clawed fingers. An image of Oscar and Emerson greeted her from the lock screen. She ran her thumb across their matching eyes and grins, then swiped across the screen to unlock it. With thick black claws tipping each finger it took her a moment to get the touch screen to respond, but she managed to get the contacts opened up and found Holt's number. She pressed send and raised the phone to her ear, growling with every labored exhale that poured out of her mouth.

If he hurts her... She tapped her claws against the desk and watched the door for unwanted company while the phone rang, and rang.

"Harper."

Holt. She snarled and dug four holes into the desk. "Where is she?"

"She's fine. Kind of cold, we've been waiting for hours."

He sounded far too at ease. She could hear him smiling – but under that tone and the sound of his breathing she heard squealing. Very angry, high-pitched squealing. "What did you do to her?"

"I didn't do anything, what did you do, Harper?"

Heat lapped her skin, starting at her forehead and working its way down. Her knuckles cracked and enlarged, turning a dark violet. "You touch her again and I'll — "

"You'll what?" He laughed. "I've got all the cards, and I know all about you now. Seems to me you don't have any room for threats."

"None of this involves her, shit for brains. Let her go, and as soon as I know she's safe, I'll give you whatever you want." *Preferably with a side-order of knuckles.* She sneered and clenched her fists.

"She's safe now," he said. "She's with me, where she belongs. Away from monsters like you."

"Did you even bother to ask her if she wanted to go with you? Or did you just take her, assuming that's what she'd want?" She snorted. "Setting aside the fact no sober woman would want to go anywhere with you. Did you assume she wanted to be kidnapped?"

"It's not kidnapping, it's rescue."

"Rescue? She needs to be rescued from you."

"She's just confused and it's not her fault. You did something to her, and I'm going to make it right. So help me God, I'm going to fix this. I promised her I'd undo this fucked up curse of yours."

"The only curse here is you."

"You're a werewolf."

Twice now someone had yelled that at her. First Emerson, and now Holt. From Emerson she could take it. It hadn't been said with such disgust. Holt used it like a swear word, something filthy and crude to spit in her face.

She growled, louder than she'd ever dared, with the hot-pink phone jammed against her jaw. "Yeah, I am. And buddy, you've got my bone."

"I'm not afraid of you. You're an animal, that's all."

If one more person said they weren't afraid of her she was going to have to break their face. "I hate stupidity," she said and moved toward the back of the store. Bootsteps approached, moving fast. Time to go, she had a party to get to. "I hate it more than anything. You know Hannibal only ate the rude? I think I'm going to follow his lead. But instead of the rude, I'll eat the stupid. You've always been a moron, Holt, but now you've crossed the line. I don't think I can forgive you."

The squealing in the background cut off and then Emerson's voice carried through without obstruction.

"Harper! Don — "

A smacking sound. Silence.

Her stomach contracted and she keeled over into a bookshelf. "Did you just…"

"This is your fault." Sounds of a scuffle followed, then the unmistakable rip of a strip of tape being pulled.

She stood back up, lurching repeatedly and holding her guts in place with a firm palm and sheer force of will. That was it, he'd signed his death certificate. The wolf raged, her skin went tight and the furious thumping of her heart stilled. Sensitive ears strained until something deep inside popped. A fresh wave of liquid heat ran down the sides of her neck. Then she heard it, soft, pained cries.

The sleeves of her already tattered shirt gave out, seams bursting around bulging biceps. Several teeth popped. She ran her tongue over the sharpened points and her mouth filled with the taste of blood.

With one hand she knocked the back door off its hinges and stood in the alley. She spit out bloody saliva and raised her nose to the air. Diesel fuel, Emerson, Holt. He'd taken her in his truck. Her nose, strong as it was, wouldn't be able to track a diesel truck in a town full of diesel trucks.

"Where are you?" she asked in a low rasp.

He answered, not with glee or even anger. His pitch dropped, deep enough to remind her of her own growls. As though he didn't want Emerson to hear, for her to understand his horrible, monstrous, and symbolic choice for their showdown.

"Where Ben died, by the tree. Where you killed him and tore up his body. That's where. We're waiting, Harper."

She crushed the phone and hopped the short metal fence separating the town from the woods.

Behind her, she heard Logan calling her name.

***

The one nice thing about the location Holt had chosen was Grady and AJ wouldn't think to look there. They would not have time to figure it out either, at least not until after the party was over

She ran through the woods, steps heavy and unfocused. Roots and snarls of dead bushes grabbed at her feet. Branches snagged her hair, scratched her face and arms. Her skin tingled as small cuts healed, over and over. The usual grace she ran with, her focus on the joy of it, was gone. She couldn't focus on anything other than reaching Emerson. Those whimpers of pain, the sound of her being smacked, imagining a red imprint left behind on soft skin – she tripped over a snow encrusted log and bounced off a thick tree trunk. Her shoulder crunched out of place, then screeched and popped back into joint.

With a groan, she pushed off and kept running. Growls rolled out of her throat constantly, increasing the pain in the back of her mouth. Wolf teeth clicked together as her feet pounded into the hard-packed snow. Bones and muscles continued to shift, pressing against her skin, then shrinking back down in rapid succession.

Not yet, she told herself, slowing as she caught a faint scent of coconut. *Not yet. Don't show your hand.*

Never before had she felt such harmony with the wolf. Instead of fighting her, the changes reversed. Her teeth returned to normal, her biceps shrank, claws shortened and her vision dimmed.

Fully human she walked toward the clearing, panting and wincing at the burn in her feet and hands. Holt's truck came into view, tucked up against the tree-line. She paused near the tailgate and curled her lip. His stench was all over his beloved douche-mobile. She grabbed the oversized tire and squeezed until her nails pierced the rubber. It popped, air exploding out around her fingers. She pried her hand free, retracted her claws and stalked past the now slanting vehicle.

Her nose led her straight and true toward coconut, toward Emerson. She stopped as the road spread and gave way to the place where Ben died. In an instant it changed from the present to the past. Her new accord with the wolf allowed access to previously buried memories. Snow melted, the scene darkened, leaves returned to the trees and revitalized the landscape. She saw muddy muck, highlighted and shining with fresh rain in the light of a full moon. Ben's breath gurgled in her ears, blood bubbling up over his lips and down his ruined neck.

She shook her head, looked again. The image that replaced the memory wasn't much better. Emerson squealed at her from behind a thick band of duct tape, eyes wider than ever and gleaming with tears. Her skin had a blue tinge to it, and just as she'd pictured, a bright red hand print marred one beautiful cheekbone. He'd wrapped her in a dirty camouflage blanket, but she shivered, and tried to scream.

Without her stylish dresses, and her makeup running and smudged, she looked as vulnerable as any other woman. Not like the classy, smart Emerson Grey that Harper knew. It unsettled her to see Emerson stripped down to a frightened, trapped, and battered creature.

Her vision re-sharpened, and Wolf teeth sprouted again. She clenched her fists and turned fiery eyes over to the other person in the clearing. The one responsible.

Holt uncrossed his arms. "You killed Ben."

Emerson screamed louder, shook her head and pulled at the rope tying her to the base of the tree.

"I did," she said and raised her chin. No point in avoiding it now. "It was an accident."

"Which part? The part where you ripped him into bite sized chunks? Or when you ate parts of him?"

"I don't have to explain myself to you. You're the one who abducted and tied up a woman you supposedly care about. Look at her. Look at what you did." She pointed at Emerson. "Let her go. This is between us. She doesn't need to be here."

He sneered. "It's your fault she's here. I thought you two were cozy. What is it? Afraid to let her see the monster? Think if she sees it, she'll run from you as fast as she should?"

"I am not the monster here you delusional asswhistle." She took a step forward and Emerson's muffled screams rose in pitch.

"You're a fucking werewolf and I have proof," he said and grabbed a backpack resting next to Emerson. He took out a file and threw it at her. It landed, open, nowhere near her, but with her wolf eyes she could read it. In

PURE OF HEART

black and white, AJ's tight cursive spelled it out. Her healing abilities, strength and speed, even notes on her transformations. The picture of the wolf had fluttered out, and glared up at her from the snow. "That's a monster. But hey, don't take my word for it. There're pages in there about how you lost control and killed your boyfriend. And a really interesting read on how you imprinted on Emerson."

"It's her choice."

"Is it?" He scoffed. "Really? It's her choice to let you brainwash her and put her under your thrall?"

"There's no thrall. I'm not a vampire, you idiot. Do I look like Count Dracula to you?" She threw her hands in the air and took another step.

"Mmmm!" Emerson jerked, crying and shaking her head. The tape covering her mouth dented in the middle with every heaving breath.

"You did something to her. I don't know what the game is, and I don't care. If you ate Ben because you realized you like pussy, that's on you. Emerson's not like that, and I won't let you warp her into a plaything. Let her go."

"Fuck you," she said and planted her feet. She felt Emerson, inaudibly warning her not to walk forward. She listened, even though every muscle screamed for action. "Fuck you. I tried to let her go, and she came back, on her own. I didn't do a thing to her, you did, tying her up, hitting her. Things I would never do."

"Show me the monster." He jabbed a finger at her, face a horrible red. "Show me what you are."

"You want to see a monster, look in a mirror." Her feet moved on their own, shifting forward an inch. "Or better yet, take a nice long walk off the cliff behind you."

"Show me the monster," he repeated and threw his hands in the air. "Show it to me."

She snarled, exposing her canines. "What's the matter, big boy? Did you actually grow a conscience? Can't kill me with a human face?"

"You're not human. You've never been a human being. You're a dog that needs to be put down. Show me the monster, I want to see your ugly face before I blow a hole in it."

"Well with that as an incentive, how can I say no?"

"You want incentive?" He stomped toward Emerson and her heart fell into her stomach. Acid crawled up her throat, her lip fell back over her teeth. She took another step forward, fists clenched and body vibrating.

He grabbed a handful of wet, blonde hair and pulled. A high pitched whine floated to her ears. He removed a knife from his belt and hitched up against her chin. "Is that incentive enough?"

"You wouldn't," she said with a growl. A chill that had nothing to do with the weather and temperature outside snaked through her limbs. Her chest constricted and cut off the furious rumble of her growl.

"This isn't Emerson, it's a zombie, and I'm here to save her. I don't want to hurt her, but anything that happens now is your fault." The gut hook on the blade nicked the side of Emerson's jaw. A bright trickle of blood seeped out. "You're right this is between us, but you put her in the middle. Show me the monster. Do the right thing for once in your miserable life. Don't hurt her anymore."

She held her hands up, swallowed hard. "Don't – Holt, don't. I'll do it."

Emerson whined. The knife moved away, back into its sheath. She leaned away from Holt and pinned Harper in place with a terrified look. Her eyes had never been clearer, icier. Fat tears hung on the edges of her thick lashes. She mumbled something, eyebrows drawn together.

"I have to," Harper said to her and yanked her torn shirt off. A stiff breeze stirred the trees and snow particles rained down. Each droplet sizzled as it hit her skin. She shivered and tugged down the zipper on her jeans. "Look away, Emers."

Pants gone, she dropped to her knees, planted her hands, and called the wolf forward.

CHAPTER THIRTY

Emerson

Harper knelt in the snow in her underwear, eyes clenched shut, forehead bunched. Steam came off her bared skin in thin wisps. Holt took a step toward her, fingers twitching, breath puffing out in streams of fog.

Emerson glanced at him and then back at Harper. She wondered if this was part of a plan. To do something as dramatic as disrobing in the snow, only to pop back up with her crooked grin and explain Holt was insane. Silly man, there was no werewolf.

Please, let that be what's about to happen, she thought. *Then we can leave, and no one will get hurt. He won't poison you and you won't rip him to pieces.*

Fed to a wood chipper, that's how Harper had described it. She didn't want to see that, or the damage it would do to Harper's already wounded psyche if she killed again.

Wide gold eyes re-appeared. Emerson's goosebumps puckered further under the loaded look. Icy air burned her nose. She shook her head, the tape holding back the "no" she said out of reflex.

"Don't watch," Harper said. "Please. Don't look."

Emerson shivered, wet jeans rubbing against her sensitive skin. Holt had wrapped a blanket around her, tucked it under her legs. Her pants were soaked through anyway. She'd never been so cold or felt so helpless in her life. Not to mention terrified. The bear traps he'd laid out were right there, waiting, inches away from Harper's hands. She closed her eyes, loosing a fresh round of tears. At the first dull crunch she opened them again, eyelashes sticking together.

Harper's back arched, the ridges of her spine prominent, straining against pale skin. Muscles rippled and bunched between her shoulders. Her mouth hung open. White teeth cracked, one by one, blunt ends whittling down to sharp, gleaming points.

Holt made an odd choking noise. He swayed and reached out, his heavy hand landing on top of her head. Emerson jerked away from his touch, wishing she could do anything else. Something to help. Do anything other than sit there and contract hypothermia while Harper charged headlong toward certain death.

Dark fur sprouted in a shadowy wave, down Harper's chest, arms, her back. Both of her shoulders wrenched out of place, sloping downwards. Her sternum and ribs flared out into the cavernous chest of the wolf with a staccato of snaps.

"Holy mother of God," Holt said, scrubbing at his eyes. "It's for real. She's really a – it's real."

Of course she's real you dumb bastard. She glared at him. *She's real and you're going to kill her for no good reason.*

Harper's already impressive physique thickened from the lean build of a runner into the mass of a body builder. The thin bones in her arms doubled in size, muscles swelled, veins bulged. Her back contorted again and she fell into the snow. Legs twisted up, reshaping. One gold eye continued to stare at them. Both ears rolled up the side of her head, grew upwards into soft, rounded tips. They flattened back against her skull, black fur racing to cover them as well.

Holt gagged and spit when Harper's face pushed out into a long muzzle. Her entire head broadened to fit the wolf jaw, realigned those dangerous, flesh-tearing teeth. The heap of black fur moved, sections of Harper's body shrinking or growing. The odd gurgle and crick punctuated the remaining changes.

Finally it stopped. Harper's transformation complete, she lay in perfect stillness.

One-one hundred, Emerson counted.

Two-one hundred. She couldn't breathe, not until Harper did.

Three...

Harper's side expanded with a mighty breath. Massive paws gripped the snow. A growl thundered and her snout came up from its snowy pillow. White clung to the fur on one side of her face. She raised her lip, then the fur around her neck, down her spine. Her size was intimidating enough, but the puff of her mane, the glint of those teeth, the boom of her growl, and the murderous look in her gold eyes – even Holt recognized the danger.

He stepped back, eyes wide, chin on his chest.

Harper snarled at him, black lip trembling over bright pink gums. She surged to her feet and shook off the snow. Her head tipped back and she loosed a howl – a war cry. Small flurries of snow fell from tree limbs, as though rattled free by the vibrations of the mournful wail.

Emerson's hair stood at attention, all over her arms and the back of her neck. Her frigid muscles quaked.

"Oh shit," Holt whispered.

Harper lowered her head, the last note lingering in the air between them. Her ears flicked. She didn't move past that, didn't blink even. Her gaze remained unwavering, aimed at Holt. A stiff breeze ruffled her fur, her tail swayed.

They just needed a solitary tumbleweed to roll through the clearing. Right between them to make the metaphor of a showdown complete.

Holt came back to life, resuscitated from his stupor with one deep breath. "Come on, bitch. I'm not afraid of you."

Harper snarled, wrinkled snout bunching further, twitching with renewed fury. Her ears flattened. She snapped at the air and dipped low, ready to spring.

The traps, the traps, it's a trap! Emerson screamed against the sticky tape and bandana shoved in her mouth. Her hands were tied and taped. Shoulders and back pulled tight against the unforgiving surface of the tree with the heavy rope that held her. The bark scratched at her, pulled her hair as she struggled. *Harper, don't! Don't!*

A snowflake tumbled past her eyes, landed on her hand. More followed, trickling at first, then fell heavier. They melted in her hair, tickled her frozen cheeks.

Holt took another step back, stretched his arm behind the tree, where he'd left both the shotgun and tranquilizer rifle.

She'd watched him load the dart, filled with toxic wolfsbane. But she couldn't do anything about it. Couldn't stop him, couldn't warn Harper or fight back at all. She screamed again, muffled but longer until her abused throat constricted and cut it off.

Holt raised the rifle and that spurred Harper into action. She gathered back on her haunches and with something akin to a roar jumped forward. Her jaws gaped, teeth eager for flesh.

She was fast. So fast. He shouted in surprise and threw himself to the side, barely avoiding her. Harper's teeth clicked together, closing on air instead of Holt, inches from Emerson's nose.

Emerson recoiled with a shriek, smacking her head against the tree. Hot, moist, wolf breath rushed past her face.

Harper whipped around and charged, snapping and growling. Holt left the rifle where it had fallen, and scrambled for the trees. Toward his boundary of traps. She followed close behind.

Harper, no! She struggled with the rope, leaning her weight against the bonds in an attempt to loosen them.

She heard a metallic snap, a horrific messy crunch, and a strangled yelp. Afraid to look, but powerless to stop, she held her breath and turned her head.

Harper staggered, whining and shaking her head. One of her back legs jerked in the teeth of Holt's trap. Blood turned the snow an awful reddish-brown. Holt rushed the wolf, and it lunged for him again, despite the trap still clinging to her leg. She toppled to the snow on her belly, a chain visibly securing her leg to the ground. Drool dripped from her muzzle. She growled and tugged in a futile attempt to free herself.

Just like she'd imagined Buck and White Fang. But it wasn't a fictional animal caught in the monstrous teeth of the snare. Harper was bleeding, terrified, and crippled. Her pained cries and whimpers interrupted her ferocious growling. She twitched and sneered at Holt, following him with her head as he traipsed past her without a care. Like she was just another animal, and not a person he'd witnessed twist into the shape of a wolf. Or a person he'd grown up with, and should have compassion for.

"Told you that would work," he said with a harsh sigh. He grinned and scooped up the rifle. "Wasn't perfect, but I didn't expect her to be that fast. I can snare anything. Bear, wolf, mountain lion. Werewolf's nothing special. And now..." He winked at her. Winked. Then pressed his cheek to the stock and took aim.

Time lagged. Adrenaline smacked her. She tried to gasp for breath, or scream, cry, anything. All she could do was watch, every other option unavailable. Her heart pounded in her throat, stomach clenched violently.

The rifle popped.

A poison dart struck Harper's side. One second it wasn't there, the next a pink tuft was visible, peeking out from her fur.

Harper howled, then her voice trailed off to a whimper. Their eyes locked.

Emerson trembled harder than before. Her lips, chin, everything shook. Gummy eyelashes and gritty eyes made it hard to keep them open, or blink. They burned and blurred. She lost definition of shapes, but colors remained. Black, white, red, red, red. Her heart picked up its tempo again, beating fast enough to make her sick.

The whimpers died. A new, more menacing growl took over.

She blinked and blinked until she could see again. Harper turned her head and snagged the chain in her teeth. She leaned all her weight to the side and the stake came out of the ground with a clump of bloody snow and dirt. She limped two steps toward Holt, back leg dragging with the burden of the trap. Her growl gained volume and rage with each painful step.

"Shit." Holt fumbled backward for his shotgun. "That stuff's supposed to work faster than this."

Emerson added a growl of her own. She twisted her body, despite the immediate and incredible pain, and kicked at him. He lurched when she

PURE OF HEART

caught his leg and she smirked in triumph.

He yelped, grabbing for his shin. "Emerson! Knock it off!"

Harper pounced while he was looking at her. Her jaws clamped down onto his arm, released and bit again. He screamed as she dragged him to the ground, shaking her head and tossing him around. They rolled, kicking, clawing, punching and biting.

Emerson banged her head against the tree, fighting the ropes with renewed fervor. The wolfsbane would kick in any moment and she needed to get free.

Harper cried out. Holt hit her again, swinging a punch at her eye. She staggered off of him and he scurried away, gained his feet, and drew his knife. The wicked curved tip of the blade glinted in the light. He waved it at Harper and swiped at his face, smearing blood. "That's the best you got?"

Branches snapped. Emerson angled her head away from the fight and widened her eyes.

Logan. Logan stood there in the woods. Pale as the snow around them, doubled over with his hands on his knees. He leaned to the side and threw up, wiped his mouth, and then ran forward.

He slid in the snow next to her like a baseball player. "I followed her," he stammered. "God, I followed her – she was – she was bleeding and – I saw – I saw her. I don't believe it. How could I have missed this?"

She ignored his ramblings, bouncing to convey her urgency. *Hurry, hurry.*

Once he had the rope off of her wrists, she stripped the tape off her mouth, gasping at the pain of pulled skin and hair. He yanked the bandana out of her mouth and tossed it away.

"Harper's a – she's a – we have to get out of here. We've got to call someone. Do something. I didn't know," he babbled, working on the knots holding her to the tree. "I didn't know. How could I not know?"

Later. Later they could deal with him.

"He poisoned her," she said, flinging the ropes free of tingling limbs. "We have to stop them. Him. Both of them. The fighting, it's only going to pump it faster through her system. I don't know how much time we have. He'll kill her!"

"He what?" Logan shook his head and grabbed her under the armpits to hoist her up on her numb legs. "No. Do you see her? Did you know about the – I just – she'll kill him? That's what we should be worried about?" Blue eyes stretched wider. "She killed Ben! Oh my God. She killed Ben. We have to get out of here. Right now."

His hands held on tight, too tight for her to get out of his grip with her weakened arms and legs. She struggled anyway, shoved at him limply, wincing at the bite in her extremities as blood rushed back in. "No, no, we can't. He'll kill her. You're not listening!"

"I'm more worried about you!" He wrapped his arms around her and dragged her back toward the truck. "You're not making any sense and you're blue. We have to get out of here."

"No!" She stomped down on his foot and wheeled around. He caught her around the waist and picked her up. She'd had enough of men dragging her around. She snapped her head back, heard his nose crunch.

"Damn it!" He dropped her.

Her knees hit first and she sucked in a breath, seeing a trap nearby. She reached back and grabbed his pant leg. "Bear traps. There are bear traps set up. Be careful!"

"What?"

She couldn't respond, her tongue dead in her mouth.

Close to the edge of the cliff, Holt slashed at Harper with the knife, she snapped back. Both of them were bleeding and limping, panting. He yelled and charged her. She snarled and reared up on her hind legs to meet him. They crashed together. Harper's jaws closing on Holt's shoulder.

He drove the knife into her side.

"No!" She shouted, too late.

They fell to the snow, Holt's fist around the hilt, Harper on top. Neither moved. Holt stirred first. He shoved Harper off and crawled back, out from under her bulk. One booted foot lashed out, kicking Harper in the head. He rotated over and headed for the tree on his hands and knees.

Harper's front legs pushed down, she came up halfway, but both back legs dragged. She dropped again, whimpering and stirring up snow. Red foam gathered around her gums, a richer, darker shade pumping from her side. Steam rose from the steadily expanding puddle beneath her.

"Holt, don't! Holt!" She screamed, screamed and cried and snatched her wrist away from Logan.

Holt picked up his shotgun, bracing against the tree for balance.

Harper keened, tried to get up again, failed and slumped down on her side.

Emerson ran for her, stumbling and sobbing. She slammed down next to Harper's head and pulled it into her lap. Up close she saw more blood dribbling out of Harper's eyes, ears, and nose. "Harper, Harper, it's okay. It's okay, Harper. Harper."

"Emerson, get out of the way."

"No!" She tucked Harper's head against her stomach and leaned over her, both arms around her, shielding her. The massive body shook and heaved. Sticky blood saturated her already wet jeans, the heat burning against her cold skin. She choked and put her hand under the knife, pressing gently to staunch some of the flow. Keep some of Harper's life from leaking out. She fumbled against Harper's other side, searching for the dart. The feathers on the end tickled her fingers. She grabbed what she could of it and yanked until she had the needle in her palm. The plunger had pressed all the way down, shooting all the poison into Harper's veins. Not a drop left. She tossed it away and hunkered down over Harper's shoulders.

"Get out of the way!"

"No! You want to shoot her, you'll have to shoot me." She set her cheek against soft fur and Logan stared back at her, mouth slack. "Logan, help! It's Harper, Logan. She's your best friend."

Harper whined and gurgled. Her front paws curled up against her chest, which shuddered with every wheezing breath.

"Loogie?" Holt laughed. "Didn't even know you joined the party, man. He can't help you, Emmy. He can't even help himself." He sneered at Logan. "You're too much of a pussy to do anything but stand there, aren't you? Hell, you never even told Harper you're in love with her. Take a good look at what you've had a pathetic hard on for. You see that? You should be helping me. It's probably got you under the same spell."

"Spell?" Logan asked.

"There's no spell!" Emerson rubbed Harper's ears, scratched her neck, stroked her bristled fur. They needed AJ, or Grady, someone who knew how to fix this. She didn't know anything about poison, or Harper's healing abilities. "Hold on, Harper. Hold on."

"Right, there's no spell. You're sniveling over a monster, both of you." Holt grunted. "Maybe that was the master plan. To turn us all into love sick zombies. Slaves for the monster."

"You're the only monster I see here," she said. A warm tongue tickled the inside of her arm. She smiled through her tears and kissed the top of Harper's bloody head.

"You're not right in the head, that's all. I'm going to stop it all. Right now. I'm going to save you. Even if it's from yourself."

"Fuck off," she said, thumbing away the stream of blood seeping from the golden eye facing her.

"Emerson, I mean it, get out of the way. I'm not playing anymore."

"No!"

"Emerson, damn it, get out of the way! I've got to end this. I swear to God I'll shoot you too if you're that far gone. I have to save the town. Think of everyone else. No more death's like Ben's. Or the hikers we assume get lost. It ends right here, right now."

"Do it then!" She tightened her grip on Harper's head, bent her torso farther over her.

"Emerson, please. Get out of the way. Let me save you. You don't even like her. It's not you, you're brainwashed."

"Close your eyes, Harper," she whispered into a twitching, bleeding ear. Harper whined a sad high-pitched note and nuzzled closer.

"Fine!" He racked the shotgun.

"Logan, please," she said, looking to him one last time. Their last chance.

He stood there, hands open at his sides, staring.

"Logan, please. Please, help."

"Don't you move, Loogie. I don't want to have to shoot you too." He raised the gun, long barrel pointed at her head. It swayed. She saw his hands shaking. "You can help me clean up. You're in this now too. That's what you get. How many years did you follow it around, begging for it to notice you. This is your fault too, you know. You should've figured it out."

"Logan, please, please stop him."

"Shut up!"

"Logan, please!"

"Shut up, you little whore!"

Logan's jaw hardened, his fingers curled into his palms. He turned to Holt. "Holt."

"You can shut up too."

He licked his lips. "Holt, put the gun down."

"I'm not going to, and you can't make me. So why don't you run back to mommy and cry about it, you ball-less coward." Holt sighed and the gun stopped swinging. "Last chance, Emmy."

"Holt!" Logan stepped forward.

Emerson closed her eyes and dug her nose into Harper's fur.

Instead of the gunshot she expected, she heard a grunt and the sound of flesh smacking. She looked over her shoulder and saw Logan wrestling with Holt for control of the weapon.

"Let go you idiot!"

Logan shoved and twisted his hands. The barrel wavered between them, pointing up at the sky then back at the ground, all over the place. Neither would let go, but Holt kept backing up, pulling and sneering at Logan.

The gun boomed, a bright flash exploding between them. Logan staggered and Holt swung the butt around into Logan's face, crumpling him.

"Son of a bitch," Holt said and spit. He racked the gun again and aimed it at Logan.

Harper dragged herself out of Emerson's lap. She fell, got up again, shaking her head. Blood dripped from her face and side in heavy droplets. She snarled and rushed at Holt, head low.

"What?" Holt jerked the gun around. Too late.

Harper hit him like a battering ram, head turned to the side, driving her massive shoulder into his gut.

The gun went off again. Holt fell backwards, screaming.

Silence.

Harper's back legs went out from under her. She keened and belly-crawled to Logan, nudged him with her nose. He groaned and shifted over, a hand swatting at her.

"Harper?" Emerson stood, a hopeful flutter in her stomach. Maybe the healing magic of the wolf had kicked in. They would be fine. Harper would finish healing and change back and they could go home.

Harper's ears pricked up, she grunted and panted, back legs sliding under her. She made it two wobbly steps before she collapsed back onto her side.

Emerson hurried to her and fell to her knees once again. "Harper?"

CHAPTER THIRTY-ONE

Logan stayed where he'd fallen at the edge of the cliff. Emerson could hear his ragged breathing, loud in the sudden stillness. Bright blood ran down the side of his face, but he didn't seem to notice or care. He rocked, back and forth, the shotgun resting beside him.

The snow stopped falling. It wasn't raining either. Not like it should have been. She couldn't think of anything else as she split her attention between worrying about Logan and Harper.

If they were in a book, or movie, it would have been storming. Thunder and lightning, torrential rain, or at least thick sheets of snow and cutting wind. Instead, they had silence and clear skies. Rather than puddles and muddy earth they had blinding white snow. Pure snow rapidly staining with dark red.

Wrong. All wrong.

And all her fault. She'd caused all of it. If it weren't for her, Holt would still be alive; Harper wouldn't be bleeding. None of it would have happened. She couldn't leave well enough alone and now...

Harper wheezed against her stomach, the hind leg not encased in a bear trap kicking feebly. The handle of the knife stuck out from her side, sheathed between her ribs, shiny wood against dark fur.

"Harper," she said and tugged at her fur. "Harper, change back. Come on, please, it's safe now. It's over. Change back."

A high pitched cry, more like a puppy, barely made it out. Heavy muscles spasmed under her fingers, but Harper stayed a wolf.

She waited, blinking tears out of her eyes, breath and sobs stuck in her chest. Harper hadn't healed like she thought. She'd used the rest of her precious energy to save them. Her fault. "Harper, please."

The sun shone. The fur remained, hiding the woman beneath.

She knew the length of the blade buried in Harper's side. Holt had sharpened it in front of her, explained the gut hook. He called it his lucky knife, the best hunting companion he ever had.

Blood poured out around it, thick and tacky, near black. She knew it had probably pierced organs.

If they were in a movie she imagined there'd be some sort of music playing. A quiet, gentle, haunting melody to add to the emotional impact of the scene – perhaps a composition created by a master. Or one of those sorrowful folk songs. The ones that never failed to make her feel like her heart had been placed in a vise.

She didn't need music to feel like she was being crushed to death. Not in reality, where they were. Not a movie. Not a book. She felt the weight of it. Steel bands constricted around her chest and tightened every time she saw Harper shudder, which she did with every other breath.

All her life she'd wanted to be like the heroines in her favorite books. Full of adventures, epic love stories, drama, intrigue. Now she had it, her own story. She'd been so wrapped up in the tale she'd been living, she forgot an important part. An essential piece to the plot.

Sacrifice. Cost.

Harper, bleeding, broken and dying in her lap.

Emerson licked her lips and bent down to kiss her wolf between her drooping ears. Harper's breathing faltered and slowed. Her pain-filled mewls and low growls petered out.

"Harper," she said again, her voice a thready, painful rasp. It burned, inspiring a new round of tears to cloud her eyes. She gasped when Harper's ears twitched. A sliver of gold appeared under a leaden eyelid.

She hiccupped and kissed her again, babbling an incoherent stream. Until it all condensed down to one word – the most important word.

"Harper, Harper, Harper…"

She stroked bloody fur, marking her shaking hands in red. Found that to be poetic, symbolic. Harper's blood on her hands.

Harper moved again and she gasped, sobbed Harper's name again and grabbed two handfuls of fur.

Do something. Help her. Do something. Your fault. Fix it.

"Logan!" She whipped around, Harper's head held in the crook of her arm. "Logan!"

"What?" he said, and didn't cease his rocking.

"Logan, help me! She's not dead!"

He shivered and gasped. "Holt's dead."

"Logan! Your best friend is bleeding out and poisoned. Help me, right now. Don't let her die here too."

Both of Harper's eyes opened, rolled up toward her. The gold had dimmed and a green ring surrounded her pupil. She knew in her bones that wasn't a good sign. Blood welled up in the corner of those strange eyes and ran into her fur.

"Logan!"

He came up beside her, face blotchy, eyes bloodshot, and dropped down to his knees. "What do – what can we do?"

"Do you have your phone?" She kept Harper's head cradled in her arm and reached for his wrist. *Please, let one thing go right.*

"Yeah, I – yeah." He fished in his pocket and held the device out to her. His fingers shook so hard he dropped it. She tried to smile at him, to assure one of them things were okay, but her lips and chin were shaking worse than his hands.

She choked and swallowed bile when his lock screen showed a picture of Harper. A candid – she'd obviously been unaware he'd taken it. He'd caught her in the middle of a laugh, green eyes glittering, mouth open in a wide grin.

In the crook of her arm Harper coughed and gagged, sounding like Mr. Darcy when he had a hairball. Warmth splashed down her arm. Blood, tar-like and nasty, clung to her skin like syrup.

They were out of time.

"Logan, talk to her. Talk to her, keep her calm." She searched his contacts for Grady, clicked it and shoved the phone to her ear. Logan hesitated, hands hovering over Harper's back. She nodded at him. "It's alright. It's Harper."

He shook his head and dragged his palm down Harper's back. "Okay, Harpy," he said with a shaky exhale. "Okay. You're okay. I don't – you know I don't care that this is you. I wish you'd told me sooner. Under better circumstances. We're best friends. You could have trusted me." He swiped his cheek against his shoulder. "You're my best friend."

The phone line rang and rang. Her heart thumped in her ears, leaping and falling every time Harper whimpered or struggled for breath.

"Logan, I can't talk right now. You're in charge at the bar. Harp and I aren't going to –"

"Grady!" She managed not to sob his name. Things needed to be clear, concise. They didn't have time to waste with hysterical, unintelligible sobbing. "We need help. Harper's – Holt poisoned Harper. He stabbed her. She's bleeding. I think she's dying."

She's dying.

"Where are you?" He swore, and something banged and clattered in the background. A feminine voice murmured.

"I don't know." She thrust the phone at Logan. "Tell them where we are."

"Grady," he said, wincing. "I'm so sorry. We're at the clearing, the cliff that goes out over the lake. Where..." He choked and glanced at Harper. "Where they found Ben."

He dropped the phone and scrubbed both hands at his cheeks. "They're on the way."

Harper cried out and jerked. She panted, yelped, while her body bucked and twisted on itself.

"What's happening?" Logan fell backward.

"Harper!" Emerson grabbed for her head again and held on through continued tremors and hard twitches. Harper writhed away with a high pitched squeal. She rolled onto her back, legs kicking, head thrashing.

Emerson and Logan shared a look, their hands in the air.

Bones cracked and groaned as they reformed Harper's human skeleton. Her ears shriveled, her face shrank, long wolf snout pulling back. She screamed as soon as her mouth was able, a half-human, half-wolf wail.

Emerson shivered and jumped back to help. She saw the knife, still in place, and thought about how the blade must've cut into shifting organs and muscle, making everything worse. Harper's screams turned into heaving sobs and horrible wrenching gasps that jostled the knife even more.

"Harper, you'll be okay. It's okay, it's going to be fine. Help's coming. Hold on, please. Look at me, Harper, look at me." She cupped a damp cheek, desperate to get through. "You have to calm down. I know it hurts, but – look at me. Please."

No magical healing saved the day, or stopped the pain. Blood continued to spill and collect everywhere. Harper's shaking hands clutched fistfuls of dirty snow. Agony was written into the lines on her face, in the tears, in the whimpers that continued to escape from behind her bared teeth. There was no magic here. Only Harper and her pain and Emerson's 'please' hanging in the air.

"Em-mers-on."

It sounded like a question, or maybe a plea, and it hit Emerson like a solid blow to the diaphragm.

"Hold on, Harper. Hold on. You're going to be fine, okay? I called for help and you're going to be fine. Everything's going to be alright." She rubbed her thumb against Harper's cheek, smearing a streak of red. "I'm sorry, I'm so sorry. This is all my fault."

Harper's head lolled, blood drenched hair sliding across her bare shoulders, painting more red in thin lines. The tendons in her neck stood out, along with the veins. Every vessel bulged, a sick dark green color instead of the normal blue. They painted a map on every inch of exposed skin, the path the poison had taken outlined for them.

Glassy green eyes turned upward, a moan snuck out between Harper's teeth. The same strange discoloration had followed over to her human half, but reversed. The eerie amber color of the wolf circled her pupils, glowing like the edges of an eclipse.

"Pro-tect you," she said, hooting the last word.

PURE OF HEART

Emerson shook her head and maneuvered Harper back into her lap. "You brave, silly, wonderful woman." She glanced at the knife and gasped when she saw red, raw flesh marring the opposite side of her ribcage. The skin bubbled and split, like she'd been burned. Further down the bear trap lacerated Harper's shin, muscle and bone visible through shredded skin.

Blood continued to sink into the ground at an alarming rate. They needed help. She didn't know what to do about the knife. To leave it in or take it out. But the bear trap, they could at least get that off of her.

"Logan," she said, turning to him. He held one of Harper's hands, his eyes directed over his shoulder, back toward the cliff. A muscle jumped in his jaw.

"What can I do?" he asked. "How do we fix this?"

"Can you get that off of her? The trap?"

He shuffled around Harper on his knees and set his hands on either side of the jaws. "This is going to hurt."

"Just do it," she said and put both hands on Harper's cheeks, directing her face up. "Look at me, Harper. Look at me."

Steel groaned and then snapped again. Harper howled, back bowing up off the ground. Logan had opened the trap but it had reattached, slipping from his grasp.

"Damn it!" He wiped his mouth with his forearm. "I'm sorry, I'm sorry."

"Get it off!"

He pulled again, arms trembling and face red with exertion. "Harper, move your leg out!"

Harper screamed and jerked her leg free. A bone stabbed up through her torn skin.

Logan fell back into the snow, both hands over his face. "God!"

Harper groaned and pushed her face into Emerson's stomach, cheeks puffing out as she dragged in breath after breath.

Shock. "Logan, get the blanket by the tree."

Logan scrambled to his feet, paused to vomit, then staggered away, weaving from side to side. He returned with the scratchy wool blanket, but stood and fidgeted with it. He stared at Harper with wide eyes and a gaping mouth, as though he'd just noticed her nakedness.

Emerson grabbed the corner of the blanket and snatched it out of his hands. She covered Harper and tucked it under her, leaving her arms free. At her pointed look he hastened to tuck the rest under Harper's body. He then retook his spot beside her and took Harper's hand back in both of his.

Harper groaned, her teeth chattering together, and arched up onto her shoulders. She rolled to the side and threw up black into the snow, the end of a tooth visible in the bloody goo.

"Harper," she said, fighting down panic. Heroes only puked blood when it was bad.

"Can't – breathe. Hurts."

"He poisoned you. It's wolfsbane," she said, using the blanket to clean some of the blood off Harper's face. Her nose was one big blood slick and her cheeks were coated, crying blood.

"Wolfsbane?"

"Yes." *Keep her awake, keep her talking, stay calm.* She glanced at Logan and shook her head. "I don't know what it does. I didn't do any research. Do you know how we reverse the effects?"

More blood bubbled out between Harper's red lips, she coughed, gagged and tossed her head from side to side.

"Harper, I…" *Give her something to hold onto. Forget your head, use your heart. Your big, stupid heart.* "You know that – you know I – that you mean so –"

"No!" Harper gasped and shook her head. "Don't – don't now."

"Why?"

She wheezed, eyes closed. "Books. In story. Wrong. Time. Hero dies when – when girl says it. You think – beautiful – but it's sad. Sad."

More tears swarmed and ran hot down her face. "You do read."

Harper nodded, whining. "You have to wait," she slurred. " 'Til I'm better. Then say – say nice things."

"Then you have to promise me, Harper. You have to promise me you're going to get better. Harper?"

"Promise promise."

Emerson got so wrapped up in watching Harper's eyelids flutter and the way her breathing got more labored that she didn't notice the sound of a vehicle approaching. She looked away when forced to, when strong hands grabbed under her arms and hoisted her off the ground. Harper growled and moved to follow, but AJ took Emerson's spot and held her down. She raised the blanket, exposing the knife.

"Wait!" Emerson cried, fighting against the strong grip.

"Emerson, it's okay. It's okay, it's us. AJ's going to fix this."

"Grady," AJ said, struggling to keep Harper still.

The hands holding Emerson slid away. Grady knelt on the other side of Harper, he held her down while AJ gripped the knife handle and…

Harper screamed, loud and broken. Emerson lurched forward, but a new pair of arms circled her.

So much blood. Too much. AJ pushed a cloth against the wound, chewing on her bottom lip.

"Stop." Emerson gasped, squirming in Cooper's hold. They were hurting her more, not making it better. "Stop!"

AJ peeled back the saturated cloth and peered at the injury, her free hand finding Grady's and squeezing. "We have to get her to the house. Quickly."

PURE OF HEART

Grady scooped Harper up into his arms, tears dripping into his beard. AJ followed him, keeping the rag against Harper's side. Emerson pulled away from Cooper and rushed after them.

"Someone's going to have to stay, clean this up," Grady said.

"I'll do it," Logan said, shakily. "Like you did last time. For Ben."

AJ paused, her hands on the back door handle of the SUV. She shot Grady a look, lips pursed. Grady tensed and pulled Harper tighter against his chest.

"I forgot you were..." he shook his head and glanced at Emerson. "Logan, this isn't what you..."

"We don't have time for a big discussion or past regrets!" Emerson grabbed the door and opened the hatch with a glare at AJ. "Let him do it."

Logan crossed his arms over his stomach, holding himself together. "What do I have to do?"

"Clean up the blood. The wolf prints. Make it look like an accident." Grady grimaced and Logan glared at him.

"It was." He moved off toward the biggest puddle of bloody snow, but stopped and turned back around, forehead furrowed, eyes on the ground. "You'll call me if..."

"She's going to be fine," Cooper said, chin quivering and ruining his sure expression. "Harper's indestructible."

Not right now she isn't, Emerson thought and climbed into the back of the vehicle. *She won't be fine at all if you don't all shut up and act like this is a problem.*

AJ winced as she got into the back with Emerson. "We need to get this bleeding under control."

"Give her to me," Emerson said and stretched her arms out.

Grady stared at her, frowning, and adjusted Harper against his chest. She wanted to scream at him. It wasn't the time to doubt her. Even if it was her fault. They'd have to time to point fingers later.

"Grady, give her to me."

"Grady!" AJ smacked her hand against the back seat and he jumped. "Damn it, we don't have time for all of this. Give her to Emerson."

He leaned into the back with a grunt and a grimace. Harper whined plaintively as he set her down, her head in Emerson's lap.

"Harper," Emerson said, stroking Harper's hair, clearing the blood off her face. AJ clamped both hands, and the rag, against the wound.

Grady slammed the hatch. He and Cooper slid into the front. The vehicle sputtered to life and tore off down the trail, slipping and lurching in the snow.

Out the rear window Emerson saw Logan watching them go. She turned her attention back to Harper, whose lips had gone white with a ring of red foam around them, her face a sickly gray color.

"You said he poisoned her?" AJ wiped her forehead and tossed the sodden rag away, replacing it with a clean one. "I've never seen her bleed like this. She's not healing."

"It was wolfsbane. He used a rifle and a dart from your office." She swiped at her eyes. "Can you – is there an antidote or something?"

"I don't know."

Harper gurgled, eyes and mouth going wide. She threw both her hands out and arched back. Her chest caved in.

"Harper!"

"Jesus!" AJ grabbed for a flailing hand and poked her head up over the seat. "Grady, drive faster. She can't breathe!"

"Harper, Harper, calm down, calm down," Emerson said, grabbing Harper's chin. The gold ring around her pupil glowed hot up at her. "Breathe, breathe."

"Em-er." She gasped, flung out her hand and caught Emerson's shoulder. "Can't –"

"AJ, what do we do? What do we –"

Horrible rattling coughs rocked Harper's shoulders, she whined, legs kicking and hand at her throat.

"Grady!" AJ yelled.

"I can't go any faster! You want to get pulled over with her in the back?"

"Christ almighty," AJ said. She grabbed Harper's bucking hips and pinned them to the floor. "Harper, Sweets, calm down, you have to stay calm."

Short, shallow gasps filled the small space, the windows fogged up. Harper's chest barely moved. She thrashed, short nails digging into Emerson's shoulder. Her eyes rolled back into her head. She shook and then went wild, bouncing against the floor.

"She's seizing. Let her go!"

"Let her go?"

"Let go!"

Emerson held up her hands and watched Harper pitch from side to side.

"Grady, nobody is going to stop us," AJ called. "Floor it!"

Harper went limp and didn't move again. AJ lunged forward, two fingers pressing against the side of Harper's throat.

"Shit." She started CPR, bloodied hands together pushing down hard on Harper's chest. "Emerson, breathe for her. You know how? Good. Come on, Harper! Come on!"

**

Harper screamed. She screamed and howled and screamed some more. AJ had her strapped down to the exam table in the vet office. One of the light stands placed next to the table crashed to the floor and shattered when Harper seized again. Her arm snapped the strap across her chest, struck out,

PURE OF HEART

snagged the pole and toppled the light.

"Harper!" Grady grabbed for her arm and held it to his chest. His other hand remained plastered against her ribs, holding another blood soaked rag to the knife wound. "Harper!"

"It's fine – let her go. Let her go!" AJ rushed across the room and slammed into a counter. Drawers banged open, one after the other, while she dug through them and tossed several items onto the countertop.

More foam gathered around Harper's lips. She choked and spit, spraying Cooper and Emerson with flecks of red.

Emerson pressed her elbows against her sides. Her shoulders quaked with silent sobs, her voice too far gone to pronounce them. She held a clammy hand over her mouth and flinched with every thump and clatter, growl and screech.

Cooper stood next to her, ashen, swaying. He grasped her wrist, held her hand tight.

"What do we do?" Grady asked, tucking a limp hand back onto the table. "AJ, what do we do?"

"I have to try and filter the wolfsbane out. I think it's keeping her from healing. Stop the poison, stop the bleeding."

"Can you –" Cooper licked at his lips and wiped his eyes. "Can you give her something for the pain?"

AJ slumped against the counter, jerked around when Harper groaned. "I don't – she's had so much over the past few days. I don't know what it will do to her. It could overload her system, which is already compromised."

Harper's muffled keening rose in volume. She pulled her hand free again and held it out to the side of the table, fingers reaching.

"Emerson," AJ said and approached the table, arms laden with supplies. "Emerson, she's looking for you."

Emerson moved to the head of the table and caught Harper's freezing hand. Bleary red filled eyes looked up at her. Emerson's lips and chin wobbled when she tried to smile. "Harper, I'm here. It's okay, you're safe. You're safe now. We're at the clinic." She raised the green veined hand and kissed the back of it before cradling trembling fingers to her cheek. "You're safe."

"Mers," Harper murmured, blinking rapidly. "Hurts. Hurts."

"I know, I know it does." She glanced at Grady, then to AJ. "Do it, give her something."

"I can't just administer something."

Harper's teeth chattered, her eyes rolled back again and again. She hissed out a breath and squeezed Emerson's fingers. "Hurts. Burns."

"AJ," Grady said.

"We have to start cycling this shit out first, okay?" She set up an IV and bit into her bottom lip as she stuck the needle into the back of Harper's hand. "I don't know if this will even work. I don't – I just don't know. It's all I can think of to do."

Harper whined through clenched teeth. Her body stiffened and then jerked in another bout of seizures. Emerson held her hand through them, helpless again but refusing to let go.

"AJ," Grady said again as Harper calmed and continued to mewl. "Jay."

"I can't – I – Grady, I'm a veterinarian, whatever I try could make it worse. I don't know enough about her physiology. She could be completely…"

"AJ." He touched her hand and dipped his head to look her in the eye.

"No. No, I could make it worse." She shook her head. "We need to get her to the hospital. The actual hospital. We can make something up, please. I can't –"

"She's a wolf."

"She's human!" She glared at him, tears dripping off her chin. "She's human. She's your damn niece and she's…"

"Ava," he said, almost whispered, raising his hand to touch her cheek. "Ava, please, you're the only one — you have to do this. We trust you. Harper trusts you. You know what to do, you do. Please."

Emerson ran her hand through Harper's filthy hair. "Please, I can't stand to see her hurt like this. Please."

"Do you understand what you're asking? What you're asking me to do? It could kill her faster. Put her in a coma. I don't even know the right dosage. I'm guessing."

"Jay," Harper slurred, eyes full of pain and confusion, glazed over and distant. "Jay?"

"Do something," Cooper pleaded, back against the wall with his hands over his ears. "Do something! You're all standing there and – just do something, anything!"

AJ went back to her cabinets and opened a drawer, shaking from head to toe. She lifted a vial out and got a syringe.

Under the remaining light by the table her ghostly pallor intensified. Every freckle on her face stood out. Dark eyes darted to each face and then landed on Harper's and stayed there. She took a deep breath and loaded the syringe, but did nothing beyond that. Simply held it in her hand like it contained nuclear waste and water from the fountain of youth at the same time.

Grady stretched across Harper's heaving torso and gripped AJ's hand with the syringe. "I'll do it."

"Grady."

"I'll do it."

Emerson bent and kissed Harper's sweat soaked hairline. "Hold on."

Grady wiped the sweat and tears off his face. AJ came around and took over holding the rag against Harper's ribs. He smiled down at Harper and stooped to kiss her cheek. "Alright, Harp, no more pain. Okay?"

She moaned in response.

AJ checked the IV, not bothering to wipe her own eyes. She sniffled and nodded. "Go ahead."

Emerson smoothed the hair at Harper's temples and held her woozy gaze. "Stay with me."

Grady grabbed the IV catheter and held the syringe in his other hand. The needle shook as he lowered it. AJ finally covered his hand, wrapping dainty fingers around the back of his, and helped him guide the needle in. He pushed the plunger.

Seconds ticked by and then Harper's repeated soft cries dropped off. Her legs stopped scraping at the table. She exhaled and her eyes dimmed.

"Stay with me, Harper, stay," Emerson said, choking on tears. "Stay."

Gold rimmed eyes disappeared behind heavy lids. Her chest relaxed.

It stopped moving altogether.

"Harper?"

"Harp?"

"Harper?" she said, crying harder when the head in her palms turned to the side. "Harper – stay, stay with me."

The beat of the heart rate monitor stuttered. Slowed.

Slowed.

Stopped.

CHAPTER THIRTY-TWO

Harper

Something jostled her. Harper whined and turned her head into her pillow with a frown. She opened her eyes when she realized it wasn't as soft as before. To her knowledge pillows also weren't supposed to move.

Then she heard panting and a fast heartbeat. Her mother's scent tickled her nose along with a new smell, sour and sharp. She jerked, little fingers holding tight to the straps of her mother's sleep shirt like handles.

A warm palm cradled the back of her head and pulled her back against a racing heart. "Mam?"

"Shush."

They were running. Running where? Away from the house. She smelled the trees and wet grass and dirt. "Mama?"

She squeaked as they fell forward. Cold seeped into her pajamas, even with the warmth coming off her mother. She pressed in closer. "Why are we outside?"

The world tilted. Strong hands gripped her under the armpits. She shivered as she was placed on the ground just under the reach of a bush, then pressed back, deeper under the cover of wide leaves.

Her mother's eyes, the same pale green as hers, pinned her in place. She leaned in and kissed her forehead, holding the connection longer than she ever had before.

Something was wrong. Very wrong. They were outside at night, in the cold. She didn't even have shoes on. Tears welled and spilled down her cheeks. "Mama."

"Stay here, baby. No matter what you hear, or see, stay here and don't make a sound. Do you understand?" Her bottom lip wobbled, her own tears splashing against Harper's tiny hands.

She nodded, crying harder and clutching at her mother's arms when she pulled away. Gentle hands pushed her back down into the mud. She scooped up a handful of the muck and rubbed it in Harper's hair, on her face and bare arms.

"Mam."

"I love you, little growl," she said and ran back toward the house.

Cold, wet, covered in mud, she stayed under the bush, hiccupping in an attempt to stay quiet. The house was close. There were no lights on. She strained her ears to hear over her heart and choking breath. Nothing. Not even a breeze.

Two pops sounded. She saw a flash of light in an upstairs window. Her room. Three more flashes and pops followed.

"Mama?"

"Harper."

The house melted, running and dripping. It drained away to nothing. The landscape went next. Branches and leaves melded together into a wash of greens and browns. The starry sky swirled, leaving nothing but the moon. A half-moon that grew larger, into a full moon. It flew toward her, filling her vision. She gasped and tripped backward.

"Harper."

She covered her face. "I am not eight years old anymore. This is a messed up dream. A really messed up dream."

"It's a memory. Your memory."

That voice. She shook her head. "No. You're dead. I'm dreaming. One of those scary, vivid dreams. You're dead."

"Little growl."

"Don't call me that!" She stood up and spun around, expecting anyone else. Someone else daring to speak to her with her mother's voice. Grady, AJ, Emerson, even Holt.

She fell back to her knees. "Mama?"

A pale hand brushed rich dark hair out of green eyes. Her mother's familiar smile inspired an eruption of butterflies in her rock hard stomach.

"Harper."

"Am I dead? Did I – this isn't real. Not unless I'm dead, and I think I'd remember dying." She covered her ears. "Not real. I'm not dead. Nope. This is a bad Telazol trip."

"Harper, honey."

"Stop talking to me! You're not my mother!"

"Harper." Those same gentle hands from her memory, her dream, wrapped around her wrists.

She whined and shook her head again, eyes screwed shut.

"I'm proud of you, little growl. You've grown into the woman I always hoped you would."

Harper snorted. "Right. Now I know this is a dream."

Her dream mother laughed. A low, melodious sound. Just like she remembered. "I suppose I didn't picture you as a foul-mouthed bartender. But you're loyal, loving, strong, and as beautiful as I knew you'd be. My idiot brother raised you right."

"Alright, I give up, figment." She peeked and found the same smile gracing her mother's features. "If you're my mother, and I'm dead, now seems a perfect time for me to ask. Why didn't you tell me about the wolf?"

Fake mother sighed, tucking a few loose strands of Harper's hair behind her ear. "You were a puppy, a baby. It wasn't the right time."

"You could have had…" She swallowed. "You could have written a letter or something, in case –"

"In case of something like what happened."

"Yeah. That," she said and licked her lips. "About that."

"Your dreams are memories. It wasn't an accident. If that's your next question."

"What was it?"

"Murder."

She curled her fingers around fake mother's wrists. "Someone – someone was there that night. A man."

"Yes, there was. But Harper, I can't talk about that."

"Oh, is there some dream-slash-death bed-ghost-visit rule I'm not aware of?"

"No."

"No?" She growled and glared.

"Honey, I can't tell you for your safety," fake mother said, smile dimming. "And I'm not a ghost and you're not dead, or dreaming. You did die, but you're not dead. You're asleep, but not dreaming. This is an in-between. A gift."

"I remain skeptical," she said and reached out to grasp slender shoulders. She crumpled fabric under her hands, tested the realness of the figure beneath. There was no scent in the non-space they were in, so she didn't smell her mother. Not the lavender and chamomile she knew. But the heat coming off the fake mother felt real, as did the muscle her fingers dug into. "Okay, somewhere skeptical."

"I'm here. Think of it like a visitation."

"Because I died, but I'm not dead."

"That's the simplest explanation I can think of." She smiled again. "Or at least the vaguest simple explanation I can think of. You have your father's habit of freaking out, after all. Ask me anything else. Anything."

"Because telling me I'm dead but not dead is keeping me from freaking out. That's great, thank you. What about the imprint, can you talk about that?"

Maybe-not-fake mother's smile broadened, dimples deepening. "Emerson. I like her. Not exactly what your father and I had in mind, but she's lovely. A good match."

"Right," she said. "Great. Parental permission. Does it – why her though?"

"Because that's who it was."

"You realize that's like saying 'because I said so'?"

"Is it?"

"Seriously. Isn't there some time limit or something to this limbo whatever? Now you've got jokes?"

She shrugged. "I've had time to develop my sense of humor."

"Jesus H. God, I've had time to develop a headache." She rubbed at her temples with a wince. The headache wasn't a joke. It came out of nowhere, throbbing away, along with an increasing ache in her side. "Why would this magical imprint happen now and with a woman?"

"It's not always based on procreation, if that's what you're thinking. It's about compatibility. A true life partner your wolf recognizes and accepts. Her strengths complement yours. She's what you need and vice versa. If it were purely about making little werewolves we would only ever imprint on purebreds, never humans. This way the lines stay mixed. It keeps them clean."

"I'm not sure if I feel better or utterly grossed out." She threw her hands in the air, heat staining her cheeks. "So it's werewolf magic, or whatever, but I'm still confused and I still have questions."

"There are..." she scraped a hand through her hair. "There's a lot to it I don't have time to explain. But you have family, other than Grady and Cooper. Wolves. In Ireland. Cousins that will help."

"Strange family members to give me the werewolf and the human talk? I've done that, sort of, and I'm not looking for a repeat. I thought these near-death visitation experience things were supposed to be mystical, not mortifying."

"You'll figure some of it out on your own," she said with a chuckle. "They can also tell you more about what you are. Things you need to know."

"Why can't you tell me? Are you sending me on a quest? Do I look like Frodo Baggins to you?"

"You don't have to. It's a suggestion. Right now, little growl, you need to go back. They're waiting."

"And how would I do that?" She huffed and flapped her hands around at the nothingness surrounding them. "Great chat, now wish yourself into a real girl?"

"Close your eyes."

PURE OF HEART

Harper did as asked and clicked her heels together. "There's no place like home."

"The sarcasm isn't helping."

"Yes, Ma'am." She peeked open one eye and smirked. "If this is real — or not — it doesn't matter. I love you, Mama. I miss you."

"I miss you too. We all do." She stepped forward and hugged her. Tears clogged Harper's throat immediately. She returned the fierce embrace and ducked her head into her probably-actually-real-mother's neck. "Close your eyes, Harper."

"I don't know how you're expecting this to — "

***

Harper's eyes opened to slits. She dragged in what felt like her very first breath ever. Something rattled in her back and chest. She coughed, wheezed, coughed again and blinked to clear the sleep cementing her eyelids together.

She wasn't in her room, or in the basement. The mattress under her was too stiff to be hers, and the walls were the wrong color. Tan, not green. Grady's room.

"What?" She frowned at the croaky whisper that came out of her mouth. Her lips were chapped and split. She licked at a cut in the corner and with effort turned her aching head.

Blonde hair spread out on the pillow next to her.

Emerson. It had to be Emerson.

When did this happen? Harper reached for the slender shoulder beside her, pulling gently, thinking it would wake Emerson up without startling her. Emerson's body rolled, limp; her head lolled to the side.

Her throat was torn down to the vertebrae. Dried blood caked the underside of her chin and what flesh remained. Her chest had been opened, sternum, ribs, her whole chest cavity. The organs beneath had been pulped to nothing but indistinguishable masses.

Harper tried to scream. Her mouth opened wide, but nothing came out. She looked down and saw AJ laid out at the foot of the bed, belly torn, guts strewn around her.

She pitched away from the body and crashed to the floor in a heap. Pain flared in her side, worse than the agony she remembered from her self-inflicted knife to the heart area. A strange sound, like a bell, rang in her ears.

She looked up and keened in disbelief.

Cooper sat below the window. Half of his face had been stripped away. Nose, ear, his cheek, missing. A chunk had been bitten out of the base of his neck and shoulder.

No! No, I didn't do this! She crawled away as fast as her weakened body would allow. Her bare feet slipped in the tacky, stale blood covering the floor. The happy jingle of a bell chasing her all the way. *It's a nightmare, just a nightmare!*

Her hands smacked into something at the base of the bed. She trembled, eyes closed, and peeked around the footboard.

Logan lay stretched out in a puddle of dark red, his back sliced into and chewed on.

She gagged and rolled onto her back, slipping and sliding toward a dresser on her palms and heels. Her elbow struck something. She jerked around. Grady sat in the chair, completely shredded. His biceps torn away, his fingers curled in unnatural angles around the shotgun clutched in his cold, dead hands. He still had a look of shock on his blood-speckled face.

Tiny whimpers burned her throat. Tears blurred her eyes, but refused to fall. Her mouth gaped open, and vomit swelled. She choked, coughed, and doubled over clutching at her ribs.

"Close your eyes, Harper."

She groaned and shook her head, eyes screwed shut.

Please no, not my family too. Please.

***

With a wheezing gasp Harper surged upwards. The immediate fiery pain in her ribs knocked her back down. She groaned and grabbed for her side. A strange cloth wrapped her chest, winding under her armpits and down to her navel. Stark white bandages with a red spot right where it hurt the most. She undid the butterfly clips holding it in place and partially un-mummified herself. Her skin came back into view. An angry red patch marred her side from just below her breast down to her hip.

"What?" She touched the mark, and hissed as pain and heat blossomed under her fingertips.

You died, but you're not dead.

She shook her head and grimaced at the motion sickness that followed. The same jingling noise from her terrifying day-terror sounded. She touched her neck, felt something small and metallic resting against her breastbone. A bell? She flicked it to be sure and it jingled again. A bell, someone had put a bell on her.

She ground her teeth together and threw the blankets off her legs. *At least I'm wearing pants,* she thought, and pulled at the fleecy fabric someone had put on her. They weren't hers and were too short, riding up the bottom half of her long shins. She struggled to get her legs over the side of the bed. Her toes brushed the bristles of the rug on the floor and scrunched the ticklish fibers. She grabbed the bedpost and heaved herself upright, but her legs quivered and ran out of strength too fast. Back onto the mattress.

Eyebrows drawn together, she smacked her thighs a couple of times to encourage some blood to return to them. She tried again, grunting with effort.

The bell rang again. She caught it in her fist, silencing it.

PURE OF HEART

One hand busy holding her new jewelry, she yanked open the dresser. It took forever to get one of Grady's undershirts over her head, and by the time she had it on she was out of breath and in tears again.

She shuffled to the door, hunched over to protect her ribs from further aggravation. Outside the bedroom she caught richer scents and relaxed. Grady, Cooper, AJ, Emerson. Alive, downstairs. She raised her nose to take a stronger sniff. Besides the comforting odors of her family she smelled breakfast. Coffee, eggs, toast, bacon. Her stomach growled and panged.

The stairs proved tricky. She stopped on each step to regain her breath, and had to concentrate on not tripping and falling. Her feet finally hit the bottom landing. She sighed, looking around, and didn't see any of her family. No one came running to greet her and explain all the weirdness.

Maybe I should have let the bell announce my presence? She craned her neck to get a glimpse of the shiny, silver object.

The scent of coconut drew her toward the living room, away from the tempting smell of hot breakfast. She used the wall to stay upright and peered around the corner. Blonde hair, the same she'd imagined seeing upstairs, covered the armrest, messy and tangled. She couldn't see anything else of Emerson besides a blanket covered lump. After two lurching steps into the room, she stopped again, eyes wide.

On the floor beside the couch, burritoed in Cooper's old Superman comforter, was Oscar Grey. He grumbled in his sleep, one hand crawling across the floor. One of Emerson's hands fell free from her own blanket cocoon and landed on the back of Oscar's. He sighed and stilled.

Twins, she thought with a fond smile and an eye roll. She snuck up to the couch and touched the top of Emerson's head. A jolt swept up her arm from fingertip to shoulder, then continued upward to buzz in her ear. At least that was still there. She sighed and backed away.

A different scene played out in the kitchen. She leaned against the doorway and drank it all in. Cooper sat at the table, upper body sprawled out across the surface, face plastered against his arm, dead asleep. Across from him at the kitchen window Grady stared outside, a steaming cup of coffee in his hands. AJ stood at the stove, stirring eggs around a frying pan, her bottom lip in her teeth.

Harper cleared her throat and raised an eyebrow.

Cooper blinked his eyes open and tilted his head up. Sleepiness vanished. His jaw dropped as he pitched upright. He banged his hand on the table and stammered at her.

"Hey?" she said.

A coffee cup shattered on the floor, followed by a pan clattering. All her future breakfast spilled out on the linoleum. She looked from one stunned face to the next with a confused smile. "Guys?"

"Harper!" Cooper stood up so fast his chair toppled.

Grady and AJ came at a run. She couldn't get out a word of protest. Before she knew it, she was being lowered into another kitchen chair, like she was made of glass. Grady kissed her forehead and hugged her against his chest, laughing and crying in the same breath. AJ dashed out of the kitchen and came back in just as fast, bare feet slapping against the floor. Cooper handed her a glass of water, tears running down his cheeks and into his blinding smile.

She took the glass of water and managed a cautious sip. Her body responded by demanding more. She chugged the rest and slapped the glass to the table, coughing at the sudden rush of moisture in her parched mouth and throat.

AJ pushed Grady and Cooper to the side and lifted Harper's eyelids. A penlight shined into her eyes, one then the other. "Pupils reacting normally. No sign of the wolf color around them."

"What the hell –" she growled when AJ cut her off by sticking her fingers into her mouth and pulling her jaw down.

"No blood. It's red, probably sore, but looks better. Much better. And all of her teeth have re-grown." Cold, always cold, hands reached for the hem of Grady's borrowed shirt.

Harper grabbed AJ's wrists and shook her head. "Hey, can we not? How about we start by answering the what the hell happened question?"

Three sets of eyes blinked back at her.

"You don't remember?" Grady asked.

"Remember what? Being burned? Or why I'm in your room when I wake up? Nope. Don't remember any of that."

"What's the last thing you do remember?" AJ asked with a worried frown.

Making out with Emerson on her couch. A weird dream, vision-quest thing starring my mother. She rubbed at her cheek. "I had a date with Emerson."

"Sweets," AJ said and knelt down. "You don't remember Holt?"

"Holt?" She growled. "No. What's the moron got to do with anything?" *You died, Harper, but you're not dead.* She sucked in a deep breath and clamped a hand over her ribs. "Did that ass candle try to kill me?"

"He abducted Emerson," Cooper supplied, fidgeting. Grady glared at him and he shrugged. "What?"

Her eyes bulged. "He what?"

"She's fine, she's fine." AJ held up her hands and pointed at the living room. "She's asleep. You went to get her."

"Are you all trying to build up suspense? Because I'm not in the mood." She huffed. "I saw Emerson before I came in here. What's Oscar doing here?"

"He flew out." Grady winced. "He knows about you."

"You told him?"

"Sort of."

"Great," she said and leaned her head back against the wall. "Way to keep that secret."

"We didn't have a choice."

"Because Holt kidnapped his sister and I rescued her?"

"Harper, Holt's dead," AJ said.

"Oh, and Logan knows about you too, now," Cooper added and ducked the swat Grady aimed at his head. "Quit it, she has to know!"

Logan knew, Oscar knew, Emerson. Holt probably knew... oh God, before he died. *Shit, Holt's dead.* She chewed on her bottom lip. The circle of trust had gotten big all of the sudden, not to mention she might have... *One problem at a time.* "Did I – Holt?"

"We don't know," Grady said and winced. "It's possible. You'll have to ask Emerson."

Harper closed her eyes. Another victim added to her list, and this time a witness. Emerson had seen the whole thing. She hoped it hadn't been a blood bath like with Ben.

One problem at a time.

"How did this happen? Did he do this to me?" she gestured at her side.

"It was wolfsbane. He shot you with a dart filled with it."

"Okay, well, that at least... how did I get here? And does it possibly have something to do with why all of you are looking at me like I'm a ghost?"

"You've been in a coma for nine days, Harp," Grady said.

She frowned at him, at all of their solemn faces. "What? No. I was asleep for an hour or something. No way that dream went on for nine days."

"What dream?" AJ asked, cocking her head. "Wolf dreams?"

"No." She stared up at Grady and swallowed. "Can I have some more water? Please?"

Cooper jumped to the task with the eagerness of a puppy chasing a ball.

"I dreamt about Mom," she said. "I thought it was a dream, anyway. It was very real and kind of weird. Even for me. She said I died, but wasn't dead. Asleep but not dreaming." She laughed and swiped at her mouth with the back of her hand. "Could have just said coma."

The fresh cool water felt wonderful spilling down her throat. She smiled at Cooper. "Thanks, Cousin. So I — "

"You died," a trembling voice said. "Twice."

Emerson stood in the kitchen doorway, Oscar right behind her.

Harper gripped the back of the chair in one hand, flattened her other against the table to leverage herself up. Grady and Cooper helped her onto her feet, hands hovering near her waist just in case. She brushed them away.

Emerson didn't smile, but she didn't frown either. She stepped closer, glacier eyes wet, and raised a shaky hand.

The light touch against her cheekbone zapped her. Harper staggered back into waiting hands as images flooded her already full mind. Snow, Holt, bear traps. Emerson, pale and shivering, crying and screaming against a wide piece of tape. Pain, blood, pain, pain, pain.

"Harper!"

"Get her to the couch!"

Dizzy and nauseas, she didn't argue when Grady scooped her up. They all paraded with her into the living room. The couch cushions felt wonderful under her battered body. Grady's ugly duck hunting blanket, the one Emerson had been sleeping under, was tucked around her.

She shook her head and squinted at all the worried expressions staring at her. "I think I just remembered."

Emerson's fingers scratched against her scalp and untangled a few snares in her hair. She tilted her head into her hand and looked up. "Nine days?"

"Yes," she said with a nod and sank to her knees with enviable grace. "Nine days."

She saw the quaver in Emerson's chin and turned to AJ. "I'm kind of hungry. Breakfast smelled good before you dropped it on the floor."

"Of course!" Grady and Cooper barreled out of the room, knocking into each other. "Hungry. She's hungry!"

AJ pinned her in place with a stern glare. "I know what you just did and I'm going to let you do it. But you are not to move off of this couch. You're still weak and recovering."

"Yes, Ma'am," she said with a small smile. "I'll stay right here. Promise promise."

Because she didn't think she could move anymore, but she wasn't going to admit it.

AJ left with one last glare and a firm point at the couch. Pots and pans clanged in the kitchen. The fridge door opened and slammed multiple times.

Harper looked over at Oscar, who hadn't said a word so far. He sat on the coffee table, sandy-colored eyebrows mashed together, hands clasped between his knees.

"I don't think we ever were properly introduced," she said.

"No, we weren't." He sighed and leaned forward. "I'm Oscar Grey. You've been dating my sister for a handful of days and she's been kidnapped, nearly froze to death, and witnessed the death of a friend. Though I use that term very loosely, considering he's the one who kidnapped her. Oh, and you're a self-healing werewolf. Which I wouldn't believe if I hadn't had evidence shoved under my nose for the past nine days."

"Nice." She grinned at him and arched an eyebrow. "I'm Harper Cahill, your sister's girlfriend. I'm a foul-mouthed bartending werewolf. I've been in a coma for nine days because I went out to rescue your sister from the local playboy after he kidnapped her and tied her to a tree. It's nice to meet you."

He snorted and stood up. "You sure can pick them, Em."

"I actually like this one though," she said and smiled at Harper. "She's infuriating and wonderful."

"Right, and the werewolf thing has nothing to do with it, I'm sure." He patted his rumpled clothes. "I'm going to go help in the kitchen, if I can. You," he said and pointed at Harper. "You and I are going to talk more."

"Absolutely." She sat up on her elbows as he walked away. "Oscar?"

He paused and turned around.

"I want you to know I'm always going to protect your sister. Hopefully not so dramatically in the future, but I will. I know what she means to you, and I need you to know she's important to me too."

"Better be ready to kill a lot of spiders," he said and cracked an easy, slow smile. "We'll save the 'be good to my sister or I'll kill you' lecture for when you're better, alright?"

"Deal."

He left the room, leaving her and Emerson to stare at each other.

"I think he likes me," she said to break the building tension.

Emerson sighed and slid onto the couch, settling Harper's head down in her lap. Her fingers resumed their soothing combing motions. "You should have seen him when he first got here."

"That bad?"

"You were dead, Harper," she said with a sniffle. "Dead, and then in a coma. We didn't know if you'd ever wake up. If the wolfsbane had already destroyed your ability to heal. I wasn't in the best frame of mind to explain things to him."

"So he doesn't like me?"

"He's adjusting still. I think by the time he heads back to New York he'll have calmed down. Plus, your charming personality is sure to win him over."

"You think I'm charming?" She almost purred at the thought, and turned to nuzzle against Emerson's warm stomach. "Is it weird that I feel like I missed you?"

"No, not at all. I missed you. These past few days I felt like I was in a coma too." Her fingers stalled and Harper whined. "Sorry, I just – I was wondering if – about the wolf too."

"I am the wolf," she said with confidence. As though to back up her statement a rush of warmth flooded her. Her vision sharpened and she smiled at Emerson's uncertain expression. "It's me. We're the same. I think

— I think I needed to stop fighting it to realize we're not two minds in one body."

"AJ's going to find that absolutely fascinating." Emerson chuckled and started the wonderful petting again. "We bonded quite a bit while you were upstairs. That woman can talk."

"Yeah, she's kind of an adorable nerd." She pulled a hand out of the blanket as a thought struck her. Fingers tangled in the soft leather of her new necklace's strap. "Speaking of adorable. Did you put a bell on me?"

Emerson blushed and ducked her head. "I – I wanted to be able to hear if you woke up. I know I joked about putting a bell on you and if you –"

"I like it," she said. "It's like I belong to someone."

Her breath stuttered and dry eyes dampened again. "You mean it?"

"Of course I do. Didn't we talk about this?"

"Not as bluntly, somehow." She reached down and cradled the jingle bell in her palm. "I may be showing my possessiveness here, but I had Cooper help me carve your name on one side. My phone number is on the other side."

Harper laughed until it turned into an aching cough. "Oh, ow, tender ribs, don't make me laugh anymore. That's so cute it actually hurts."

"You're not offended?"

"Nope. Not even a little. In fact, I'm kind of proud to have it." *Proud to have you*, she thought and picked up Emerson's hand to kiss her fingertips. "You're sweet."

Emerson smiled at first, but it soon slipped back into a small frown. She cleared her throat and pulled her hand back. "We should probably… talk."

"About what happened," Harper said, eyes closing. "I killed Holt."

"You did. Protecting me, and Logan, and yourself."

"I'm sorry you saw that, Emers. I'm sorry about the whole thing. It wouldn't have happened if I — "

A slim finger tapped Harper between her eyebrows. "Harper. Yes, it was a terrifying experience, and I'm not sure how to deal with all of it. Holt kidnapping me, his death, you sacrificing yourself. The past nine days. It's a lot. But please, don't think it was your fault."

Harper whined. "I killed another person. In front of you."

"He was going to shoot both of us. Probably Logan as well. If it weren't for me none of it would have happened. I'm the one that showed up and made a mess of everything. If I'd just told Holt I wasn't interested in him, all of this could have been avoided."

"You're not allowed to blame yourself either. I'm not trying to justify murder, but he kidnapped you. He threatened your life. That's on him, not you." She opened her eyes and found Emerson looking down at her with such concentration. "Where do we go from here? How do we handle this? I don't know what to say. I can't make this better."

Emerson smiled again, the corners of her mouth barely curling up. "A day at a time. Right now we focus on getting you healthy again. We'll have time to talk."

"You're not scared of me now?"

"No. I was scared for you. You're not a monster, Harper. What happened in that clearing doesn't change that. You're not a monster and I'm still not running."

"So later, more talk. Serious talk." Harper tried for a smile. "I'm glad you're safe, Little Moon."

"You too, *Mon Loup*."

"I still don't know what that means."

"Wolf. My wolf."

The others came trooping back in, carrying enough plates to feed an army. Emerson helped her sit up and a plate heaping with eggs and bacon was set in her lap.

She struggled with the fork to mouth movement for a few seconds before succeeding in getting it right. "Guys," she said, after she swallowed. "You know I love all of you, but can you not stare while I'm eating? Makes me self-conscious."

AJ laughed. "Since when? Normally we have to stand back to avoid getting food thrown at us."

Her fork scraped at the plate as she set it back down in Mount Egg. She picked up a strip of bacon and took her time chewing, watching AJ the whole time. "So... your name is Ava?"

"Oh," AJ said and blushed. "I was hoping you didn't hear that."

"Uh-huh." She crunched some more bacon, smirking. "Wolfy hearing."

"My, what big ears you have."

"Don't I know it," she said. "What's the middle name, Ava?"

"No." AJ shook her head and crossed her arms. "Bad enough you all know the first."

"Come on, it can't be that bad."

Grady grinned and pulled at his beard. "At least we know she's feeling better. She's already back to torturing us."

"There's a reason I shortened it. Eat your food, Harper."

"I think Ava is a beautiful name."

"Thank you, Emerson. It was my grandmother's."

"Please, Jay?" She asked with her best pout. "I promise I'll never call you Ava again." She batted her eyelashes and whined in the back of her throat.

"God, you insufferable thing. It's Jolene."

"Jolene, Jolene, Jolene, Jolene," Harper sang, a blush burning her cheeks at the raspy, rough tone to her voice.

"And that's why I use my initials. Thank you." AJ rolled her eyes and raised a hand as though to smack her.

"Hey! None of that, Pol-Pot. Use your words." Harper shrank back into Emerson. "I'm wounded, remember? Poisoned and recovering from a coma. Do you want to see the scar?"

She reached for the hem of her shirt and five pairs of hands reached for her among a chorus of "No!"

"Harper," Emerson said and groaned.

She giggled, and stuck another forkful into her mouth.

"Definitely feeling better." Cooper shook his head and moved his bacon over to Harper's plate. "Here, Cuz, get your strength up."

"Thanks!"

The comfortable sound of forks against plates and happy chewing was broken by three loud knocks on the door. Harper frowned and looked around the room, confirming everyone was there that should be, besides Logan. "Is it Logan?" she wondered out loud.

Grady stood and handed his empty plate to Cooper. "Logan's been running the bar while I've been here. It's not him."

Harper perked her ears and raised a hand for everyone to be quiet. The front door opened and the smell of metal and cigarette smoke made her wrinkle her nose.

"Sheriff Blalock," Grady said. "This is a surprise, what can I do for you?"

"Grady, how many times I have to tell you to call me Tom?"

"Sorry. Tom. Old habit. We're just finishing up breakfast, if you're hungry."

"I'm afraid I can't today. I heard about Harper's accident and I've been meaning to come by and check on her."

"Oh, I'm sure she'd be happy to see you."

"That's not all."

Harper tensed and grabbed Emerson's knee.

"I know she's been laid up, but I need to talk to her. It's about Holt."

THE END

ABOUT THE AUTHOR

Danielle Parker is a musician and lives in Boise, Idaho with her dog and her boyfriend. She has been writing and publishing short stories online since 2004. As a child she told her parents that when she grew up she was going to be an author. When she's not writing she enjoys working on cars and riding motorcycles. Despite the rumors, she is not a werewolf.